SPUD -
Exit, Pursued by a Bear

John van de Ruit

PENGUIN BOOKS

PENGUIN BOOKS

Published by the Penguin Group
Penguin Books (South Africa) (Pty) Ltd, Rosebank Office Park, Block D,
Parktown North, Johannesburg 2193, South Africa
Penguin Books Ltd, 80 Strand, London WC2R 0RL, England
Penguin Group (USA) Inc, 375 Hudson Street, New York, New York 10014,
USA
Penguin Group (Canada), 90 Eglinton Avenue East, Suite 700, Toronto,
Ontario, M4P 2Y3, Canada (a division of Pearson Penguin Canada Inc.)
Penguin Ireland, 25 St Stephen's Green, Dublin 2, Ireland (a division of
Penguin Books Ltd)
Penguin Group (Australia), 250 Camberwell Road, Camberwell, Victoria
3124, Australia (a division of Pearson Australia Group Pty Ltd)
Penguin Books India Pvt Ltd, 11 Community Centre, Panchsheel Park, New
Delhi – 110 017, India
Penguin Group (NZ), 67 Apollo Drive, Rosedale, Auckland 0632, New
Zealand (a division of Pearson New Zealand Ltd)

Penguin Books (South Africa) (Pty) Ltd, Registered Offices:
Rosebank Office Park, Block D, Parktown North, Johannesburg 2193, South
Africa

www.penguinbooks.co.za

First published by Penguin Books (South Africa) (Pty) Ltd 2012

Copyright © John van de Ruit, 2012

ISBN 978-0-14-353024-4

Cover design: mr design
Cover photograph: Matt Rosin, by Carla van Aswegen

This book is dedicated to my Dad,
Dave van de Ruit, *who always told me stories.*

John Milton proved fruitful in still one more respect. He was versatile, and Major Major soon found himself incorporating the signature in fragments of imaginary dialogues. Thus, typical endorsements on the official documents might read, 'John, Milton is a sadist' or 'Have you seen Milton, John?' One signature of which he was especially proud read, 'Is anybody in the John, Milton?' John Milton threw open whole new vistas filled with charming, inexhaustible possibilities that promised to ward off monotony forever.

Catch 22
Joseph Heller

Dramatis Personae

Family	Mom Dad Wombat (my gran)
Ex-Girlfriends	Mermaid Amanda Christine (one night stand)
Teachers	The Glock: Headmaster Viking: Housemaster/Drama The Guv: English Lennox: History Mr Bosch: Geography Mongrel: Afrikaans Mrs Bishop: Maths Eve: Hot counsellor Sparerib: Unpleasant former housemaster
Crazy Eight (Matric)	John *Spud* Milton (Prefect) Simon Brown (Head of House) Robert *Rambo* Black (Prefect) Sidney *Fatty* Smitherson-Scott (Prefect) Alan *Boggo* Greenstein (Non-prefect) Vern *Rain Man* Blackadder (Cretin) Garth Garlic (Malawian) Henry *Gecko* Barker (RIP) Charlie *Mad Dog* Hooper (Expelled)

Normal Seven (3rd year) Spike
Thinny
Darryl (the last remaining)
JR Ewing
Barryl
Runt

Fragile Five (2nd year)   Stutterheim
Rowdy
Plump Graham
Sidewinder
Meg Ryan's Son

Harmless Half-Dozen (1st year)
Albert Schweitzer
Small & Freckly
Enzo Ferrari
Shambles
Plaque
Near Death

Sunday 17th January 1993

MEN'S BREAKFAST

09:15 I was woken by devious whispering from outside my bedroom door. My parents were definitely up to no good because the only time they whisper in the passage is when I'm sick or if they think I'm suicidal. Stupidly, I grew curious and sauntered out to reconnoitre for any potential landmines. Dad was whistling Roger Whittaker and frying sausages in the kitchen, while my mother greeted me in a high-pitched and unnatural voice from the lounge before disappearing out of the front door jangling her keys.

'Just taking Mum out for her tea and crumpets at the Bot Gardens,' she called from the driveway and with an unpleasant grating of the gears she was gone.

'Send the old bag my love!' hollered Dad before plunging a steak knife into an extremely large Russian sausage which in turn squirted boiling juice in his face and onto his arm.

My father issued a hysterical scream and retaliated by kicking the door off the washing machine. The broken washing machine door led to further tirades about the Japanese (DEFY), my father's Jonah tendencies, and the diminishing quality of your standard Eskort sausage. Having made my tea while nodding sympathetically at Dad's rant, I attempted to extricate myself from the scene of acrimony and make a break for the safety of my bedroom where Tom Wolfe's excellent *Bonfire of the Vanities* awaited. I didn't quite pull off the plan because my father scampered across the dining room and slammed the door shut before I could reach it.

'A men only father and son breakfast,' he said, ushering me to a seat and darting back to the kitchen to turn the Russians and chop a tomato in half. I sipped at my tea and gazed out of the window at the half-mowed lawn. The lawnmower's lid was open and most of the engine lay in a heap of spare parts on the slasto beside the pool.

I didn't have a good feeling about this at all.

'Good old English breakfast just the way your grand-mother made it,' Dad announced rather emotionally slapping an enormous tray-sized plate of fried breakfast down in front of me.

'Been dry,' said Dad to get the ball rolling.

'Helluva dry,' I agreed and set to work cutting through a Russian.

'They reckon it's called El Niño,' added my father gravely, shoving a fork load of food into his mouth.

There was a brief period of silence as I salted my eggs and Dad poured orange juice with a shaky hand, before carefully rearranging the breakfast on his plate.

'So ... how goes things on the girlfriend front?' he asked without the slightest shred of warning.

'Very, very slow,' I replied gravely, and attempted to look like the kind of boy who might never think about sex, girlfriends, let alone bizarre sex acts with girlfriends.

'Really, boy?' said Dad with some concern.

'Extremely slow ... barely off the mark,' I said, hoping that Dad might register the cricket reference and that would be the end of it.

Unfortunately, it wasn't.

'I thought we might have a little chat over our men's breakfast,' he said.

'Right,' I replied and felt terribly nauseous.

'Brekkie okay?' asked Dad, while looking despairingly at my untouched plate.

'Delicious,' I lied, miming further chewing.

And then out of the dark end of left field came:

'Johnny, you could think of the male penis as very much like your average Russian sausage.'

The blood rushed to my face. My father had already speared the Russian with his fork and held the dripping creature aloft for examination.

'Size is important, my boy, but no lady south of the Vaal likes a freak.' He nodded knowingly like he was deeply knowledgeable about such women.

'Right,' I replied through gritted teeth and we both stared at his sausage.

'Just like the fairer sex, Johnny, fried eggs are all about timing and probably enjoyed best when flipped over.'

I watched in horror as Dad wrapped a tomato skin around the end of the Russian in a suggestive fashion. When I say 'suggestive fashion' I mean that he kept looking at me oddly and saying, 'Watch closely, my boy, this is life and death ...'

'Just for precautions,' he said firmly, after accomplishing his fairly lengthy mission of wrapping the skin of a fried tomato around the uneaten side of his Russian.

'Trust me, boy; there is no greater disaster in a man's life than hearing the terrible news that his wife is pregnant.'

I nodded.

'Your life is over, Johnny,' he said desperately.

'I understand,' I replied and really did.

'If you haven't had a threesome by twenty-five, then kiss the fantasy goodbye!' blurted my father growing increasingly upset and red faced about matters.

There followed a fairly long pause while I wound down

the clock by re-salting my already re-salted fried tomato.

'Use protection, Johnny. At the very least it will keep your jalogi free from the VD plague.'

I stared at my plate and nodded again.

'Frank says it's all over the place,' he added.

Then without doubt God answered my silent prayers and the phone rang.

It was Amber from next door asking if Dad could help her with a blocked drain. He was gone in seconds and one of the most excruciating moments of my short life was over. In case my father returned and tried to stoke up his men's breakfast again, I jumped on my bike and rode the streets of lower Durban North at a furious pace while trying not to think of sex, threesomes, and the VD plague.

Thankfully, I never did find out what the bacon meant.

Monday 18th January

18:20 I didn't want to go in. I just stood there staring at those red brick walls feeling greatly about the contradiction of this being both an end and a beginning. The setting sun dipped behind the line of trees to my right and I reluctantly ended my procrastination. One deep breath and I heaved up my bags and staggered towards the great archway and the heart of the school where the depraved and the insane awaited.

The place was oddly deserted, and for a moment I hesitated, considering the unlikely possibility that I had arrived at school a week too early. It was only the prefects who had been summoned tonight but it genuinely appeared like I was utterly alone. The main quad was trimmed and serene and Pissing Pete must have been serviced in the holidays because the spray of water from his sword flew high into the air before crashing back into the pond at his feet. His face looked a good deal shinier too.

I skirted the clipped grass of the quad and strode swiftly towards the house door. It was wide open but I couldn't detect any sign of life from inside.

'Hello!' I shouted and heard my voice echo up the stairs and down into the bogs. There was no reply. I dropped my bags and poked my head into the common room which now boasts a blood red carpet and two new armchairs. On the television Adrian Steed was reading the news but the volume was turned down.

Up the stairs and onto the landing, I hovered outside the head of house's room.

'Simon?' I knocked gently.

There was no response so I continued along the passage to the second year dormitory which was equally deserted. Then onward to the first year dorm where the air was dank and unexpectedly cool.

I reclined on the house bench and surveyed the quad for any signs of movement. The bell tower glimmered pink and silver in the fading light. Nothing stirred. It was truly as if I was the only schoolboy left alive in the world. Just me and ten million desperate schoolgirls. It was a mightily positive thought.

After scoping the bogs, which I am happy to report have been retiled and painted a brilliant white, I tried the handle on the prefects' room door which, surprisingly, twisted and opened.

'Get out!' hissed an icy voice from the gloom inside.

'Sorry,' I replied instinctively, and hurriedly closed the door.

Out in the passage the realisation dawned on me that this was 1993 and I was a prefect and well within my rights. I turned the handle again, kicked the door open and entered. All I could see was an unmoving figure seated in an armchair across the room.

'So what's the answer, Milton? Are you retarded or did you just forget that you were a prefect?'

'I'm probably retarded,' I replied.

The dark figure snorted and I immediately knew who it was.

'So, 1993, Spuddy ... what you say – a bang or a whimper?'

'A bang,' I responded, sounding positively inspired.

'There's a bottle of vodka on the table to your right,' he said rather matter of factly. 'It's the only liquor that can't be smelled on your breath.'

There was a glow of light about Rambo's face, his lips pursed together around a cigarette as he slowly bowed his head to the flame.

'It's going to be one hell of a year.'

'Bring it on,' I said.

He didn't reply.

Fifteen minutes later I found a drastically slimmed down Fatty on the house bench staring intently at Pissing Pete. When I asked him how his holiday had been, he turned to me and said, 'My oath to God, Spuddy, it was like the best ever and I lost like twenty kilograms in six weeks.'

'Penny?' I asked. This was a loaded question because only Fatty's barely legal, but very pretty, thirteen year old girlfriend could have inspired such a dramatic weight crash.

'It was kinda like a scene from Grease meets Romeo and Juliet, but only set in Port Shepstone,' he said with wonder in his voice. 'You know, like summer loving on the beach with two star crossed lovers and all that ...'

I considered this for a moment.

'So who was it this time, Mermaid or Amanda?'

'Neither,' I said.

'Oh well, there's always more fish in the ...' he faded off as a new idea seemed to strike him. 'I actually know for a fact that Brenda – you remember Brenda from *A Midsummer Night's Dream*, right?'

I nodded.

'Well, she told Penny on New Year's Eve that she was still willing to kiss you anytime.'

'Great,' I replied without much enthusiasm.

'And maybe a bit more ...' he added hopefully.

There was a longish pause while I considered the barren wasteland of my love life.

'Hey, and remember to book your room. It's first come first served,' he added.

'Okay,' I replied still trying to shake off the dismal vision of having to resort to young Brenda as my girl-friend, and first ever girl to touch my Russian. I think I'd rather become a monk or a Rastafarian or something.

Rambo and Fatty had already booked the rooms upstairs diagonally opposite Simon's head of house room. Despite Rambo occupying a double room, he made it abundantly clear that should anyone (read me) even think about asking to share with him, he'd kill them (me) slowly with his bare hands. He went on to add that the corpse (mine) would then be incinerated with concentrated lime stolen from the store room at the cricket pavilion.

On the landing halfway up the stairs was another option, although this was a tiny room with barely enough space to stand up straight. Besides, this was Pike's old matric room and is bound to have terrible karma due to his depraved behaviour and disturbing bullying.

Another flight down and under the stairs itself was the room that was most famously home to Gavin, the weird prefect under the stairs. It's a thoroughly disturbing space and I didn't linger before moving on.

The bog room occupied last year by Meany Dlamini is large and spacious but suffers from three obvious problems:

1. Its proximity to the bogs
2. Its proximity to the urinal
3. Its proximity to the house phone

That left the prefab double room outside that attached to the rear end of the first years' classroom. I immediately liked the look of the long and narrow room which, although outside the house itself, was close enough not to feel out of the action. Three problems immediately presented themselves:

1. The proximity of Viking's office window offers the maniac a clear view of the door which could be tricky if I have to unexpectedly bring a buxom blonde back to my room for some late night jiggery.
2. The room is attached to the first year prep classroom which will make it noisy unless fear is instilled into the new boys the very moment they arrive. Depending on their general sizes, this could be achievable. The flip side, however, is that Eve's counsellor's office is attached to the opposite end of the first year classroom, so with us regularly crossing paths there should be plenty of opportunities to hone my spadework over the coming months.

   (If I did take the room, it would probably be worth my while writing down and memorising a number of classic one-liners that I could use in passing conversation with Eve. Nothing too obvious, but just the kind of stuff that would make me look witty, cool and well worth a shag.)

3. It's a double room. That could mean I am opening myself up to a possible room mate (Vern, Boggo or Garlic) and definite disaster. Still, there are three decent-ish rooms in the house for the others. After some considerable thought, I decided the double room was a gamble worth taking.

I hurriedly made the bed and unpacked enough clothes from my trunk to make the room look taken. I checked the basin taps which, after spluttering out some chocolate water, seemed to rectify themselves and run true. Thereafter I locked the door and pocketed the key with the confidence of a proud new owner.

Spud Milton has staked his claim! At last, a room of my own.

Tuesday 19th January

07:45   After enjoying a sumptuous breakfast at the prefects' table, Rambo, Fatty and I dawdled across the quad with our coffee in the general direction of Viking's office. Simon was waiting for us at the bench.

'Hey, Simon,' I said cheerfully. 'How was your holiday?'
    'Cool,' he replied without much enthusiasm.
    'What's this meeting all about?' asked Rambo, looking uninspired.
    'Flippin' new boys, what else?' hissed Simon, rolling his eyes.

Viking was as furious as ever although it was impossible to know what he was so livid about. All I could really glean from his introduction was that the new boys were arriving in two hours' time and that he had recently had a vivid nightmare about one of them attempting to commit suicide on his watch. When Fatty asked our housemaster whether this had been a bad dream or a premonition, Viking refused to elaborate other than to say that the dying boy was naked. A long silence followed before he cleared his throat and moved on to general protocol. After repeated instructions on what to say to the parents of the new boys as they arrived, he scavenged through his filing cabinet and brought out yet more instructions. We were each given a folder and told to familiarise ourselves closely with its contents.

Before having to read out the entire document together in unison, Viking made it clear that during the first years' two week period of grace we were to keep interactions with the new boys to the minimum and that Simon was the only contact point should any of them need help or assistance. It all seemed a little odd but then again Viking isn't exactly the heartland of normal.

Since the document accurately demonstrates my housemaster's (fragile) state of mind, and is perhaps the most ridiculous set of guidelines ever dished out by a high school teacher, I have decided to stick some of its contents into my diary for safekeeping and future proof that I in fact received a scholarship to the monkey asylum rather than to a top private school as previously advertised.

How to Spot a New Boy is Homesick

Crying Usually involving tears/sobbing/red eyes/or boy covering his face with his hands for prolonged periods. Beware!!! Prolonged periods of crying can lead to depression, loneliness and SUICIDE (see below).

Depression Loosely means permanently sad moods which could result in crying (see above), or loneliness (see below) or a combination of both (see above and below).

Loneliness Leads to depression (see above), crying (see above), SUICIDE (below) or a combination thereof (see everywhere).

Tell-tale signs of SUICIDAL tendencies include impressionable young boys **exhibiting some or all of the following behaviours**:

1. Jabbing at their wrists with Swiss army pocket knives, razor blades or sharp nail scissors
2. Lethal overdose of pills
3. Leaping naked out of the dormitory window/s
4. Placing gun in mouth/electric drill in ear etc ...
5. Self-drownage with backpack of bricks/stones/ gymnasium equipment

Most common reasons for suicide:
- Poor family life (Abuse, divorce, incest)
- Late development
- Poor financial decisions (Gambling/thievery/fraud victim)
- Insanity (Due to possible birthing problems/blows to the head/drinking paint or detergent etc ...)
- Iron deficiency (See sanatorium for assistance)
- Prolonged constipation (See sanatorium for assistance)
- Victimisation and bullying (This must be weeded out!)
- Homosexuality

Warning*******
Should a boy demonstrate SUICIDAL behaviour in any shape or form he should immediately be subdued by means of wrapping his entire head in a towel or bedspread. His arms and legs should be tied together and, if possible, his body should be attached either to the floor or to an immovable object such as a sturdy wall or bolted to a roofing panel. A particularly effective ploy is to lock the distressed boy inside the boot of a car while professional help is found. On rare occasions a responsible yet solid blow to the back of the head may be necessary. Once the boy has been subdued, make sure he doesn't swallow his tongue, and report directly to your housemaster ...

V.A. RICHARDSON
B.A.(Hons) UED (cum laude) RHODES UNIVERSITY

Meeting the new boys and carrying their trunks to the first year dormitory thankfully went off without a hitch. Although nervous, none of them seemed suicidal. They seemed quite an unassuming bunch apart from the black boy, Ntoko, who was extremely confident on arrival.

While head of house Simon was forced to attend The Glock's laborious speech about discipline in the theatre,

Reverend Bishop's sprawling feel-the-spirit sermon in the chapel, and an awkward buffet lunch in the quad with the parents and new boys, Fatty, Rambo and I spent the afternoon drinking tea, eating toast with honey, and discussing the finer points of seduction. Despite it being close to thirty degrees outside Rambo poured an entire steel bucket of coal into the fireplace and soon had a raging furnace under way. He took off his shirt and sat before the smouldering coals smoking his cigarettes and tracing the lines of his biceps and triceps with a piece of coal while we continued our discussion.

In the knowledge that the rest of the Crazy Eight would be arriving shortly, I locked my room and stashed the key in my pocket. Boggo has a long history of thievery, blackmail and forced removals.

17:35   Garth Garlic was the first of the rest of the Crazy Eight to arrive. We heard his excited shouting about Malawi from the passage outside the prefects' room.

'Rowdy!' he hollered. 'Where's the rest of the Crazy Eight?' We didn't hear Rowdy respond but he must have because Garlic immediately began banging on the door of the cop shop and shouting, 'Hey, guys! Fatty? Spud? You guys in there?'

Nobody replied. The handle twisted and the prefects' room door flew open. The pink and incredulous face of Garth Garlic appeared.

'There you all are!' he cried with delight like we had been involved in a game of good natured hide and seek.

'We're in the middle of a prefects' meeting, Garlic,' said Rambo sharply while exhaling a large cloud of cigarette smoke into the fire and up the chimney.

'Cool,' replied Garlic with an expectant grin like somebody was on the verge of cracking a rip-snorting joke. He closed the door and made his way to the empty armchair to my left. 'So how was your holiday, guys?' There was a long pause before Garlic continued. 'Mine was a top tenner, maybe even a top fiver!'

'Good,' muttered Rambo. 'Now sod off before I roast your face in the fire and eat it.'

Rambo sprang to his feet and made a lunging bid to catch the Malawian but Garlic, who is fast developing a reputation for narrowly escaping imminent pain and humiliation, evaded Rambo's outstretched hand, leapt over the armchair in which he had been sitting, and bolted from the prefects' room, his eyes wide with terror and his skin glowing pink.

'I swear to God,' growled Rambo once the dust had settled, 'one day I'm going to roast a piece of Garlic and taste it. No bullshit. I reckon he'll be absolutely delicious.' I didn't quite know how to respond to Rambo's cannibalism so I nodded in agreement as if eating a piece of Garth Garlic was normal if not downright sensible.

Boggo arrived when we were all at dinner. After carefully examining the available room options, he selected the bog room for its size and the fact that it suited his nickname. He said that he would rather contract cholera from the urinal than have to share with me and sleep with a cork up his bum for an entire year.

Garlic selected the tiny room on the landing which meant that whether he liked it or not, Rain Man would sleep in the room under the stairs.

Vern arrived at 21:00 and immediately began to cause trouble. Firstly, he kept banging on Boggo's door and shouting, 'Oi!' The maniac seemed furious that Boggo wasn't allowing him in and was hell bent on evicting him. But Boggo was resolute as always and refused to open the door even when Viking came knocking to welcome him back to school. Then some donkey fart suggested that Vern should share the outside room with me. Luckily, I beat the nutcase in the race for the door and locked him out. I sat triumphantly at my desk listening to Vern's banging and shouting outside, confident that if I stuck to my guns like Boggo I would eventually see the idiot off. Thankfully, Viking didn't take kindly to the terrible racket going on outside his office window and ordered the Rain Man to cease his terrible din and occupy the room under the stairs.

Vern's fate was sealed and within minutes Viking (with the help of Simon, JR Ewing, Thinny, Runt and myself) managed to force him into his room.

Strangely, once the cretin was in, he never once tried to come out again.

Wednesday 20th January

06:30 I called the morning roll call at a good lick, giving dissenters and wise guys no chance to undermine my first official duty as a prefect with lame jibes and idiotic sideshows. I even issued a stern rebuking of Darryl (the last remaining) for looking an absolute shambles and threw a nasty glare at Plump Graham for being forty seconds late. The first years seemed genuinely afraid of me which was heartening to see. It must be added that they do look pretty much terrified of everything right now so I probably shouldn't take too much masculine credit at this stage.

Vern wasn't at roll call and didn't open his door when I knocked. Considering Rain Man's oddball behaviour last night, I thought it wise to inform Simon in case Vern had run away or done something disturbing.

Simon rapped sharply on Vern's door but there was no reply. I spied through the keyhole and found myself locked onto Vern's demented eyeball which was peering through the other end.

'Vern,' I said in a kindly voice, 'I just wanted to check

that you were all right.'

There was no reply other than the sound of Rain Man muttering to himself and pushing his desk against the door.

'Quick, attack!' shouted Simon. He shoulder charged the door and managed to prise it open before Vern had his barricade in place. Vern tried his best to keep the door closed but the collective muscle of myself, Simon and Sidewinder, who was wandering past clad only in a yellow towel, was enough to heave the door open and reveal a wild looking Rain Man dressed in khaki.

'Grab him!' ordered Simon and lunged for Vern's arm. Despite there being nowhere to hide in his spooky little room, Vern nevertheless made a valiant attempt to escape by diving head first into the wall. The bang to the head settled him down and we were able to escort him out of his room, down the passage and into the bright sunshine of the main quad.

'Come, Vern, it's time for breakfast,' I called as normally as possible.

The cretin grinned and followed me rather unsteadily to the dining hall for a breakfast of scrambled egg and sausages which he drenched in tomato sauce and wolfed down without using any of his cutlery.

(DIS) ORIENTATION DAY

Simon, Rambo, Fatty and I led the new boys off for an introductory tour of the school to the sound of loud and obvious sniggering from a tea-drinking Boggo Greenstein on the house bench. Simon led the tour which meant that Rambo and I dawdled at the back, with Fatty falling further behind before calling it quits at the squash courts.

Viking called us in for our second prefects' meeting of the day and was relieved to hear that none of the new boys had plunged to their deaths on the school tour. His big announcement was that Eggwhite, last year's mostly ineffectual house prefect returning for post matric, would be back on Friday and that we would have to cover his duties this week. He handed us further lists and instruction documents before sending us on our way with a curt nod.

Back in the prefects' room, which we have taken to calling the cop shop, we bemoaned our lot over milky tea and cheese sandwiches. Rambo even reckoned that he was thinking of packing it in if Viking didn't stop with his endless meetings about naked boys committing suicide. I returned to my room to ready myself for tomorrow's lessons and glanced through the variety of textbooks filled with reams of knowledge and information that I will have to devour, digest and regurgitate in November. I wonder if my brain will have the capacity to take it all in? My matric maths textbook looks particularly nasty with its small unemotional writing and vomit yellow cover. At least I have the space and serenity of my own room to make a decent stab at it.

I bumped into Eve on the way to dinner and I would be denying the truth if I didn't say that she looked absolutely ravishing in her knee length skirt and high heels. We spoke about Roger the cat's banishment to Sparerib's brother's farm near Komga due to his endless spraying and destructive behaviour around the house over the holidays. She reckons he ripped up all their lounge cushions during Christmas and extensively soiled Sparerib's thermal underwear drawer while they were at The Glock's New Year's Eve party. I nodded sympathetically about the situation and stole a glance at her cleavage as she leant forward to adjust her left heel. Eve seemed rather concerned about the way Vern had taken the news about Roger no longer being at the school and asked me if he was behaving unusually. 'Vern always behaves unusually,' I replied, making her laugh and then briefly ruffle my hair. We must have chatted against the wall of the passage for at least fifteen minutes about Roger and Vern and I sensed a growing ease in each other's company. Overall, it was an excellent conversation and Eve smelled terrific.

21:30   My first lights out duty went rather smoothly, all things considered. The first years even called me sir. I was careful not to open up any meaningful conversations but a small boy with ginger hair and the unfortunate name of Michael Wiggle asked me with a deeply troubled expression on his face if Vern was insane.

'Definitely,' I replied and switched out the lights.

The second year dormitory was a little livelier than the first but the Fragile Five immediately obeyed when I ordered them to their beds.

'Hey, John, can I ask you a question?' asked Plump Graham, as he tried to squeeze himself into an extremely tight pair of white long-johns. 'Why is Alan Greenstein charging a toll on the urinal?'

The Fragile Five were adamant that Boggo had charged both Runt and Sidewinder R1.50 each to use the piss trough. I promised the worried second years that I'd look into the problem.

(Surely it's only a question of time until people begin whispering about the relative sizes of Plump Graham and Fatty, considering Graham's vast expansion and what Boggo is now calling Fatty's 'anorexia-paedophilia'.)

I was mildly dreading the Normal Seven dorm as they were most likely to pull something on me or challenge my authority. As it turned out my fears were unfounded

18

and even the likes of Spike and JR Ewing were polite and obedient when I called them to order. If I didn't know better I'd say they were up to something.

'Where's Runt?' I asked after discovering his empty bed.

Barryl stepped forward and in an exceedingly deep voice replied, 'He's helping Rambo and Viking push Vern back in his room.' I headed downstairs to where Viking was shouting and Vern was shrieking and clawing at people's faces because he didn't want to go back into his room again.

Thursday 21st January

School began properly today and it was the usual grind of boredom that passes for higher education in this place. Handed out were piles of papers detailing various syllabuses, approaching large projects, and dire threats of what cocking up matric will do to the rest of your life. There wasn't even any comic relief because The Guv hasn't returned to school. Boggo said he overheard Mr Cartwright telling Norm (I don't believe in spinners) Wade that The Guv was in hospital for an operation.

I ran down to The Guv's house after lunch but the place looked deserted and nobody answered when I knocked and yelled. I should have called him in the holidays, if only to say Merry Christmas and to check on how he was doing. Hopefully, it's nothing serious and only the gout in his drinking arm playing up again.

19:30 During prep I took a stroll across to Boggo's room to have a little chat about the increasing complaints that I have received concerning his toll charge at the urinal. Boggo reluctantly let me into his bog room which is plastered wall to wall with pictures of beautiful naked women striking sexy poses, mostly under waterfalls. I decided to confront Boggo directly about his controversial new way of raising capital and, unsurprisingly, he pretended to be utterly shocked and outraged, saying that 'people with agendas' were already spreading malicious rumours about him.

Boggo flopped down on his bed and appeared to be thoroughly disgusted with life. I allowed some time to pass before saying, 'I have three boys willing to testify that they saw you charging Runt R1.50 for taking a piss.'

Boggo's eyes narrowed and his look of disgust was instantly replaced by one of raging defiance.

'Well, obviously I charged Runt, but then who wouldn't? He's the weirdest little creep south of the North Pole.'

'Still,' I said in my most reasonable voice, 'you can't charge a guy for having a piss. It's completely dictatorial and borderline insane.'

'They do it in Europe,' retorted Boggo with a broad smirk like he had gone some way towards winning the argument.

'What do they do in Europe?' echoed a surprisingly loud but mumbled voice from the doorway. We turned to see Garlic standing there in his crimson dressing gown with a buzzing electric toothbrush in his mouth.

'Shag animals,' replied Boggo, looking deeply displeased with life once more.

Garlic was astonished by this revelation about Europeans but thankfully couldn't ask any more questions because his mouth was too full of toothpaste. He raced off to the basins to spit and Boggo took the opportunity to slam and lock his bedroom door.

'You see, that's the fundamental problem with life, Milton,' he said. 'Too many lurkers.' Boggo looked wistful as his eyes took in a large poster of a shapely brunette with a python sliding through her naked cleavage.

'If it's not Garlic with his questions or Vern with his screaming and banging, then it's Runt peeping into my room and lingering around with suggestive intent.'

'But you can't blacklist boys from using the bogs just because they're lurkers,' I argued.

'On the contrary, they are completely and utterly free to use the bogs for no payment whatsoever,' stated Boggo with his open arms demonstrating his generosity. 'It's just the urinal that falls under my jurisdiction.'

I found myself nodding absent-mindedly as I took in the splendour of a poster of a feisty old granny in leather riding a Harley Davidson. Underneath it was written:

CAN YOU GO THE DISTANCE?

There was an excited knock on the door.

'Piss off, Garlic!' shouted Boggo immediately. He hurled a hockey boot which missed the door by some distance and clattered into his bookshelf instead, sending half a shelf of pornography and both of his primary school hockey trophies crashing to the floor. Boggo appeared not to notice his blunder as his focus remained on the door where Garlic was attempting to jimmy the handle with his electric toothbrush. When that failed, the Malawian commenced pounding on the door and shouting questions at Boggo about the Europeans as the shrill ringing of the telephone sounded from the room next door.

'You see what I have to put up with down here, Spud, my oath to God it's sheer hell.'

I had to concede that things were a little chaotic when most of the Normal Seven struck up a lewd war cry outside and the house began ringing once again.

'Chaotic!' snorted Boggo. 'Oh, I'd settle for chaotic all right, this is worse than a frikkin' Bombay fish market.

My oath to God it's chronic. Could easily cost me ten per cent in my exams.'

'Okay, I can understand Vern, Garlic and Runt getting blacklisted from the urinal,' I reasoned, attempting to return to the original purpose of my mission, 'but why Sidewinder?'

'Hygiene, pure and simple,' replied Boggo like the matter was out of his hands and beyond his control.

'Hygiene?' I repeated, wondering where he might be leading me with this new line of thinking.

'Well, do the trigonometry, Milton,' he said. 'The dude's dongle points due west, if you get my drift.' Boggo used a long bony finger to demonstrate the left leaning nature of Sidewinder's sidewinder. 'So unless he faces the window at right angles to the urinal when firing off, then he's definitely going to spray on the wall or the step and contribute dramatically to the aroma problem which I'm sure you've picked up around here.'

Boggo sauntered over to his cupboard and gave his armpits two short blasts of deodorant each before continuing. 'Nothing personal against Sidewinder but, let's face it, the guy could cause mass devastation on a full tank with a morning glory.'

Once again I found myself nodding away in agreement as the sly Boggo defused my questions with his typical cunning and warped logic. With a friendly pat on the back I found myself out at the urinal and the door of Boggo's room snapped shut behind me.

'Which animals do they shag, Spud?' blurted Garlic with eyes filled with wonder and desperation. 'Please tell me.'

'What?' I asked in confusion.

'The Europeans!' trumpeted Garlic.

'Giraffes,' I replied, and made a break for it, leaving the sound of hysterical laughter from the Malawian echoing around the bogs.

Friday 22nd January

06:10   Just awoke from a sublime dream involving Eve and a taller version of myself enjoying a romantic picnic with champagne and fine cheeses in a grassy vale beside a lake. Unfortunately, nothing physical happened but it was obvious in the way that Eve ate her cherries that she was being deliberately flirty. I had less than five hours of sleep but felt my most rested in years.

Inspired by my vivid dream, I pretended to be making a full and lengthy inspection of the first year prep classroom after breakfast but despite Eve's office door being wide open, I didn't so much as lay eyes on her. No doubt Sparerib has bailed her up at home with boring conversations and unnecessary demands to iron his underpants.

08:20   The Guv still hasn't returned. Rumours of his operation it seems are true. Reverend Bishop refused to say what was wrong with him but made it sound like it wasn't all that serious. Not sure why everybody is being so evasive when talking about The Guv?

11:00   The announcement of the trial cricket teams usually indicates what side you'll make for the coming year and the jostling crowd around the notice board meant that the moment of truth had finally arrived. The whole thing is a diabolical lottery and what with the sudden and unexplained disappearance of The Guv who was meant to coach the 1sts, one would presume that goblin man chose the teams instead. I sensed that my karma was definitely bad with Sparerib after dreaming about romping his wife for three nights in succession. The unhealthy energy in the air reminded me of last year's fiasco when spinner prejudice sentenced me to three weeks of vermin cricket with the likes of Garlic and Vern. Understandably, I approached the notice board with some hesitancy and began with the 5ths/6ths trial match and moved upwards without breathing. My name wasn't down in the 3rds/4ths trial match either. Eventually, I could bear the agony no longer and allowed my eyes to scan down the first team for Saturday's trial. And there it was – J Milton, down to bat at number 8.

I refused to allow myself any emotion until I was back in the safety of my room where I celebrated uncontrollably in fluent gibberish.

Dare I say it and curse myself? For the first time in my life I feel like I'm on a bit of a roll.

18:00   Boggo talked the Crazy Eight into signing up for the senior social at St Mary's Convent next Friday night. I initially gave it the thumbs down but since momentum is on my side I thought it could be a strategically clever move, and besides Boggo reckons convent girls are notoriously filthy between the sheets.

20:30   Rumours of a midnight Fragile Five nightswim have been circulating. Fatty and Rambo have elected to keep guard and attempt to catch them in the act.

Saturday 23rd January

05:45   Fatty shook me awake and hauled me out of bed because he said major shit was about to hit the fan. Over a cup of tea and a buttermilk rusk he excitedly filled me in on the dramatic events of last night.

The Fragile Five's (FF) nightswimming effort, which appears to have been planned by Plump Graham and Meg Ryan's Son, deteriorated rather dramatically upon return from the dam. The FF discovered the chapel window, through which they had just escaped,

24

was locked from the outside by means of Rambo's unbreakable Japanese combination lock. True to form the FF panicked and galloped down the gallery stairwell only to find all the lower doors bolted from the outside. In desperation, the second years sprinted back up the stairs and into the bell tower where they chanced upon a large figure shrouded in a white sheet (Fatty) who had been instructed by Rambo to make like Macarthur on the bell ringer's platform. The FF took one look at the enormous apparition looming over them, screamed like a bunch of small girls, and fled. Poor Rowdy exploded into hysterical sobs as they careened back down the steps to the gallery and had another yank at the chapel window which stubbornly refused to budge thanks to Rambo and the Japanese.

Then Rambo fired up his reign of supernatural terror. It began with playing one long and creepy note on the organ and ended with him screaming, 'I'm gonna eat you!' and leaping off the pulpit with his arms outstretched onto a huge pile of cushions set out below. The overall effect of Reverend Bishop's ceremonial robes was that Rambo apparently looked like some terrible flying Satanic creature. The shattered FF gave up on escape and spent the rest of the night huddled together for safety in the gallery of the chapel.

06:00 A straight-faced Simon phoned Viking and alerted him to the fact that all of the second years had gone missing in the night. Our housemaster arrived at 6:07 half-dressed and already in an immense rage. He immediately sent the prefects out on a search of the house and surrounds for the missing boys. With utter fury he shouted, 'By fuckery, if these little shit-stirrers are found to be bunking out I'll meat cleaver them to death!'

It didn't take long for Rambo to make the 'discovery' and Viking was led to where a pile of sleeping bodies lay huddled together in the chapel gallery.

'What in God's name is the meaning of all this?' he roared after galloping up the steps.

'We weren't bunking out, sir,' said Plump Graham in a quivery voice. 'We just wanted to make sure that we were early for chapel, sir.'

Three major problems with this feeble-minded excuse immediately presented themselves:

1. Nobody arrives early for chapel
2. There are no chapel services on Saturdays
3. Two of the Fragile Five were dressed in speedos and the others only in their underpants

17:00 My winning momentum has stalled. I made a duck in our batting innings in the trial match against the 2nds, although it must be said that Yobbo Skelton took a blinding catch in the gully to see me marching back to the pavilion without troubling the scorers. Even worse, I didn't even have a chance to bowl because as I was measuring my run-up for my first over, a cloud burst and within ten minutes the field was waterlogged. Sparerib made us hang around for an hour and a half of watching the rain fall before he finally called the game off. Will I still be in the 1st team when the side is announced on Friday? That will be the true test of whether momentum is still going my way or if the worm of happiness has turned south and sour.

20:00 I opted against watching the house movie (*Dangerous Liaisons*) despite it starring the beautiful Michelle Pfeiffer and the disturbing John Malkovich. I'm very close to finishing *Bonfire of the Vanities* so I made for the cop shop hoping to find a quiet spot on a comfy armchair to read. Instead I found Fatty eating a chip bunny and Rambo smoking at the fire grate. It appeared as if they were having a debate about the fate of the Fragile Five.

'Spuddy, you're never going to guess what happened,' gabbled Fatty excitedly.

'Viking wants to lash them eighteen strokes each,' interrupted Rambo on a smoky exhale before chortling to himself and taking another deep drag. I wasn't really sure if beating somebody eighteen strokes was even legal, let alone good form.

'Viking scoured the school rules this afternoon and found nothing limiting the number of strokes a boy may be caned,' added Fatty as he licked his fingers and mopped up the remaining crumbs on his plate.

According to the residents of the cop shop, Viking has accused the Fragile Five of a multitude of crimes, including truancy, nightswimming, deviancy, vandalism, bunking-out, bunking-in, crass deception, blasphemy, soiling hymnbooks, and being underdressed in the chapel within thirty hours of the commencement of a service. This all added up to eighteen strokes each to be dished out at 20:00 tomorrow evening in Viking's office.

'One of them could definitely die,' said Rambo, looking rather pleased about developments.

'Eighteen strokes is pushing the line of barbarism even by apartheid standards,' cautioned Fatty.

'Perhaps one of them will commit suicide,' ventured Rambo in a low voice. 'Now that would be deeply ironic.' I left Fatty and Rambo to their disturbing conversations about death and headed to my room with a cup of tea. There's nothing quite like the feeling of drawing close to the end of a great book and *Bonfire of the Vanities* was screaming for attention.

Despite not having any pictures or posters up yet, I really do like the feeling of being alone in my long skinny room. School is far more enjoyable when you have the right place to hide from it.

Sunday 24th January

How fantastic to be in matric and finally shot of the laborious institution of free bounds. I always wondered if sending the majority of the school off the premises on a Sunday afternoon ever did any good. Now I see that it most definitely does. Matrics, post matrics and staff get to have the run of the place and for three short hours the school is a place you would never want to leave.

After seeing all the boys off from the house bench, Rambo and Boggo took on Fatty and me in a three-set marathon tennis match. Rambo continued his one man rebellion against the school rules despite being a prefect. His large juice bottle was filled with strong vodka, ice and Oros, which he forced us to taste before knocking up. We lost in the third set tie-breaker when Boggo's relentless goading of Fatty's anorexia-paedophilia finally took its toll as my partner lost his temper and smashed a forehand into the net and the next over the back fence. He then served two double faults to end the match and shouted, 'Shot a lot, Boggo, for screwing up a great tennis match!' and stormed back to the house without shaking anyone's hand.

Weirdly, Rambo's tennis improved with every cup of 'jungle juice' he drank, although his voice was slurring terribly when he called out the score in the final set.

17:00   Roll Call

I knew something was wrong the moment I noticed Plump Graham's expression.

'Where are Rowdy and Stutterheim?' I repeated, this

28

time in a far sterner voice. Whispering and murmurs of interest flared up among the other boys, so I ordered the three remaining members of the Fragile Five to see me afterwards in the cop shop and continued with the roll call.

As expected, the three offered very little information about the whereabouts of the missing boys other than to say that Stutterheim and Rowdy were last seen sitting together at breakfast. I ordered a house search which turned up nothing. I went through their possessions and by the looks of things some clothes, toiletries and bags were missing from both their lockers. Simon wasn't in his room and Rambo had passed out after too much jungle juice and tennis. Instead I took matters into my own hands and marched down to the phone room where I kicked Meg Ryan's Son off a call and dialled up Viking's internal extension.

'Yes!' barked the voice of my housemaster.

'Sir, it's Milton,' I said.

'What's going on, Milton?' he replied with terrible dread lining his voice.

'Sir, I think Rowdy and Stutterheim might have run away.'

'Fantastic, just fantastic!' he roared with hideous sarcasm. 'Milton!' he barked. 'Meet me outside my office in three minutes and bring along anybody who can shed light on the matter, or anybody else who needs to be interrogated or beaten!'

I roped in the remaining members of the Fragile Five and headed downstairs to wait for the housemaster. A haggard looking Plump Graham, Sidewinder and Meg Ryan's Son followed me out the house door, ignoring the commotion under the stairs where a large crowd of boys were carrying Vern head first into his room. Outside the light was fading.

Viking arrived in a billowing white Hawaiian shirt open to the stomach, blue tracksuit pants, and brown ethnic sandals. He was nowhere near as furious as expected, although this proved to be only a temporary lapse as he blew his top when I summoned the remaining Fragile Fivers into his office.

'You bastards again!' he roared and stood up violently. He pointed aggressively at Plump Graham and boomed, 'When I'm done with you lot, you will know the true meaning of suffering!' The tirade continued for at least five minutes as the Fragile Five wilted under the firestorm of Viking's wrath once more. After the shitting-on ended with several vile and imaginative threats in quick succession, Viking composed himself and in an acid voice said, 'Now I hope you lot have some news about the disappearance of Rowdy and the other boy?'

Meg Ryan's Son admitted that besides seeing the missing boys at breakfast they had nothing further to report. Viking blew his top again and gassed all over the remaining members of the Fragile Five with incredible force and from a dizzying height. After threatening them with prolonged torture, he upped their nightswimming punishment from eighteen to twenty strokes for wasting his time on a Sunday and kicked them out of his office. I felt a little bad about being responsible but reasoned that after eighteen strokes from Viking, a further two would make little difference.

Thankfully, Simon became involved after spending four hours hitting cricket balls from a bowling machine in the nets. After hearing my story he said he would take it from here and disappeared into Viking's office for further meetings.

19:00   With Simon in Viking's office, Rambo man down with a hangover, and Fatty on a marathon call to Penny,

I finally found some tranquillity to finish off *Bonfire of the Vanities*. I fell well short last night when a sudden dreamless sleep overcame me. I made a cup of tea in the annexe and returned to the deserted cop shop where I reclined on the couch with the book in my lap.

Unfortunately, my tranquillity only lasted long enough to read three quarters of a page, before there was a timid yet relentless knocking on the door.

'What?' I shouted, attempting to sound ferocious and unapproachable.

I immediately regretted not staying silent when the glowing face of Garlic poked around the door.

'Spud, you're in here!' he announced. 'I thought you would be out looking for Rowdy Stutterheim?'

'Rowdy **and** Stutterheim,' I corrected.

'You mind if I pull in and hang snake?' asked Garlic in an obscenely loud and pleading fashion.

I found myself in a terrible predicament. All I wanted was to be alone to read in the cop shop with my cup of tea and, to be honest, having lame chats with the Malawian about Rowdy and Stutterheim made me want to abandon everything and retire to my room.

'The cop shop is only meant for prefects,' I ventured boldly, hoping that Garlic would take the hint and press on. He didn't.

'Simon and Rambo said that a matric could come in if he had permission from a prefect,' retorted Garlic.

'Oh really?' I replied.

'Hey, you're a prefect, Spud! That means technically you could invite me in.'

'I suppose technically I could,' I replied, desperately attempting to think of an excuse that could fend Garlic off.

'Please could I come in, Spud?' he begged in a pitiful voice. 'I don't mind even sitting on the carpet.'

It was impossible to refuse and Garlic was hugely delighted finally to be allowed official entrance into the cop shop.

'Please feel free to carry on reading,' he said, graciously indicating my book.

The Malawian seated himself on the armchair closest to the door and reclined with a contented sigh. I returned to *Vanities* and scanned the page for the place where I abruptly left off. Just as I'd found it Garlic said, 'So I heard the Fragile Five beatings have been postponed?'

I nodded and said, 'Yip.'

There was a silence so I returned to the book despite the fact that Garlic was watching me closely.

'Good book, hey, Spud?' he asked.

'Excellent,' I replied.

'What page you on?' he asked with great interest.

'472,' I replied.

Garlic nodded as if hugely impressed and there was another pause. This time I didn't attempt to read because I sensed that the next inane question wasn't too far off. It wasn't.

'So how many pages in the whole book altogether?' he asked.

'589,' I guessed. Garlic nodded and whistled to himself like he was quite blown away by this.

'Hey, that means you've nearly got there. That's totally impressive, Spud, I can see why they gave you a scholarship.' Garlic continued to whistle as his eyes ran up the walls over the ceiling and onto the curtains where they paused for some moments before moving down the far wall and zoning out on the top of the fireplace.

'Hey, I'm serious, Spud, you must come to Malawi, hey,' he said. 'You'll love it.' I sensed my evening was doomed. 'It's like the best country in the world ...' Nevertheless I pretended to read on. 'Have I ever told you how crystal clear the water in the lake is?' I nodded inanely when he asked me a question. 'For Christmas we went up to my uncle's house there by Nkhata Bay.' And otherwise ignored him when he didn't. 'Most monitor lizards I've ever laid eyes on ...'

Suddenly, the cop shop door flew open and Fatty dragged himself in and collapsed into the armchair beside my couch. He studied his watch for some time and said, 'Three hours and four minutes. One call ... now that's called true love!' He shook his head like he was the luckiest guy in the world and huskily hollered for service.

'Where the hell is everyone?' he asked.

'Looking for Rowdy Stutterheim,' replied Garlic.

'Rowdy **and** Stutterheim, they're two people Garlic,' I snapped.

Fatty shouted hysterically again for service but there was no response.

'Hey, Garlic,' said Fatty in an excited voice, 'do you want some tea?'

'I would love some tea!' roared the thrilled Malawian.

'You're welcome,' beamed Fatty. 'Won't you make us a cuppa, too, while you're about it?'

'Score!' shouted Garlic, punching the air with his fist, unaware that he had just been duped.

'Better make it three cups, Garlic,' said Boggo as he marched through the doorway and threw himself onto the far end of my couch.

'Chronic!' he said. 'My oath to God ... is the shit hitting the fan or is the fan hitting the shit or whatever? I mean, it has to be the joke of the century: a mute and a stutterer on the run together.'

Garlic exited in a hurry to make tea and Fatty looked less than pleased about Boggo swanning in like a prefect and making himself at home in the cop shop without permission.

'Nobody invited you in here, Boggo,' spat Fatty angrily. 'And I'd rather you left if you're going to mention my girlfriend and her age and all that other disgusting stuff.'

A rare but convincingly warm smile spread across Boggo's face.

'Fatty, I was only pulling your leg on the tennis court about Penny,' he swooned. 'You know I think she's a babe ...'

'Really?' gasped Fatty. 'You agree that she's a babe?'

'I'd definitely bang her,' replied Boggo and flashed me the merest hint of a wink. He then realised that Fatty was scowling and quickly countered, 'Hypothetically, I mean ... if you weren't around ... and she was begging for it.'

There was a long pause.

'So you agree she's hot?' said Fatty eventually.

'Flaming hot.'

'Hey, thanks for saying that, Boggo, it means a lot.'

'No prob, so may I stay?'

'Make yourself at home,' gushed Fatty, unable to stop himself grinning.

Boggo must have taken Fatty literally because he put his feet up on the table and screamed at Garlic to make it snappy with his tea.

'My oath to God,' cursed Boggo. 'Malawians are flippin' useless.'

'That kettle took ages,' complained Garlic, as he entered with a circular tray laden with mugs. 'Water boils much quicker in Malawi.' He didn't seem to notice that he had sloshed tea over the sleeve of his white school shirt.

'I wasn't sure who wanted sugar or not so I gave everyone three spoons just in case,' he added, passing the tea around. He raised his mug and shouted, 'Cheers, everyone!' This was met with absolute silence.

'Oi!' shouted a deranged man at the door.

'Oh God, it's Frankenstein,' grumbled Boggo.

'Rain Man!' announced Garlic.

Vern said, 'Cop shop' in a loud voice and skulked into the prefects' room pretending to have a gun in his pocket despite it quite obviously being his hand with a pointed finger. His face was mostly glued to the floor but his eyes darted around in unexpected directions. After a moment's hesitation, he sat down on the carpet with a naughty smile and warmed his hands over the fireplace where there was no fire burning.

Friday 29th January

I can see that keeping up with regular diary entries this year is going to be difficult. Despite having my own room and personal space, it is impossible with the ridiculous amount of work demanded by all my teachers. Mongrel is by far the worst culprit after setting three quarters of all Afrikaans novels ever written to be read and reviewed by Monday. Clearly the man is unhinged and the violence he meted out on Noddy Worthington yesterday should have him arrested, jailed and vilified on Carte Blanche.

Report back:

- The missing duo of Rowdy and Stutterheim returned to school on Monday and claimed to have become lost and disorientated during free bounds.
- Viking wasn't able to beat the Fragile Five twenty strokes each because the boys' disappearance had attracted the attentions of their parents and the board of governors. In the end the punishment was commuted to five hours of hard labour in the housemaster's garden, which involved digging a

huge pit and then filling it up again with Viking hurling personal abuse from a deckchair on his veranda.

- Vern is still refusing to enter his room if he is out or exit if he is in. This prompted Eve to conduct a thirty minute counselling session in Vern's room on Tuesday afternoon which made absolutely no difference to the cretin's behaviour whatsoever.
- After hearing about Eve's 'house call', Boggo promptly barricaded himself in his room for a day and a half and demanded that he, too, have a counselling session with Eve. His thirty-seven hour stand-off with authority ended with Viking kicking the bog room door off its hinges on Thursday morning and dragging Boggo roughly into the showers where nasty shouting followed. The laughter and mockery of the assembled crowd did little to improve Boggo's mood, although he did somewhat silence the peanut gallery by swearing on his mother's life that he would sprinkle rat poison in the house water tank and kill everyone.
- Spud Milton has been selected for the first cricket team to play St James tomorrow! I have been summoned to a team talk tonight in the Barnes cop shop at 21:00. Simon is obviously captain and Rambo and I make up the other representatives from the house. I phoned Dad at the pub to break the news and he went ballistic with joy. Unfortunately, The Guv still hasn't returned and three different sources have said that he is having an operation in hospital. I slipped a note under his door wishing him a speedy recovery and added that I was missing our luncheons.
- More than a week after his supposed arrival, fellow prefect Eggwhite is yet to materialise. Viking has assured Fatty and me (who have been covering his duties in his absence) that Eggwhite has been

dealing with family issues and is certain to arrive by the end of the weekend.

- I took my own laundry for the final time in my school career. It is a task that I won't be missing. From next Wednesday morning I won't have to make my bed again either.

21:00 The team stood against the far wall and Simon called forward Sparerib as our stand-in coach to say a few words. Sparerib rambled on in his unique and unpleasant way about us being iconic ambassadors for the school and that the way we play sets an example to all boys. He then introduced The Glock who repeated what Sparerib had just said except slightly louder and significantly slower. Thereafter they moved down the row and handed out our red and white striped cricket caps. I looked down at mine and felt the material between my thumb and forefinger. How many hours of blood, anguish and disappointment has it taken to reach this moment? I wondered if it had all been worth it.

In the end there wasn't much spoken in the way of tactics but rather a great deal of tea drinking and munching of toast was done instead. Here I was in the prefects' room of another house late on a Friday night shooting the breeze with ten other boys looking ridiculous in their khaki uniforms and striped caps. I've never felt more important.

Saturday 30th January

Once again the weather gods were against us and by the time the first team minibus left for St James shortly after 8am thick black clouds were rolling in from the west. It was raining when we reached Pietermaritzburg and upon arrival at the school it was pouring. We went through the motions of getting ready and dressed up in our whites but all we could do was sit outside the change room and watch large pools of water appear on the outfield. By noon the game had been called off and we were back in the bus returning to school.

20:00   House video was *Terminator 2: Judgement Day* starring Arnold Schwarzenegger who Rambo swears is on steroids. As the film ended a brief punch-up broke out in the common room after Thinny declared the film better than *Star Wars*. JR Ewing seemed to take this personally and punched his supposed best friend Thinny in the face. Fatty and I quickly broke it up and Darryl (the last remaining) was dispatched to Boggo's room for painkillers while a sobbing Thinny slowly ascended the stairs clutching his jaw and shaking his head in utter shock and bewilderment.

Sunday 31st January

17:00   I summoned Thinny and JR Ewing to my room for a 'chat' about last night's punch-up. They both appeared rather pathetic standing there beside the basin. Thinny's jaw was swollen and JR's right hand was wrapped in a bandage. In hindsight, I should have ordered them to shake hands and get lost. Instead I foolishly asked JR Ewing why he had punched his friend in the face.

'Because he insulted *Star Wars* ...' was the sullen reply. I nodded slowly to buy myself some time but either way one looked at the situation it was absurd. For twenty minutes I attempted to make JR Ewing acknowledge that his behaviour was extreme if not completely insane but he stubbornly refused to see sense. Thinny kept shaking his head sadly like he was the victim of a heinous crime but added nothing at all.

After forcing JR Ewing into a reluctant and rather

insincere apology, I sent the two on their way with a bland warning to stay out of trouble.

Minutes later there was a timid knock on my door which turned out to be Thinny again. This time he was alone.

'Hey, Spud, I mean John,' he said softly. 'I just wanted to tell you why I think JR hit me in the face.'

'Why?' I asked.

'Because I sort of boned his ex-girlfriend in the holidays.'

'Why did you do that?' I asked.

'Because she was hot,' he replied.

'Right,' I said, momentarily lost for words.

'It's not my first time,' he said proudly.

'Oh,' I said.

'Not even my second.'

'Really?' I was unable to hide the surprise in my voice.

'I even boned a girl in a car over Christmas,' he added.

I was beginning to feel a little jealous of Thinny's numerous sexual conquests so I cut him off abruptly and sent him on his way. I then spent the half hour before dinner feeling like a complete virgin. How is it possible that somebody who looks like Thinny can have sex with so many women? Where are all these girls out there begging for bonings in cars? I decided Thinny had to be lying and strode off to dinner where I watched Fatty snort an entire saucer of milk through his nose and take a tenner off an astonished Boggo Greenstein.

Tuesday 2nd February

FIRST YEAR INITIATION CEREMONY
Venue: Cop Shop
Time: 20:30

A hyped-up Crazy Eight were already gathered inside

the cop shop and the kitchen annexe was crammed with the Fragile Five whom Fatty had placed on tea and toast duty. Each new boy has been instructed to prepare a brief speech/performance/introduction. This was my idea and although Boggo initially called me gay for bringing theatre to the initiation ceremony, Rambo and Simon thought it was excellent and the idea was adopted.

'Hey, Sidewinder!' shouted Fatty above the din inside the cop shop. 'Make it another round of Bovril cheese, and not so stingy with the cheese this time!'

'And another round of Milo!' hollered Boggo. 'And make it stronger. That last mug tasted like rectal discharge.'

When the door flew open I thought it would be Rowdy or Plump Graham with the Milo, but instead it was the wild and bearded face of Viking.

'Viking!' shouted Garlic in alarm and hurled himself over the top of his armchair, disappearing from view. The happy hubbub abruptly ended and all eyes turned to our housemaster.

'Gentlemen!' he roared. 'Good evening.'

'Good evening, sir,' replied Garlic from behind the vacant armchair.

It seemed he planned to remain in hiding until Viking had left.

'So I believe it's initiation night,' said our housemaster wearily. He glared around the room in a concerned manner.

'Beat 'em up!' announced Vern.

'I beg your pardon, Blackadder?' replied Viking, a deep frown creasing his forehead. Vern didn't respond, instead he pretended to be fast asleep against Rambo's shoulder. This rattled Viking who seemed torn between

40

screaming at Vern and pretending that he didn't exist at all. In the end he did neither and merely repeated, 'Right, right, right,' and seemed to be pondering something of great significance. 'Take it easy on the youngsters,' he concluded before leaving the cop shop. 'You wouldn't want their suicide on your conscience.'

'My oath Viking's pre-menstrual,' said Rambo, lighting up a cigarette once the housemaster had left.

'He busts you smoking he'll go ape shit,' warned Simon.

'What's he gonna do – send me to Robben Island?'

The relieved face of Garlic appeared over the top of the armchair. 'Phew! That was a close one! I thought he had us there.'

Once Rambo had finished smoking, the first member of the new group of slaves was summoned to a little wooden stage in the cop shop.

It was most certainly an unusual and unexpected start to the initiation proceedings. Despite having a weird half-American, half-African accent, Ntoko 'Nzone' Vilikazi had us all grudgingly clapping at his clever rap song and dance routine in which he used all of the prefects' names which impressed the audience greatly. Despite being small in stature, he wasn't intimidated, even when Boggo hurled half a mug of hot Milo over him after he referred to Boggo as 'Bro'. The icing on the cake was when Nzone (which is apparently what even his grandmother calls him) demonstrated his skills by keeping a soccer ball in the air by using most of his body parts before ending the routine by mysteriously catching the ball with the back of his neck. Garlic gave the performance a loud whoop and a standing ovation and was later quite rightly reprimanded by Simon for being overly supportive and laming us out.

'It's not the bloody Royal Variety Show, you wop,' blasted Simon and banned Garlic from any further cheering and applause.

Surprisingly, it was Vern who inspired Nzone's new nickname. After announcing to us that he didn't need a nickname since he already had one in Nzone, he was interrupted by Vern who declared, 'Enzo!'

Almost in unison we chorused:

'Enzo Ferrari!'

'What's Enzo Ferrari?' asked Garlic.

'The guy who invented Ferrari, you dork,' replied Simon, rolling his eyes.

'But Ferrari wasn't black!' boomed the incredulous Garlic.

'Nothing wrong with a black Ferrari,' declared Rambo drily.

And so it was official.

Marco Delaney was next and before he had even stepped onto the stage Boggo called him to a halt.

'What's on your shirt, Delaney?' Marco Delaney looked down at the stain on his khaki shirt. He grinned sheepishly at Boggo, shrugged his shoulders, and said, 'Sir ... I think it's tomato sauce from dinner.'

'Looks like dribble to me,' commented Boggo after taking a closer look at the small stain on the boy's shirt.

Upon further inspection it was discovered that the boy had his shirt un-tucked at the back, both laces undone and his fly hanging at half-mast.

Marco Delaney said that he had a comedy routine planned but this was cancelled when nobody indicated any interest in hearing his jokes. After desperate pleading from Marco (and Garlic) for a few crackers to be told, Simon relented and allowed him a single joke to prove his mettle. Marco stepped onto the stage and delivered an incredibly lame joke about a barman serving a pint of milk to a cow. To make matters worse he initially delivered the punch line from another joke before correcting himself and apologising and then repeating the correct punch line to no response whatsoever. (The irony is that Vern and Garlic howled with laughter at the wrong punch line.) In the end Marco was christened Shambles and banished from the cop shop under no illusion that the laugh was firmly on him.

After the exit of Shambles, the ridiculously toothy Gregory St James was ordered in and from this point onwards the ceremony began to regress at a steady rate. Just as the grinning youngster stepped onto the stage to begin his story of the St James family's history since 1821, Vern set fire to a cushion and began screaming in alarm. The flaming cushion inspired general chaos and a loud argument between Fatty, who demanded the cushion be left burning in the fireplace, and Boggo, who wanted it doused with water and removed from the cop shop. Nobody could agree and the cushion continued to burn while Gregory's high pitched ramble was drowned out by general arguments, squabbles and personal insults. In the end Rambo christened the boy Plaque because of his huge teeth, before sending him packing. We never found out why his great-grandfather switched from farming bananas to cabbages.

Thereafter Simon called for a ten minute break during which the acrid smell in the cop shop was attended to by the Fragile Five. Boggo and Fatty's bitter argument about the cushion continued all the way to the urinal and back some minutes later. Rambo eventually lost patience with what he called their 'feminine' bickering and threatened to scorch their crotches with a burning log should they continue. They didn't.

The grandly named but weedy looking Julian Marshall

Tinsley was next. He looked disconcertingly pale as he shuffled into the cop shop and gingerly made his way towards the wooden block like he was facing the guillotine. He began his 'performance' by mumbling in an extremely soft monotone with his eyes fixed on his shoes. He soon stopped his laborious mumble and said he was feeling sick and urgently needed the loo.

Tinsley was packed off to the bogs immediately and the ginger haired Michael Wiggle was ordered in. It was clear that Wiggle was an emotional mess from the off and after taking one look at us, promptly burst into tears. Wiggle's weeping set Vern off with his sniffing, sighing and eye rubbing which only aggravated the situation further. Rambo wasn't impressed with the spineless new boy and told him so. He threatened to roast the skin off Wiggle's face in the Snackwich maker should he continue with this dismally over-emotional behaviour. This made the freckly boy begin sobbing uncontrollably and whimpering about going home. Wiggle received no sympathy from the Crazy Eight, was christened Small & Freckly, and ejected from the cop shop.

The opening and closing of the door brought in a blushing and eager Russell van Rensburg. 'Sirs!' he said with a nod. 'Tinsley isn't feeling well and collapsed in the bogs. People say that he could even be near death.'

'Near death!' gasped Garlic in alarm.

'I'm going to take him to the san,' declared the new boy in a defiant tone.

'What are you – some sort of Albert Schweitzer?' sneered Boggo through machine gun laughter.

'Albert Schweitzer,' repeated Vern with his thumb wedged into his left nostril.

'Who's Albert Schweitzer?' asked Garlic.

'He's the ambulance driver who saved hundreds of lives during the First World War,' explained Boggo. 'If you don't know that, you're bound to fail matric.'

With our focus diverted, Russell van Rensburg fled from the cop shop to help his ill friend to the safety of the sanatorium.

The Harmless Half-Dozen (HHD)

Enzo Ferrari
Shambles
Small & Freckly
Plaque
Albert Schweitzer
Near Death

Wednesday 3rd February

08:00 Simon announced that the assignment of slaves to prefects would be done by means of a lucky draw in Viking's office which nobody believed. Small & Freckly has been placed on suicide watch by Viking after hearing about the boy's emotional breakdown in the cop shop last night. As such, he was assigned to Simon along with Enzo Ferrari. Rambo chose Plaque after declaring himself fascinated by the size of the boy's teeth and Fatty was dealt Shambles. I have been assigned Albert Schweitzer and Near Death is slaving for the Missing Eggwhite.

13:30 I officially met up with Albert Schweitzer and showed him around my room so that he could familiarise himself with the way things work. He was extremely polite and respectful and promised to keep my room in an orderly state. I left him to it and headed to the nets to sharpen up my skills for Saturday's match against St Giles.

16:45 Returned from cricket practice to find my room

transformed. Every item of clothing has been neatly folded and packed away and all my shoes are gleaming and smelling of polish. Clearly Albert Schweitzer didn't think much of my original organisation because everything has been relocated, refolded and repacked. The small locker that I had been using for textbooks now houses my socks and shoes and all my textbooks have been assigned into subjects along the shelf above my desk. I noticed, too, that my laundry had been taken and the sheets and duvet cover had been changed.

There was only one blemish. I couldn't find my towel, face-wash, shampoo and slops anywhere in my room. I marched into the house and found Albert Schweitzer in the annexe on afternoon tea duty with Plaque. Despite his industrious work I decided to remain hard to please and questioned him aggressively about the whereabouts of my missing items. Albert Schweitzer didn't seem too concerned with my bristling intimidation and replied, 'I left them all in the prefects' cubicle in the showers so that you could go straight in after cricket practice.'

'Oh right. Thanks,' I replied and felt oddly unsure of myself in front of a youngster displaying such confidence and ruthless efficiency.

'I didn't know if I should take through your razor and shaving cream too,' he said while fishing a tea bag out of Simon's mug. 'But then I figured that would be pointless.'

I felt the blood rising to my face. Was this young whipper-snapper mocking my sluggish development on his very first day of service?

'What do you mean that would be pointless?' I demanded through clenched teeth.

'It's pointless because you obviously would use the basin in your room to shave and not the bogs.'

'Obviously,' I repeated and felt stupid for being so

sensitive.

'You'd better get into the showers pronto,' he advised while buttering three slices of toast with ease, 'because Mr Greenstein has been showering since 2:30 and the hot water is apparently going fast.'

'Right,' I replied and lumbered off to the bogs where Boggo was discussing the basics of tantric sex with a number of riveted juniors. The water was barely luke-warm.

Thursday 4th February

Missing Eggwhite has been spotted on the school grounds by Thinny and Runt. He must be well rested after his ten week holiday. Missing Eggwhite didn't report to the house, though, and no other sightings of him have been made but Viking has nevertheless assured everybody that he has in fact returned. Rambo wagered Fatty permanent use of the enormous blue tea mug that the sighting probably wasn't Missing Eggwhite at all but Ryan (Free Willy) Cotton, the school squash champion, to whom he bears a striking resemblance from behind.

Friday 5th February

I crossed paths with Eve after chapel outside the junior classroom. She gave me a beautiful smile when I greeted her. Unfortunately, I haven't got round to that list of suave pick-up lines yet so I stared at her gormlessly and said, 'Nice weather today, hey, ma'am.' She smiled weakly and disappeared through the archway. I gazed up at the sky only to discover that it was overcast.

Why can't I be cooler in front of hot girls and teachers?

Saturday 6th February

09:00 Albert Schweitzer may be pushing things a bit far with his excellent slave service. Not only did he lay out all my cricket clothes on a coat hanger but he cleaned out my cricket bag, washed my pads, shined my boots, and even sandpapered my bat. I'm not complaining but I do question the boy's sanity.

I'm happy to report that my bowling form has returned. I only took one wicket in the easy win at St Giles, but even Simon reckoned I deserved a few more. Sparerib complimented me on my effort by saying 'Bowled' under his breath as he passed me outside our change room.

17:00 Returned to my room to find Albert Schweitzer perched on a chair which itself was perched on my desk. He had a tin of white paint balanced in his left hand and seemed to be doing some touch-ups to cracks on the far corner of the wall.

'How was the cricket?' he asked. Albert Schweitzer doesn't know the first thing about cricket so I left it at, 'We won.'
    'Your showering stuff is waiting and I need to know whether you are wearing shorts or longs tonight.'
    'Shorts,' I replied.
    'Polo-neck or V-neck jersey?' he questioned.
    'V-neck,' I answered.
    'Tea or coffee after your shower?' he asked.
    'Tea,' I replied and strode off to the showers, carrying nothing.

Sunday 7th February

Assessment tests begin tomorrow which means a gruelling week of eighteen hours worth of mock exam conditions. The teachers say these tests are for their own assessments and mean absolutely nothing in terms of our final matric marks. Since teachers usually mean the opposite of what they say, wide scale panic has broken out in the higher grade classes. Lucky Vern (functional grade) has no tests, unless of course you count writing the date without making a spelling mistake a test. I grafted hard all morning on maths and geography and decided to head down to the courts to smack some tennis balls after lunch. I strode across the quad and through the great archway where a number of third years were gathered in their full school uniform waiting for a bus.

'Hey, Spud!' barked Garlic, looking wide-eyed and holding out his hand. 'We really need to talk.' I didn't reply as I hoped to make it to the tennis courts without interruption.

'There's something I really have to tell you,' he said rather desperately as he looked about us for a suitable place to spill the beans.

I kept walking, hoping to shake him off.

'Quick, Spud!' bellowed Garlic, attracting the attention of a sizeable crowd of boys standing about the archway. 'Let's do it behind the tree!'

I heard some sniggers from the Normal Seven and others.

'I'll be quick, I promise,' pleaded Garlic to louder chortling from the boys behind me. Instead, I pretended to have my Walkman playing in my ears and continued down the grass bank towards the tennis courts.

'Please, Spud!' wailed Garlic as he sped up behind me. 'We seriously need to talk.'

'Just stop being so embarrassing!' I shouted, surprising even myself. Garlic nodded and apologised with watery eyes that naturally made me feel guilty.

'I have a secret,' he whispered.

'So why are you telling me then?' I asked.

'Because it's a secret,' declared Garlic like I was a complete moron.

I gave up attempting to reason with the Malawian and waited for what he would say next.

'Rambo's trying to eat me again,' he blurted with a tortured expression.

'I think he's definitely a cannibal,' he said, this time in a quieter voice, 'I really do.' He showed me a bite mark on his arm and a nasty purple one on the back of his thigh.

'He bites me all the time,' added Garlic sadly. 'He even attacked me last night at one in the morning!'

'You know Rambo,' I said in a reasonable voice. 'He's only trying to psyche you out.'

He didn't seem to hear my advice and immediately blurted, 'Boggo says that Rambo even had sex with his own mom.'

'His step-mom,' I corrected, but Garlic didn't seem to hear that either.

'And Eve.'

'Can't deny that,' I admitted.

'... and your girlfriend on New Year's Eve,' he said uncomfortably loudly.

'What girlfriend?' I asked, sure that I hadn't heard him correctly. Garlic flushed pink and his hand rose to cover his mouth in that familiar manner when he's blown something that he swore not to.

'What did you say, Garlic?' My voice was surprisingly full of rage.

He took one look at my face and sprinted off like his life depended on it. 'Who told you that?' I screamed as we sped across the rugby field towards the railway line. I was gaining on him and he knew it because he kept whipping his pink face around to check if I was still in hot pursuit. I heard the blast of an approaching train from the left and had a terrible premonition of Garlic being crushed and me being arrested for his manslaughter. I stopped running.

If I could have caught him, I would have bitten him too.

Monday 8th February

Didn't sleep very well thinking about what Garlic said yesterday about Rambo having sex with my 'girlfriend' on New Year's Eve. It had to be Amanda as I doubt Gavin the Umpire would have stood for a threesome. Even if it is true, Amanda never really was my girlfriend and I have no right to feel jealous about this news. Still, it felt like a stab in the nuts.

Wednesday 10th February

12:30   As predicted, the teachers were all lying and the 'meaningless assessment tests' turned into real exams with outside invigilators. Fatty says this is meant to be the best year of our lives, but with all the pressure and intensity being heaped on us I'm not so sure that will be possible.

Boggo reminded us that the St Mary's orgy/social on Saturday will be just the tonic we need after a brutal academic week. He said he was going to carry out a perverse and thorough boning on Saturday and set off to the English assessment/exam with a determined expression and an excessive amount of stationery under his arm.

Friday 12th February

Everything felt positive today with the last of the assessment/exam tests behind us and the weekend ahead.

16:45   Boggo kicked up such a firestorm in the showers about the orgy/social that a number of boys tried in vain to sign up at late notice.

Simon was also full of Friday positivity and gave a stirring speech at the first team talk. He even labelled us 'unbeaten' which, although technically correct, is hardly much of an achievement since two of our three games so far have been rained out. Nevertheless the speech wound us all up and even Rambo looked the most excited he has all year. Lincoln College had better bring their game tomorrow because I'm betting we'll be on fire come 10am.

Saturday 13th February

09:30   There were some astonishing scenes at the cricket oval where a fight broke out among the Lincoln team shortly before the game was supposed to have started. Up until the fracas broke out Lincoln, despite their reputation for being one of the weakest schools that we play, appeared to look fairly efficient about how they were carrying out their warm-ups. Then the tallest boy on their side lobbed the cricket ball to his captain who wasn't paying attention. Despite a loud call of 'Chips!' 155 grams of shiny red leather crashed into the Lincoln captain's forehead.

The captain, who also apparently moonlights as a DJ and deputy head boy, marched up to the tall and gangly culprit and whacked him straight in the face with a cricket bat. The lanky boy's parents became involved as did the Lincoln coach, Sparerib and Mongrel, who streaked out of his garden gate in his jogging shorts to join the heated argument. Thankfully, Dad hadn't arrived yet as I'm sure he too would have become heavily embroiled.

Eventually, the fight petered out and the lanky boy was sent to the san with a bleeding nose and blurred vision. The game was delayed by half an hour while the Lincoln coach lectured his team under a tree near the scoreboard.

10:20 A white Mercedes carrying two insane people roared up to the field and the two occupants made an embarrassing scene of setting up their bar/picnic table on the boundary. Mom hollered across to me, making everybody turn their heads just as I walked into the change room. Inside the change room I heard the distinct sound of an exploding champagne cork from outside, followed by a loud shriek and chorus of 'Cheers!'

'Hey, Spud!' said Stinky, entering the change room with his helmet on. 'Your folks have arrived.'

'Shot, Stinky,' I said in a nonchalant fashion like the news didn't mean much to me.

Then Martin Leslie entered. 'Hey, Spud, your Mom and Dad are here,' he said with a hint amazement in his voice.

'Thanks,' I said.

'I think your mom's looking for you,' he continued, as if I should do something about it sooner rather than later.

'Cool,' I said, casually lacing up my spikes.

'Yoo hoo!' came Mom's strident call from the window behind me. I sprinted out of the change room, turned the corner and saw my mother perched on a drainpipe peeping through the window into our change room.

'Mom!' I bellowed.

She turned to me with her mouth open in surprise. 'There he is!' she screamed and darted over to me with champagne splashing over the sides of her wine glass.

'Hello, handsome!' she shrieked in front of the entire Lincoln team who were standing in silence at the edge of the field. I quickly ushered Mom back to the car and into her deckchair before she could cause more of a scene.

'Where's Dad?' I asked.

'Checking the pitch,' she replied, motioning out towards the middle with her glass. With barely fifteen minutes until the start of play my father was standing at the wickets and pretending to play a series of flamboyant shots with his blue Standard Bank umbrella. By the looks of things his shadow innings was attracting some attention.

'I see your father has all the shots,' hollered a smug Mr Leslie from the picnic next door. I laughed politely and watched as Dad's flailing around at the wicket became more forceful as he laid into the imaginary bowler. Thankfully, the maniac must have done something to his back because his umbrella innings ended abruptly and he staggered towards us in a decidedly flatfooted and sideways manner.

'Done my back in again, howzit my boy,' groaned Dad all at once as he sank into his deckchair and floored his champagne.

'That's what happens when you try and show off for all the ladies,' said Mom rather smugly. She winked at me and topped up her plastic wine goblet.

'I was conducting a memory exercise of my fifty-six not out back in 1961,' said Dad rather loftily.

'Oh ... a memory exercise,' mocked Mom. 'Let me guess – you were finding yourself.' The way she emphasised 'finding yourself' made me think that my mother doesn't think much of it at all.

'I found myself in the bath at thirteen,' retorted Dad and my parents erupted into peals of hysterical laughter. Mom poured the rest of the champagne into Dad's glass and asked me to fetch another bottle from the cool box in the boot. I was pleased to see that my parents had only brought up two bottles of champagne, but less thrilled at the sight of a further three bottles of red wine that lay partially concealed beneath Dad's anorak behind the driver's seat.

At lunch my parents were in high spirits; by afternoon tea they were completely sozzled. Dad took up most of my tea break with his conspiracy theory about Sparerib deliberately coaching our team into the ground to kibosh my chances of making Natal Schools. I returned to the change room to find an anxious Sparerib in urgent conversation with Simon. Unbelievably, the warring Lincoln team were well and truly beating us. With only 137 runs needed for victory our top order batting fell apart and we found ourselves in desperate trouble at 33 for the loss of seven wickets with an hour and a half of play left after tea. Worse still was that The Glock took it upon himself to deliver a threatening speech to the team in the change room. Unfortunately, he delivered it mainly to Rambo, Stinky, myself and Spearmint as our team's only remaining batsmen.

'I don't know about you, Spuddy, but I don't want to be remembered for losing to Lincoln,' hissed Simon who had seated himself next to me on the stands as we watched Rambo and Stinky face the music in the middle. I think our captain was intending to be supportive but his continuous advice and pointers were only making me feel more nervous.

'Our only chance is to fight for the draw,' he said through clenched teeth like he was worried somebody might read his lips through binoculars from afar. 'If we're still batting come five o'clock, then we're still unbeaten.' I nodded and kept watching the pitch where

Stinky was looking decidedly unsteady at the crease.

'Focus, Stinky!' bellowed Simon who had also picked up on his sudden fragility. Stinky looked around and nodded at Simon like he had got the message. He then proceeded to conduct a wild swing and miss as the ball flew narrowly over his off stump.

'Focus, Stinky!' roared my father from behind the boundary.

'Stinky's such a turdhole,' muttered Simon. He turned to me again. 'Okay, Spuddy, now listen up,' he said. 'I don't care if you don't score a single run but I want you to stay out there.' I nodded again and watched Stinky's middle stump being uprooted as a despairing groan sounded around the ground.

Simon grabbed my arm as I stood up. 'Tell Rambo to wind down the clock.'

I nodded and trudged in to bat. My Remex read 15:44 which meant that I would have to bat for 76 minutes and either Rambo or Spearmint would have to do likewise. A massive scream went up from the Milton Merc parked on the deep cover boundary, followed by urgent hooting and a brief snatch of deafening music from the car's stereo.

A seething Rambo met me halfway to the wicket. 'I'm gonna kill Stinky, my oath to God,' he said.

'Simon says you must wind down the clock,' I told him. He nodded and said, 'Spud, look at me.' I looked into his eyes which were burning black. 'We're gonna do this.' I nodded. 'We're going to do this – you and me,' he repeated. I nodded again.

Slowly but surely the minutes slipped by. I blocked out at one end and Rambo at the other. The clouds were beginning to roll in and the atmosphere around the ground steamed like a pressure cooker. Every blocked ball was cheered and every over that was successfully negotiated was met with thunderous applause and strident hooting from the white Mercedes at deep cover. At exactly 16:37 Rambo was hit on the glove by a medium pace bowler and fell to the ground screaming. Then there was a long delay after Simon 'struggled' to find ice in the pavilion to treat Rambo's hand. Lincoln were visibly livid by Rambo's obvious time wasting tactics and their coach/umpire wasn't exactly what you would call sympathetic to Rambo's declaration that his hand might be broken. In the end Rambo's theatrics used up valuable time but twenty-four minutes still to be negotiated.

By 16:50 and with only three overs remaining, I met Rambo in the middle of the wicket for another brief chat.

'Did you shag Amanda?' I heard myself say.

'What? Why are you asking me this now, Milton? Are you retarded?' spat Rambo, looking at me incredulously.

'Did you?' I asked again.

'Of course not,' he said and walked away from me.

A delicious sensation of relief washed over my body. Eighteen balls remained and the end was in sight. The thing was that I just could not get the image of Amanda out of my mind. Even as the Lincoln opening bowler was running in all I could imagine was her face watching me. I heard the snick as the ball took the edge of my bat and flew low to second slip. But then I was surrounded by groans and somebody swore angrily. The fielder buried his face in his hands. He had dropped a half chance and my idiocy about Amanda went unpunished.

'Steady on, Milton,' came the sharp order from a bench on which a long-legged man in tweeds was sitting under a blanket. His face was obscured by a large brown hat although the tip of his smoking pipe was just visible. The Guv nodded to me and I nodded firmly back.

Amanda was gone from my mind.

When I saw off the final delivery of the day a relieved cheer filled the ground. We shook hands with the dejected Lincoln players and Rambo and I strode off to our waiting team mates. I looked up to where The Guv had been sitting on his bench but it now stood empty. Rambo grinned at me and placed his arm around my shoulder. He leant closer and whispered, 'Oh, by the way, Milton, I did shag Amanda on New Year's Eve.' His eyes never left mine. 'If it's any consolation, she's a hell cat between the sheets.' Seconds later we were engulfed by our team mates.

23:30 All things considered, it has been a thoroughly extreme and unpredictable day in the life of the lesser Milton. What with the tumultuous drawn cricket match, drunken parents cavorting on the boundary, Rambo's revelations about bonking 'hell cat' Amanda, and the momentary arrival and disappearance of The Guv, it has quite literally been impossible to predict. With this in mind I shouldn't have been gobsmacked by what occurred at St Mary's, but I was. Just as it seemed as if this social would be as dreary and mortifying as any other of my school career, something unexpectedly sexy and amazing happened.

Shortly after 9pm, I was casually dancing in a circle with Boggo, Fatty, Penny and Garlic when a tall and extremely hot brunette materialised on the edge of our circle. Boggo immediately commenced with some savage pelvic thrusting in different directions as he gyrated himself towards her. The girl smoothly evaded the spasmodic Greenstein, and began dancing with me. She smiled and I smiled back. We kept watching each other. Later, we slow danced to Prince's Purple Rain and kissed for most of the song. Later outside on a hockey field we kissed again, this time for longer. Dotted around the field were other couples doing the same thing and yet it all felt so natural and easy like it does in dreams. We didn't talk much but she told me her name was Sarah and her breathing changed when I ran my fingers over her body.

Sunday 14th February

I only realised that it was Valentine's Day when a fight broke out between Thinny and JR Ewing in the common room after breakfast. JR Ewing's ex-girlfriend (whom Thinny recently confessed to boning) sent Thinny a box of chocolates and a sexy card via special delivery. What with there being no normal post on a Sunday it didn't really feel like a typical Valentine's Day. I spent the rest of the day in my room attempting to work but fantasising about Sarah instead. After the events of last night, the news about Rambo and Amanda doesn't seem to matter any more.

Monday 15th February

I received a Valentine's letter! Unfortunately, once Fatty had torn open his large pink envelope, devoured the chocolates and read his card from Penny he charged straight down to my room and asked me if I had received my card from Brenda. I had already convinced myself that it was from Sarah despite it having being posted last Tuesday and containing the handwriting of a seven year old. To make matters worse, Brenda had sent identical cards with similar messages to Rambo, Boggo, Spike and Meg Ryan's Son.

Tuesday 16th February

I spent most of the day having an internal debate on the merits of calling up St Mary's Convent and asking for a hot brunette called Sarah. Decided against it on the basis that the school is probably half crawling with hot Sarahs and I'm not sure the nuns would be impressed with that kind of request. When we kissed each other for the final time she didn't mention seeing me again and I didn't want to appear desperate and needy so neither did I.

So there it is – a glorious one night stand. As always with Spud Milton, the pathway to the Garden of Eden ends in a disappointing cul de sac. The problem is that I haven't thought of much else since Saturday night. The condition is so serious that I've even lost interest in stalking Eve.

After lunch I set off for a jog to clear the mind and ended up running along the bog stream and past The Guv's house. The curtains were open so I knocked and called, but there was no reply and only silence from inside. I was about to leap back over the bog stream and rejoin Pilgrims' Walk when I heard the familiar drone – 'Milton!'

'Sir!' I called, looking up at the ashen face that was glaring at me through the curtains of the living room.

'What in Fanny Higgins are you doing cavorting about in my garden?'

'I came to see if you were all right, sir,' I replied.

'I'm dying, Milton,' The Guv said immediately and slowly dragged his finger across his throat.

'What do you mean, sir?' I shouted, fervently hoping that he was joking.

'Gangrene,' he said grimly and took a hefty swig from a bottle of wine.

'It began in the toenails shortly after Christmas and grew steadily northwards,' he said, staring out at the fields like it might be his final afternoon.

It was impossible to ascertain whether The Guv really was dying of gangrene or merely making dark jokes about himself while drinking heavily.

'Come closer, Milton,' he ordered and I walked up to the window. Upon closer scrutiny The Guv looked terribly pale and completely drunk. It was difficult not to laugh at him in his red and yellow striped pyjamas standing on a footstool and peering through the window with a bottle of red wine in each hand. 'Milton, you've met Private Pinotage and Colonel Cabernet?' he said, holding out the wine. He winked at me and out of the side of his mouth whispered, 'I couldn't in all conscience split the platoon.'

I nodded in agreement as The Guv took a swig from Private Pinotage.

'Art Garfunkel, Milton!' he shouted unexpectedly loudly. 'You've bloody grown. Or should I say you've sprouted?' He angled Colonel Cabernet in my direction and said, 'Just as well, old boy. If you ask me, you were beginning to take on the appearance of a consumptive David Bowie.'

I laughed loudly, but The Guv remained deadly serious.

'Between these four walls, I may have picked up a case of the pox from a large nurse in the psychiatric wing.' He pointed Private Pinotage at his nethers and said he planned to go down all guns blazing. By this stage I wasn't sure if he was referring to the nurse, death, wine, or the pox.

I also pondered a possible link between the pox and the VD plague.

When I pushed him for further details about his disease he shouted, 'No bloody comment!' and slammed the window shut.

Wednesday 17th February

15:00   Garlic, Boggo and Vern took up residence in the cop shop on account of having apparently received permission from Rambo who was fast asleep in his room with the door locked and a *disturb and die* sign on his door. It seemed that evicting the non-prefect matrics would be impossible. Fatty made a break for the archives while I attempted to master the googly in the cricket nets.

17:05   I returned to the house where a deeply impressed Albert Schweitzer was waiting for me.

'Hey, John,' he said, 'Small & Freckly said you had a telephone call from a girl at ten to four.'

'Thanks,' I replied and made my way to the showers where my stuff had been neatly laid out. Albert Schweitzer marched along beside me and had much to report back on.

'I've made a list of things you need to stock up on this long weekend. All the usuals – toothpaste, soap, cop shop stuff ...'

'Thanks.' As I was slipping out of my clothes Albert Schweitzer turned his back politely and double-checked the soap bar in the soap box. My clothes had barely hit the floor when he snatched them up and raced off without saying anything further. The showers were all taken but both Plaque and Near Death stepped out when I approached. I nodded my thanks to Plaque and claimed his steaming shower.

After a good soaking I dried off and made my way along the passage towards the house door. Out of nowhere Albert Schweitzer appeared and began walking alongside me again, talking at a furious pace.

'Just spoke to Small & Freckly,' he said. 'The girl on the telephone call didn't leave her name or a message.'

'Thanks,' I replied.

'Who do you think it might be, John?' he asked eagerly.

I shrugged and closed the door, leaving my slave looking rather forlorn outside. Inside my heart was thumping at the thought that it might have been her. I allowed the towel to drop and studied my naked body in the long mirror fastened to the inside of the cupboard door. A tad more meat and muscle than before perhaps, but still not much to write home about. A shaft of sunlight slid over the chapel roof and beamed through my window like a light sabre. It was golden and warm and I loved the feel of it across my face. On the bed my khakis had been carefully laid out for dinner, but a part of me resisted putting them on.

Thursday 18th February

Never sit next to Garlic at school hymn practice. Not only is he tone deaf and sings at the volume of a shout, but he weeps during the school hymn.

The Malawian, despite being in floods of tears minutes earlier, was in sprightly form at breakfast because he is leaving this afternoon for his beloved Blantyre. Thankfully, he isn't heading to the lake which means we will be spared a series of inane stories about his windsurfer, monitor lizards and evolutionary fish with upside down faces. He did, however, invite us all to visit whenever we wanted and narrowly avoided being stabbed in the head by Rambo's fork which flew across the table and sailed millimetres over the top of Garlic's luminous left ear.

08:20   I returned to my room to brush my teeth and gather up the books that had been neatly readied on my desk. Despite having locked my door, Albert Schweitzer was inside ferreting away in my cupboard.

'How did you get in here?' I demanded.

Schweitzer didn't wilt in the face of my threatening approach and aggressive tone. Instead he looked at me like I was a simpleton and said, 'You left the window open.'

Friday 19th February

11:15 While soaking up a rare minute of not having anything immediate to do, a tall shadow blocked out the sun and I found myself squinting up at Simon who shouted 'Catch!' and flicked a turquoise envelope in my direction. The motley gathering of sun-tanners on the house bench, consisting of JR Ewing, Barryl, Darryl (the last remaining), Meg Ryan's Son, Stutterheim, Enzo Ferrari and Shambles, demanded that I open the letter and read its contents. I immediately agreed, opened the envelope and pretended to read a note inside. My (porno) graphic reading of my imaginary letter had the idiots hoodwinked and when I said I couldn't read aloud any more because the letter was becoming too sick and sexually disturbing, I had to flee the mob and hurtle back to my room where I locked the door and windows, all the while laughing hysterically and gasping for breath. I opened the envelope again and inside was a tiny slip of silver paper on which was written:

Sarah Silver 774 3031

What a way to start the long weekend!

Saturday 20th February

19:00 Wombat was half pissed upon arrival at the Royal Natal Yacht Club. Not only was she embarrassingly loud and shrill but her breath reeked of whisky and she yelled 'All aboard!' at the maître d' as we stepped into the dining room. Fair enough, the yacht club lies on the banks of the harbour, but to spend the entire evening thinking you're on a ship sailing for Southampton with the Duke of Edinburgh hosting a party on the deck below is just plain daft. When the distinguished Indian waiter with grey hair came to take our food orders, Wombat blasted him for being a slacker and ordered the man to roll up his sleeves and pump the bilges. The waiter stared at Wombat for some time before clearing his throat and recommending the prawn curry.

Wombat pointed at me and announced, 'David will have the kingklip, as will Roy his father.' She pointed at Mom and said, 'My sister will have cottage pie, and I'll have the hake and pilchards.' The waiter obviously figured out that he was dealing with a jabbering nutcase as he had by now ceased writing on his pad. Meanwhile, Mom seemed genuinely appalled at being referred to as Wombat's sister and was furiously applying make-up to her face while scowling into a small hand mirror which she held below the level of the table. Thankfully, Dad called the waiter aside, ordered a double round, and requested a few more minutes to study the menu.

Wombat excused herself after dinner and said that she needed the loo. Mom offered to accompany her but Wombat snapped back that she wasn't an invalid, snatched up her handbag and strode off angrily.

'What a lady!' quipped Dad, before belching loudly and stacking a few empty beer cans in a pyramid formation. Mom berated Dad for his poor manners and blamed his hanging around the pub with seedy characters for his lapse in standards. My father appeared unconcerned by Mom's lecture, kicked me under the table, and whispered, 'Have you seen the jugs on the bride's mother?' I shook my head. 'Bigger than Parton,' said Dad with a naughty look in his eye.

'What's that?' questioned Mom in a menacing tone.

'I just said ... I beg your pardon,' replied Dad, casually pouring another Castle into his tilted glass.

Suddenly a terrible wailing noise started up on the veranda. It would be best described as a combination of an old air raid siren, screeching tyres, and the beginnings of a serious cat fight. All the diners ceased eating and craned their necks to see who could be responsible for such a shrill and bloody massacre of God Save the Queen.

Our waiter and the concerned maître d' ushered Wombat back to her seat after she had completed her hideous rendition of the British national anthem. Thankfully, nobody ordered dessert or coffee so once Mom had forged Wombat's signature on the bill we bundled my grandmother into the car before she could cause further trouble and set off for Wombat's flat via Umbilo to avoid possible roadblocks.

Sunday 21st February

17:30 I was shivering, could hardly breathe, and my tongue felt as thick as a cricket bat. I couldn't back out now, what with Mom out walking, Dad spraying his roses, and Blacky fast asleep in his basket – there would never again be such a perfect time to make the call.

'Hello, Sarah speaking.'

An explosion went off in my head and I heard myself saying, 'Hi, is that Sarah?' In hindsight this was a hugely embarrassing start since she had already identified herself.

'Um ... I think I just said I was Sarah,' she said, sounding a little peeved.

'Hi Sarah, sorry, it's John Milton here.'

There was a pause on the other end until I remembered that I hadn't revealed my surname on the night of the social.

'It's John. You know the guy at the social ...' I prompted, feeling the blood rush to my face. I was in the process of making a colossal fool out of myself.

'What social?' Her question shocked me to the core. I began doubting everything, even my own sanity.

'This is Sarah Silver, right?' I asked in a high voice that sounded like it had run out of air and was now fuelled by desperation alone.

'Right,' she replied.

Come to think of it, now even her voice sounded different too.

'And you go to St Mary's Convent, right?'

'Right ...' she replied. I could detect a note of caution in her voice like she thought I might be some kind of heavy breathing stalker.

'And you were at the social last weekend ...' I continued, praying that something would register.

'Yes, I was.'

'And I kissed you ...'

'What?' she exploded.

'It's John,' I declared, becoming desperate. 'The guy you danced with during Purple Rain.'

The maddening silence continued and I could tell that she quite literally had no idea who I was, nor did she have the slightest memory of kissing me.

'You sent the letter, the note, with your number on it?'

There was another horrendous pause and then she said, 'Um, sorry, look I don't know what you're actually talking about so please don't phone this number again.'

The line went dead and I just sat there staring at the telephone. I am officially the most forgettable human being in the world.

I picked up the phone on its third ring.

'Hello, John speaking.'

'What took you so long to call?' she asked without even saying hello.

'What?' I said. 'You remember me now?'

'Of course I remember you. I was only teasing,' she said, laughing heartily at my embarrassment. The relief was intoxicating and I collapsed back onto the telephone stool, grinning stupidly.

'We had wild sex up against the hockey goalposts, right?'

Another pop of light went off in my head and I found myself standing upright. 'What?'

'You're quite a stallion, John Milton.'

'Um, Sarah,' I said, 'we didn't have ... I mean do ...'

'What!' she gasped. Pause. 'Oh shit,' she said. 'So you must be the other guy.'

'What other guy?' I asked in a voice that sounded desperately high and womanly.

'Never mind. Okay, now I know *exactly* who you are.'

I didn't know what to say. This second telephone call was turning out worse than the first one (which by most rational standards had gone extremely badly). Then I heard Sarah laughing again.

'That was another joke, wasn't it?' I said and was treated to her howling at my discomfort.

On the plus side, in the final minutes of our rather unnerving conversation she admitted to having lost her virginity at fourteen. This was offset by the revelation of her emotional breakdown at fifteen, and the relationship with her cousin at sixteen which her parents forced her to break up. (I shudder to think what the next year might bring.)

Sarah Silver is a mighty strange girl indeed and, if I'm being honest, I was disappointed when the call was over. The bright side (her possible nymphomania) was cancelled out by her unfortunate side (her controversial personality).

To make matters worse, Mom had returned from her walk and was listening in on the final moments of my conversation. She shat me out for chasing girls like a playboy, breaking Mermaid's heart, and neglecting my studies. She said I was growing into an unpleasant young man and that if I carried on in this fashion I was bound to be a complete failure in life and would never find a decent girlfriend. I'm not sure what provoked the tirade because I've pretty much kept to myself this weekend. Mom's verbal abuse pushed me over the edge and I slammed my bedroom door so hard that the windows vibrated. I lay down on my bed and wished that I was back in my room at school where nobody bothers me and people stay out of my way.

Monday 22nd February

Dad and I had planned to fish this morning before I headed back to school tonight. Unfortunately, the wind had already been blowing from sunrise and Frank, who has bought himself a house in Umdloti, phoned through to say the sea was on its ear. Dad took me to the Hypermarket by the sea instead so that I could stock up on the various items on Albert Schweitzer's shopping list. On the way there he told me to take it easy on Mom because she's having a tough time with Wombat.

'I'm not the one doing all the shouting,' I replied, still seething about last night. Dad nodded and changed the subject.

WEEKEND SCORECARD

RAMBO	Quit smoking and has commenced serious rugby training for the approaching season.
SPUD	Has mostly stopped fantasising about Sarah Silver.

BOGGO	Acquired Madonna's book *Sex* which he claims is illegal in South Africa and contains pictures of Madonna having an orgy. We were only allowed to see the cover from a distance of fifteen feet before he locked it away in his room.
SIMON	Spent the weekend at the house of his new girlfriend Lisa in Johannesburg.
VERN	Refused to emerge from his room and wouldn't say what he did this weekend.
FATTY	Spent all his time with Penny and Brenda. He reckons Brenda is becoming a pest and refuses to leave the lovebirds alone for more than five minutes. The only problem is that Penny doesn't seem to mind.
GARLIC	Had a terrible weekend after missing his flight home and having to spend three days with his 81 year old grandfather in Pretoria. Grandfather Garlic apparently doesn't bath very often and owns eleven African Grey parrots.

Tuesday 23rd February

The Guv was seated comfortably at his desk and his attention was entirely focused on a dirty old book with a faded green cover. The English class quietly made their way to their desks and unpacked their books while he continued to read in a rapt and studious fashion. After we were settled he slowly raised his head, looked up to the ceiling and in a low groaning voice uttered, 'I have of late – but wherefore I know not – lost all my mirth.' His eyes fell upon Rambo and his expression hardened as he continued, 'Forgone all custom of exercise; and indeed it goes so heavily with my disposition that this goodly frame, the earth, seems to me a sterile promontory.'

There was something tragic about The Guv's quotation from *Hamlet*. A silence fell across the classroom. Even Rambo was staring at him, expectant.

Then Garlic charged in, pink-faced and desperate. He had just begun a shouted apology for his lateness when he tripped over Boggo's outstretched legs and flew head first across the floor.

'God almighty,' whispered The Guv as he glared intently at the fallen Malawian.

'Sorry I'm a bit late, sir,' said Garlic dusting himself off.

'It's a long walk from Nyasaland, Garlic,' noted our English teacher.

'No, sir,' replied Garlic as he limped over to his vacant desk and collapsed into his chair with a grunt. 'I just had to see Mrs Wilson.'

'I know the feeling,' replied The Guv.

'She put me through five different tests and then the computer told her what my career options were.'

'And?' enquired Rambo swivelling in his seat.

'Forestry or the clergy,' Garlic declared to a cacophony of laughter.

'May God help himself and our forests,' muttered The Guv before ordering silence. After a suitable pause he informed us that he was dying of syphilis and if he should expire during English then his orders were for his body to be cremated and his ashes to be eaten by Fatty.

Fatty didn't seem to think this would be much of a problem.

Not sure what it is with The Guv since he's come back, but he's certainly not his normal sprightly self.

17:00   During a lengthy shower after cricket practice I debated Spike on capital punishment. Unsurprisingly, considering the boy's psychopathic older brother, Spike has deeply controversial politics and possible neo-Nazi tendencies. He didn't even bother arguing his case for capital punishment at all and merely spent most of the time suggesting new and innovative ways of torturing and killing people. Surely not even the National Party would dream up the idea of lawnmowing someone to death?

Back in my room everything has been changed around again. My bed is now behind the door and my desk has been placed under the window. Shelves of uniforms are now shelves of books and, senselessly, every single poster has been taken down and pinned up elsewhere.

This time I lost my temper and marched around the house screaming for my slave clad in nothing but my towel. Turns out he was at choir practice so I had to return to my room in a foul mood where I briefly considered the sublime pleasure of slowly lawnmowing Albert Schweitzer to death.

21:00   Just issued Schweitzer with a stern ticking off outside the phone room where he was awaiting a call from his mother. I told him that if he ever senselessly moves my room around again I'll fill him with Easygas and blow him up by inserting a flame thrower up his rectum (another one of Spike's sadistic ideas, which I now realise are coming in helpful).

Wednesday 24th February

I have just completed a series of intense aptitude tests with Eve in her office. It is without doubt the most horny I have been all year and possibly ever. Not even hearing the news that I am best suited to being a teacher or researcher lessened the fact that it was a profound and memorable hour spent with my former housemaster's wife.

CRAZY EIGHT CAREERS

RAMBO	politician or lawyer
GARLIC	forestry or clergy
SIMON	sportsman or psychiatrist
SPUD	teacher or researcher
FATTY	food critic or children's entertainer
VERN	animal trainer or creative artist
BOGGO	sales executive or porn star

If the complaints in the cop shop after prep were anything to go by then very few of the Crazy Eight were altogether impressed with the results of their session with Eve. Nobody believed Boggo that Eve's computer would have spat out porn star as a career in the first place. Not unless there was a sudden demand in the sex industry for pale long-legged acne sufferers. Rambo was bragging about the fact that he had outwitted Eve and her computer by deciding beforehand what career he wanted before answering all the questions accordingly. Fatty was extremely happy about being a food critic but less so about being a children's entertainer. Boggo, after issuing an extremely long machine gun laugh, reckoned that the computer had obviously picked up on Fatty's anorexia-paedophilia and spat out children's entertainer.

I must admit that I was rather jealous of Vern being labelled a possible creative artist. Clearly the computer takes a rather dim view of creative people because it understands creativity and insanity as being one and the same. Garlic's unlucky form continued when Fatty knocked over his tea and broke his I ♥ Lake Malawi mug. Later he complained of a migraine and thanks to Boggo being the only person this side of the sanatorium with a supply of painkillers he had to pay a rather extortionist three rand per tablet.

Thursday 25th February

The following letter arrived in the post:

Dear John (Ha Ha.)

Okay so I promise that this will be a serious letter without a single joke. Not. (Ha Ha.) Okay so the truth is I have this like weird disease which turns me into an idiot on the phone. I don't know if it's nervousness or brain freeze or whether it's something that I inherited from my parents (which is possible). Shame poor me. (Ha Ha.)

I didn't know your surname was Milton. Did you know there was this old English writer called John Milton who wrote a poem for our Std 8 poetry book? That's so hilarious! (Ha Ha.) Your Mom and Dad must have a real sense of humour!

I was wondering (a little) if you were coming to the Arcade party next Saturday night in PMB? Anyway my friends and I are going and it would be great to see you there???? Also one of my friends (Loren) is totally in love with that hot guy Rambo. I think his name is Robert. Is he single? Could you bring him along next weekend? No pressure! (Ha Ha.)

Also there was that really weird and creepy guy who was dancing behind you with his hands in his pockets for most of the evening. Is he your friend? Does he go to your school? What's wrong with him?

I have so much homework to do (Yuk!!) but Mrs O'Reilly will kill me if I don't finish it by tomorrow. (She's my maths teacher and I hate her.)

Okay so I hope you write back and I'll see you next weekend at the Arcade.

Love Sarah Silver

PS Why do they call you Spud? (Potato?)

Reasons for persisting with Sarah Silver:

- She's good looking
- She's an excellent kisser
- She jumped her cousin (possible nympho)

Reasons for dumping Sarah Silver:

- Her personality seems a little dire
- Her jokes aren't funny
- She's odd
- She writes (Ha Ha!) frequently in her letters which is terribly lame even for Std 8 level
- My heart beats normally when I think about her
- She committed incest

It would seem on this evidence that I have to dump Sarah Silver. Since there is no way in hell that I am ever going to phone her again it will either have to be via letter or via ignore-ance. Letter or the latter? I think the latter.

Friday 26th February

14:15   There was considerable excitement in the house when Vern took a hostage and barricaded his bed against the door of his room, making it impossible to break in or out. Initially, it wasn't clear who the hostage was, but shrill shrieking and high-pitched crying led the crowd of onlookers outside Vern's room to believe that the unfortunate boy was Plaque. According to Plump Graham, who overheard the altercation, Vern issued Plaque a yellow slip for loitering in the bogs and surrounds. Foolishly, the first year seemed under the impression that the yellow slip was meaningless and threw it in the bin outside the common room.

Vern, who had been trailing Plaque at a discreet distance, promptly shouted 'Stop thief!' and wrestled the first year to the ground. Once subdued, Rain Man dragged him into his room and battened down the hatches. That was over half an hour ago and despite all the wailing and hysteria, Plaque is still being held captive in the room under the stairs.

Viking was livid when he heard about the hostage crisis. He strode into the house in a menacing mood, scattering the crowd that had gathered, and thumped on Vern's door.

'Blackadder!' he cried. 'If you sodomise that boy I'll bloody sodomise you!' He noticed that we were all staring at him and added, 'Not literally, obviously.'

Viking drove his heel into the door with an enormous crash but it remained intact. There was the sound of more hideous and chilling shrieking from inside which might have been Plaque but was most probably Vern.

'Right!' cried Viking. 'That's it. I'm calling in the maintenance department.'

He made it sound like he was calling in the Terminator but it turned out to be only a sickly Rogers Halibut carrying a small toolbox. Under the close inspection of Viking, Rambo, Simon, Boggo, Garlic and me, the maintenance man slowly unscrewed the hinges on Vern's door. After the hinges were dealt with, Viking issued an extremely resonant countdown from ten which served no purpose other than to alert Vern to the fact that we were coming in.

Rambo and Simon heaved the door back and a ghostly Plaque tore out and didn't stop running until he reached his dormitory. Vern, on the other hand, was nowhere to be seen which, considering the dimensions of his room, was an excellent achievement.

Boggo triumphantly threw open the cupboard but aside from an abnormally high pile of khaki shorts the space was vacant. Unfortunately for Vern, the only other possible hiding place was beneath the wooden slats under the mattress and that's exactly where we found him playing dead. Having slept next to the idiot for most of my teenage years, I can tell the subtle difference between Vern pretending to be sleeping/unconscious and Vern pretending to be dead. On this occasion he was quite obviously playing dead, a performance that he only brings out when, in his estimation, he has blundered badly. The tell-tale tongue sticking out of the corner of the mouth was in evidence after Vern was dragged from the bowels of his bed and laid out on the floor of the passage.

'What's he playing at?' shouted Viking after noticing the 'dead' Vern breathing heavily at the stomach.

'He's dead, sir,' said Boggo with a broad grin after thoroughly exploring the pockets of Vern's running shorts.

'Dead?' cried Viking indignantly. 'What do you mean he's dead, Greenstein?'

'Nothing serious, sir,' replied Boggo. 'He's died quite a few times before.'

'Sir, he died last week at cricket practice after dropping a catch,' added Garlic, his soulful blue eyes filled with concern.

'He dies all the time,' agreed Boggo, calmly pocketing a tube of Vern's toothpaste.

'Milton!' barked Viking. 'Have you ever seen Blackadder die before?'

'Yes, sir,' I admitted.

'But he's feigning death. I mean, clearly the boy is breathing,' barked our housemaster while examining Vern at close quarters. He began prodding and kicking Vern's limp body with the toe of his shoe. His plan B was to fill a glass of water which he hurled in Vern's face. Other than a loud shout of 'Oi', Vern didn't return to life.

'See what I mean, sir,' said Boggo. 'Once Vern decides to die it's not easy bringing him back to life.'

'This is preposterous!' boomed Viking, raising his hands to the heavens. He ordered the prefects and Boggo to deal with the matter and for Vern to see him in his office once he was alive again.

After lengthy debate, Vern's body was taken to the san and after a thorough check-up by Sister Collins, his corpse was deemed to be in rude health and as such he was given a private ward in the sanatorium.

Saturday 27th February

Took three wickets and scored 23 runs for the firsts today. Unfortunately, we were playing at Waterfall whose team The Guv quite rightly said were about as threatening as a bowl of cornflakes. Simon scored 104 not out and Rambo took three wickets in a single over. It's excellent to have The Guv back as coach. I'm convinced that I always reserve my best cricket for when he's watching. Perhaps it's just that he is the only master who's had any faith in my bowling. Good news, too, is that he didn't once mention his death by gangrene or syphilis except with reference to wilfully passing the disease on to the aggressive blonde lady who repeatedly barked threatening instructions to Waterfall in a strident voice from the stands.

Sunday 28th February

Rambo put his foot down at the prefects' meeting with Viking and demanded an explanation as to the whereabouts of Missing Eggwhite. Bizarrely, it seems that our housemaster was under the impression that Missing Eggwhite had returned to school some weeks ago and was fulfilling his duties.

'Have you actually seen him, sir?' asked Simon. Viking was astonished by our lack of faith in Missing Eggwhite's presence and claimed to have had a telephonic meeting with him about his lack of academic progress on Friday morning. I duly informed our housemaster that personally I haven't once laid eyes on him this entire year and as far as I was concerned he hasn't completed a single prefect's duty. This puzzled Viking greatly and he scratched away at his beard with some savagery.

'So let me get this straight, Milton,' he said finally. 'I have a living boy lying dead in the sanatorium and now you're telling me that one of my prefects is a spook?'

After more scratching, he asked, 'Who is Eggwhite's slave?'

'Near Death,' replied Simon.

'Right!' he roared. 'Send in Near Death.'

I ordered Runt, who was eavesdropping in the cloister outside Viking's office, to summon the boy immediately.

While we waited Viking asked if there had been any repercussions of the Plaque hostage crisis. Rambo said that he had spoken to Plaque who had wisely decided not to tell his parents and was seen to be behaving fairly normally yesterday.

'Good work, Black,' intoned Viking. 'It looks like we may have dodged a bullet there. But just in case, I'm placing young Plaque on suicide watch.' He looked at us despairingly. 'It is a heavy burden we bear, gentlemen.'

There was a timid knock.

'Come!' roared Viking and the door slowly opened. Near Death appeared ghostly white and terrified as he shuffled forward with stiff legs like Blacky on the verge of a compulsory bath.

'Ah, Near Death,' announced Viking, 'we would like to ask you a few questions about your prefect Eggwhite, er ... Greg Whitton.' Near Death stumbled back a pace and nodded weakly.

'Firstly, is he at school?' asked Viking.

'Well?' coaxed Viking after receiving no response. 'Is Eggwhite at school or not?' Near Death nodded uncertainly before squeaking out, 'Sir, I make his bed every day, sir.'

'You see, gentlemen,' reasoned Viking, smacking his hands together. 'Normal service has resumed. I think your concerns about Eggwhite are unfounded, although I'll be the first to admit that he has been slouching off on his prefect's duties lately.'

Swayed by Near Death's limited explanation, Viking abruptly closed the meeting.

By 17:05 there was no sign of Missing Eggwhite so Fatty called the roll. For once I agree with Rambo: this school is an absolute farce.

Monday 1st March

15:00   Back in Viking's office for yet another urgent meeting. Simon informed our housemaster that Missing Eggwhite had typically missed his duties yesterday, but Viking pretended not to hear him and brought up the late Vern Blackadder instead. It looks like Vern's death is becoming serious. He reckons the san sister is at the end of her tether with Vern and he's taking up valuable space in the sanatorium that could be used by a sudden deluge of autumnal flu sufferers. Despite being deceased, Vern is reportedly eating three hearty meals a day and was bust wanking by Sister Collins when she brought in his breakfast on Saturday morning.

'The situation is absurd!' roared Viking and thumped his fist into his desk. 'If he doesn't resurrect himself I'm going to have to advise the headmaster to have his body removed from the school.'

The Crazy Eight agreed to meet at the san at 17:00 in a last minute bid to save Vern's life and school career. It would seem that the powers that be are finally running out of patience with their resident nutcase.

THE RESURRECTION OF RAIN MAN

Until she bust him pulling his wire on Saturday morning, Sister Collins was fairly sympathetic to Vern's kicking the bucket, but since then she, too, has lost patience with the cretin. She waved her finger at us sarcastically and declared this to be his last day in the san. We filed through the sanatorium to the large room at the end of the passage where we found Vern reading in bed. When the fool noticed our arrival he flung down his comic, closed his eyes and stuck his tongue out of the corner of his mouth.

'Vern,' I said with much gravity, 'if you don't come back to life they're going to kick you out of the school.' There was no response from the corpse other than a short and furious rub of the nose. 'Okay, Vern,' I told him in a calm voice, 'Fatty is going to conduct a spiritual ritual to bring you back to life.'

Rain Man nodded to let me know that he understood that some sort of process was under way.

Fatty stepped forward solemnly and began ten minutes of Red Indian chanting and sporadic movements with his hands hidden in black leather motorcycle gloves. Vern was avidly watching Fatty's performance out of the corner of his left eye but still refused to snap out of it even when Fatty built up to his final crescendo of 'Vern arise, stand up, live and let live!'

Outside in the corridor a vociferous yet whispered Crazy Eight argument yielded two further possibilities of reviving Vern. Rambo's plan was straight out of the Mad Dog manual. His idea was to inform Rain Man that since he was dead we had a moral duty to remove all his limbs and organs and donate them to the gutless. He seized a bread knife from the sanatorium kitchen and began sharpening it menacingly against the metal doorframe. Boggo's idea was even more ridiculous. It centred on treating Vern with fictitious electric shock treatment which, as it transpired, involved no electricity whatsoever. Boggo assured us that his technique had worked last year when Vern died suddenly in the librarian's office after it was discovered that he was in the possession of a library book 21 months overdue. We agreed to try out Boggo's approach first before calling in Rambo to begin harvesting Vern's organs.

From the sanatorium kitchen Boggo pilfered oven gloves, from the doctor's surgery he brought a drip stand and a cord, and from the waiting room the plug from the infra-red lamp. Vern was clearly watching every single one of Boggo's movements as he tied the cord to the oven gloves and ran it over the drip stand towards the plug point on the far wall. Regrettably, there was a snag when we discovered the cord was too short to reach the wall socket and Sister Collins refused Boggo's request for an extension cord. To be honest, the fact that the entire apparatus was a ruse consisting of a loose cord, a plug and some oven gloves meant that electricity wasn't really needed at all, although Boggo was adamant that Vern wouldn't revive unless it was plugged in. After some discussion it was agreed that Fatty could create the fictitious electrical charge by placing the plug in his underpants and pretending to let rip. Eventually, all was in readiness and Boggo shouted 'Clear!' before dramatically slamming the oven gloves onto Vern's chest and calling for Fatty to pump out a megawatt of electricity. Garlic was so overcome with laughter at the ridiculousness of the situation that he had to chew on the curtains to contain himself. Fatty made a stupid buzzing sound and Boggo shouted, 'I've got the power!' He too began making a weird buzzing sound, but within seconds Vern was sitting bolt upright in bed grinning at us.

'He's alive!' screamed Garlic.

We all roared in mock amazement at Vern's resurrection and Rain Man cheered along with us. He then hopped out of bed, dressed rapidly in his khakis, and followed us to dinner. After the meal we led him back to his now door-less room where he happily counted out a jar of copper coins before discussing something with his tea mug.

Tuesday 2nd March

Rumours have spread about Boggo's unexpected revival of Vern. The Holy Greenstein continued with his miracles in the common room when he cured Plump Graham's stomach ache by wrapping the boy's entire body in the morning newspaper for ten minutes. To cap off an excellent day by the self-styled matric messiah, he also exactly predicted the maximum temperature for Durban tomorrow: 29 degrees. Garlic was amazed by Boggo's predictions and healings and demanded to know when he might finally lose his virginity. After some meditation Boggo informed the deflated Garlic that it was impossible for even him to predict events that would take place over thirty years down the road.

Friday 5th March

Another letter from Sarah Silver:

Dear John (Ha ha sorry that gets me every time!)
　　Okay I didn't get a response from you and I sent my last letter nearly two weeks ago and I would have expected you to respond in this time unless you have and it got lost in the post or you sent it to the wrong address or perhaps you didn't get my original letter because it went to the wrong school or something anyway I have had this sort of problem with boys before so I was just checking to see that you weren't just being a pig and not returning my letters. Anyway we'll be at the Arcade party in PMB on Saturday night so if you aren't there or if you don't phone me by the time I leave tomorrow then I'm going to take your silence to mean that our relationship is over.
　　I miss you John Milton.
　　Sarah Silver

When I don't arrive at the Arcade party tomorrow night she'll hopefully kiss some other poor sod and stop sending me demanding and disturbing letters.

18:00 An ugly fight broke out at the hot chocolate machine in the dining hall between two seniors from Barnes House. A tall stringy third year called Dobie's Itch kicked the machine because it kept filling up his cup with hot water instead of hot chocolate. A stocky matric with a big chest and spiky hair called Ice Tray took exception to this and punched Dobie's Itch in the face, causing a near riot. Thankfully, it was the Larson House duty week so they had to sort out the chaos. Rambo says Ice Tray will probably be the first team loose head prop this season. What with him and Rambo in the forward pack there should be no shortage of menacing aggression and severe injuries for the opposition.

Saturday 6th March

Excellent news is that after a dodgy start to the season, the 1st cricket team is gaining some momentum at last. With Simon scoring yet another century in the morning, St Nicholas collapsed to 77 all out in the early afternoon, with Stinky taking six wickets with his steady in-swingers. I can't help feeling that our side has always taken the long route to glory, even in the early days of U14 when we relied on the fiery pace and insanely long run-up of Mad Dog to scare opposition batsmen out. It's also fairly obvious that when Simon makes runs we seem invincible, and when he doesn't the rest of us melt like chocolate firemen. Next week is the big showdown at King's College with two unbeaten sides duelling to the death and if Simon continues his excellent form we must have a serious chance of causing an upset. The Guv set the tone for the crunch game next Saturday by barging into the change room after the match and bellowing, 'Now that was a game of cricket!' He banged the point of his shooting stick into the concrete floor and said, 'A performance on that level next week and we'll treat ourselves to a night in a brothel.' Before leaving, The Guv shook Simon's hand and admitted that for once he was lost for words and superlatives to describe his innings. He left with a great smile on his face and a stern reminder not to leave any floaters in the toilets.

Besides taking a simple catch, I had very little to do with today's victory and yet just being part of the team that has done well was enough to make me feel like I had scored the century myself. Usually I feel insecure when I have a bad or anonymous day on the cricket field but today I felt jubilant.

21:00   Boggo has cashed in on his status as the house guru and Nostradamus. He charged a number of eager juniors to hear his 'Pontifications from the Piss Trough' which was a brief yet graphic lecture on seduction delivered from the step of the urinal.

Sunday 7th March

Fierce banging on my door revealed the excited face of Fatty.

'I suppose you heard the news about the matric dance?' he panted.

'What about it?' I replied with sudden tension in my voice.

'It's been brought forward this year to avoid clashing with trials and finals.'

'How far forward?' I asked, my mouth suddenly dry and tasting of acid.

'June,' replied Fatty. 'And it's not happening at school like normal but at the Capitol Towers hotel in Maritzburg.'

If I had known that the matric dance was just three months away I might have persisted with Sarah Silver. However, after not replying to her letters and skipping the Arcade party last night, my goose must be well and truly cooked. It took considerable effort to drive the matric dance fear out of my mind and although I eventually succeeded my hands trembled for the rest of the afternoon and evening.

Monday 8th March

Double Afrikaans: Mongrel made us watch a disturbing documentary about shark attack victims which had been badly dubbed into Afrikaans. Thereafter he listed six ways to kill a great white shark should you ever find yourself attacked while surfing or swimming. One doubts whether strangling a great white with the leash of your surfboard, or plunging your snorkel up its anus would achieve much other than to rile up a two ton psychopath with big teeth and a short temper. Mongrel didn't think much of our sniggering and by way of revenge has banned English from being spoken in his classroom for the rest of the year. With people like Mongrel teaching the nation's youth, I'm not surprised that South Africa is such a violent country.

Another one! (Sent by Fastmail)

Dear John (Okay not so funny any more)
   I know you weren't at the Arcade party because I looked for you everywhere and obviously you weren't there despite all my efforts to get in touch. I can handle rejection, but I can't handle being ignored by someone who should count themselves lucky that I was with them in the first place. I hope you're feeling guilty because you have screwed me up so much that I can't go to school any more and everyone is thinking I'm a freak because I found a picture of you in your school magazine from last year when you were dressed in a tutu and playing a girl in the school play. I stabbed your eyes out with a pencil and set fire to the magazine in the library which got me in some more shit with Mrs Lambson. (I hate her guts just like I hate yours!)
   I kissed two boys on Saturday because I wanted you to feel jealous but they didn't mean anything to me like you do. You are different because you are beautiful and evil.
   Sarah Silver

Reasons for feeling disturbed:

1. It was sent by Fastmail.
2. I'm starting to feel like Michael Douglas does in most of his movies.
3. SS is clearly a psychopath.
4. The final two lines appear to be written either in red ink or blood.

5. Her admission of stabbing my eyes out with a pencil.
6. I love you forever???????
7. Not a single (Ha Ha). Things are becoming serious.

I decided to bite the bullet and call a Crazy Eight crisis meeting at 21:00. To curry favour and improve the general mood, I splashed out at the tuck shop, buying tea, bread, butter and cheese as cop shop provisions are as per usual dismally low. Simon has also been complaining about non-prefects repeatedly using the prefects' chow and facilities. Further aggravating the situation is that Garlic ruined the toaster after electrocuting himself while attempting to fish a half slice of toast out of the appliance with a metal fork.

21:00   There was widespread mockery when I alerted the gathered crowd to the fact that I had a stalker. It wasn't until Boggo read yesterday's letter that the atmosphere changed and snide comments turned to astonished interest. Even Rambo studied the letters closely and Fatty ran his tongue over where Sarah Silver had inscribed her name in red and vouched that it was definitely human blood.

Crazy Eight Advice:

SIMON says I should continue to ignore her and if her letters and general stalking continue then I should alert The Glock and the police.
RAMBO is so interested in Sarah Silver that he has offered to take her off my hands. This may sound radical but it certainly makes for a neat solution.
FATTY called Sarah Silver demonic and feels that she may need a spiritual intervention. He reckoned her initials SS (Satan's Sister) were proof of supernatural evil.

BOGGO reckons there is no point in being stalked unless you get some primitive sex out of the bargain. His advice is to write her an apology letter and pretend to have been seriously ill in the san for the last three weeks. I should then invite her to watch me play cricket after which I should give her 'a hot beef injection' behind the scoreboard.

GARLIC: 'Invite her to Lake Malawi to test her out!'

VERN was livid with Sarah Silver's letters and tried to throw them into the fire. If it wasn't for Boggo's dramatic intervention my evidence for a possible police investigation could have been destroyed.

The gathering ended at 21:50 when Viking broke up the party and said that we were making too much noise and setting a bad example. I returned to my room through the cold drizzle to write up the results and for a review of the situation.

Albert Schweitzer left a hot water bottle in my bed. Slaves rule!

Tuesday 9th March

A rumour was circling at breakfast that a first year in Larson House called Tampon Thompson tried to kill himself this morning by leaping out of his dormitory window before the rising siren. The boy broke his arm in the fall but escaped more serious injuries.

'Nickname like that, I'd also commit suicide,' snorted Boggo, scooping ants out of the sugar bowl.

'Viking is going to give birth when he hears about this,' added Simon, munching furiously on his muesli.

13:30 Word at lunch is that Tampon Thompson definitely tried to commit suicide. If it weren't for the quick thinking of a third year called Fungus who, inspired by Viking's infamous suicide directives, thumped Tampon on the head with a cricket bat and locked him in his army trunk, the boy might actually have succeeded in doing himself in. Rumour has it that Tampon's folks have already removed all his stuff and that he's leaving for good. Predictably, the school has denied everything and The Glock later announced that the boy had fallen out of his window by accident. (Where have we heard that one before?)

14:30 The Guv organised a practice match between the 1sts and 2nds. Although there wasn't really enough time for a full match we were well on top when he called a halt to proceedings shortly before 17:20, declaring that it had become too dark for him to see. Since the sun was still shining and The Guv was wearing his dark glasses, I would have to presume that he wasn't joking about having two Bulgarian prostitutes trapped in his wine cellar.

There was a sense of intensity among the members of the team and our fielding looked sharp and threatening. To beat King's College at King's College would really be something. The only real setback is being invited/ coerced into a team building braai at The Glock's house tomorrow night.

Wednesday 10th March

In my epic dream I was heroically saving numerous scantily clad schoolgirls at a burning St Catherine's school. After discovering that the scorching flames and smoke had no effect on me whatsoever, I kept charging back into the inferno to rescue yet more top drawer schoolgirls before carrying them through the flames to the admiring crowd of beauties who screamed and swooned whenever I appeared with another sexy victim in my arms. On the final deadly mission I scaled a turret, only to find Amanda stretched out on her bed in black lingerie and looking incredibly seductive. I was about to show her a few sparks of my own but a loud banging on my door yanked me out of Amanda's room and back to mine. It was Schweitzer with a large mug of tea and the morning newspaper.

08:00 Viking's prefects' meeting was far better than expected. Our housemaster was surprisingly in an excellent mood and confessed that Tampon Thompson's attempted suicide yesterday had in fact set him free from his terrible premonition about a naked boy taking his own life. The fact that the incident occurred on another housemaster's watch delighted Viking. He even apologised for excessively harping on the subject and promised not to bring it up again. 'Now we can all focus our energies on the really important things,' he said, 'like winning house trophies!'

THE GLOCK'S CRICKET PARTY

The Glock made the fatal error of inviting Sparerib along on the flimsy premise that he had filled in while The Guv was away. The Guv arrived in a jolly mood, smelling of blue cheese and whisky. He took me aside on The Glock's patio and whispered, 'I'm as pissed as a Sicilian sausage dog, Milton. Would you be so kind as to guide this syphilitic old spirit to the nearest armchair?'

'Good to see you're on the mend, Edly,' commented the headmaster as he sidled past us wearing a white apron emblazoned with the school's insignia and carrying a large tray of steak.

'I live, headmaster, I live,' replied The Guv. He raised his goblet of red wine skyward and announced, 'To kill the king.' Sparerib joined The Glock at the fire and the rest of us sat with The Guv on the patio where he entertained us with stories of his Moroccan hashish holidays in the 1960s.

After a poorly timed visit to the bathroom, I found myself sandwiched between Sparerib and The Glock at the dinner table. The Glock is the slowest eater and frequently pauses as if considering the fate of some-body before slipping a carefully trimmed fork load into his mouth and chewing relentlessly. To make matters worse, he surprised me at odd intervals with unexpected questions that forced me onto the back foot.

'Problems with my steak, Milton?' he asked as he shiftily eyed out my lack of eating progress. Admittedly, Sparerib's poor table manners to the left were hardly aiding my appetite, although I must say the idea of hovering your face a few centimetres above your plate and then scoffing ridiculously fast does mean that you don't have to worry about being included in any dismal conversations.

'What's your approach going to be in the early overs on Saturday, Milton?' I wasn't exactly sure what the headmaster meant because I never bowl or bat in the early overs anyway. In the end I opted for 'Keep things tight, sir.' The Glock nodded and chewed before nodding some more.

'You have a swimming pool where you live?'

'Yes, sir,' I replied.

The Glock seemed surprised by this and things fell silent once more.

We waited forever for the headmaster to finish eating his seconds as he had already announced that he wanted to address the team after his meal. The speech, when it did come, was certainly not worth waiting for. It began promisingly enough when he congratulated us for remaining unbeaten thus far, but undid the earlier good work by openly doubting whether we had the mental stamina to pull off an upset at King's College. I'm sure if The Guv hadn't fallen asleep in his chair he would have been outraged by the headmaster's goading and lack of good faith. Sparerib said nothing other than nodding to whatever The Glock was railing on about. Rambo quite rightly accused Sparerib of being an oxygen thief and a lead balloon at parties.

It was a great relief to be out of the headmaster's mansion. As we left the gate Simon called the team together under the lemon tree and told us to ignore what we had just heard and take revenge on the headmaster by thumping King's College on Saturday. Rambo reckoned that he had already taken revenge against The Glock and showed us a bottle of expensive looking whisky that he had pilfered from the headmaster's drinks cabinet during his marathon eating stint.

Saturday 13th March

KING'S COLLEGE

Simon won the toss and chose to bat on a sweltering day in Pietermaritzburg. We lost Rhino Jarvis in the first over to a ropy lbw decision by the opposition coach/ umpire but good karma soon followed for us when The Guv gave Martin Leslie not out after Leslie appeared to snick the ball to first slip. Unfortunately, he was clean bowled three balls later and we were looking iffy at 6-2 with karma and momentum swinging back the way of King's College.

Simon didn't appear to notice that the King's opening bowler was the quickest in the province or that we were in dire need of consolidation and began blitzing their bowlers to all parts of the field. Most of the 1500 boys of King's College crowded the ground in their school uniforms and grew increasingly glum as 6-2 soon became 102-2 with Simon on 71 and the newly promoted Omo Pringle holding firm at the other end with a timid but steady 16 not out. Simon drank a disturbing amount of Oros at the tea break before returning to the crease and producing a flurry of shots to show the King's bowlers that he was only just getting started. The Guv took the five minute break to pay his respects to my folks and slot back a gin and tonic. Thereafter he moved in a weird skipping motion back to his position at square leg.

We declared our innings closed at lunch with a score of 223-6 with Simon making a whopping 121 runs. King's had clearly been emotionally damaged by Simon's genius innings. They prodded and poked around, scoring just 23 runs in the first hour. It became increasingly obvious that they were playing for the draw and had given up on attempting to chase down our total. Their ultra-defensive tactics and lack of interest in scoring runs meant that half the crowd lost interest too, and the other half melted away to spade girls and visit the tuck shop. After exhausting all other possible options, Simon signalled for me to warm up to bowl. I began to swing my arms in a circle and a loud cheer followed by a short yet lively toot of the horn sounded from my father's car. The sight of me warming up to bowl created instant activity with my parents. Mom ran around the boundary line and presumably went to the loo while Dad obviously didn't think anyone would see him disappearing into the small clump of bushes behind the scoreboard. By the time I had finished marking out my run-up they had already charged their glasses.

I ran in, hoping that my first ball wouldn't prove an

embarrassment. It did, but the batsman missed the high looping full toss and the ball cannoned into middle stump. Mad hysteria broke out at my parents' car while a subdued groan echoed around the rest of the ground.

After eight overs of bowling I had taken five wickets. By the end of the day I had taken 6-57 and King's were bowled out for just 93. I didn't even care that Mom came into the change room while boys were showering. For once I had struck leg spinning gold and I was determined to relish the moment.

The Guv took us out drinking and I remember Rambo forcing tequilas down my throat at a pub that smelled of lemons and fried fish. The Guv also kept his promise about taking us to a brothel but the bouncer at the door wouldn't let us in because he reckoned Spearmint didn't look eighteen and I didn't even look fourteen. At that moment the police pulled up and asked The Guv what he was up to with a busload of schoolboys at an escort agency on a Saturday night.

'We're the King's College choir!' he announced to the policeman. 'Come on, boys. Onward Christian soldiers!' With that he led us back to the bus and after stalling it twice and badly grating the gears we drove off hooting and singing the school hymn.

Sunday 14th March

Terrible hangover after last night's celebrations. My head is pounding. Can't write because I have the shakes. I hate Rambo for making me drink a shot of tequila for every wicket I took.

12:00   I ordered Thinny and JR Ewing to write a 3 000 word essay on the beauty of silence. The idiots have the grounds of the entire school in which to bash each other's brains out so why must they insist on doing it outside my window when I have a hangover?

15:30 Pretended to be out when Viking thumped on the door and shouted congratulations. It astonished me how many times he repeated 'Milton!' before eventually giving up.

Was too lazy to go to dinner so Albert Schweitzer cooked pasta and Alfredo sauce for me in the cop shop annexe and served it with a cup of strong coffee. Looks like news of my bowling heroics has spread around the school because Schweitzer bowed when I let him into my room this afternoon and he now seems to have reverted to calling me sir again.

After dinner, coffee and a 45-minute shower I felt semi-revived.

Monday 15th March

I am officially over Saturday night's hazy 'six tequilas and a beer and a half' binge and my will to live has returned. The Glock used his sermon in chapel to congratulate the cricket side and singled out me and Simon for special mention. The school broke out into a roaring applause followed by a chorus of 'Eat! Eat! Eat!' after which we sang the Lord's Prayer.

Tuesday 16th March

I lost my temper when taking the first years for prep tonight. I had repeatedly warned both Shambles and Plaque about surreptitiously passing notes to each other by methods which they obviously thought were cunning but which most sane people had dumped by primary school. Shambles, who clearly had no interest in school work and appeared to be bored stiff, removed numerous pens from his pencil case and lined them up in formation across the edges of his desk. Minutes later his stack of pens and pencils collapsed all over the floor causing another disturbance. The final straw was when the idiot made deliberate farting noises by scraping his thigh against his warm plastic chair which the Harmless Half-Dozen thought was hilarious. I wiped the impish grin right off Shambles' face when I gave him a painful fingertongs using the blackboard duster. The moment I heard the cracking in his fingers I knew I had taken things too far and his subsequent sobbing didn't do much for my conscience. I had to endure watching the boy spend the last ten minutes of prep pathetically holding his injured digits and sniffing sadly at the roof. The rest of the first years watched me warily and Albert Schweitzer called me 'sir' close to a dozen times in the five minutes that he was in my room after prep. If I keep up the bowling heroics and public brutality he may be calling me Führer soon.

Wednesday 17th March

06:01 Just woke from a terrible dream. Shambles' fingers were broken and I was hauled in to face The Glock for bullying. I was de-prefected, dropped from the cricket team, and forced to swap rooms with Vern.

06:31 I tried to apologise to Shambles after roll call but he ran away from me only to be shat on by Mongrel for running in the quad. I don't have a good feeling about this.

Possible reasons for my short temper and poor form:

1. My recent drinking binge
2. Being pressured into making career decisions at age sixteen
3. Arrogance after cricket heroics

4. Suppressed phobias thanks to being stalked by Sarah Silver
5. Having to take on most of Missing Eggwhite's duties
6. Sexual frustration due to virginity

18:00 My worst possible fears were realised when I witnessed Viking leading Shambles into his office before closing the door behind him. This is how Pike must have felt every other day of his school career. Despite not being hungry or thirsty I ordered Albert Schweitzer to make me a toasted cheese and mayonnaise and a cup of Nescafé. This may well be my final night as a prefect.

Thursday 18th March

I began the day on an even keel. If Shambles had ratted on me last night, surely Viking would have hauled me into his office immediately. Unless of course he's interviewing the other new boys first, and gathering a file of evidence before bringing me in.

11:00 Gloom and doom has returned. As I made my way across the quad towards the house at tea break, Viking beckoned me over to where he was standing outside the staffroom.

'Milton, we need to talk,' he said in an icy tone.

'Yes, sir,' I stammered.

'Not now,' he boomed. 'I'll send for you tonight.'

I nodded and felt the walls of my life collapsing around me.

Cricket practice was a bit of a blur although I remember repeatedly looking at my watch and thinking about what was surely to follow. Perhaps Viking will let me off with a stern rebuke and final warning? That's about the best I can hope for.

20:30 Runt knocked on my door to say Viking wanted to see me immediately. Having waited for so long I felt rather numb about it all. As far as I was concerned my fate was no longer in my hands and there wasn't much to be done now to reverse what had happened.

'Sit down, Milton,' ordered Viking and closed the curtains. He took off his jacket and laid it over the desk. He studied me closely and said, 'This is a serious business.'

I nodded and he nodded grimly back.

'You of all people ...' he said and crunched his hands together. He removed his specs and shined them up with his silver tie.

'You of all people,' he repeated, 'have demonstrated the necessary creativity, maturity and nous for such a demanding venture.'

'What?' I blurted, thinking I hadn't heard him right.

'Milton,' he roared, his eyes alive and burning, 'I have chosen you to conceive, create and direct this year's entry for the house play competition.'

I swear I almost blacked out with relief. I'm directing the house play! What a massive breakthrough. Viking ordered me either to write or select a play for performance by the end of the first week of the second term. That was it.

'Good luck, Milton,' he cried. 'By God, you're going to need it.'

I galloped back to my room, locked the door and carried out an energetic celebration. What a week, and what a joy not to be obsessing about Shambles' fingers and being moved to a haunted room with no door.

Friday 19th March

My search for the perfect house play has begun with a scouring of the main library. So far I have four possible options, none of which I like.

Saturday 20th March

The cricket match against Wellendon College from New Zealand ended in a draw after thick mist descended over the school after lunch. That means we end the first term cricket season as the only unbeaten team in the province.

Sunday 21st March

11:47 Just returned from a brilliant twenty minute conversation with Eve after bumping into her by chance outside her office. When I mentioned that I was on the lookout for an excellent house play she said we should spend an hour or two one evening sifting through plays in the drama library. She rattled off a long list of playwrights who were well worth checking out. Unfortunately, I can't remember a single name she suggested because I became entangled in a vivid fantasy of the two of us romping naked by candlelight up against the shelves of the drama library Early Restoration section.

Tuesday 23rd March

Over a lunch of red wine and dark Belgian chocolate, The Guv and I spent considerable time discussing house play possibilities. I thought he might like my idea of condensing *Macbeth* into thirty minutes of murder and mayhem but he reacted violently and threw his television remote control at me, accusing me of conspiring against the Bard. He cheered up noticeably when I suggested a farce. In fact he leapt out of his chair shouting, 'By God, Milton, if it's farce you're after then it must be Feydeau!' He laughed heartily at something he remembered and sat down again.

'Or it could be a witty comedy?' I added.

'Coward!' barked The Guv. 'It must be Noel Coward!'

'Yes, sir,' I agreed.

'*Blithe Spirit* is as dependable as my morning ablutions,' he added, refilling his wine glass and replacing the bottle on his side table. The Guv paused as if on the verge of making an announcement but took a bulging swig of wine instead before scrambling to his feet in excitement.

'Unless, of course, Milton, you are willing to take on an entirely surprising creative challenge?'

The Guv disappeared into his study and returned some minutes later carrying a rather decaying play in his hands. He handed it over and advised me to peruse it carefully in the holidays. He also threatened to slit my throat with his shooting stick should I lose it because it was a first edition and even signed by the playwright.

'It's known as the "unstageable play". I dare you, Milton! I bloody dare you!' He handed it over.

The cover read:

A Resounding Tinkle by NF Simpson

Wednesday 24th March

Had another informal chat with Eve outside the first year prep classroom. She claimed to be looking for me and asked what profession I was leaning towards for my work experience next term.

'Actor,' I replied boldly.

Eve hesitated and asked me if I was certain.

'Dead certain,' I replied in a commanding voice. She made a note on her clipboard, flashed me her gorgeous smile and minced off. What a tease.

Thursday 25th March

15:30   Albert Schweitzer expertly packed my suitcase while I issued directions from the warm comfort of my bed. After he was done I complimented him on being an excellent slave and thanked him for his efficient service over the term. Schweitzer blushed and grinned before declaring it an honour to clean my room and take my laundry. It was getting awkward so I sent him off to make me a cup of tea.

Friday 26th March

I received my colours for cricket at the final assembly. This may sound like an excellent achievement but one has to consider that the entire team was awarded colours, including Strangely Sallow, who only played in last weekend's match against Wellendon and didn't bat or bowl. Simon of course received honours and deserved it. Colours were also dished out to the first tennis and swimming teams and, more controversially, the first squash team whose only victory in nine weeks was against the seconds in a practice match. Typically, The Glock took full credit for our famous victory over King's College declaring that he personally laid out the challenge to the team at what he called 'a secret meeting' last Wednesday.

After assembly I strolled back across the quad with Simon and Garlic. We shook hands and I ambled through the great archway across the turning circle and down onto the rolling lawns and Pilgrims' Walk. Albert Schweitzer and Near Death raced past with my bags and luggage. They were giggling and happy and drunk on the feeling of their first ever holiday. On the bus I chose the second seat from the back, stretched out and slipped on my Walkman.

Home time.

Monday 29th March

It's been a relaxing start to my Easter holidays, what with Dad spending most of his time working at the pub and the rest of his time sleeping or hammering about in the garage. Mom is also seldom around due to what she describes as her overwhelming social calendar at present. I have taken the opportunity to kick back and relax, read plays, and work on my suntan. Although Simon sometimes takes it to extremes, he maintains that with girls a good suntan can often mean the difference between reaching first and second base, and in some cases scoring a home run.

The sun's rays eased my stresses and I refused to be riled up by anything, even the sight of Blacky gulping down an unnecessary amount of pool water before urinating demonstratively against the side of his kennel.

Nor did I think of the two letters from Sarah Silver that were waiting for me on my desk when I returned home. The first was a copy of the initial letter that she sent me at school but the second arrived by post on Thursday and, disturbingly, all it said was:

PIG!

Like Thomas More, I have decided to keep my silence. How long can this crazy woman carry on with this obsessive insanity?

Wednesday 31st March

Dad was out with the car so Mom asked me if I would cycle to the café and buy bread, milk and the evening paper. Feeling useful, I raced off, greatly enjoying the feeling of vigorous exercise and the wind in my face. After paying at the till, I strode out of the café with my packet and nearly crashed into the Mermaid as she was attempting to enter.

'Hi,' I said.

'Hi,' she replied.

'Sorry,' I said.

She giggled and tossed her long blonde hair back.

'How are you?'

'Really good,' I replied.

'I didn't know if I would ever see you again,' she said, staring into my eyes.

I laughed falsely and asked her how Gavin the Umpire was. Her smile faded and although she said that he was well, I sensed that she would rather have had me not mention his name.

There was an awkward pause so I told her that I had to get home. She gave me a hug and I unchained my bike. I wasn't sure if she was watching me but, just in case, I raced off at top speed, narrowly avoiding an irate old granny with her shopping trolley.

She is still beautiful.

Thursday 1st April

Besides Dad pretending to have a heart attack in the kitchen after breakfast, there were very few April Fool's jokes at Milton HQ. For a while it was thought that Innocence was playing a joke by being late but this thought was later abandoned when she didn't rock up to work at all. Another grim reality that I wish was a joke is a looming weekend to the berg with Mom, Dad and Wombat. My grandmother discovered through her hairdresser that there is a half-price weekend autumn special running at the Sani Pass Hotel and has booked us all in from tomorrow until Tuesday. A relief is that I have my own room, although the good news is rather overshadowed by the fact that Wombat is on experimental Alzheimer's medication which Mom says has had mixed results.

Friday 2nd April

08:30 Dad showered praise over the entire German nation after all of our bags, golf clubs, fishing rods and hiking kit were gobbled up by the generous boot of the Mercedes. After numerous checks and endless fiddling with the air conditioner, we slid off down the road leaving a heartbroken Blacky with his face pushed up against the chicken wire on the gate.

Wombat was in excellent form out on the pavement of her old age home, Guinea's Rest. She shouted out and waved to everybody who passed by and was even friendly to Dad and kissed him on the cheek.

'Hoi polloi!' shrieked Wombat as we set off down Musgrave Road with a healthy roar of the engine. She pointed out landmarks at regular intervals, although it was disturbing to note that when we drove past her old block of flats, where she had lived for 32 years, it didn't seem to register at all.

There was nearly carnage on the freeway when Dad punched in a number of buttons before declaring that the car would now drive itself. My father leaned back in his seat, and folded his hands behind his head. I'm not sure if Dad punched in the wrong buttons but the Merc veered off to the left and if it wasn't for Mom seizing the steering wheel we may have crashed through the fence of the Rainbow Chicken factory. Dad blamed the Japanese to whom he said the Germans had probably outsourced the auto-pilot control.

12:30 We were welcomed to the Sani Pass Hotel with warm smiles by the receptionists and a glass of fruit punch. Wombat grew suspicious and refused even to sip her punch until she had been assured by the food and beverages manager that she wouldn't be charged for it.

12:35   My room is luxurious and the bed is so large that I could feasibly sleep in over twenty different positions. It's certainly the type of bed one should consider if planning an orgy.

Bingo!

As feared, Wombat was a total embarrassment during the bingo tournament in the lounge. The entertainment co-ordinator named Edgar was stumped when Wombat screamed out 'Bingo!' after he had called out the first number of the evening. The insane old woman shouted 'Bingo!' numerous times thereafter and never once had her card full. She became angry that all her shouting out hadn't resulted in any prizes, grew very unpleasant and had to be bribed with a hot toddy to leave the lounge and go to bed early.

Saturday 3rd April

Dad signed us up for the Sani Pass Saturday Golf Challenge and we set off to the first tee after breakfast determined to win. Mom and Wombat joined the small crowd to watch us hit our first shots. I was happy to see my opening drive land on the fairway, but slightly less happy with Wombat shrieking, 'Wonderful, David!' Dad unfortunately sliced his tee shot over the river and into the thick bush growing on the side of the mountain. He loaded up another ball and smashed it into the trunk of a nearby tree. 'Fore!' shouted co-ordinator Edgar as Dad's ball ricocheted off the tree and careened back towards the tee box. The net result was that after two savage drives my father had only advanced his golf ball by three paces.

'Pig dog!' barked my father as he slammed his driver back into his golf bag. To add insult to injury there was an extremely loud whisper of 'Roy's a terrible embarrassment, isn't he?' My mother nodded her head in agreement and the two set off to find Wombat a pot of tea and an egg sandwich for her 10:30am elevenses.

Quite frankly, it was a relief that the competition lasted only nine holes because after an excellent start my golf game regressed at a terrible rate. Dad became increasingly enraged as his disastrous round wore on. What began as loud shouting and the throwing of the odd club soon dissolved into threats of suicide and later the tracking down and bombing of the course designer's home.

21:00   DINNER DANCE

A one man band called Elf kicked off proceedings with a lively version of Eric Clapton's Cocaine and followed it up with Dire Straits' Sultans of Swing which had my mother and father gyrating in the middle of the sparsely populated dance floor. Under the ruse of helping Wombat to bed, I escaped to the far reaches of the veranda and sat down at one of the empty tables. There was no moon but the stars were as bright as I could ever remember seeing them. I traced the line where the mountains met the sky and listened intently to the sound of the river which I had hardly noticed during the day.

'Mind if I join you?'
    It was the pretty girl from the table next to ours.
    'That would be really cool,' I answered rather smoothly despite my ridiculous heart rate.
    'What are you doing?' she asked, taking a seat and wrapping her scarf tightly around her neck.
    'Looking at the sky and thinking about life,' I said rather nobly.
    There was a long silence as the girl looked out at the sky. I wasn't sure if I should say something but decided

to remain mute after realising that I couldn't for the life of me think of a single half decent conversation starter.

'They say that life works in circles,' she said.

'Vicious circles,' I replied.

She laughed and introduced herself as Leanne. I introduced myself as John Milton and she laughed again.

Later, we were snuggled up together protecting ourselves from the chill breeze when her dad came to call her to bed. I felt heartbroken that Leanne lived in Johannesburg and was leaving the next morning.

'So I might never see you again?' I heard myself say.

She shrugged her shoulders. 'Depends if life works in vicious circles ... '

'May I kiss you?'

'You may, John Milton.'

Before she disappeared through the door into the hotel, she smiled and briefly waved.

I stayed out until the cold drove me in.

Sunday 4th April

Today was a bit of a daze after last night's surreal experience on the veranda. Been having many irrational feelings about Leanne and sense that this may indicate that I'm finally ready for a proper relationship. Also on the positive side, it would be safe to say that things are finally picking up when it comes to scoring girls. (Admittedly, one of my two most recent conquests was a psychopath.)

I considered these thoughts and many others over the five hours I spent on my sun lounger at the pool. Simon is definitely right about a good suntan paying off.

Monday 5th April

Took a hike up the river and discovered a beautiful pool of slow flowing water sheltered by boulders and head high grass. I dived in without checking the temperature and emerged milliseconds later screaming in brain freezing agony. With my privates shrunken to former spudly levels, I lizarded onto a rock warmed from the sun and waited for my body to stop shuddering and convulsing.

I would have hiked further downstream but my wet shorts chafed my inner thigh and I had to turn back. By the time I reached the hotel I was walking like an aged cowboy and spent the afternoon in bed drinking tea, reading newspapers, and thinking about Leanne.

Tuesday 6th April

Dad cunningly covered the total amount on the final bill with his thumbs when holding it out for Wombat to inspect. Mom helped my grandmother out to the car while Dad wrote out the cheque and forged Wombat's signature.

Friday 9th April

Shocking development! Viking called at 06:30 in the morning to ask me if I would be willing to return to school four days early to help out with the prospective new boys' weekend. Although my housemaster made it clear that I could say no, he also hinted that a negative response would be bad for my future. It was too early for my brain to conjure up a brilliant excuse so I agreed to return to school next Thursday evening.

'Excellent, Milton,' he roared. 'I always knew that I could

rely on you in a crisis.'

'Not a problem, sir,' I said, despite coming to the sudden realisation that I only have five days left of my holiday.

'Any news on your house play selection?' ventured Viking.

'I'm getting close, sir,' I lied.

'Good, good, good,' he repeated, before shouting, 'Righto then!' and hanging up.

I have five days to choose the house play and wade through a mountain of assignments due by the start of term. Suddenly this doesn't feel like a holiday at all. After a shower and breakfast I locked myself in my room and got stuck into some earnest sloggery.

Saturday 10th April

Communist Party Secretary General Chris Hani was assassinated this morning. I heard the news on Dad's radio which he had left blaring in my parents' bathroom. I folded down the lid and sat on the loo listening to an account of how a man shot Hani in his driveway. A neighbour of Hani's who had heard the shots was being interviewed and reckoned that she saw a white man driving away in a red Ford Laser. The interviews continued and every single person mentioned the words 'civil war' and how the killing of Hani may well be the spark that sets South Africa on fire.

There are far too many maniacs in this world.

Thursday 15th April

19:10 Dad drove me back to school in a new record time of 79 minutes from gate to gate. I had to agree that if it weren't for being caught behind a lorry carrying small stones around Lidgetton, the Merc may well have broken through the 75 minute barrier. I staggered out of the passenger seat, feeling decidedly elated but a bit car sick. Dad threw me a meaty high five, ruffled my hair, and told me to go get 'em. He bragged that he was going to smash his 'down-run' record of 73 minutes. My father bent over backwards to stretch his back out and after loud groaning and an unhealthy cracking sound from his vertebrae, he leapt back into the driver's seat and raced off looking inspired. As I hauled my belongings through the archway and into the quad I bemoaned the lack of any slaves to help with the carrying and general service.

I dumped my bags in my room and returned to the house to make a cup of tea in the annexe. Surprisingly, the light was on when I opened the door of the cop shop although it was only when I registered the deafening shout of 'Spud!' that it became evident I wasn't alone.

I gaped at the Malawian for some time without saying anything.

'What are you doing here?' I spluttered eventually.

'I've been made a prefect,' replied Garlic, his face pinking with excitement.

I staggered back against the door in astonishment and felt the burning sensation of hot tea spilling over the sides of the mug and scalding my fingers.

'You're a prefect?' I asked in a voice of dread and confusion.

'For the whole weekend,' replied the Malawian, punching the air with his fist.

'So you're an acting prefect then?' I corrected.

'I'm a proper prefect until Monday night,' he corrected me in turn. 'So that's exactly 101 hours of prefectship from the moment I arrived this afternoon until 11:59 on Monday night.'

'Congratulations,' I said slipping into my favourite armchair and feeling a little more comfortable about things.

'It's a massive honour,' he added, before setting off at length about his predictably amazing holiday on the banks of Lake Malawi.

'How was your holiday, Spud?'

I sipped casually at my tea and said, 'I kissed a girl in the mountains.'

'Wow!' gasped Garlic.

I nodded and sipped at my tea.

'Did you bone her?' he asked.

'Of course not!' I replied angrily.

'Did you squeeze her gaboonies?' he demanded.

'None of your business,' I snapped, and fixed the Malawian with a malevolent glare.

Garlic backed down and looked a little sheepish.

'Sorry,' he said. 'Just checking.'

I finished my tea and contemplated the situation I now found myself in.

'So who else is a prefect for this weekend?' I asked.

'Just the three of us,' replied Garlic.

'Three?' I questioned.

'Eggwhite's also coming back early.'

I tried my best not to snigger but couldn't restrain a few snorts of laughter when Garlic confirmed that Missing Eggwhite was due back at any minute and even glanced across at the door expectantly.

Friday 16th April

09:30 'While we wait for Eggwhite,' intoned Viking glancing at his watch, 'let me once again thank you both for sacrificing your holidays to offer up service to the house.'

Viking bemoaned the series of unforeseen and unfortunate events that had kept Simon, Rambo, Fatty and Boggo from joining in this weekend.

'Poor Brown is marooned in Florence thanks to

a band of gypsies stealing his family's money and passports,' he declared with some measure of distaste. 'Fatty's grandfather sadly passed away last weekend and Black is in a race against time to be fit for the rugby season after being struck down with a nasty bout of tick bite fever.'

'What happened to Boggo?' asked Garlic.

'Greenstein has dedicated his entire holidays to helping leukaemia sufferers at a local hospice,' replied Viking solemnly. 'I couldn't in all conscience drag him back to school and let the patients down.'

I marvelled at two things:

1. Viking's gullibility
2. The ability of my peers to think of brilliant excuses off the cuff at the crack of dawn when confronted by Mr Shouty

'What about Vern? Why couldn't he be here?' demanded Garlic.

Viking fixed the Malawian with a deadly stare before uttering, 'Garlic, I hardly think Blackadder is the type of role model to show off to prospective new boys.'

'So Milton, Eggwhite and I are role models, sir?' responded Garlic, his face flushing pink with pride.

Viking scratched his beard and looked pained at the mention of Missing Eggwhite's name. He stood up sharply, marched past us, and flung open the door. He glanced up and down the cloisters before roaring, 'Eggwhite!'

There was no response other than the scattering of a few startled rock pigeons in the eaves above. Viking slammed the door and returned to his desk shaking his head in utter perplexity.

14:30   I was astonished by how small and young these

prep school kids looked. They made the Harmless Half-Dozen look like grizzled veterans which, considering their complete lack of intimidation factor, is saying something.

Viking kicked off proceedings with shouted welcomes and introductions. Despite recently declaring that he was cured of his morbid phobia about a naked boy committing suicide, he nevertheless listed eleven drawbacks of killing oneself. My thoughts began to drift but I was soon shaken back to reality by Viking saying, 'Milton, I'm sure you have more than a few words to share with these fine young lads?'

After a scratchy start, including a knack jump (where did that come from?), I gradually found my groove and set forth on a lively yet convincing overview of the school. Viking seemed highly impressed with my impromptu speech, except for the part where I mentioned that the first year at the school might be tough, for it was a mere few seconds later that he cleared his throat and tapped his watch to indicate that my time was up.

Viking introduced Garlic as a 'special weekend prefect' and encouraged him to step forward and say a few words after me. The Malawian might also have been allowing his thoughts to wander because he shouted 'Me?' and looked around like he didn't know what was cracking. He grew extremely pink in the face before kicking off with his introduction.

'I'm Garth Garlic!' he blurted, like he was talking to three year olds. 'And I come from Malawi!' His face broke into a broad grin and he shouted, 'Hands up all those who've been to Malawi!' None of the boys lifted their hands and poor Garlic gaped at them like this was the very last response he expected. He turned to me and shook his head like the world had gone crazy.

'Where is Malawi?' he demanded, changing tack slightly.

There was much whispering and shaking of heads but nobody answered.

'Come on!' roared Garlic in disbelief. 'You must have heard of Malawi?'

There was a good deal of nervous muttering but nobody raised their hand.

'Nobody?' gasped Garlic, appalled, and looked set to continue with his loud Malawi interrogation until he was sawn off by Viking who said firmly, 'Thank you very much for that, Garlic.'

Viking ended the meeting and the youngsters were packed off to the chapel where Reverend Bishop and the school wind band lay in wait.

19:00 The evening film show turned out to be a dreadful let-down. Everybody was expecting a Hollywood blockbuster but it turned out to be a badly filmed school promotional video directed and narrated by The Glock. The headmaster had cast himself in just about every single scene of the film which, if I'm honest, amounted to The Glock striking a number of different poses around the school and banging on about what an excellent place it was. In fact I'm not even sure that this dismal effort could be regarded as a film at all. Some of the more disturbing scenes were:

- The Glock swimming numerous laps of the school pool in his Speedo
- The Glock wearing the first team rugby jersey and scoring a try under the poles to the sound of canned applause
- The Glock dressed in full school uniform and pretending to be a new boy studying the school rules in bed

- The Glock being hoisted aloft by a number of unhappy boys who had clearly been coerced into it
- The Glock enjoying being licked in the face by Mr Lilly's poodle

If I were Sparerib I never would have identified myself as the cinematographer in the credits.

Sunday 18th April

09:30 Viking accosted me after chapel and demanded to know what my final house play selection was. I had to concede that although down to a shortlist, I hadn't made my final pick yet. I didn't expect my housemaster to become so agitated about the situation. He advised me to send Garlic out on the hike with the prospective new boys (now nicknamed the Small 24) while I read through my shortlist of plays once more.

12:30 Viking thundered on my door and demanded to know the whereabouts of Garlic and the Small 24. They were meant to be back at noon and despite all the other groups returning there was no sign of ours.

12:45 A panicked Viking hauled me into his office and insisted we were facing a monumental crisis.

'The parents are coming at half past two!' he cried. 'I can't just tell these people that their children are missing in the hills with Garlic, can I?'

I studied my watch closely with a worried expression.

13:00 The siren sounded for lunch and Viking's panic began to turn ugly.

'So help me God!' he rampaged. 'When I find that Garlic I'm going to slaughter him.'

13:15 Viking was in a terrible state. With only 75 minutes until the arrival of the parents things were becoming desperate. We raced off in his red Alfa Romeo kicking up large clouds of dust behind us.

'Top of the hill should provide a view, Milton,' he shouted above the roar of the engine. He passed me his binoculars and told me to keep scanning the hillsides. I kept the binoculars trained and pretended to scan around but all I could see was a green blur and a wall of brown dust. Garlic and the Small 24 were nowhere to be found.

13:45 Our thirty minutes of racing around the Midlands achieved nothing other than setting off a number of red warning lights on the Alfa's dashboard.

Viking resigned himself to his fate.

'The headmaster is going to have my head,' he muttered with dread lining his voice.

I tried to cheer him up by pointing out that Garlic's blunder wasn't his fault, but he looked at me like I was clueless.

'Headmaster's been planning this weekend for ten months,' he said. 'That's longer than a human pregnancy.'

We turned the corner with a screech and nearly ran into a crowd of sprinting boys in the middle of the road following a larger boy with white hair and pink face who was galloping towards the school gates.

'Thank cock!' screamed Viking his right hand clasped across his chest.

He swerved violently around the boys and sped ahead to pull level with the Malawian who nearly fell over when the great bearded head of Viking leered out of the car window and commenced with the mother of all tirades. After driving alongside and lambasting Garlic for over 400m, the irate housemaster sped ahead while barking instructions at me.

'Milton, you make sure these boys are showered, dressed and packed up by 14:20 and I'll have a word with the caterer about a late lunch! Go! Go! Go!'

14:45   Viking collapsed onto the house bench after the last of the Small 24 had been claimed by their parents. 'What an ordeal, Milton,' he gasped, taking a few deep breaths and looking a little more human. 'Right,' he said getting to his feet in a determined fashion. 'Send Garlic to my office immediately.'

15:05   I opened my door to be confronted by a large tear-stained face.
'I've been de-prefected,' Garlic stammered, stifling a sob. 'A whole day early.'
'Sorry,' I said.
'All my special weekend prefect privileges have been revoked,' he sighed.
'Sorry,' I said again.
'You mind if I make myself a cup of tea and hang snake in the cop shop for old times' sake?'
'Go ahead,' I replied.
'Thanks, Spud,' he said and with a loud sniff he turned and walked sadly away.

Monday 19th April

CRAZY EIGHT HOLIDAY SCORECARD

RAMBO	Stayed in a luxury hotel at the Victoria Falls with his dad and stepmother, where he didn't contract tick bite fever. After a head shave on number two he's taken on the appearance of a wanted criminal.
SIMON	Spent Easter in Tuscany which he said wasn't all that bad. Although

a young gypsy had attempted to steal Simon's wallet, the thief wasn't successful and he was roughed up by Simon's dad, a passing priest and numerous bystanders.

FATTY   Wasn't very communicative about his holidays. In fact he seemed terribly depressed and on the verge of tears. I assume his grandfather really did die.

BOGGO   Worked the entire holiday in his stepdad's betting tote. He says he's saving up so that he can splash out next year in Amsterdam where he plans to sample every prostitute in Holland twice. When asked about his work with the leukaemia patients he laughed so hard that he snorted tea out of his nose and had to leave the cop shop.

GARLIC   The only boy in the school's history to be prefected and de-prefected during a holiday.

SPUD   Made a strong emotional connection with (and kissed) a girl called Leanne under the stars in the mountains.

VERN   Vern shouted 'Mozambique!' during a lull in conversation. He proceeded to muddy the waters somewhat by repeating the word 'Helsinki' into the vacant fireplace and listening carefully for an echo. It's still more likely that Vern went to Mozambique than Helsinki.

Tomorrow I turn seventeen years old. It certainly feels like a massive leap forward from sixteen which now seems embarrassingly young. As of tomorrow I can legally drive a car (providing I pass the learner's test and have a licensed driver in the vehicle with me at all times). Still, it's a major milestone and leaves me just twelve months short of finally being classed an adult. I'm sure somebody has a sneaky and vile surprise lying in wait for me tomorrow but I plan to unleash a counterattack of terminator proportions.

This will be my last birthday as a schoolboy.

Tuesday 20th April

Happy 17th birthday, Spud Milton!!!

Any thoughts that my birthday would be forgotten were blown out of the water when Albert Schweitzer charged into my room minutes before the rising siren brandishing a birthday present. I thanked him for the jar of Peck's Anchovette and my slave responded by snatching it back and neatly stashing it on the shelf with my other provisions.

The Fragile Five sang happy birthday to me in the showers which I later discovered to be a case of brownnosing because Simon bust them having a pillow fight last night and they wanted to curry favour with the prefects and avoid punishment.

After roll call I was approached by most of the Normal Seven. My instinct was to back away, thinking they were the lynch mob coming to capture me. As it turned out they only wanted to shake my hand and wish me well. I'm thoroughly unsettled by all the friendliness. As Boggo says, when somebody around here pats you on the back he's only looking for the perfect spot to plunge the knife.

11:20 A number of interesting letters/cards arrived in the post:

- Mom and Dad sent me a card and fifty bucks.
- Wombat sent me a card, although the writing was completely illegible. If the envelope hadn't contained a five pound note I wouldn't have known who it was from.
- Mermaid's card was only from her and thankfully not Gavin the Umpire. She also signed off: *Forever your Mermaid.*
- Brenda's card was very sweet but by far the easiest to throw away.

After tea break I found it difficult to concentrate on school work because my brain was mostly taken up with thinking about ex-girlfriends and sordid sex acts.

18:20 Rambo, Simon and I left the dining hall together but were held up by a traffic jam of boys squeezing through the door. I felt myself being jostled, hands gripping my shoulder and then my legs were seized and I was lifted into orbit. Within seconds I felt myself hurtling through the air before crashing into the freezing water of the pond. I heaved myself out of the water and everywhere boys were sprinting away. I pulled off one of my sodden shoes and branded the nearest boy on the back, who happened to be JR Ewing.

'Hey!' echoed a booming shout away to my left. It was The Glock who had charged out of his office to see what the rumpus was all about. Aside from a drenched Spud, the quad was utterly deserted. The headmaster studied me closely as I squelched up to him. 'Happy birthday, Milton,' he said with a smug grin and strode back into his office.

I slopped my way into the house and ignored the cretinous shout of 'Birthday boy!' as I passed Vern's room.

Wednesday 21st April

Something is dreadfully wrong with Fatty. He was crying during maths and is refusing to speak to anyone. A concerned Sidewinder reckons he's sleeping rough in the archives and Shambles reports alarmingly that Fatty has stopped eating between meals. After geography I offered him my condolences about his grandfather but he just walked away.

13:30   Lennox and I had an excellent discussion about the murder of Chris Hani after history class. He said that somebody called Clive Derby-Lewis and his wife have been arrested in connection with the killing. We agreed that it could very possibly be a security police conspiracy. Outside the sun was shining, turtle doves were cooing, and autumn leaves blanketed the fields in a picture of tranquillity. Lennox reckons that chaos works in disguise. He may well be right.

20:30   Albert Schweitzer was in one of his cleaning moods so I vacated my room and headed to the cop shop to check on the insane. Rambo and Simon were arguing the merits of various breeds of dogs.

There was a loud rap on the door and Boggo's head appeared.

'I've got fresh porn, you guys mind if I come in?'

'Make yourself at home,' replied Simon and lunged to catch a flying magazine.

'That's illegal Dutch,' advised Boggo settling into a chair. 'There's some pretty trippy stuff on page 61 involving a transsexual Santa and a guy with a large knob dressed up as a reindeer.'

'Slave!' roared Rambo.

There was a timid knock on the door.

'Come!' boomed Simon, thoroughly engrossed in Boggo's Dutch magazine.

Shambles and Small & Freckly entered.

'Right,' said Rambo. 'Tea and toast for Greenstein, and coffee for me. Simon?' Simon waved to indicate he still had a full cup.

'Oh, and another Milo for Spud,' added Rambo without so much as consulting me.

Boggo smacked his lips together and let out a contented sigh. 'Just nailed down my matric date and she's bloody hot and a real goer.' He refused to indicate who she might be.

'You'll all have to wait until June 11th, I'm afraid.'

'Who's your unfortunate date, Milton?' asked Rambo with a barely disguised smirk.

'He could always invite his stalker nun,' chirped Simon, still without looking up. For some reason the others thought this was hilarious.

'It could be worse,' cried Boggo. 'He could be Fatty and have no date at all.'

'What about Penny?' I asked, sending the trio into cackling laughter once more.

'Penny blitzed Fatty big time in the holidays,' chortled Simon with considerable delight.

I said I thought Fatty's grandfather had died in the holidays, which only provoked further laughter.

'Jeez, you been living under a rock or what, Spud?' asked Rambo. 'It's like the fourth time Fatty's lost a grandfather in two years.'

'Penny dumped him last week over the phone. Apparently it got messy,' ventured Boggo and reached out for his tea which Shambles had just carefully brought through. 'Fatty was begging and crying and pleading with Penny not to bullet him.'

'How do you know all this?' I asked.

'I have confidential sources that witnessed the carnage,' he replied and carefully sipped at his tea to check the temperature.

'I see somebody's been molesting Brenda in the holidays,' chirped Simon.

Boggo's strident denials were interrupted by frantic knocking on the cop shop door.

'Come!' roared Simon.

The door creaked open and Garlic and Vern entered.

'You mind if we join in?' asked Garlic, looking at Rambo with pleading eyes.

'Yes, we do,' replied Rambo and returned to his magazine.

'Please, guys,' whined Garlic.

'Only if you have a matric dance date,' replied Boggo smugly.

'I have a date!' shouted Garlic. 'I'm taking Myrtle Pienaar.'

'Not Myrtle the Mountain from St Catherine's?' retorted Boggo, his bottom lip turned down as if he was on the verge of vomiting.

'For a large girl she's a surprisingly good kisser,' declared the Malawian and happily made his way to the vacant armchair beside mine. The fool gave me a huge grin and ridiculous thumbs up which I ignored.

'What about you, Vern?' asked Simon, removing his face from the magazine for the first time since he had opened it. 'Who's your date?'

Vern grinned deviously and folded his arms, his focus moving upward until he was staring at the roof.

One would have to say that the chances of poor Vern finding a date even with somebody as large as Myrtle Pienaar are highly distant. All this talk about the matric dance made me feel uncomfortable and I left the cop shop before Rambo had the chance to order me another Milo.

Thursday 22nd April

11:00 I have decided to destroy Albert Schweitzer. The only question that remains is what method of torturous death would create the most pain, agony and horror. During geography Mr Bosch issued us with an unexpected open file test on rock strata. I immediately snapped open my geography file only to discover that bloody Schweitzer had turned my entire ordering around so I didn't know where anything was. Quite why the moron has changed my notes from chronological to alphabetical order is a complete mystery and I'm determined to make him pay, this time with his life.

I thundered about the house at tea break issuing threats but Schweitzer was nowhere to be found. He has an uncanny ability to sense when I'm after him and disappears like a ghost into the surroundings. Still seething, I returned to my room and checked all my other files. It would seem that history and drama have also been tampered with in a similar manner.

After lunch there was no sign of the little worm so I ordered the Harmless Half-Dozen to find the swine and bring him to my room immediately.

14:30 No sign of Schweitzer. I bet one of the HHD has tipped him off and he's hiding in the hills, hoping that I'll calm down and forget about it. Still deciding on suitable punishment, but I am determined to rattle his cage.

17:00 Still no sign of my slave. I can't hang around the house because Viking is lurking and if he sees me then he will demand to know my house play selection which I obviously haven't made yet. It's a terrible catch-22.

18:00 Schweitzer is officially missing. The sun has set and he's not at dinner, nor in the house.

18:30 I am beginning to feel a little concerned and slightly responsible. How long does somebody have to be not around before he's declared missing?

19:00 I marched up to Simon's room to declare my slave AWOL and found our head of house listening to Enigma and sitting cross legged on the carpet. I managed to spell out the problem, despite the chanting monks and Simon having his eyes closed and being in some sort of trance. 'San,' was all he uttered.

I raced down to the sanatorium and found Albert Schweitzer in the general ward with another small boy. Their conversation ceased abruptly when I entered.

'Hey, John!' croaked Schweitzer. 'Thanks for coming to see me.' I could see Schweitzer was fairly sick and he seemed so delighted with my visit that I decided to postpone his reprimand and slaughter until his health had improved.

'Are you Spud Milton?' asked the small boy with prominent ears in the bed next to my slave. I casually informed the boy that I was indeed the man.

'First team cricket,' said the youngster with some reverence. I wasn't sure how to react to the boy with the large ears so I turned my attention back to Schweitzer and asked him what was wrong.

'Bronchitis,' said the boy with big ears before Schweitzer had a chance to respond. 'Did you really kiss Amanda Lawrence?' continued Big Ears, staring at me intently.

I was a little taken aback by such a direct and personal question but cunningly countered by asking him how he knew about Amanda Lawrence.

'My brother says she's the hottest girl in the world.'

'Who's your brother?' I asked.

'James Wilkens, but at school he was called Bongo,' replied the boy.

I remembered Bongo Wilkens. He was the first team spinner when I was in second year.

'My name is Jeremy Wilkens,' continued the boy, 'although round here I'm known as Wingnut.' It wasn't hard to see why. 'My brother told me Amanda Lawrence sent you a picture of herself in the nude with a horse.'

'It was actually a painting,' I corrected. 'And there was no horse involved.'

Wingnut Wilkens looked dubious but I made a break for it before he asked me any other personal questions about my lack of sex life. On my stroll back to the house I considered the beauty of Amanda, the chances of her agreeing to be my matric dance date, and the growing confidence of the modern slave. In my day I would never have dreamed of asking a prefect about his private life even if it did involve a hot girl and a horse. Perhaps Boggo has a point when he says discipline and standards are slipping. I returned to my room to study for tomorrow's history test on the rise of the National Party 1924-1948. Now that I am getting used to Albert Schweitzer's alphabetical ordering, my history file isn't so bad after all.

Friday 23rd April

I narrowly avoided the passing Viking by hiding behind a wall in the cloisters. Darryl (the last remaining) asked me what I was doing so closely pressed up against the bricks and I told him I was searching for structural defects. This can't go on. I need to make my play selection today!

11:00 The rugby trial teams have been announced.

I have been placed at fullback for the 6th team which is a two team jump on last year. Further good news is that I have narrowly avoided Mongrel (7ths coach) and Sparerib (5ths) and have ended up with Bony Cartwright who seems a far safer bet. Tomorrow's trial match against the 5ths could be crucial. Play too well and I could be promoted to the goblin fifteen. Play poorly and I might end up under the control of a sadist and spend my season running up and down mountains carrying logs and hyperventilating.

Albert Schweitzer has been gone 24 hours and my room is already a shambolic mess. I sent Plaque down to the san to check on his progress and he returned with good news. My slave is returning tomorrow and it's not a moment too soon. I'm still determined to have stern words with him about tampering with my files without permission.

Saturday 24th April

Rugby trials

10:00   I did my best to maintain mediocrity at all times on the rugby field and mostly succeeded. I thought I had blown it when I scored a try after intercepting a pass on the halfway line. Thankfully, however, my conversion attempt scuttled along the ground and had the 5ths forwards chortling. I hoped that my two standout moments had cancelled themselves out in the final reckoning and that I'll remain under the coaching guidance of Bony Cartwright for the foreseeable future.

14:30   Visited The Guv who was reading a thick book on his veranda when I arrived.

'Milton?' he called as I opened his garden gate. 'Have you nothing better to do than pester a ripe fig on a Saturday afternoon?'

'Sorry, sir,' I said.

'No, you're not,' he retorted. 'How did you know that I wouldn't be ravaging a nymph up against the ironing room door?'

'Lucky guess, sir,' I said.

'Sarcasm, Milton!' he boomed. 'It's the bastard child of a lugubrious wit.'

I informed The Guv that the time had come to make a call on the house play and I couldn't decide between the final three contenders.

'This calls for refreshments and floor space,' he cried as he sprang to his feet and strode into the house. I followed at a polite distance.

'Heave ho, Milton!' shouted The Guv as I entered his study. My English teacher was desperately attempting to push his piano aside and didn't seem to be having any effect on it. We eventually succeeded in creating an acting space and The Guv called for a fifteen minute hiatus while he drank wine and recovered from the exertion of moving the piano.

The Guv reckoned the only way to choose between the three plays would be for us to deliver staged readings so as accurately to gauge each play's potential. When The Guv said 'we' would deliver a staged reading it turned out to be 'he' doing all the reading. The maniac would assign me various parts before kicking off and proceed to steal all the roles when it came to the actual performance. The problem was that both *A Resounding Tinkle* (NF Simpson) and *Blithe Spirit* (Noel Coward), although excellent when in the hands of The Guv, had some major issues. *Tinkle* lost points because it really only has two major parts, one of which is a woman. *Blithe Spirit* was excellent but far too long. When I suggested to The Guv that we could cut the play in half he glared at me with menace and said this would be an 'uncowardly act'.

I was reluctant to reveal my third option because I had a very strong feeling that The Guv would hate it and call me a cretin or a Philistine. Firstly, it was a spoof. Secondly, it was written by two people (Wayne and Schuster) and finally, and most alarmingly, it was a rip-off of Julius Caesar. Its name ... *Rinse the Blood off My Toga*.

Predictably, The Guv was horrified. He refused even to touch the script, let alone begin reading. After much pleading and cajoling he eventually agreed to scan the first three pages despite the fact that this went against the very fibre of his being. He insisted on opening another bottle of wine to help him through the ordeal and loped off to the wine cellar, shaking his head like he was being cruelly treated. When he returned clasping Major Merlot he had an inspired expression on his face.

'You hungry at all, Milton?' The Guv asked.

'Not really,' I lied.

'Thought I might fry up a few sausages,' he said and turned back to the kitchen where he shouted, 'Ophelia, you wretched feline! Can't keep the old felis cattus out of the boutros boutros ghali, Milton,' he said when he returned a few minutes later. 'I'm afraid she hasn't been the same since my last wife left. They have very similar characteristics in fact.'

He poured himself a glass and produced another for me which he half filled. 'Just to grease up the old joints,' he said and handed it over. We clinked our glasses and The Guv began reading *Toga* while I held my breath. He barked with laughter lower down on the very first page and within minutes he was snorting so much that he repeatedly had to stop to drink more wine and unfog his glasses.

Afterwards he called it 'Hideously funny in the worst possible way'.

'Should I do it, sir?'

'By crikey, yes!' he roared. 'But if you tell anyone that I said so I'll have your skin removed in the night.' He paused as if remembering something before erupting into mad laughter once more.

'Oh God, Milton!' he screamed scrabbling to his feet. 'The bloody sausages!'

22:30 I staggered down the garden pathway with my stomach aching from too much laughter, wine, and burnt sausages. The Guv stood on his porch and raised his glass to me. 'Exit, pursued by a bear, Milton.' I held my fist aloft, opened the gate, and began running across the fields through partial moonlight.

Sunday 25th April

Just my luck it was pork sausages for breakfast. I decided that I needed a thorough cleaning out of my system so I only ate fruit and muesli which was deeply dissatisfying. Despite slow reflexes, I don't have a hangover after yesterday's wine with The Guv. Now that I'm seventeen this is surely an indication that I have outgrown hangovers once and for all.

For the first time in a week I haven't had to avoid Viking, although typically now that I don't need to avoid him he is nowhere to be seen.

Further good news is that Albert Schweitzer has returned from the san and seemed to take the mess and filth in my room personally. I waited until he had finished his hour of feverish cleaning and finally raised the re-ordering of half my files issue, but he misunderstood me and apologised for not finishing all of them before he was struck down with illness. Since I am now rather enjoying the new alphabetical system I decided it would be senseless to tear a strip off the lad for using his initiative. He did such a good job of cleaning up that I allowed him to make himself tea in the annexe. This thrilled him no end and inspired further unnecessary work in my room.

20:00   I knew Viking was in his office because I could see the large shadow moving about through his window. I knocked on his door which stood ajar and entered to find him scribbling furiously in red ink all over Garlic's drama essay.

'What is it, Milton?'
   'I have selected the house play, sir.'
   'Well?'
   Rinse the Blood off My Toga, sir.'

There was no immediate response so I passed him the script. I thought he would send me on my way but he began reading it right there and then. Almost immediately Viking let off a hideous bark which turned out to be him laughing and, like The Guv yesterday, he was soon doubled over with hysterics at the spoofy silliness. He stopped reading after five pages and appeared flushed with happiness. He said he would finish up the rest tomorrow morning and give me the all clear at breakfast if he was satisfied.

After the meeting I popped my head into the cop shop where the others were having yet another discussion about the matric dance so I headed back to my room. After staring at my chest in the mirror for some time I decided that I need to work out more. I completed ten press-ups and seventeen sit-ups before concluding that being creative is far more important than having a six pack and called off the workout.

I'm yet to hear anybody asking how big Shakespeare's triceps were.

Monday 26th April

Viking gave me the all clear on *Rinse the Blood off My Toga* and instructed me to hold auditions as soon as possible. 'Good luck, Milton,' he said, followed by, 'Please avoid a disaster.' On that promising note I conducted my morning house check and chanced upon an unusual sight. Boggo's door was partially open but through the gap I could see Vern making Boggo's bed. I pretended to be having an extended slash and kept an eye on Rain Man as he began folding clothes and stashing them away in Boggo's cupboard. Boggo wasn't in his room and there was no explanation to be had from Vern who bleated like a sheep when I enquired what he was up to.

Tuesday 27th April

The rugby team lists have been posted and I was mightily relieved to remain as the 6th team fullback. Rambo has been made the first team captain and 8th man, although the real surprise is that JR Ewing is the first team scrumhalf. That is almost unbelievable considering that he is only in third year. Ewing was leaning up against the common room wall with his hands in his pockets surrounded by numerous well wishers.

'Congratulations, JR,' I said.

'Hey, shot,' he replied as if I was a complete stranger.

The good news about making the 6th team was tempered by the fact that Thinny is one of our locks and Garlic the hooker. On a more positive note I have been made vice captain which means that I get to run onto the field second after our captain Scum Rogers.

I was also rather shocked by the fact that Vern is playing left wing for the 4ths. That means a man with no brain is currently two sides higher than I am. Not sure if this says more about Vern or the sport of rugby?

Wednesday 28th April

After breakfast it was with great pride that I attached the following to the house notice board:

> *1993 House play competition official entry*
>
> *Rinse the Blood off My Toga*
> *A comedy in one act*
> *Written by Wayne and Schuster*
> *Directed by John Milton*
>
> *Auditions Friday Night 20:00 in the Cop Shop*
> *Audition pieces should be no longer than 3 minutes and must be comic*

Thursday 29th April

I have been bombarded with wannabe actors asking unnecessary and moronic questions about tomorrow night's auditions. There has also been a fair amount of brownnosing which I have largely ignored, apart from accepting a gift of a block of gouda cheese from Darryl (the last remaining) which I donated to the cop shop reserves. Thankfully, Vern didn't ask any questions but skulked outside my room for an hour after lunch repeatedly announcing 'Toga!' through an empty toilet roll.

- How much will I be paid to audition? (Boggo)
- Can I do a hadeda impersonation as an audition piece? (Runt)
- Was the play written by Leon Schuster? (Albert Schweitzer)
- Do we have to audition naked? (Near Death, Barryl, Plump Graham and Thinny after the idiots fell for Boggo's erroneous rumour)
- Do you have to be gay to audition? (Rambo)
- Will there be hot girls in the cast? (Spike)
- Is a toga the same thing as a tog bag? (Garlic)
- Do Wayne and Schuster attend our school? (Garlic)
- Who is John Milton? (Garlic)

14:30   Rugby practice

The 6ths rugby team suffered their first (and probably not last) defeat of the season against the 5ths. It might have been closer had our scrum not repeatedly collapsed. Our two props, whom Bony Cartwright has nicknamed Mutt and Jeff, blamed hooker Garlic for binding like a moron. I made a conscious effort not to impress the watching Sparerib and concentrated hard on being where the ball wasn't wherever possible.

I returned to my room where Albert Schweitzer had his hands full fighting back a mob of desperate actors wanting to ask me further moronic questions about the auditions. I refused to answer anybody and pushed past them and headed to the showers where more excited questioners awaited.

Friday 30th April

HOUSE PLAY AUDITIONS

I can see why very few people make a career out of directing. It could also explain why Viking is perpetually enraged and has high blood pressure. I cast my mind back to *Noah's Ark* in second year and the mutiny against Julian and what a dog show the rehearsal process was. If the auditions are anything to go by, *Rinse the Blood off My Toga* could be heading in a similar direction.

The farce began at 19:50 when I entered the cop shop to set up for my auditions and discovered the first rugby team inside. How wonderful of Rambo not to offer advance notice about using the cop shop tonight. I relocated to the junior classroom but was evicted by Mongrel who sidled past on his evening patrol and forced me out on the flimsy premise that classrooms are for study and not theatre. I sent Albert Schweitzer out on a mission to check if the theatre or drama room were open but he returned looking glum.

By 20:15 I was still floundering about searching for a suitable venue when a scuffle broke out after Spike jumped the audition queue and subsequently kneed Plump Graham in the nuts. After quelling the riot I cut my losses and began auditioning people in my room. This only played into the hands of Rambo, Simon and Boggo who have been spreading rumours that the only way to make the house play is to offer me sexual favours. I decided to leave the door open to avoid suspicion but this proved a blunder when a large crowd hovered around the doorway watching the auditions and Garlic kept applauding and shouting encouragement. In the end I slammed the door and pressed on with the debacle.

An hour and a half later I closed my door for the final

time and drove the remaining lurkers up to their dormitories for lights out. I lay on my bed covering my eyes and wondering how I had been suckered into this job in the first place. If the terrible lack of talent on display is anything to go by, this may be an extremely abrupt end to my career as a theatre director. After making myself a large cup of tea I returned to my room and began sifting through the wreckage of the auditions.

Promising
Meg Ryan's Son

Passable
Spike
Thinny

Poor
Enzo Ferrari
Barryl
Plump Graham
Sidewinder

Very Poor
Darryl (the last remaining)
Small & Freckly
Runt
Plaque

Barely Audible
Rowdy
Stutterheim

Astoundingly Bad
Garlic
Near Death

Off the Charts
Vern

Saturday 1st May

06:30 Awoke from a horrendous nightmare where Sarah Silver marched into my room and demanded an audition for *Toga*. When I refused on the grounds that she isn't a member of the house, she took her clothes off and demanded sex. At that precise moment Mongrel stormed into my room, berated me for having a naked girl bent over my desk and ordered me to report to his 7th team rugby practice on Tuesday.

10:00 After the dodgy dream, things improved on the rugby field when the mighty 6ths narrowly defeated St James 13-10. It wasn't exactly sparkling rugby but Bony Cartwright seemed happy enough with the result and my performance was solid and steady, but in no way spectacular.

By 14:30 most of the talk around the ground was of the looming battle of the 1sts. St James old boys were overheard bragging about having their best team in a decade, while nobody was sure what to expect from our team other than frightening aggression under the captaincy of Rambo Lecter. The rest of the talk around the ground was of Vern Blackadder's various cretin attacks for the 4ths.

At high noon the 4th team charged onto Trafalgar in front of a healthy crowd and it would seem that the pressure of the occasion had an adverse effect on Rain Man.

Vern's initial blunder was running too fast down the bank and wiping out before he even made it onto the rugby field. He fell awkwardly against a low picket fence and sliced his knee open. Medics were called to the scene and the start of play was delayed by five minutes while Vern was being bandaged up. The embarrassing fall rattled Rain Man who became visibly agitated on the left wing. He spent most of the first half staring at his bandage and shouting angrily at nobody in particular. At half time the cretin became carried away with devouring a number of orange quarters and sprayed juice in his eye. Vern's play deteriorated in the second half mainly because he kept his left hand cupped over his left eye and therefore struggled to catch or tackle. Rain Man had everyone in hysterics, including the ref who at one stage was laughing so hard that he couldn't blow the whistle properly. Vern's final clanger was his attempt to catch a high up and under. The cretin misjudged the catch and the ball rebounded off his face and into the arms of the approaching opposition forwards who went on to score what turned out to be the winning try.

15:00 The first team, despite appearing extremely macho and aggressive when charging onto the field, were soon trailing by ten points to an extremely slick St James. However, in one of the most exciting games ever, we clawed our way back into the match and Ice Tray crashed over for a try in the corner with just three minutes to go for a single point lead. Joy soon turned to horror when the flying St James winger caught the ball from the kickoff, burst through a wall of players and scorched down the touchline to score what the entire crowd thought was the clincher. That's when we noticed our linesman standing on the halfway line with his flag raised. Boggo Greenstein ignored the loud boos from the St James supporters and pointed his flag accusingly at the touchline to indicate where the flying winger had breached the line. The ref came over and asked Boggo if he was sure about his decision, considering the context of the match. Boggo held his hand solemnly across his heart and declared, 'I swear to God on my mother's life.' The ref was convinced by Boggo's earnest swearing and disallowed the try. He briefly glanced at his stopwatch before blowing the final whistle for a famous victory.

Boggo took flight immediately after the game as a number of large and irate St James old boys seemed intent on lynching him. Using his local knowledge, he was able to evade the angry old boys and barricade himself in the tuba room of the music centre where he remained until darkness fell and the baying crowds had finally dispersed.

Sunday 2nd May

Spent most of the day mulling over my options for *Toga*. If I could only cast the two lead roles, the smaller parts should fall into place. Flavius Maximus needs to be a cool cat private investigator and Brutus a sly and manipulative schemer with good comic timing. Ideally, I would cast Rambo and Boggo as the pair but Boggo has made it clear that he wants a ridiculous salary for his performance and Rambo no doubt thinks himself too cool to be directed by me. Fatty is another option for Flavius, although in his post-Penny bat depression, it's unlikely that he would agree or put in much effort anyway. I considered my options once more and began hypothetically filling up the minor roles with the best of the rest.

Directing a play is like anything else in life: You start at the bottom and slowly grovel your way upwards hoping things will improve.

Monday 3rd May

15:00 I have been plagued by desperate idiots demanding to know if they have made the play. You would think I was Steven Spielberg offering up million dollar film roles, such was the feverish excitement outside my room after lunch.

To end the incessant knocking and questioning I placed the following on the house notice board:

Please Note:

Rinse the Blood off My Toga *cast list to be announced soon! Please be patient while the process is under way.*

J Milton

20:00   Obviously, my original notice wasn't clear enough because the knocking and questions have increased with everybody wanting to know how soon 'soon' is. Replaced the original notice with the following:

Please Note:

Rinse the Blood off My Toga *cast list will be announced on Sunday 9th May at 18:00.*

J Milton

PS No further questions about casting will be answered.

Tuesday 4th May

I witnessed Vern taking Boggo's laundry this morning. When I asked him what was going on he sniggered at me like I had just told him a naughty joke and galloped off. Later, I spotted the cretin shining Boggo's black school shoes in his room but once again he refused to answer any of my questions, responding to them all by crudely bending over and pretending to shout 'Toga!' out of his bum hole.

The showers were oddly deserted for the entire afternoon despite numerous boys hanging about the common room and surrounds with towels and soap dishes. I asked Plump Graham why nobody was showering and he said it was because Rambo has declared that if there was no hot water left after his rugby practice, he would physically maim every single boy who had showered before him.

Typically, King Rambo sauntered into the showers at 5:55pm, meaning there was chaos in the bogs and the entire house was late for dinner. To make matters worse, I was sternly rebuked by the caterer because I was meant to be covering for Missing Eggwhite as prefect on duty and therefore held responsible for the repercussions of Rambo's megalomania. It's a cruel world.

Wednesday 5th May

Disaster struck early this morning when Viking spotted me crossing the quad and beckoned me over to his office door. I hoped it might be a quick word in the cloisters but it turned into eleven uncomfortable minutes in the office.

'I hear the casting is going great guns, Milton?'

I was rather taken aback by Viking's opening gambit, considering I haven't cast a single role or spoken to anyone (other than myself) on the matter.

'Who said that, sir?' I asked.

Viking's eyes narrowed and in a rather icy tone he said, 'I meant it in general rather than in the specific.'

His reply made no sense to me at all, although I nodded as if it did.

'Well?' demanded Viking.

'Nothing is set in stone, sir,' I replied.

'Yes?' he said.

'It's kind of all up in the air, sir.'

'Right.'

'Although I have a couple of strong possibilities.'

'Who are your two leads, Milton?'

Viking eyed me suspiciously as if a great deal hung on the names that were about to tumble out my mouth.

'Sir, I was thinking about Rambo as Flavius Maximus and Boggo as Brutus.'

I spoke in as vague a voice as I could muster in case I was forced into an urgent retreat.

'I didn't realise they'd auditioned for the house play,' replied Viking, scratching at his beard before studying his fingernails for signs of wildlife.

'They didn't, sir. I was hoping that I could persuade them.'

'Well, I'd get about that chop-chop, Milton,' advised my housemaster. 'I hope you have a plan B?'

Simon burst into the office looking hassled and didn't appear to notice me seated in the chair. I was mightily relieved for the interruption.

'Sir,' said Simon.

'Ah yes, Brown. Apparently our third years were dicking around in the dining hall at lunch.'

Viking's voice began to rise in volume and blue veins appeared across the fringes of his forehead.

'I heard about it,' said Simon. 'It looks like Spike and JR Ewing were the ringleaders.'

'Who was the prefect on duty?'

Simon glanced at me momentarily before his attention returned to Viking.

'Eggwhite, sir.' Simon spoke with a flatness in his voice like he may have had this conversation many times before.

'Not again!' roared Viking.

'Afraid so,' sighed Simon, glancing across at me.

'Well, that is all about to change, gentlemen,' spat Viking, snatching up his telephone receiver and dialling the school switchboard.

'It's Richardson!' he boomed. 'Put me through to the post matric residence immediately.'

While he was waiting to be transferred, Viking slid open his desk drawer and withdrew an envelope. He lobbed it over to me, telling me it was my house play budget allocation for small running costs. I waved my thanks and took the opportunity to make a break for it. I closed the office door behind me but could clearly hear Viking screaming, 'Well, where in the hell *is* he?'

Outside in the cloisters I opened the envelope and found two crisp R50 notes inside. I have a budget and a play. Now I just need a few half-decent lead actors.

'You tell Eggwhite if he doesn't report to my office this evening he can consider himself de-prefected!' roared Viking, his voice piercing through the walls and echoing around the quad.

'Hey, Spud, what's in the envelope?' demanded a pink face looming into my field of vision.

'None of your business, Garlic,' I replied acidly.

'Is that the cast list?'

'What?'

'In the envelope!' howled Garlic in exasperation. 'You know, like the Oscars!'

'No,' I replied.

A pile of textbooks and files crashed into my arms.

'Geography, double maths and history,' panted Albert Schweitzer. 'Oh, and Viking was looking for you.'

'Viking!' shouted Garlic in excitement. 'Is he also in the play?'

20:00 Viking called the entire house into an emergency meeting in the common room. He was spitting mad and lost no time in announcing that Missing Eggwhite was officially de-prefected for gross dereliction of duty. 'Let that be a lesson to you all that abrogating house responsibilities will not be tolerated,' he said. Then he ordered the Normal Seven to his office immediately where he thrashed them three strokes each for causing mayhem in the dining hall at lunch.

Thursday 6th May

The dramatic de-prefecting of Eggwhite had very little impact on the house as a whole, and apart from Boggo pointing out that a new prefect ought to be selected in his place, it was business as usual at the northern end of the main quad.

After lunch I decided to bite the bullet and knocked on Boggo's door. After considerable time passed it opened and I was confronted by Vern Blackadder.

'Vern?' I said in some surprise. 'I want to speak to Boggo.'

'Tell him I'm busy.' It was Boggo's voice from inside.

'Tell him I'm busy,' repeated Vern, glaring suspiciously for some reason at my shirt pocket.

I heard a creak from Boggo's bed and soon the man himself pushed past Vern at the door.

'Well, if it isn't Dud Milton,' said Boggo by way of a greeting.

'I wanted to know if you would consider playing Brutus in *Rinse the Blood off My Toga*?'

'It would be an honour,' he replied.

I felt a surge of excitement. Perhaps this wasn't going to be as difficult as I feared.

'My fee is one hundred bucks a rehearsal and two hundred per performance including dress rehearsals.'

The door slammed in my face and I could hear sniggering from inside and Vern saying 'Toga!' I returned to my room feeling deflated.

20:10 Near Death celebrated his fourteenth birthday by enduring a brutal bogwash that had him retching and sobbing in the bogs for over half an hour. Once he had showered and recovered himself he returned to the dorm where a beaming Thinny was waiting to congratulate him for surviving the ordeal. Thinny issued Near Death a friendly slap on the back with a stick-on sign in red paint that read 'Please kick me it's my birthday'. Near Death didn't realise that he was carrying a 'kick me' sign on his back and was later nearly stampeded to death by a bloodthirsty crowd in the bogs when brushing his teeth.

Back in my room Albert Schweitzer finished off his nightly cleaning and straightening while I lay on my bed catching up on *The Merchant of Venice*.

'John,' Albert Schweitzer said in a quiet voice.

'Yip.'

'Did you hear about Near Death's birthday present this evening?'

'Yip.'

'I'm so relieved my birthday is in the holidays.'

'Lucky,' I replied, attempting to visualise Venice of four hundred years ago. Strangely, when I picture the merchant himself I can't help imagining Sparerib with a cloak and walking stick.

'My birthday is on January 4th,' he added.

Albert Schweitzer fell silent again but he was still clearly disturbed by the events that he had witnessed this evening.

'There are some crazy people in this house, hey, John?'

'Yip.'

'They never tell you about that before you come,' he said, refolding my khaki shirt.

'No, they don't,' I mumbled.

'Mr Vern is the maddest,' continued my slave, seemingly unaware that I was only half listening. 'Small & Freckly saw him squeezing an entire tube of toothpaste into his mouth this morning and then eating it.'

'That sounds like Vern.'

'I don't know if you noticed,' he said, 'but Mr Vern pulls the hair right out of his head like all the time!'

'I've noticed,' I said drily and made a deliberate point of turning the page.

There was silence while Albert Schweitzer considered the matter as he gently folded my khaki shirt and placed it back in the cupboard.

'Did Mr Rambo really have sex with Eve in first year?' he asked unexpectedly.

'Yes, he did,' I replied.

'In first year?' he repeated like the mere thought of it amazed him.

'Yip.'

'Wow!' gasped my slave. 'That's bloody lucky.'

Friday 7th May

11:00   Vern has been dropped from the 4ths to the 5ths for this weekend's match against St Paul's. I imagine his embarrassing cretin attacks last Saturday must have counted against him.

14:30   I reasoned that what with rugby tomorrow and Rambo being the captain of the 1sts, this wasn't the right time to approach him about playing Flavius Maximus in the soon to be legendary house play *Rinse the Blood off My Toga*. Instead I headed up the narrow turret hoping to find Fatty in the archives.

'Hey, Spud,' Fatty said mournfully, barely turning in his chair to look at me.

I did my best to bring some positive energy into the place and spoke in a bright and loud voice about how splendid the weather was today. My positive intent had absolutely no effect on Fatty who continued to look grim and speak as if continuously on the verge of giving up on life altogether.

'I heard about you and Penny,' I said.

'Who told you?' he asked immediately.

'Boggo heard from Brenda.'

Fatty rolled his eyes and continued to stare mournfully out of the window.

'She said she was too young to be in a proper relationship,' he sighed. 'I just couldn't understand it, you know. It made no sense to me how somebody could feel something for somebody one day and not the next.'

'Girls are weird,' I agreed.

'Now I'm probably not even going to the matric dance any more.'

'You could still invite Penny as a friend,' I suggested.

'Nought,' replied Fatty, trapping a fly against the window pane and squashing it with the palm of his hand. 'I think Penny's with somebody else now.'

'What?' I blurted. 'Who?'

'My oath if it's true I'm going to wait for the right time and kill him with my bare hands,' hissed Fatty through clenched teeth.

'You know him?' I asked.

'Oh, I know him all right. It's that little back-stabbing shit-eating traitor Spike.'

'Spike?' I shouted.

Fatty ordered me to keep it down and looked around

like I may have blown the secret. He then swore me to secrecy.

'I think she may have been cheating on me,' he said, his voice sounding oddly detached.

'That's unbelievable.'

Fatty nodded. 'When I asked her she denied it, but she could have been lying.'

I nodded.

'I can't trust her any more, Spuddy, but I'm still going to find out one way or another.' He wiped the perspiration away from around his mouth and gazed out of the window again.

Fatty is unhealthily obsessed with Penny and over the course of our conversation I came to the realisation that he wasn't right for Flavius Maximus at all. Ironically, as I stepped out into the quad the first person I saw was the grinning Spike cruising across the quad with his hands in his pockets seemingly without a care in the world.

Saturday 8th May

It was a long and successful day at St Paul's with most of the rugby sides winning easily. The mighty 6ths won 23-12 and the 1sts won 32-9, with Rambo scoring a try under the posts. The trip back to school took an age and it was already 20:30 when I finally made it back to my room. The Saturday movie was already under way so I opted for a long shower and early bed instead.

The bogs were deserted and the water was stinging hot against my back. Steam billowed up around me and what with my soap, shampoo, body and face wash, a thorough personal cleaning and preening lay in store.

'Don't drop the soap, okes, looks like Milton is running loose in the showers!' Boggo thought his joke hilarious and cackled as he pulled off his trousers and swung them over the wall of the toilet stalls.

'Big game today,' he said as if he had played in it himself. He proceeded to suggest that being a linesman was far more physically demanding than actually playing in the team.

'My oath to God,' he said, adjusting his water temperature slightly, 'if I don't get rewarded for all this effort it will be a complete stab in the litchis.'

Boggo began whistling Def Leppard to himself as he vigorously cleaned his groin with a soapy facecloth.

'Watch this, Spuddy, my oath it's classic.' He made sure that I was watching him before hollering, 'Vern!' Boggo grinned deviously and gazed at the entrance as if expecting Rain Man to materialise.

'Hey, Vern!' he shouted again, this time far louder.

There was no response and the smile faded from Boggo's face.

'Is Vern slaving for you or what?' I asked casually.

'He's just offering personal service to a man he respects,' replied Boggo haughtily as he squeezed an alarming amount of Clearasil into his palm.

'So you won't do the house play, hey, Boggo?'

Boggo studied the blue liquid for a moment and said, 'Don't get me wrong, Spud, I'd dig to be your leading man, but as I said before it would have to be worth my while.'

I didn't push the matter any further as I didn't want Boggo to think I was too desperate.

'I can fully understand why you asked me to be your numero uno,' he continued. 'I mean I'm probably the most naturally talented actor in the house and as you know true talent costs money nowadays.' Boggo paused to retrieve something out of his ear before continuing, 'Also, my oath I have so much going on, like schoolwork and being first team linesman and ...'

He ran out of things to list and instead ended the sentence by blowing his nose on the webbing between thumb and forefinger.

His theatrical arrogance irritated me and I decided there and then that I would sooner cast Garlic as Brutus than pay Boggo a single cent for his 'performance'. My shower was up and I called for Albert Schweitzer. When there was no immediate response Boggo chortled and reckoned he didn't think Schweitzer was coming.

'Oh he's coming,' I replied calmly, although this inspired further sniggering from Boggo who thought I was being overly optimistic. I silently counted a further ten seconds, switched off the taps and paced across the bogs as the tapping of light footsteps approached. Schweitzer appeared round the corner carrying my towel, a fresh T-shirt and slip slops. Without uttering a word he laid them out on the prefects' bench, gathered up all my soaps and shampoos and disappeared.

'Cheers, Boggo,' I said casually and left Greenstein alone in the showers and unusually lost for words.

Sunday 9th May

09:30 I fear my dream of being the next great directing wunderkind is imploding. Tonight my cast list goes up and I still have no idea who my two leads will be. I decided that despite the grim situation, I had nothing but face to lose and marched up the stairs to find Rambo after breakfast. My knocking on the door was met with a muffled 'Come'. I entered boldly.

'Spuddy,' Rambo said in a delighted voice from his bed, 'what an unpleasant surprise.'

I congratulated Rambo on his brilliant rugby match yesterday (it's common knowledge in directing circles

151

that actors are susceptible to praise and compliments). He nodded but didn't say anything so I jumped right in and asked him if he would be willing to play the lead role in the house play. I expected him to laugh and order me out of his room but instead he pulled back the duvet and languidly got up from his bed, stark naked.

'Who else is in it?' he asked, searching through his desk drawers.

'I've cast quite a few of the smaller roles,' I said, 'but I need to nail down the two main parts and I was hoping it would be you and Boggo.'

Rambo lit a cigarette and stood by the open window enjoying his smoking in the nude.

'Which is the bigger part, mine or Boggo's?' he asked and exhaled.

'Yours by far,' I replied immediately. 'That's why I wanted you for Flavius.'

Rambo nodded to himself for a while and continued with his smoking.

'I thought you'd quit?' I commented to break the awkward silence.

'Only smoke on Sundays,' he replied and stubbed out his cigarette on the window sill before flicking the stompie out the window and into the gutter below.

'I'll do it if Boggo does it,' he said finally. 'If Boggo's out then I'm out.'

This was a massive and unexpected breakthrough. To have Rambo semi-committed was a major coup for *Toga*. Having the first team rugby captain heading up the cast will mean that people take the play seriously and due respect will be shown. Galloping down the stairs I felt the thrill of the casting process fitting together exactly how I'd imagined it. Now all I needed was to convince Boggo to sign up, which I hoped would be easier now that Rambo was tentatively in.

Boggo was nowhere to be found.

11:50   Discovered Boggo in the bike shed in the nick of time. He was on the verge of setting off for Nottingham Road to buy provisions and supplies. While he worked away at Thinny's bike chain with a hacksaw I filled him in about Rambo coming on board to play Flavius Maximus. Unfortunately, this didn't have the desired effect and Boggo told me to make him an offer before pedalling away in a tiny pair of maroon Polly Shorts that accentuated his long furry white legs.

12:30   I am furious with Boggo. After giving the matter some thought I've come to the realisation that he is in fact holding the entire house to ransom with his ridiculous demands for money. So I have decided to cut Greenstein loose and select Spike or Meg Ryan's Son to play Brutus instead. I marched off to break the news to Rambo.

12:34   Rambo refused to be in the play unless Boggo was Brutus. He said if I really wanted him to star in it then I should pay Boggo and be done with it. I asked Rambo why he insisted on Boggo being cast and he said it was because of their brilliant comic rhythm together on stage. I returned to my room to reconsider the situation.

16:35   A livid Thinny and I were waiting when Boggo returned from Nottingham Road with a rucksack full of supplies. He refused to talk to either of us and locked himself in his room. Thinny and I hurled some choice language at the swine through the door but he didn't respond.

I returned to my room and considered directing a play with Spike and Meg Ryan's Son as the lead actors. It would be dismal. I even considered playing one of the leads myself but that would mean directing and acting which The Guv and Viking both agree is courting disaster.

18:55 I found Boggo reclining on the house bench with a book called *The Semantics of Rugby Union*. Crouched at his feet was Vern, shining Boggo's brown Grasshoppers with a tin of Nugget and a holey shammy cloth.

'I'll give you fifty bucks to be in the house play,' I said.

Boggo glanced up from his book. I felt Vern watching me too, but chose to ignore him in case I became sidetracked with his idiocy. Boggo returned to his book and after some seconds of reading said, 'Two hundred.'

'One hundred. Final offer,' I countered, and waited for his response. A cold, bony hand slid out from behind the book and gripped mine.

'Deal,' declared Boggo.

'I have two conditions,' I said. 'One, you have to be professional, and two, tell nobody I'm paying you.'

'Agreed,' he said. 'I also have two conditions.'

Boggo's first demand was that his character Brutus may carry around a scroll at all times with his lines written on them. I reasoned that he'd managed to get away with this kind of trickery last year in *The Dream* and carrying around scrolls is exactly what they did in ancient Rome anyway. (I tried not to focus on the fact that I was paying my entire budget to an actor who was in essence refusing to learn his lines.)

'The second condition is that I want payment in advance.'

After some hesitation I reached into my back pocket and pulled out the two crisp fifties that Viking had given me. The bony hand shot out from behind the book once again and the money was soon safely stashed away in Boggo's breast pocket.

I knew in my heart that I was wasting money but it wasn't my cash and the deed was done. With long strides and blood pumping in my ears, Schweitzer and I raced off to the computer room to print out my final cast list minutes before the 20:00 cut off.

Rinse the Blood off My Toga
Final Cast List

Flavius Maximus	Rambo
Brutus	Boggo
Mark Antony	Spike
Claudius	Enzo Ferrari
Regulus Bibendus	Thinny
Calpurnia	Garlic
Announcer	Meg Ryan's Son
Drinkers	Sidewinder
	Barryl
	Plump Graham
	Darryl (the last remaining)
	Albert Schweitzer

20:00 There was a near riot in the common room when I pinned up the cast list for *Rinse the Blood off My Toga*. It was an immense relief finally to have done it and I retired to my room where Albert Schweitzer brought me celebratory tea and toast with honey. He seemed overjoyed that he had been cast in the play, although I didn't mention the fact that as a drinker he doesn't have any lines. I breathed out all the stress of the weekend and slipped Nirvana's Smells Like Team Spirit on the Walkman to drown out the endless knockers, questioners and shit-stirrers at the door.

'Here we are now, entertain us!'

Tuesday 11th May

This week is turning into sheer drudgery with three assignments due and a massive history test tomorrow. It made me wish that the year would speed up and that I could be let loose into the real world to find fame and fortune. Yesterday, while slaving away at my desk, I had a tremendous daydream that I was drifting through theatrical schools of Western Europe wearing a beret, visiting famous sights, and sleeping with tall Swedish girls.

Today marks exactly one month until the matric dance and I still have no partner, which is not only embarrassing but highly alarming. With all the excitement around the house play I had postponed worrying about it until today and now I'm so desperate about the matter that I've postponed obsessing about it until at least tomorrow. It's reached the stage where I have even seriously begun to consider Brenda as a possible contender. Perhaps I should write back to Sarah Silver? At least the night would be interesting. Amanda is at UCT, Christine is scary and Mermaid ... I could ask Mermaid to come along as a friend but I can't help feeling that a night of polite conversation with an umpire's girlfriend kind of defeats the purpose of a matric dance which, as far as the Crazy Eight is concerned, is to get drunk or laid and preferably both simultaneously.

Thursday 13th May

17:10 Simon burst into my room and caught me in the middle of my newly instituted late afternoon workout which comprises ten press-ups, ten stomach crunches, and a bout of aggressive shadow boxing in front of the mirror. He laughed at my boxing so I stopped and ordered Albert Schweitzer to throw me my towel and water bottle.

'What's all this shit about Vern slaving for Boggo?' he demanded, like I should know.

'Beats me.'

'It's totally against school tradition,' he barked, appearing livid about the matter. 'A matric should never be seen slaving for another matric, it sends out mixed messages to the slaves.'

'Either Boggo won a bet or he's somehow tricked Vern into it.'

'Vern's a menace,' replied Simon. 'How the school let him in at all is still beyond me.'

'He's only getting worse,' I said.

Simon gazed out of the window towards the crypt. 'Vern won't say anything and neither will Boggo so it's impossible to know.'

He turned away from the window and cast a look around my room.

'I've always thought this room was a complete shithole,' he said, 'but it's actually not all that bad.'

'Thanks,' I said, wondering if this was a compliment or an insult.

Simon's gaze ran briefly along my bookshelf and across the wall to my desk. He sauntered to the door, and, as if speaking to himself, muttered, 'I think I'll hand the matter over to Viking.'

I was about to respond but he was already gone, leaving the door open.

'What was that all about?' demanded Garlic, stepping into my room uninvited.

'None of your business,' I told him. I returned to my shadow boxing.

'If you ask me, Boggo is blackmailing Vern like he did

to me last year,' said Garlic, watching me shadow boxing in the mirror.

I delivered a series of savage jabs that surely would have rattled Mike Tyson.

'Hey, shot a span again for casting me in the play, Spud.'

'No problem,' I replied.

'What kind of character is this Calpurnia anyway?' he asked. 'I was thinking of playing him with a physical defect on his leg.'

Garlic demonstrated a ridiculously over the top walking style that appeared more orang-utan than human.

I brought his lively demonstration to an abrupt halt by stating, 'Calpurnia is a woman, Garlic.'

'A woman!' he blasted, turning pink. 'What do you mean, a woman?'

'She's Julius Caesar's wife.'

'Oh my God!' cried Garlic. 'Who's playing Julius Caesar then? Please don't tell me I have to kiss him.'

'Julius Caesar is dead, you moron, he's not even in the play.' I attempted to figure out how Garlic came to be reclining on my bed and annoying me with his incessant questions and irritating personality.

'Thank God,' he gasped. There was a brief pause before Garlic asked, 'How did he die?'

'Murdered by Brutus,' I groaned and attempted to touch my toes but succeeded only in reaching halfway down my shins.

'Who's playing Brutus?' questioned the Malawian.

'Boggo,' I said.

'So Boggo killed Julius Caesar,' reasoned Garlic.

'Yip.'

'That figures,' he said and shook his head like Boggo is always up to no good.

I hoped that Garlic might run out of questions and press on to irritate somebody else. Instead he flopped back down onto my bed and stared at my ceiling. A brief and pleasant period of silence was shattered when the Malawian, who had been in my room now for quite some time, finally noticed Albert Schweitzer sitting on his small footstool behind the cupboard organising my socks into pairs.

'Albert Schweitzer!' roared Garlic, leaping up from the bed. 'What are you doing in here?'

'He's my slave,' I said in a deliberately calm voice.

'Oh,' he replied and collapsed back onto my bed with some measure of relief. 'It's cool to hang snake in your room, Spud.'

'Cool,' I replied without much enthusiasm.

'I'm not allowed in Rambo's or Simon's room and Fatty's never around any more. Vern's room smells funny and with it having no door people can eavesdrop and stuff. Of course I've been banned from Boggo's room.'

'Why's that?' I asked.

'Last time I got a boner looking at his pictures.'

Thereafter I forced Garlic from my room, citing having to learn for an imaginary geography test. After he had reluctantly moved on, Albert Schweitzer asked me why Garlic was always so pink in the face.

'He's Malawian,' I reasoned and gave up on my fruitless attempts to develop my manly physique.

'Mr Rambo says it's because Mr Garlic is made out of ham.' The way he said it made me think my slave most probably believed this too.

Friday 14th May

I have finally made a call on the matric dance. I can't say that I'm particularly proud of my decision, nor is she the romantic ideal of a matric dance date, but I cannot postpone any longer. I will bite the bullet this evening.

11:00 Vern has been dropped once again, this time from the 5ths to the 6ths. This means I'll be sharing a field with Captain Cretin on Saturday against St David's.

17:30 While I was hanging around the vicinity of the phone room summoning up the courage to make the call, I heard a terrible rumpus from the vicinity of Vern's room. I spied Viking blasting out Rain Man about his unexplained slaving for Boggo.

17:44 I heard ringing at the other end and almost hung up but didn't. Instead I prayed that nobody would answer.

'Hello?' It was a woman's voice.

'Hi,' I said, my voice quivering slightly. 'Please could I speak to Christine?'

'May I ask who's calling?'

'John Milton,' I said with a little less quiver. The woman laughed and I heard her calling for Christine.

'Is that Oliver Twist?' Christine's voice was loud and squawky and by the sounds of things she was eating something.

'Hi, Christine,' I said.

'Hi, baby,' she said and continued with her noisy eating.

'Um, I was wondering ...'

'Ja?'

'If you would like to be my date for the matric dance?'

There was some harsh giggling at the other end.

'That's hysterical!' she hooted and chewed some

160

more. 'You asking me to your matric dance!'

'Will you come?' I repeated.

'I can't,' she said abruptly. 'Too late. I've already been asked and accepted.'

'By whom?' I blurted in an unnecessarily desperate voice.

'Alan,' she replied rather smugly.

'Alan who?' I demanded unaware of anyone in our year called Alan.

'Greenstein,' she replied.

Bloody Boggo!

'I would swap dates because you're much better looking,' she added. 'But he's already sent me love letters and flowers and stuff so I can't.'

Rejection on my first call! I headed to dinner where I was barely able to eat and had to put up with Boggo bragging about how he had hired a suite at the Capitol Towers Hotel for the night of the dance. I gave up on the stringy lamb stew and returned to my room where I stared at the ceiling and felt a little pathetic.

After motivating myself, I rose from my bed, strode into the house and made a beeline for the phone room. I dialled through to the switchboard and waited to be connected.

'Hi, I'm looking for Amanda.'

'Um ... she's in Cape Town,' replied the man's voice in a vague tone.

'When will she be back?' I asked.

'Um ... around the end of June, I think. Hang on, let me get her digs number.' There was some scratching around and the man seemed to be whispering to somebody else in the room.

'Sorry, man,' he said. 'I've lost the number. Call back tomorrow.'

The line went dead. I wonder if that was Amanda's dad? He sounded a little bozed out. I guess it would make sense considering he sketched his own daughter in the nude and artists are notoriously bozed out – they work better that way.

I returned to my room where I decided my luck was out today and gave up on any more attempts to find a date for the big night.

Saturday 15th May

Fatty made an appearance at breakfast and besides appearing terribly gaunt in his ill-fitting clothes, he was overall in exceptional form.

'Penny and I are back together,' he whispered in a gleeful voice.

'Nice one, Fatty.'

'I asked her to the dance and she said yes.' His voice rose in excitement.

'What about Spike?' I asked warily.

Fatty shrugged and reckoned that in his woe he might have become a little overwhelmed with jealousy. 'Same thing happened to Othello,' he noted and waved his hand around like it was commonplace.

I informed Fatty that I was struggling to find a date and would probably come alone to the dance or even not at all.

He said I was being ridiculous. 'Something will happen for you, Spuddy, it always does.'

11:30 The mighty 6ths rugby team warmed up on a small patch of grass behind the weights' room toilet while captain Scum Rogers led some inspirational shouting of, 'Come on, ous! Let's kick some butt!'

Vern didn't seem to know anybody in our team so he stood directly behind me at all times and performed a

number of ridiculous exercises, including removing his rugby boots and socks and stretching each one of his toes. After a brief war cry and more shouting of 'Come on, ous' from Scum Rogers, we followed him out from behind the gym, across the road and onto the field of play where a small but appreciative crowd had gathered.

'Come on, my boy!' echoed a loud shout from a voice that sounded alarmingly like my father's.

'Go, Johnny!' screeched Mom and waved her wine goblet from the touchline.

'Give them hell, boytjie!' boomed Dad, cracking open a Castle.

I noticed Albert Schweitzer gaping at my parents before turning and whispering something to Small & Freckly who nodded.

Mongrel blew the whistle to signal the start of the game. Thirty seconds later we were all standing under our poles after St David's had scored the easiest of tries. 'Come on, ous!' shouted Scum Rogers, glaring at us like we had let him down, this despite it being Scum himself who had missed the crucial tackle.

Four minutes later St David's burst through again and the ball was swung across into the hands of a small but speedy ginger boy who hurtled along the touchline. I sprinted across to cut him off and crashed into him with all my might. The crowd roared as the two of us collided and my momentum forced the flying winger into touch. The skin was gone from my right knee and my elbows were on fire. I staggered to my feet as people slapped me on the back.

'Eat him, my boy!' shouted Dad. 'Don't take any shit from that ginger ninja!'

I looked in the direction of my father's voice and

locked eyes with the Mermaid. She grinned and her mouth silently said 'Hi!' I attempted to grin back but I was gulping for air at the same time with a gum guard in my mouth so I probably looked a little psycho.

For the following 45 minutes I played the game of rugby like I have never played it before. I scored two tries, kicked every ball between the poles and tackled everything within sight. We won 26-18 and Bony Cartwright said I'd played like a superstar. Goes to show just what can be achieved when showing off for a hot blonde. Standing before the Mermaid after the game I felt like I was thirteen again and all the love and mystery was back.

I raced up to the house with Vern following behind me repeatedly shouting 'Mermaid!' I ignored the cretin altogether and showered and changed into my school uniform at double speed despite the grazed knee and elbows.

'Is that your girlfriend?' asked Albert Schweitzer as I combed my hair and studied my face in the mirror.
    'Used to be,' I replied.
    'Wow! She's very hot.'
    'Thanks. I know,' I said and galloped off to find her.

Mermaid and I took a languid walk around the estate and to the dam where nobody was around. There she told me that she had broken up with Gavin the Umpire and left the church. It was such thrilling news and I was so deliriously happy that for a moment I forgot to say 'I'm sorry'. When I did succeed in getting the words out I might as well not have said them because they sounded mightily insincere.

'He was so constricting and everything I did was wrong

or needed to be improved,' she replied after I had delicately probed the matter.

'How do you improve perfection?' I said and locked eyes with her. She kissed me.

'I love you, Johnny,' she whispered. 'Always.' We kissed again and I told her that I loved her too which made her cry and kiss me once more.

'I want us to start again,' she said.

'You mean like in a relationship?' I asked.

She nodded and stared at me like she was looking for an answer.

'Okay,' I said. I got down on one knee, held her hand and gazed into her eyes the colour of the ocean.

'Will you come to my matric dance with me?'

'Yes!' she screamed and leapt into my arms. I looked out over the dam and up towards Hell's View and almost dared myself to wake from the dream because a moment like this shouldn't happen. At least, not to Spud Milton.

The burning of my knee and elbows and the sweet taste of the Mermaid made me realise that I wasn't dreaming after all but experiencing a life defining moment.

The 1sts won 18-12 but in the overall context of the day this mattered surprisingly little.

I am officially in a relationship, and I have a date for the matric dance!

Slamdunk!

Sunday 16th May

I awoke madly in love like never before. I read back over yesterday's diary entry and it still seems unbelievable to me. Forty hours ago I was inviting Christine to the matric dance and a mere seventeen hours later I found myself head over heels in love with the Mermaid and in a committed relationship. How splendid.

By breakfast I was longing for my girlfriend so much that I had an uncontrollable desire to call her. We talked for an hour and she called back and we talked for another hour until Marge angrily forced her off the phone and threatened to ground her. I could have called her right back and talked for another hour.

By 15:00 I was missing Mermaid so desperately that I almost called her once more but feared her mother may take action. Every single second of time that stands between now and Friday seems a torture to be endured.

15:25 I finally pulled myself together by focusing on Mermaid's notorious fickleness and how she has not only cheated on me with a surfer and an umpire, but scarred my teenage years with a double dose of her infamous Valentine's bat. Dredging up all these negative thoughts righted the ship and I was able to cast my mind towards tonight's first official reading of *Rinse the Blood off My Toga*. I read the play twice through in preparation and considered my general approach and what I would say to the actors. To keep my mind off the goddess of lower Durban North I even made notes for each actor about their respective characters. Thereafter I attempted to work on maths theorems but became distracted and, instead, with a ballpoint pen I drew an intricate sketch of Mermaid on an exam pad. Other than her boobs being four times their actual size it was a fairly accurate portrait, I thought, that captured her shapeliness.

19:00 The first read through of the house play was a roaring success and the cop shop was abuzz with laughter and positive energy. The play sounded far better than I thought it would and Rambo and Boggo are already finding some excellent comedy with their unique love/hate combination. The second read through was even funnier than the first and if the early indications are anything to go by, this could be a hit. After the readings I congratulated the actors on their brilliant work and scheduled our first rehearsal for Tuesday evening. It was gratifying to see the likes of Rambo and Boggo going with the flow. Even Garlic demonstrated professionalism and self-control by keeping his incessant questioning down to the bare minimum.

Monday 17th May

I woke in the middle of the night sweating and screaming after enduring a cruel and shocking nightmare. If only it was one of those bad dreams that you can instantly forget I might have been able to drift back to sleep. However, the terrible image was ingrained in my mind and I found myself wide awake and extremely anxious. I glanced at the Remex and it read 1:32.

In my dream I found myself on the verge of losing my virginity with the Mermaid. We were naked and I licked her entire body with a tongue three times its normal size which came in handy considering the giant licking that lay ahead.

'Let's make love,' groaned the Mermaid in a deep voice that made me pause my licking. She turned, revealing herself to be not Mermaid but her mother Marge! To make matters worse, Marge had black teeth and seemed to be well over a hundred years old. I glanced down at the skin that I had just been licking and it was a lifeless dull grey and terribly wrinkled. I leapt back screaming in horror but Marge chased me down the driveway demanding sex in payment for the enormous telephone bill that Mermaid and I had run up. I vaulted the fence, galloped down the street, veered left into Broadway and careened down the hill like my very life depended on it.

14:00   Viking's prefects' meeting was the usual litany of disgust, threats and shouting, most of which was directed against Missing Eggwhite for repeatedly not being around. Since de-prefecting Eggwhite, Viking's rage has only increased in velocity and he seems hell bent on ensuring that he is expelled once and for all.

'As such,' he said, 'I have decided to suspend Eggwhite from school for a period of two weeks.' I had to fight to keep myself from laughing, as did Fatty, who snorted and then recovered quickly with a complaint of a post-nasal drip due to the change in season.

'Sir,' enquired Rambo in a charming voice, 'what exactly is the point in suspending somebody from school if they aren't even here in the first place?'

Viking grew angry. 'Black!' he shouted. 'It's the rules. First suspension, and then expulsion.'

'Obviously the rules didn't apply to myself and Mad Dog in second year,' said Rambo with an eyebrow raised.

Viking hesitated before declaring, 'That Mad Dog was an animal.'

Tuesday 18th May

Toga rehearsal was cancelled at the last minute because Rambo had to attend a meeting with the school rugby committee. I suppose I could have read Rambo's part but without my lead actor present, pressing on seemed pointless. I have postponed the first rehearsal until tomorrow evening.

Tomorrow is Wednesday and that's just two days away from Friday.

Wednesday 19th May

20:00 Rambo said he had to study for tomorrow's maths test and couldn't rehearse tonight either. I hoped to push on with the rehearsal anyway since the rest of the cast were assembled and eager but Vern arrived with the news that Boggo was bedridden with flu. With both leads missing I was forced to cancel the first rehearsal again. I will have to try my luck after the long weekend. With over six weeks until the big night there is still plenty of time in hand and no reason for panic and stress.

20:30 Caught Boggo playing a highly charged game of soccer in the second year dormitory and by the manner in which Greenstein was jumping around and delivering flying headers, I would have to suggest that he wasn't very ill at all.

I lambasted Boggo for being unprofessional and said that seeing as I was paying him a hundred bucks the least he could do is rock up to rehearsals.

'You only paid me twenty,' responded Boggo rather sulkily.

'I gave you a hundred,' I shouted.

Boggo rolled his eyes like I was the slowest human being alive. 'You gave me a hundred, I kept twenty and I gave eighty to Rambo.'

'Why?' I asked.

'Because it was his idea,' he replied and sulkily set off down the stairs to his room.

I should have known Rambo was behind it all. What a sly dodgerian.

Midnight counts as Thursday, and according to my calculations, that's just 1 440 minutes away from Friday.

The maths test was even more diabolical than expected. I dread the results and I genuinely fear mathematics. The only dim light at the end of the tunnel is that everybody thinks they've failed and Garlic definitely has failed after his mind inexplicably went blank for ninety minutes, leaving the Malawian only half an hour to complete the test.

20:00   There were jubilant scenes in the cop shop where the Crazy Eight gathered around a roaring fire to braai marshmallows on wire coat hangers stolen from the Fragile Five. There was much debating going on about the whereabouts of a woman's G spot. Boggo was demonstrating, using an oddly shaped piece of wood, while Rambo chirped that Boggo couldn't hit the G spot with a banjo. Boggo scoffed and suggested that he was such a renowned expert on the matter that the G spot was in fact an abbreviation for the Greenstein spot. Garlic piped up and admitted that he always thought that the G spot was at the back of a woman's head. This sent Rambo into hysterics and he ended up holding his stomach as if he had been stabbed.

Plaque knocked and entered. Under his arm he carried a scale which he handed over to Rambo.

'Call in Plump Graham,' ordered Rambo. 'Oh, and tell the duty slaves to take more orders.' Plaque exited as Enzo Ferrari and Near Death entered.

'Another round of tea,' called Simon above the hubbub. 'And keep the toast rolling, hey.' The boys nodded and left hurriedly.

Rambo raised his hand and waited for silence. 'There has been much debate over who holds the mantle of the fattest boy in the house,' he announced. Fatty chortled and shook his head like he thought Rambo was joking.

'Plump Graham!' called Rambo. The door opened and Plump Graham entered.

'Gentlemen – meet the challenger.' Rambo pointed to Plump Graham who blushed and grinned.

'And now the reigning champion himself – FATTY!' Despite the hearty cheer, Fatty refused to leave his seat or be weighed.

'What's the point?' he argued.

'There can only be one true Fatty,' reasoned Rambo, holding up the scale, 'and the Scales of Injustice will be the decider.'

He carefully placed the scale in the small clearing beside the door and demanded Fatty stand up and be weighed.

'To hell with you bastards,' grumbled Fatty, lurching to his feet and making his way over to the Scales of Injustice. 'Name like that, it's probably rigged,' he muttered and stepped up.

The needle came to rest at 99kgs. Fatty seemed satisfied that although a drastic drop off on former glories, this was still heavy enough to rebuff the challenger and he returned to his armchair in a confident mood.

'Plump Graham, step forward,' ordered Rambo in a stern voice.

Plump Graham stepped onto the Scales of Injustice and the dial came to rest on 102kgs. The cop shop erupted.

Rambo silenced the roaring and laughter and declared that a re-christening had to be done immediately. Plump Graham was immediately promoted to Fat Graham, leaving poor Fatty looking humiliated after being rebranded Plump Sidney.

'You can thank your anorexia-paedophilia for that,' ventured Boggo, finishing off a slice of toast and greatly enjoying himself. In desperation, Plump Sidney attempted to eat his way out of trouble. He ordered the duty slaves to create a conveyer belt of cheese and bully beef sandwiches. Fat Graham, who seemed thrilled at how everything had turned out, was ordered to sit on the floor by the door and wait for Plump Sidney to finish his panic eating before the rematch commenced.

In the end Plump Sidney polished off six beef and cheese sarmies before provisions ran dry. Bizarrely, his second visit to the Scales of Injustice saw his weight remain at 99kgs while Fat Graham, who hadn't eaten a thing in half an hour, went up a kilogram to weigh 103kgs. Plump Sidney had a complete sense of humour failure and went to bed citing a stomach ache. The newly crowned Fat Graham was rewarded with tea and toast, although the toast was deferred because Fatty had cleaned us out of all foodstuffs.

Tomorrow is Friday! A Mermaid awaits ...

Friday 21st May

Long weekend begins.

I was drunk with excitement knowing that Mermaid would be waiting at the bus stop. I saw her long before the bus ground to a halt. She was leaning against Marge's car in her short denim skirt and her left hand was playing absent-mindedly with her hair.

'Hey, ous, check out that hottie!' cried a boy from somewhere near the front of the bus. A number of boys leapt up to study the Mermaid.

'Too bad, donks, she's already taken,' said Plump Sidney, pushing through to the front with his suitcase held aloft. Mermaid created quite a spectacle when she

charged up to the bus and leapt into my arms. Besides staggering a few feet backwards I thought I kept up my side fairly well and responded by kissing her on the lips to a healthy roar of approval and sporadic applause from the disembarking boys.

I greeted Marge and tried not to think of the vile skin licking dream. Thankfully, her skin was normal and not at all grey and wrinkly, so I was able to return my attention to her daughter. Mermaid jumped into the back seat with me leaving Marge alone up front like a chauffeur. We were all laughing hard at something, although I cannot remember what initially set it off. For the rest of the journey my eyes never left the Mermaid's face (apart from when we went over the grid in the road and her boobs bounced up and down). We drove to Verulam where we booked our learner driver's test for the July holidays. It was strange to be in an Indian area and not to see other white people around. From what I briefly noticed there didn't seem too much difference between here and where we live. Except we have nicer gardens and we can see the sea.

Back at Mermaid's house we had a bout of kissing on Mermaid's bed which I found highly stimulating. Although tempted, I didn't try anything else because the door was ajar and I could hear Marge walking up and down the passage at regular intervals. After the kissing session, Mermaid made me lie on her bed while she disappeared into the bathroom to try on outfits for the matric dance. She kept reappearing wearing one possibility after another. After calling the first five options 'beautiful', Mermaid said I was a typical male, slammed the door and disappeared. She returned minutes later wearing an extremely sexy and revealing dress that barely covered her thighs. 'That's definitely the one!' I declared. She rolled her eyes and vanished once more. After two more demonstrations Mermaid lost patience with her wardrobe, marched out into the garden and informed her mother that she needed a new dress for the dance. Marge refused, citing money being tight and Mermaid having a full cupboard of dresses that she buys and never wears. Mermaid flew into a rage, accused her mother of ruining her life and stormed back inside.

I followed my girlfriend back to her room at a polite distance. After agreeing that her mother was completely unreasonable, more splendid kissing and rolling around on the bed followed.

Saturday 22nd May

Dad insisted on escorting me into town so that I could try on my rented tuxedo from Lord Louis Suits in the centre of the city. The drive into and through the city was taken up with us reliving my best cricket performances of the season, and my father berating the African sprawl taking place in the city centre.

'Frank got mugged in broad daylight last weekend,' he said and shook his head in disgust.

'You mark my words,' he said, 'come the year 2000 there won't be a single whitey left in the place.'

On this promising note we entered Lord Louis.

'Debbie's going to be looking blitz hot,' he said, 'so you're going to have to up your game, my boy.'

Dad's advice and generally loud demeanour made me nervous.

'I'm looking for a top quality suit for my boy's matric dance,' announced my father at the top of his voice. 'And don't think you can just give us any old combo, I know you buggers.' The Indian manager responded by studying me closely before pulling out his tape measure and firing off a number of measurements. He strode off and returned almost immediately with a suit on a hanger.

The man pressed the suit against my body and said, 'I'll give you the entire combination plus bow tie and cummerbund for 135.'

'What you been smoking?' countered my father. 'I won't pay a cent over 70 bucks.'

The manager laughed at Dad's counter offer and said that the price was set at 135. Dad continued with his haggling and threats to leave until he eventually scored a 14% discount.

'Deal,' replied my father immediately. 'You accept Visa?'

I asked Dad if I shouldn't at least try it on first and he reluctantly agreed. Thankfully, it fitted perfectly and I have to admit that I didn't look far off handsome in my regalia – just goes to show what a tux can do.

In the end the manager had the last laugh when, after taking off my father's 14% discount, he added 14% for VAT returning the total to R135. Dad still maintained that he had scored.

The drive home became a bit of a trial.

Dad's Matric Dance Advice:

- Remember to brush your teeth on the day of the matric dance.
- Don't mess on your shirt over dinner. Rather use a serviette or even the table cloth for protection.
- Don't look at anyone else's dates during the dance. This will make your date jealous and remind you of what you could have had but didn't quite get.
- If you get involved in a punch-up, make sure you win it even if it means using underhand tactics.

- Don't get her pregnant, and if you do, deny that you're the father.

'Hot, hey?' said my father after a long silence had descended on the car.

'Quite hot,' I replied, realising that I was still wearing a jersey. Dad looked up at the sky with a grim expression and said, 'Unusually warm for May.'

I nodded.

'Means we're in for a cold winter,' he ventured.

'Why's that?' I asked, thinking that my father might have some interesting climatological explanation for this.

'Just goes like that,' replied Dad and nodded knowingly at the sky.

19:00 My date with Mermaid at RJ's Steakhouse, Beachfront

Highlights

- She moaned pleasurably when I felt her up when we were kissing in the moonlight on the pier
- We kissed an uncountable number of times over the course of the evening
- Sharing alcoholic drinks and a meal together like proper people in a relationship
- Mermaid getting drunk and giggly
- Walking barefoot on the sand together

Lowlights

- The waiter refusing to serve me alcohol
- The waiter serving Mermaid alcohol and not me
- Having to be fed sneaky drinks by my girlfriend (I ordered Sprite and she ordered vodka)
- My girlfriend having to flirt with the waiter for a second round

- Mermaid's revelation over dinner that she's still a fervent believer in no sex before marriage

Sunday 23rd May

Mermaid wasn't allowed to attend the Milton braai with Wombat because she has two tests this week and Marge refused to let her out of the house. She reckons Mermaid and I have spent sufficient time together this weekend. How can the words 'love' and 'sufficient' ever be used in the same sentence? We exploited the one gaping hole in Marge's defence, allowing her daughter out for a late afternoon jog. I cycled to the park near Mermaid's house and found her sitting on the swings waiting for me. It was an incredibly romantic farewell that ended with a lingering kiss. I picked up my bike and cycled away desperately trying to resist the urge to pop a wheelie.

Monday 24th May

16:20 Dad insisted that he was happy to drive me back to school despite my offer to take the bus. The answer to why somebody would unnecessarily choose to undertake a round trip of 300km came when he made me beep the stopwatch at the gate and raced off so fast that my head flew into the windscreen. The entire journey back to school was a commentary on all the dodgy drivers that forced Dad to take numerous illegal measures, like overtaking in the emergency lane and swerving through traffic at 160kph. Dad broke his up-run record by two minutes and twelve seconds and the manner in which he hurtled back down Pilgrims' Walk led me to believe that, barring a fatal crash, he was certain to break the down-run record too.

WEEKEND SCORECARD

RAMBO	House sat his dad's new penthouse in Camps Bay. Must have been a tough weekend ...
PLUMP SIDNEY	A very long weekend of working through numerous relationship problems with Penny.
BOGGO	Passed his learner's licence test and reckons he can drive perfectly already. 'It just comes naturally to me,' he said, 'like sex.'
SIMON	Went gambling at an illegal casino with his cousins. He didn't say exactly how much money he made but he said it was 'a fair whack'.
VERN	Unknown. Spent most of the evening watching me with his left eye, while covering his right with a red coffee mug.
SPUD	Legendary three days with his beautiful girlfriend.
GARLIC	Weekend with his folks at Lake St Lucia. He called the place a complete embarrassment compared to Lake Malawi.

Tuesday 25th May

06:10 I struggled to leave my bed this morning. Outside my door lay the chaos of the second half of the second term. Duties, tests, teachers, Viking, matric dances, nutcases, rugby matches, a house play waiting to be directed, and more of the bizarre and the ridiculous. Like a man staggering towards the guillotine, I snatched up my towel and stumbled to the door before throwing it open as if daring the world to take me on. A blast

178

of Antarctic air punched me in the face. I slammed the door shut behind me and ran towards the house entrance where a crowd of boys were trying to flick a distressed Small & Freckly in the groin with the tips of their towels.

'Hey, cool it!' I shouted, scattering the crowd. After a shower I headed back to my room where a hyped up Albert Schweitzer was waiting with an enormous list of impending things. Maths was first up. I sent my slave off to make me a strong cup of coffee while I readied myself for the results of last week's test.

07:15 36% was all that I could manage for the maths test. If that was my score in the final exams I would not only bomb out in maths but fail matric too.

17:00 Further bad news – if this afternoon's practice is anything to go by, I have been promoted to the 5ths rugby team. Obviously, my showing off for Mermaid at the last match has come back to haunt me as I am now being coached by the unlikeable Sparerib. Bony Cartwright released my former 6th team comrades from practice at 15:45 while Mr Personality kept the 5ths on for a further 45 minutes of gruelling fitness drills.

Wednesday 26th May

Feeling slightly better after discovering half the class failed the maths test too. Garlic scored 17% and Dog Johnson only mustered up 8%. Mrs Bishop berated the entire class for our poor efforts and said she would be setting another test soon which would allow us an opportunity to redeem ourselves. Despite finding maths incredibly boring and nonsensical, I have resolved to spend more time working on it so as to avoid being the first scholarship winner in the history of the school to fail matric.

20:00   It was a massive relief to find Boggo and Rambo among those gathered in the cop shop for the first proper rehearsal. After Schweitzer and Plaque had moved the chairs aside we began marking out (blocking) the play on the floor.

20:20   A nervous Near Death knocked repeatedly at the door while Boggo was trying to work out where Brutus would stand when discussing Caesar's death with Flavius. I hoped the knocking would cease but it continued with regular monotony and at the same volume. Eventually I lost my patience, flung open the door, and swore viciously at the boy.

'What do you want, Near Death?' I demanded, advancing on the terrified youngster.

'Um, sorry, Mr Milton,' he gabbled in a high pitched voice, 'but there's an urgent telephone call for Mr Rambo.'

Rambo looked slightly concerned and left immediately. Thinking he would be only a few minutes I stepped into the character of Flavius and we continued blocking the play. Rambo never returned.

Thursday 27th May

Sparerib had us running our guts out at rugby practice once again. He seems to agree with Mongrel that boys produce better rugby after being tortured instead of coached on Tuesdays and Thursdays.

17:10   Called Mermaid because I needed cheering up after my afternoon spent under the sadistic control of goblin man. We talked for so long that I missed dinner and Albert Schweitzer made me toast soldiers and instant noodles instead.

20:00   Rambo was back for tonight's rehearsal but

wasn't very focused about his acting. To make matters worse Spike (Mark Antony) farted, adding to the numerous stoppages during which Boggo repeatedly mocked and ridiculed any actor smaller than himself. Garlic's incessant questions are also becoming a problem and he still hasn't dealt with the fact that he's playing a woman and can't use his ridiculous disability walk for the character. The Malawian followed me back to my room limping away in his exaggerated fashion while everywhere people were pointing and laughing at him. 'You see how funny it is, Spud!' he declared. 'Please let me use it for Calpurnia?'

I promised Garlic that I would think about it and locked myself in my room. I had barely dropped my script notes on the desk when there was a loud knocking on the door.

'Go away!' I shouted, collapsing onto my bed in exhaustion.

Further knocking.

'Who is it?' I demanded.

'It's me again,' replied Garlic.

'I'm busy.'

'No you're not, Spud,' he cried, 'I can see you lying on your bed through the keyhole.'

'I'm memorising stuff,' I replied. For a moment there was silence and I fervently hoped that he had moved off, but there was a loud knocking on the window. With gritted teeth I flung it open, hoping it would crunch a large hole in Garlic's head and knock him out. Unfortunately, it narrowly missed.

'Hey, I forgot to ask,' Garlic said. 'Why not come to Lake Malawi in the holidays?'

I slammed the window shut and listened to my Walkman so that I didn't have to be driven mad by the knocking and shouting about Lake Malawi that went on for at least another twenty minutes.

Friday 28th May

As expected, I have been officially promoted to the 5ths rugby team to play against Arlington tomorrow. Poor Vern suffered another calamity when he was dropped yet again, this time from the 6ths to the 7ths. Considering Rain Man began the season in the 4ths, it's a pretty poor show even by cretin standards. Boggo goaded him at lunch for a reaction, but Vern showed no embarrassment whatsoever, responding to the taunts by shoving an entire roll in his mouth and sniggering through his nose.

Saturday 29th May

My new rugby team (the fighting 5ths) easily beat Arlington (53-0). I was largely anonymous in general play. In fact, I think our team would have easily won without me even on the field.

Mermaid called in the early evening and reminded me that it was only two weeks until the big night.

'By the way, where are we staying after the dance?' she asked. I deftly changed the subject so that she didn't think I was devoid of a plan and commenced racing through the possibilities. I can't afford a room in the hotel and, unlike some of the other boys' parents, Mom and Dad would never cough up for such a luxury. Boggo has booked a suite with an extra room so while I was in the neighbourhood I paid him a friendly visit. Loud techno music was playing on his ghetto blaster and his room smelled strongly of deodorant. Boggo was involved in a game of Patience on his bed while Vern folded a pile of Boggo's laundry on the floor.

'Spud the crud!' announced Boggo upon my entry. 'What brings you to the bowels of the house?' Vern ceased folding and stared at me with his mouth agape.

'Howzit, Boggo,' I said. 'I was just wondering if you have anybody staying in your spare room after the matric dance?'

An ominous tube of light appeared in Boggo's eyes. 'Leaving accommodation a little late, aren't we, Milton?' he commented gathering up the cards and shuffling them very quickly.

'I was thinking of partying all night,' I said boldly, 'but in case my chick gets tired I thought I should have a back-up plan.'

Boggo sniggered heartily and replied, 'Funny your chick didn't get tired when she jackhammered me the whole of last night.'

'Hilarious,' I responded in a deadpan fashion, ignoring Vern's loud announcement of 'Mermaid!' and the lame sniggering that followed.

'You're welcome to use the spare room,' said Boggo suddenly, 'although it will mean that Mermaid obviously falls under my jurisdiction.'

When I asked Boggo what he meant by jurisdiction, he said he would be compelled to bone, grope, kiss or fondle my girlfriend while she was staying in his suite.

'There's no way in hell she'll allow that,' I replied.

He shrugged nonchalantly. 'Then I'm going to have to resort to sniffing her undies when she's sleeping.'

I ignored the mocking laughter and returned to my room where I obsessively considered the matter until well after 11pm.

Sunday 30th May

There seems to have been some sort of a breakthrough with regards to the matric dance sleepover problem. Plump Sidney reckons he's crashing at Penny's house and that Penny's mom is picking them up after the dance. He assured me that it wouldn't be a problem if we stayed over too, but promised to check with Penny. At least this would guarantee that my date won't have to sleep on a park bench or have her underwear sniffed by Boggo in the middle of the night. There are, however, two major drawbacks:

1. Penny's parents' house doesn't strike one as the place to cavort with your date after the dance.
2. Penny isn't even allowed to attend the after-party at Take 5 because her mom says she's too young to go to nightclubs. That would mean we would miss it too, which is a bit of a bummer. At least it's a reserve measure should all other streams of possibility run dry.

Plump Sidney is still furious about having his name changed and says he spent the long weekend (when not with Penny) planning his strategy to regain his rightful name and knock Fat Graham down a peg or two. When I asked him what his approach would be, his response was, 'My oath, Spuddy, the day after the matric dance, I'm going on a crash binge.' He glanced down at his thin frame with disgust and rumbled off to look for Sidewinder.

Monday 31st May

It would seem that our housemaster has finally succeeded in checkmating Eggwhite whose two week suspension for being missing is now officially over. Since Eggwhite hasn't reported in after his suspension, Viking has now pinged him for bunking out and gross avoidance.

'This so-called Eggwhite is a stain on the house!' roared Viking as he tore viciously and unsuccessfully at a small packet of peanuts and raisins. He went on to say that Eggwhite had seven days in which to return to school and explain his continual absence. Failure to achieve this would see him expelled. 'Then at last this farce will be a thing of the past,' boomed Viking, unaware that he had used three rhyming words in the same sentence.

I didn't feel like working on maths all afternoon so I called Mermaid instead and we talked for nearly two hours. Marge was out shopping so, aside from Runt having a forty-five minute lurk at the urinal, we were able to have some measure of privacy for a change. When Mermaid brought up the accommodation question, I lied and told her that it was all sorted out. 'My mom's freaking out about it,' she said in a concerned voice.

'Don't worry, I've got it covered,' I assured her.

Wednesday 2nd June

A dim-witted rock pigeon flew into The Guv's English classroom as he was about to announce the debating topics and match-ups. The poor creature flew about crashing into the walls and ceiling while we all tried to guide it towards the doors and windows. The Guv was horrified by the flapping bird and seemed intent on beating it to death with Roget's Thesaurus.

'Hitchcock wouldn't have stood for this nonsense!' he declared, advancing on the flapping pigeon as if it might attack him. In the end Turk Andrews pounced on it with his jersey and released it in the quad.

'Now, plebeians,' The Guv began, rocking vigorously on the balls of his feet, 'a debate isn't a competition, it's a civil war.' We laughed but he held up his walking stick for silence. Then, with a sternly raised eyebrow, he said, 'Done badly, a debate can shred one's nerves and grate one's foreskin.' The Guv paused as if a momentous thought had possessed him. 'But, done properly, a fine debate is the very entertainment of the gods, every bit as satisfying as a night of rumpy pumpy with a woman of sparse morals.'

I drew Simon in the debate and our topic is:

School traditions are outmoded and puritanical

Simon elected to argue against the motion which means I will be arguing for it come the big showdown at the beginning of next term.

16:45 Received an irate call from Dad who had just opened last month's telephone bill from the school. He accused me of driving the family to bankruptcy with my marathon calls to the Mermaid and threatened to thrash me within an inch of my life. I informed my father that I couldn't be blamed because I was madly in love and had lost complete control of my senses. Dad must have thought that I was joking because he snorted with laughter and called me a cheeky little shit.

'Hey, guess what?' he announced suddenly sounding like he didn't care about the telephone bill at all. 'I'm buying a Venter trailer this afternoon.'
    I asked Dad if this meant that we weren't on the verge of bankruptcy after all, and he laughed again and said, 'Don't be silly, my boy, I put it all on the credit card.' Thanks to my father's spendthrift ways and my Mermaid telephone addiction, the Miltons are sinking beneath the breadline.

20:00 Feeling better about *Toga* although nobody has bothered to learn their lines yet. I have given them all until Sunday and then no scripts will be allowed on stage, apart from Boggo's scroll, of course.

Thursday 3rd June

The school is kicking into overdrive for the big match against King's College on Saturday. The morning newspaper said King's will be too strong for us and that we had little chance of success despite being unbeaten thus far.

Mermaid called for a quick chat. She's also in trouble for a nasty phone bill on her side so we agreed to a strict limit of ten minutes from now on. Unfortunately, while discussing the new time limits we ended up talking for over half an hour. Mermaid asked about the accommodation again and said that Marge was harassing her for more details. I pretended that I couldn't remember where we would be staying and promised to let her know soon. More pressure – that's exactly what I need right now.

Boggo had obviously been eavesdropping on my call because he reiterated his offer for a room in his suite in return for Mermaid jurisdiction. When I told him to get lost he said my big problem with girls was 'too much phoning and not enough boning'.

21:00   Just completed a disastrous rehearsal of *Toga*. Rambo didn't rock up because he said he was mentally preparing for the big game on Saturday, so not for the first time I stepped into the shoes of Flavius Maximus. Unfortunately, this meant that I was busy playing the role and not keeping the rest of the cast in check. Thinny and Spike became bored standing in the background and discovered new and inventive ways of being irritating. I kept stopping and ordering them to be quiet but within a few minutes another scuffle would inevitably break out. Boggo tried to help restore order by hoofing Thinny in the shins and smashing Spike in the face with his scroll. He may have overdone things slightly as Thinny was doubled over in agony for the rest of the rehearsal and Spike had to lie on his back because of a nosebleed. To make matters worse, Garlic followed me back to my room after the rehearsal doing his stupid walk again and invited me to Malawi in the September holidays. He reckons that Vern is keen and Fatty has agreed to go if I go. I told Garlic that I would think about the matter and forced him out of the door.

I am ravaged with fear and doubt. I thought life was meant to become easier as you grew older, but it appears that it only becomes more stressful. Back in my junior years the sum total of my worries extended to avoiding Pike and Devries and hoping my parents wouldn't be too embarrassing at cricket matches. Now I'm beset with obligations and realise that this so-called freedom is just a myth as my worries hang around my neck like a school tie made out of lead.

Despite his suspicious personality and disturbing tests on Vern and other animals, the old school counsellor Dr Zoodenberg once said something that I have never forgotten. He maintained that if you wrote down all your fears and worries you would realise that there were actually far fewer genuine problems than you first expected.

SPUD MILTON'S GENUINE FEARS AND WORRIES

- I fear the house play will be a disaster
- I fear this will ruin my dream of becoming a great actor/director
- I fear that I won't find accommodation for the matric dance
- I fear we will have to stay at Penny's
- I fear that the most important night of my youth

will be a terrible let-down
- I fear that Mermaid will soon grow tired of me and leave me for someone else
- I fear leaving school a virgin
- I fear being a virgin at 30 because of Mermaid's warped beliefs about sex and marriage
- I fear mathematics
- I fear failing mathematics
- I fear failing
- I fear my father's bankruptcy
- I fear the end of the year
- I fear my world changing and nothing staying the same
- I fear not having the courage to wander the Earth

This list has made me realise two things:

- I'm a neurotic nutcase like Woody Allen
- Dr Zoodenberg was insane

Friday 4th June

11:00   Mass hilarity erupted in the quad when Boggo announced that Vern had been dropped from the 7ths to the 8ths. Surely this must be some sort of school record? A mere month ago he was in the 4ths. I suppose the one positive for Vern is that he cannot plummet any further as there are only eight rugby teams. Obviously his new coach (Mr Lilly) felt sorry for the cretin after his numerous droppings because he has made Vern his vice captain.

I'm still in the 5ths. Our coach Sparerib said at yesterday's practice that we should bear in mind that a narrow loss to King's College would be as good as a moral victory. He really is quite inspirational at times.

18:30 'They say we aren't good enough,' shouted Rambo, his voice growing hoarse with rage. 'They say we won't have the power or strength or will or desire,' he continued, as the school stood in rapt silence interlocking arms over shoulders. The first rugby team stood on the wall of the fountain and the rest of us crowded into the quad looked up at them, awaiting the command to chant. 'Let's kill them!' screamed Rambo and the entire school went bananas. A chorus of 'EAT EAT EAT!' echoed through the quad and I found myself stomping the ground like a maniac. After numerous renditions of the war cry the school was dismissed and the entire house charged into the common room to watch 100 Greatest Tries. I planned to watch, too, but Mermaid phoned and we chatted for half an hour before one of us even looked at our watches. After the call I returned to the cop shop where a fire was blazing. Plump Sidney was seated beside it in an armchair reading a book on crop circles in the United States.

'Oh, Spuddy,' he said, 'I'm glad I caught you. I'm afraid Penny's mom says you and Mermaid can't sleep over.'

'Oh great,' I replied unable to hide the sarcasm in my voice.

'Sorry, bud. But I hear Geoff Lawson has booked out a double room and may have space,' he said and shrugged like it was well worth an enquiry.

'Thanks for trying,' I replied and decided to drink my tea in my room instead because my mind was racing about the accommodation crisis.

'Hey, Spud!' shouted a pink face outside the cop shop.

'Not now, Garlic,' I said and pushed past the Malawian.

'Have you thought any more about coming to Malawi in September?'

I decided to end the Malawi thing once and for all and informed him that with my maths on the very edge

of failure I couldn't afford the time away from studying. Garlic argued that the final exams were six weeks later and that I would need a relaxing break after the trials exams in August.

'Please come, Spud,' he begged. 'It will be totally radical!'

I told him that I would think about it again and drove him out of my room.

Saturday 5th June

King's College Report Back

I'm lying on my bed writing this while Albert Schweitzer applies mercurochrome to my knees. King's College fielded a massive pack of forwards against our poor 5ths team. The King's lock was a Greek giant who went by the name of Ari Pelagos and I'm flummoxed as to why he wasn't playing for a higher side. He scored four tries and was responsible for removing all of the skin and scabs growing on my already wounded knees. I did my best to tackle the giant but on the one occasion that I did manage to hold on to him, the monster dragged me down the length of the dormant cricket pitch which lay slap bang in the middle of the field. It may have been a comical sight for the spectators to see me dragged a fair distance along the ground, but it felt like I had been dropped knees first into an active volcano. The final score was 36-3 to King's which coach Sparerib smugly admitted was exactly the score he had been expecting.

In a bizarre and unexpected turn of events Plump Sidney recognised Missing Eggwhite in the crowd at the King's old boys club bar where he seemed to be in high spirits with a group of friends. He didn't remember us very well but mentioned that his nickname at varsity has changed from Eggwhite to Groggo. When Plump Sidney asked him what he was studying, he replied 'Fine arts'. I told him about Viking still thinking he was attending school, and he mumbled something about his father and a tax certificate. The rest of his explanation was drowned out by war cries indicating the main match was about to start. As we hurried off to the stands at the far side of the field we tried to make sense of how Eggwhite was studying at university and simultaneously facing expulsion from school?

'Something shifty is going on,' remarked Plump Sidney as we pushed our way through the crowds.

The first team, despite Rambo's speech, lost 24-16 which sounds quite close but wasn't really because two further King's tries were disallowed thanks to linesman Boggo who was probably our best defender of the goal line on the day.

The school is unusually silent. Even the cloisters smell of defeat.

Sunday 6th June

After chapel I trekked across the school in search of Geoff Lawson. I found him playing video games in the Larson common room. I asked him if he had a spare room or even a couch for the Mermaid and me. He said all the space had been taken up already and advised me to try Stinky whose family owns a flat across the road from the Capitol Towers Hotel. I couldn't find the Stinkmeister anywhere but the prefects in the Barnes cop shop reckoned that he had been overwhelmed with people asking him for sleeping space. I returned to my room in a grim mood. It now looks highly unlikely that I will find a place for us to sleep which means her dad will be picking her up after the dance at 11pm. That means I either leave with the school bus at 11:30pm or attend the after-party at Take 5 with no partner and sleep in a gutter. Worse is that I have kind of led Mermaid to believe that I'd already sorted a plan. So now I either have to risk Boggo behaving perversely with my date's underwear or break the news to Mermaid that I have been lying about the sleeping arrangements all along.

Plump Sidney has been conducting further investigations into the Eggwhite mystery. He reckons he's found/stolen proof that Eggwhite's father still makes a healthy annual donation to the school. Perhaps that's why his son remains registered as a schoolboy when he's halfway through a degree in fine arts at the University of Natal. Boggo reckons he can smell tax fraud from a mile off and declared that the Eggwhite saga reeked like the bogs after breakfast.

Garlic burst into my room without knocking and demanded to know if I had thought any further about going to Malawi. I stopped him in his tracks with a tongue lashing that would have made Viking proud. In fact I shat on Garlic from such a dizzy height that his eyes grew wide and his face went bright pink. After I had completed my unexpected rant, Garlic studied me with a quizzical expression and said, 'Gee, Spud, I've never seen you get properly pissed off before.'

'Neither have I,' I replied feeling rather elated.

'Your face went all crazy,' he said and pointed at my forehead.

I told Garlic that it wasn't personal and he had just caught me at a bad moment. There followed an extremely frustrating five minutes of me refusing to tell Garlic what was bugging me and him pleading and begging for me to spill the beans.

'It's the matric dance, it's driving me crazy,' I said after eventually giving in.

'You haven't got a date yet?' he cried in amazement.

'I've got a date,' I replied. 'I'm going with the Mermaid.'

'What mermaid?' he demanded, wrinkles creasing his forehead.

'Her name is Debbie but I call her Mermaid,' I said.

'Why?' he asked.

I explained to Garlic that the first day I met her way back in February 1990 I was with her in the pool.

'Did you bone her?' he asked suddenly.

'I was in first year, you wop!' I said and felt close to another rant.

'Oh, right,' he said and motioned for me to carry on.

I told him that I had experienced this fantasy about her having a tail and being this mysterious water creature that I had instantly fallen in love with. Garlic didn't seem all that impressed with my story and added that he hadn't come across a single mermaid in Lake Malawi.

'So what's the problem with the matric dance?' demanded Garlic.

I almost drove him out for sheer irritation but ended up explaining my problem with the accommodation.

'Why not stay with me then?' he cried, his face turning immensely pink once more.

'Where are you staying?' I cried back in confusion.

'At the Capitol Towers Hotel. Mum booked me a room,' he said. 'I would have offered but I thought you were staying with Fatty, I mean Plump Sidney.'

'You have space?' I asked.

The Malawian looked deeply concerned and said, 'It's a tiny spare room and only a pull-out couch.

'Anywhere, I'm happy,' I said.

He grinned and held out his hand. I shook it and grinned back, my heart pounding with relief and excitement.

'Please come to Malawi, Spud.' Garlic was still holding my right hand and his eyes were locked onto mine. 'Please, Spud.'

'Okay, I'll come,' I said.

Monday 7th June

Mermaid mentioned the word 'orgy' during my call to her this afternoon. Unfortunately, it was with reference to one of her mother's greatest fears rather than a saucy plan for Saturday night. Still, it was thrilling.

I called Dad immediately afterwards to wish him happy birthday. Surprisingly, my father wasn't very responsive to my hearty best wishes and offered me mumbled thanks for my present (a book on marlin fishing). He soon passed the phone to Mom who reckoned that my father had his lip on the ground because this is his last year of his forties. 'He's practically a senior citizen!' shrieked Mom and erupted into loud hacking laughter.

17:30 Viking called the house in for an emergency meeting in the common room shortly before dinner. With unrestrained glee he triumphantly declared that he was meeting the headmaster tomorrow to finalise the expulsion of Missing Eggwhite.

'This boy has pushed me too far,' he ranted. 'His dereliction of duty in this house has been nothing short of appalling.'

There were some stifled sniggers from the seniors when he said Missing Eggwhite would be ordered to leave the school grounds by the end of the week. Viking began a strong applause that resounded around the common room.

Rambo still doesn't know his lines for *Toga* and has asked to carry around a scroll with crib lines like Boggo. As the director, I felt compelled to put my foot down and said it would look ridiculous to have both leading actors continually opening and closing their scrolls in the middle of general conversation. Most of the smaller role actors have their scripts down apart from Spike, whom I now regret casting as Mark Antony due to his poor concentration and continual horsing about in the wings with Thinny. Garlic, playing Julius Caesar's grieving widow, has thankfully memorised his only line: 'I told him, Julie, don't go! Don't go, Julie!' Unfortunately, the Malawian has to repeat his line at regular intervals throughout the play and hasn't the faintest idea when those regular intervals should be. I have allowed him to keep his ridiculous walk for Calpurnia only because he refuses to take no for an answer. I fear *Toga* may well be funny for all the wrong reasons.

Tuesday 8th June

18:30 Boggo overheard Viking receiving a tongue lashing from The Glock in the headmaster's office. Our housemaster was gesticulating wildly and feverishly arguing his case but The Glock apparently gave him short shrift and sent him packing. Plump Sidney is convinced that it must have been about the Eggwhite saga, furthering rumours about his father's secret donations.

19:45 Albert Schweitzer burst into my room in the middle of prep to say that I had an urgent phone call and a woman was wailing hysterically at the other end of the line. I immediately came up with two possible horrors:

1. Somebody has snuffed it
2. Mermaid has been grounded and can't come to the dance

I sprinted into the house full of dread and certain that my life was just seconds away from imploding.

'Hello?' I said, my voice trembling and strangulated.

'David!' screeched Wombat. 'It's your grandmother.'

'Hi Gran,' I replied.

'David, I'm phoning from the cloakroom. I need you to corroborate the spelling of vermouth.' My grandmother was whispering desperately like somebody phoning the police while there's a burglar in their house. After providing the spelling Wombat didn't even bother to thank me and hung up. Albert Schweitzer's worried face loomed into the phone room. 'Everything okay?' he asked, looking rather shaken by the entire experience. I told him everything was hunky dory but called home just to be sure. Mom said everyone was well apart from Blacky who has worms again and has been dragging his bum slowly across the grass with a disturbing expression on his face. Turns out Wombat is attending Scrabble night at the yacht club. I asked Mom if phoning family members from the cloakroom constituted cheating, but Mom said that all the old ducks cheated and Scrabble night was just an excuse to get drunk and have a raging argument. I left the phone room, passed Runt pretending to use the urinal, and returned to my room where Albert Schweitzer had left a cup of hot Milo beside my bed. I'm not sure I could survive in this place without a slave.

I couldn't sleep for ages, and when at last I dropped off, I couldn't dream either.

Wednesday 9th June

Mrs Bishop described this new maths test as a shot at redemption after last month's 36% debacle. Overall, it felt more like torture than redemption, but it was certainly less impossible than the previous one. Either way, it should steer me well clear of any threat of imminent failure.

Rambo is still carrying his *Toga* script around with him and the final performance is a mere eight days away. When I asked his lordship when he intended to learn his words he looked at me disdainfully and suggested I take a chill pill. Actors can be extremely temperamental.

20:00 Viking called yet another house meeting. This time he sported a sheepish expression. In consultation with the headmaster, he told us, mitigating evidence regarding Missing Eggwhite had come to light.

'As such, his expulsion has been quashed, his suspension rescinded, and he has been fully reinstated as a prefect in this house.'

'Congratulations, Eggwhite,' shouted Viking and initiated a strong but confused round of applause for Missing Eggwhite who predictably didn't bother to rock up.

'Just goes to show,' observed Boggo later in the cop shop, 'not only can money buy you sex and happiness, it can also let you be in two places at once.'

The siren rang for lights out. There was a moment's hesitation among the prefects as to whose duty it was. Rambo lit up a cigarette and stretched back in his chair. 'Don't worry, gents,' he said, 'I'm sure Eggwhite is on to it.' We laughed until we were weak.

Thursday 10th June

My right kneecap continues to seep blood and gunk. Fearing a weeping knee might ruin my hired tuxedo pants, I popped into the san after lunch and showed it to Sister Collins. Sister C wasn't very impressed with the state of my knees and asked me why I hadn't had them treated sooner because one had turned septic and the other was just short of septic. When I described my encounter with the giant Greek Ari Pelagos dragging me across the cricket pitch, she shook her head and said she hated rugby season and that her cousin married and recently divorced a Greek.

So now I am sporting bandages on both my knees and am not allowed to play rugby this weekend. I had to find Sparerib at lunch to break the news that I was bailing on him. He didn't respond to my story, which included a demonstration of my bandaged knees, with any words. Instead he nodded curtly and continued eating his baked beans. Since this weekend's match against Westwood is the final game of the season, I have played my last rugby game for the school. In fact I've probably played my last game of rugby ever. In news that is bound to shake the world, Spud Milton has officially retired from rugby at the ripe old age of seventeen years and two months.

21:00   After rehearsals Vern lit the fire in the cop shop using his history notes as kindling. The orange flames soon attracted the Crazy Eight who entered in lively form and high spirits.

'If your chick is an eight,' ventured Boggo to Simon, 'then my chick is a nine!'

'Christine isn't a nine,' I commented drily.

The cop shop fell silent and all eyes turned to Boggo whose face reddened. 'How did you know I was taking Christine?' he asked in amazement. With Boggo's 'gorgeous' mystery date revealed to be the slightly above average Christine, the cop shop buzzed with further taunts of mockery and harsh laughter. Rambo said that he had heard news that Christine had kissed so many schoolboys that she was moving on to animals. Plump

Sidney reckoned the only way Christine could be a nine out of ten was if you turned the number six upside down. For once I was able to sit back and feel excited about the dance but mostly I just want it to be Saturday night when it's all for real and I can see the Mermaid dressed up like a princess.

Friday 11th June

11:00   There was more hilarity in the quad outside the dining hall after the rugby team lists had been posted for Saturday's match. Poor Vern capped off a drastic season when he was dropped to the last on the list reserves for the 8th team and has been stripped of the vice captaincy.

Saturday 12th June

Mom and Dad brought up my tuxedo and corsage along with a bag of Mermaid's clothes. My father was in a grim mood after his latest attempt to break his up-run record was foiled by roadworks at Key Ridge. He accused the N3 highway construction company of falling into the hands of lazy commies and threatened to take the Old Main Road in future as a sign of protest. Since I am officially retired from rugby, I joined my parents for a picnic lunch under the trees and watched my old team the 6ths lose badly to Westwood.

I said goodbye to my parents and thanked them for all their help with the tuxedo. Mom became a little weepy and wished me luck for the dance while Dad punched me on the shoulder and said, 'Give her one for me, my boy.' Mom slapped Dad on the back of the head and ordered him to stop clowning around and making an arse out of himself. Despite the resounding smack my father threw me a double thumbs up before racing back to the car. Through the windows I could see Mom lecturing Dad about his poor form but he ignored her, revving the engine at a high pitch while staring at his watch and waiting for the second hand to reach twelve. When it did there was a dramatic screeching of tyres and a vast amount of mud and gravel shot out from under the Mercedes. Thankfully, Lord Louis provides covers for their suits or I might have been off to the dance in my school uniform.

I walked up the road and came across Boggo warming up for his linesman's duty on the lawn outside the old boys' club. I wished him well for the big game and he nodded and said he was totally psyched. He asked me what was in the bag and I told him it was my tuxedo.

'No, you helmet,' he sneered. 'The pink bag.'

I glanced down at Mermaid's bag and tightened my grip on the handle. The first team linesman approached with his school flag pointing accusingly at the bag. After turning down a number of generous offers for a peek at Mermaid's underwear I strode off along Pilgrims' Walk with my head held high and a great sense of destiny before me.

I changed in Plump Sidney's room because he was a nervous wreck and had no idea how his tuxedo worked. Neither did I really, but Albert Schweitzer took charge and by 17:30 he had us both looking incredibly swish. Plump Sidney sprayed aftershave in his underpants in case he got lucky with Penny at her parents' house after the dance. I decided not to tempt fate which turned out to be a good decision because within minutes he was complaining of an intense burning sensation in his goolies. A swift ice application behind the cupboard saw things slowly improving and soon Plump Sidney was back in the game and ready for action. Despite the childish wolf whistles from the Normal Seven and other brain donors in the common room, we strode out into the quad with the look of men who knew their place in the world. I reckon a tuxedo raises your appearance by at least twenty-five per cent. No wonder James Bond is always having it off with so many hot women.

We ambled over to the great archway and sidled up to Boggo who was bragging to Garlic and Vern about how he had had the Westwood 1st team captain sent to the cooler for ten minutes.

'If I hadn't taken out their captain,' he bragged, 'there was no way in hell we would have won so easily.' Garlic told Boggo that he was the best linesman that he had ever encountered. Boggo pretended to be coy and merely said that it was fitting for him to end his incredible season with such a flourish. Boggo was less pleased when Pig suggested that his red bow tie and cummerbund made him look like a waiter. Boggo retorted with a vile comment about Pig's mom and high-tailed it for the bus.

'Let's do it, gents,' cheered Plump Sidney and slapped me on the back. 'Tonight boys will become men!'

Rambo and Simon drove down to Pietermaritzburg in Rambo's dad's Porsche despite Rambo not having a driver's licence. Some guys have all the luck.

Nobody's sure what to expect of Vern's date. Most of us reckon that he won't even have a partner at all or that he might rather pretend to have an invisible date instead or, if all else fails, play dead. The cretin looked in good form although he obviously didn't know that the white hanky in his top pocket was for show rather than for repeatedly blowing his nose on.

'Best night of our lives,' I nodded to Geoff Lawson for lack of anything else to say.

'This is nothing,' shouted a loud voice from the seat behind. 'You wait for Lake Malawi.'

18h50 'The name is Garlic,' he announced to the hotel receptionist. 'My mum booked a double room.' The receptionist punched a number of words into his computer but couldn't find Garlic's booking. The Malawian kept shouting out the spelling of his name and saying, 'Mum definitely booked!' to just about anybody who was willing to listen. Then he noticed a tray of juice on the table and hollered, 'Hey, orange juice!' The receptionist stopped Garlic dead in his tracks and said that we couldn't drink the juice unless we were checked into the hotel.

'Mum definitely booked,' Garlic repeated. 'She even told me and everything.'

Garlic's unnecessary volume attracted a studious looking manager who listened patiently to his loud retelling of recent events surrounding his mum's missing booking. The manager thrashed away at another computer keyboard for some time before whispering something to the receptionist and disappearing through a door marked 'private'.

'This would never happen in Malawi,' whispered Garlic raucously.

Boggo and Vern began checking in beside us. Vern carried all of his and Boggo's bags and I'm not sure what the cretin had done to himself in the bus but his tuxedo was badly dishevelled.

'What's the problem, retards?' questioned Boggo, noticing the concern on our faces. Garlic set forth with yet another retelling of the sad story of our reservation that wasn't.

'Hey, Garlic, maybe it's hotel policy, strictly no vegetables allowed!' quipped Boggo and snapped a gold credit card between his fingers.

It wasn't looking good for us and I became rather downhearted about our chances. My nemesis of accommodation had won the battle at the very last minute.

'There's your key, Mr Garlic, I apologise for the delay,' said the manager suddenly.

'We're in!' trumpeted the Malawian and gave me a thrashing high five. 'Does this mean we can have some orange juice?'

The manager extended his arm to indicate that we could help ourselves.

'Woo hoo!' hooted Garlic and bolted back a glass.

'Come on, Spuddy!' he hollered blissfully unaware that literally everybody in the lobby was watching us. 'Let's go test out the beds.'

Garlic wouldn't be half as bad if he wasn't so damned embarrassing. He really needs to be sent off to extra whispering lessons.

19:20   After half an hour of more talk at high volume about Lake Malawi and some final touches to our appearance we headed down to the gathering area where a sizeable crowd of boys awaited their dates.

'I should have had a last pee before we came down,' confessed Garlic, staring blatantly at the breasts of Steven George's girlfriend.

'At least Myrtle isn't the kind of girl you would lose in a crowd,' he said optimistically. I nodded and glanced along the street where a silver Jetta had pulled up.

'Hey, Spud,' called Garlic catching me up, 'is that Penny?' I nodded and Garlic whistled, 'She's flipping hot, hey?'

Penny really was looking hot. It was astonishing to see how much she has grown up in a year. Even Boggo grudgingly admitted that she was worth a squirt before elbowing me in the ribs and showing off a pack of banana and lemon condoms. He promised that the entire pack of five would be soiled by sunrise.

Simon's date was a brunette called Jade who wore

a short dress that showed off her sensational legs. Christine arrived soon after Penny and she and Boggo made a spectacle when they snogged directly in front of everybody. Christine's dress left very little to the imagination and she didn't seem to mind us all staring at her. Vern was left among the group of boys still awaiting their partners. I could tell that he was becoming agitated by the increased muttering and the fact that he was holding himself tightly by the groin.

'You okay, Vern?' I asked.

He nodded.

'When's your date getting here?'

He didn't reply.

Loud hooting drew the crowd's attention back to the street where a black Porsche pulled up flashing its headlights. Rambo, wearing a brown suit, approached with a blonde who walked like a ramp model and was nearly as tall as he was. 'Leigh Bezuidenhout,' whispered Boggo. 'Hot as a house fire.'

And then Mermaid was there and I stepped forward to meet her. She looked gorgeous in a cream dress that accentuated her cleavage and made me unsteady. She kissed me and said, 'Johnny, I'm so honoured to be your partner.'

We moved through the crowd who were laughing and cheering at Garlic who had just kissed Myrtle Pienaar. Myrtle was the only girl at the dance wearing pants instead of a dress and she didn't seem to mind all the cheering and the odd harsh comment about her girth. Garlic was only too delighted to be the centre of attention and excitedly led Myrtle along like she was Julia Roberts.

20:00 Poor Vern was the last man standing. He mostly studied his watch and muttered urgently to himself, and on occasion he would step out and scan the street. Then he would return to his spot and examine his watch once more. Some time later he began pulling out his hair so I went back to distract him.

'Hi, Vern,' I said.

'Spud!' he replied.

'Are you sure your date is coming?' I asked.

'Just now,' he responded and pointed towards a side street that ran behind the hotel where Boggo and Christine were in a vigorous clinch up against the wall.

A yellow Eagle taxi sidled up the road and out of it stepped an extremely pretty blonde woman who looked about thirty-five but Boggo later swore her to be a grandmother of forty-six. She was extremely sexily dressed and was smoking a cigarette. She wasn't shy either because she shouted out, 'Which one of you is Vernon?'

'Cop shop,' said Vern and raised his hand.

'Come here, Vernon,' said the woman and beckoned Rain Man over. Vern blushed and began pulling out more hair. I urged him forward and the nervous cretin stumbled up to the woman like he thought she might eat him. She grabbed him by the face and kissed him savagely on the lips causing those watching to applaud.

Hand in hand, a blushing Vern Blackadder led his date along the red carpet and into the hotel. The rest of us fell in behind him. After receiving our welcoming glass of punch and having our photographs taken, the doors to Conference Room A were thrown open for the 1993 matric dance.

To suggest the third years had outdone themselves with the decorating would be an overstatement. Aside from the draping of a few school flags and one or two discreetly placed streamers, there were no decorations at all. The Crazy Eight were seated at table thirteen and it was good to see individualised name tags for each setting. Mine read **Spud Milton** and the one to my right read **Mermaid Milton**. I pulled back the chair for my partner. 'Thank you, Spud Milton,' she purred seductively. 'Pleasure, Mermaid Milton,' I replied in a suave fashion.

'Nice buns,' chirped Boggo seizing up a bowl of bread rolls. He nonchalantly tried to flick one into his hand but only succeeded in sending the rolls flying across the table.

'Nice co-ords,' retorted Rambo as he settled into his seat at the far end of the table. Vern's date had frozen him up with terror and he stared fixedly at his fork while she tried to make conversation with him. I wondered how the poor woman was ever gimped into being Vern's partner.

Smoked salmon and fruit punch were served as The Glock grandly rose to his feet and made his way over to the lectern to make his welcoming speech. Count Killjoy did his best to throw a wet blanket on the party by droning on about the deadly peril of under-age binge drinking and spent a considerable amount of time reading out the most recent drunk driving statistics. Christine didn't think much of The Glock's speech and was feeling up Boggo under the table all the way through it. Greenstein had a delirious look on his face and slid well down in his chair so that only his shoulders and head were visible above the table. I blocked the cavorting couple out and returned my focus to The Glock who had moved on to pedestrian safety.

'Your headmaster seems quite angry,' whispered Mermaid.

'Boggo says he's a cross dresser,' interrupted Garlic, forgetting to whisper.

The atmosphere in the room took another drubbing when Reverend Bishop delivered the grace. During his lengthy twelve minute diatribe he compared our matric dance to a wedding, a pack of wolves, and the seed of Satan. When he was finished, I picked up my knife and fork and noticed that Mermaid and I were the only ones at our table who hadn't finished our starters yet.

The Glock began a slow tour of the room, engaging each table in awkward conversation. He made his way grimly towards the Crazy Eight with his hands clasped behind his back and a ghoulish smile plastered to his face.

'Good evening,' he said in a creepy fashion. His large face loomed over the table with a slightly raised eyebrow like he might be expecting some nasty surprises from us for some reason. There was a generally mumbled reply with most of us avoiding the headmaster's gaze in case he tried to strike up an embarrassing conversation.

'Enjoying yourselves?' asked The Glock after an excruciating pause.

'The salmon was excellent, sir,' barked Garlic.

'Thank you,' responded The Glock like he had caught, prepared and cooked the fish himself. His eyes ran from Penny across to Mermaid and then on to the sparsely dressed Christine, where they lingered.

'You all look rather ... pretty,' he said awkwardly and fumbled with his tie.

'Thank you very much, sir,' chirped Rambo.

We all laughed and The Glock laughed along too although it was terribly cringy and awkward. After repeating the word 'lovely' a few times he rocked on his heels before pitching forward and placing his hairy hands on my and Boggo's shoulders. The headmaster leaned in like he was about to reveal an important secret about himself. Instead, he said 'Enjoy' and sauntered off to creep out table fourteen.

Once Count Glockula had moved on, energy and life returned to the table. Rambo, Simon and Boggo began discussing today's rugby match, Garlic bailed up the Mermaid with incessant talk of Lake Malawi, while Christine's hand was steadily making its way up my thigh. With the Mermaid literally sitting right next to me, Christine was insane enough to lick my ear and whisper, 'Come visit after.' I grinned at her but only because I was shocked and didn't know what to say. She stuck her tongue out at me and slowly removed her hand from my inner thigh.

'Lake Malawi is definitely in the top three holiday destinations of the entire world,' declared Garlic to a rather bemused Mermaid. 'Right up there with the States and the Alps.'

Mermaid seemed to be playing along and acted like she was impressed by all his bragging about Lake Malawi.

'You must pull in for a holiday,' continued Garlic. 'Even if you're not with Spud, feel free to come along anyway.'

I drew the line at Garlic inviting my girlfriend to Lake Malawi and boldly intervened. I refilled Mermaid's punch and we chatted avidly until head boy Rooster Illingworth stood up to make his speech. I've always thought Rooster to be a bit of a nob, but he spoke brilliantly about how this dance marked our coming of age as men. He finished his speech by raising a toast to our dates, but then called up all the boys to perform the school war cry. It felt all wrong and for some reason I was embarrassed by it. (Perhaps my retirement from rugby has meant that I have become distanced from school spirit?)

After the war cry, Plump Sidney pulled me into the

corridor outside the conference room. 'How hot is Penny?' he gasped, and shook his head like he was quite literally astounded. 'Mermaid is looking really good too,' he added as an afterthought, despite obviously rating his date hotter than mine. Before I could say anything, Plump Sidney continued, 'Hey, I just wanted to warn you to lay off the punch.'

When I enquired why, Plump Sidney looked around suspiciously before whispering, 'Rambo spiked it with vodka.'

'What!' I roared and noticed that the corridor was spinning slightly.

'He did it under the table during The Glock's speech.'

'Why did he do that?' I asked, attempting simultaneously to tally up the number of glasses of punch that Mermaid may have consumed.

'Because I asked Rambo for help with getting Penny to ... you know ... to get down and dirty and stuff and he reckoned it was the only way.'

Feeling instantly drunk, I staggered back to my table to save my date from the Malawian and the effects of Rambo's vodka. While I was gone, Garlic had moved his chair right up beside the Mermaid's and was remonstrating violently with her about something. The Mermaid thought this was hilarious and hooted with laughter. She turned as I approached and I could immediately see that she had drunk far too much of the tainted punch. In fact, her eyes had glazed over and she had this great goofy smile on her face.

'Spuddy!' she squealed, causing the entire table to laugh raucously.

'Hey, Spud!' boomed Garlic. 'I was just telling Mermaid about when you told me about those Europeans shagging giraffes.'

I had no idea what Garlic was on about and swiftly

replaced Mermaid's half-filled glass of punch with iced water and did likewise with mine. The main course was chicken á la king, which only Plump Sidney and Myrtle ate with any relish. Eating sobered me up slightly, although it seemed to have very little effect on the Mermaid who sat resting her chin on her fist and looking a little vacant. It was good to see Mermaid flooring an entire glass of water moments before Plump Sidney nudged me in the ribs and whispered, 'Word's out that Rambo spiked the water as well.'

I sampled the iced water which certainly didn't taste like iced water should, and immediately snatched away Mermaid's glass. She stared at me like I was insane and then leant across and kissed me without warning.

'I love you, Johnny,' she slurred.

After my date had made a scene by singing loudly with Garlic to Neil Diamond's Sweet Caroline, I decided to take her out for an intake of some fresh air. Unfortunately, Garlic followed along behind us and I had to send him back to the table. I led the Mermaid out into the chill night air hoping it would sober her up.

'I feel so strange,' she confessed, after stumbling on the stairs outside the entrance. I broke the news to her about Rambo spiking the punch and she didn't react well at all. At first she was angry and threatened to call the police. Moments later she found the whole thing hysterically funny and laughed so hard that she collapsed onto the ground and I had to help her up. Thereafter her laughter died away and she became depressed. 'I've ruined your matric dance,' she wailed and sobbed so hard that her make-up ran down her face and smudged her eyes like a badger. After weeping for ten minutes, she told me again that she loved me and kissed me with a tongue that smashed around my mouth like a trapped sea creature.

When I asked if she was ready to return to the dance Mermaid shook her head and said she wanted to go back to the room to fix her face. I returned alone to the dance where things were loosening up somewhat, although the dance floor was still sparsely populated thanks to The Glock and his wife waltzing around it in an intense manner. I found Garlic in deep discussion with Vern's partner, Plump Sidney and Penny. I asked him for the room key.

'Is Mermaid okay?' questioned Garlic with deep concern.

'She's excellent,' I replied.

Back in the room things began to look up. Mermaid said that she felt terrible about how drunk she was and wanted to make it up to me. She then began unzipping her dress like she meant business. For a brief time span I felt certain that this would be the defining moment of my youth. Unfortunately, while attempting to escape from her dress, Mermaid caught sight of her face in the mirror and squealed at how ghastly her eyes looked. She ordered me to hang five and disappeared into the bathroom. While I waited for the Mermaid to sort her eyes out, I took off my jacket, bow tie and cummerbund. I then decided that for once I wouldn't be a complete loser and quickly stripped down to my underwear and hopped into bed to wait for her. I've seen this tactic many times on TV.

Seconds later I heard the unmistakable bark of vomiting. Poor Mermaid. It sounded terrible. After a suitable time had passed I knocked on the door and enquired if she was doing okay.

'Coming,' came the distressed and pathetic call from inside. I backed off again and returned to our little room where I lay down on the pull-out bed once more. A while later Mermaid stepped out of the bathroom in her lacy white underwear, her face a ghostly pale mask. She slipped into bed beside me and wrapped her arms around my shoulders.

'Sorry, Johnny,' she said.

'What are you talking about? It's been a great night,' I replied.

Mermaid didn't answer because she had already passed out. I glanced at my watch in the lamplight and the time read:

21:22.

I lay in bed with my sleeping date simmering about Rambo spiking our drinks and imagining how I could exact revenge on him. The door flew open and Garlic charged in looking desperate.

'Where's the Mermaid,' he gasped, like I may have killed her.

'She's sleeping,' I whispered and pointed at the comatose body lying beside me.

'Did you bone her?' he asked in a voice so loud that it made me jump out of bed and drag him out of our room and into his. Myrtle was in the bathroom and Garlic continued jabbering. 'Just about everyone's left for the after-party.' The toilet flushed and there was the sound of a shower being switched on. After a minute Garlic admitted that Myrtle was calling it a night too.

I informed the fool that I intended to stay with the Mermaid and forgo the nightclub.

'What!' he roared. 'Are you mad, Spud?'

I shrugged and told him that I wasn't feeling up to it. Garlic was furious with my defeatist attitude.

'This is the biggest night of your life,' he argued. 'You can't go to bed at half past nine!'

I shrugged and said that I didn't feel like an after-party anyway.

'It's a nightclub and you can't get bounced,' Garlic

pointed out. 'When does that ever happen?'

'Okay,' I said eventually. 'I'll go.'

21:42   Dressed in jeans and a collared shirt with my hair combed back like John Travolta in *Grease*, I felt ready for a wild evening. Leaving our dates to sleep, Garlic and I took the lift down to the ground floor, sauntered through reception, and out onto a street littered with kissing couples. We passed Plump Sidney but didn't speak to him because he was locked in an intense discussion with Penny as they waited for her dad. Garlic and I marched on down the street until we were alone and the deserted buildings about us loomed like a ghost town.

'Spud?' asked Garlic.

'Yip.'

'I think I've fallen in love.'

'With Myrtle?' I asked, failing to hide the surprise from my voice.

'With Mermaid,' he replied and whistled to himself. 'You're so damned lucky, Spud. You really are.'

'I know.'

'Don't worry, I would never try to steal her from you,' he added.

'I'm not worried.' I felt a bit for him.

'Spud?' he asked again.

'Yip.'

'Do you know where we're going?'

'Haven't a clue.'

'Me neither,' he admitted.

Luckily, we spotted two boys in tuxedos running in the opposite direction and we charged after them along a narrow lane, cut across some vacant land, and down a far busier street. It seemed that everyone was heading in the same direction towards the throbbing music of

Take 5.

The huge bald bouncer gave us grief due to Garlic completely botching up our arrival at the club. 'Matric dance, sir! We're together,' he blurted as we made it to the entrance.

'This is not a gay club,' replied the bouncer who, thanks to Garlic's ambiguous greeting, now thought that we were a couple.

'Our dates went home,' I interrupted, hoping to swiftly clear up any confusion.

'They're actually sleeping in our hotel room,' added Garlic, muddying the waters further.

'The barman won't serve under 18s any drinks,' grumbled the bouncer in a rather unfriendly tone.

'That's okay, I'm 21,' lied Garlic unnecessarily when a simple nod would have seen us into the nightclub unscathed. Instead the bouncer seized him by the collar and accused him of being a wise guy. I managed to talk the bouncer down by explaining that Garlic was Malawian and wasn't right in the head.

'That figures,' he muttered, releasing his grip. 'Any shit from you two and I'll deal with you personally.' The bouncer cracked his knuckles and stared at us in a menacing fashion. I nodded and pushed Garlic up the stairs before he could say anything else. The staircase was dimly lit by ultra violet light which made people's faces distort and their teeth gleam an otherworldly white. A beautiful woman with bronzed skin and mesmeric teeth appeared in front of us. She seized my hand, twisted it upside down, and stamped my wrist.

'What's that for?' I asked staring at the stamp.

'Oh my God,' she replied. 'How old are you, like thirteen?'

'Twenty-one,' replied Garlic. The woman laughed and stamped his wrist too.

Garlic tapped my arm and said, 'It's so you can

prove to people that you were in a nightclub.' I nodded and followed him up the stairs into the throbbing mayhem. The first person we saw was a delirious Vern Blackadder dancing by himself outside the gents' toilet and licking the stamp on his wrist.

'Sex!' announced Vern the moment he saw us.

'What?' shouted Garlic above the din.

'Sex!' repeated Vern and pointed at his privates. We made our way past the pool table where a number of the first rugby team were involved in a game. Their partners stood around looking bored and beautiful. Away from the dance floor was an open veranda that overlooked the street. 'Where are your dates, gaylords?' hollered a drunken Boggo, lurching up to us in exceedingly high spirits.

'Passed out,' I replied.

Boggo sniggered like a machine gun and said, 'Blind one.'

'Where's your date?' asked Garlic.

'Recovering from our second shagging of the evening,' bragged Boggo while swigging lustily from his beer bottle. 'Lost my virginity tonight, boys,' he declared.

'I thought you said you lost your virginity in first year,' I said.

'Not properly,' he slurred. 'Tonight was the night.'

'Vern also lost his virginity tonight,' said Garlic.

Boggo thought this was exceedingly funny but said that there was no way in hell that Rain Man had got any nookie. When Garlic asked how he knew this, Boggo threw his hands into the air and cried, 'Because I paid for his bloody partner, Garlic, and the only extras I paid for was a side guy.'

'What's a side guy?' demanded the Malawian.

'A backhanded pulling of the wire,' replied a smug looking Boggo, demonstrating rather dismissively with his left hand. 'It was well worth the bargain of having a slave for the entire term.' That's when Boggo admitted that he had hired an escort for Vern and that the woman was actually a 46 year old grandmother.

'A prostitute! I wish I'd thought of that,' admitted Garlic as we retired to the far end of the veranda where an impressive palm tree grew up from the pavement of the street below.

We discussed Vern's side guy for a few minutes and watched the others chatting with their dates or tearing it up on the dance floor. I felt like I always do at parties, socials, bars and nightclubs. I felt like an outsider.

'You want a drink?' asked Garlic after a particularly long silence. I told him that there was probably very little chance of a barman serving us because we looked too young.

'Nonsense,' he declared. 'They all think I'm 21.'

The Malawian set off towards the bar with considerable confidence but returned cursing a few minutes later.

I waved at Christine flitting past with a girlfriend on each arm.

'Spuddy!' she shrieked and immediately wrapped her arms round my neck. Her two friends obviously didn't think much of us because they hung back at a safe distance. Once I had prised Christine off me I asked her if she could help us with buying some drinks.

'Shame, Babyface,' she teased, tugging playfully at my cheek, but she agreed to buy Garlic and me drinks provided we also paid for a round for herself and her friends. Garlic pulled out a fifty and handed it over. He seemed to be rendered a little speechless by Christine and once she had left us he asked, 'Does Christine really do it with animals?'

'Happy hour!' shrieked Christine, and handed us Carling Black Labels and three shooters each which she ordered us to down. Thereafter the complexion of the night changed once more. I found myself dancing, playing pool with Rambo and Simon and generally having an excellent time. At one stage Christine returned with even more tequilas and whispered in my ear that she planned to fool around with me later.

I think I will always remember staggering through the streets of Pietermaritzburg at 3am on a Sunday morning, as drunk as a skunk, with a crowd of hooligans keeping themselves warm by raucously singing the school hymn and attacking unsuspecting rubbish bins.

Sunday 13th June

Waking up was a dreadful experience. I had planned a bold approach with Mermaid in the morning in the hope of losing my virginity but neither of us felt very well and she spent so long in the shower that there wasn't enough time in any case before Marge arrived and rang us from reception. I kissed my girlfriend goodbye and waved her and Marge off. Then I picked up my bag and boarded the bus to take me back to school.

19:00 With a mere four days to go until the final performance, *Toga* rehearsal was cancelled because both leading actors and the director were 'not feeling well'.

MATRIC DANCE SCORECARD

RAMBO	Romped with his model girlfriend Leigh.
SIMON	Gave 'multiple orgasms' to his partner Jade.
BOGGO	Lost his virginity five times in twelve hours.
PLUMP SIDNEY	Had to leave the dance early and sleep in a separate room from Penny.
VERN	Received his debut 'side guy' from a 46 year old grandmother-prostitute.
GARLIC	Snogged Myrtle and fell in love with Spud's date.

SPUD	Came within seconds of a life changing sexual experience before his date passed out after having her drinks spiked by Rambo.

Monday 14th June

It was a terrible morning. Albert Schweitzer soured my mood when he brought in my coffee and started interrogating me about *Toga* rehearsals. To make matters worse, I was on duty and the house was in an uproar after Vern paraded about in the bogs with a morning glory shouting 'Side guy!' at people. His escapade terrified the blazes out of the Harmless Half-Dozen who refused to come downstairs for roll call and stood to attention on the vestry roof instead.

Thankfully, my morning funk had worn off after breakfast. I suppose I should be panicking about the house play considering the performance is only three days away and the whole thing is dreadfully under-rehearsed. However, news that West and Barnes haven't even selected their plays yet has made me feel considerably less urgent about *Toga*.

I struggled to concentrate during classes today as my brain was fully occupied with thoughts of Mermaid prancing about in her lacy white underwear. There are drawbacks to having a hot blonde girlfriend.

17:15 Viking made a scene about *Toga* during his house meeting. He even made me stand for a bow while the house applauded. Our housemaster pointed up at the honours board and said, 'Nothing would give me greater pleasure than seeing house play winners inscribed on that very board.' Now I'm feeling utterly terrified and desperate about *Toga*.

'Finally,' he barked, 'it gives me great pleasure to announce a new house prefect.' The boys fell silent. 'Let's put our hands together and congratulate Alan Greenstein!'

An astonished Boggo rose unsteadily to his feet and crossed the room to shake Viking's hand.

'Greenstein will be picking up some of the slack when Eggwhite is otherwise committed,' continued Viking while his eyes darted from side to side as if attempting to make eye contact with the entire house at once. After the meeting the new prefect ordered tea and toast to celebrate his appointment, despite it being less than ten minutes until dinner time.

20:00 Rambo still hasn't learned his words but has assured me that he will know them backwards by Thursday night. I told him that I would rather he knew them forwards by tomorrow morning. He just laughed and walked away.

Despite being a prefect for just two hours, Boggo handed out numerous punishments during the rehearsal. Thinny and Spike were each given hard labour for messing about offstage and Garlic, Albert Schweitzer and Enzo Ferrari received fingertongs with Brutus' scroll after they entered the scene late and threw Boggo off his comic timing. Afterwards I asked the new prefect to tone things down a bit as I wanted the rehearsal environment to be a happy space rather than a concentration camp. Unfortunately, he was too busy firing off commands to his new slave Near Death to answer me properly.

Since the authorities are determined to keep up the myth that Missing Eggwhite isn't at university, Near Death has been officially listed as having two prefects to slave for.

Tuesday 15th June

Boggo and Plump Sidney have taken up permanent residence in the cop shop. While Boggo seems to be relishing his new found authority, Plump Sidney is on a crash eating binge and has devoured 24 eggs, a kilogram of cheese, four loaves of bread and a large roll of polony since Sunday afternoon. That, of course, is in addition to his usual meals in the dining hall and afternoons spent in the tuck shop.

19:00 Final dress rehearsal on the theatre stage was a debacle. Rambo still hasn't learned his words and doesn't seem to care that he could ruin the entire play and look like a complete moron on Thursday night. The cast were completely distracted by being in the theatre and there was a considerable amount of horsing about in the wings which was only inflamed by Boggo dishing out harsh punishments left, right and centre. Vern didn't help matters when he started up with his loud announcements of 'Toga' and 'Side guy' from behind the back curtain. It also took several minutes to quell the riot after the cretin strode onto stage naked from the waist down. After the rehearsal I gave the cast a savage lecture on discipline and professionalism that would have made Viking proud. I fired Spike from the play altogether for his persistent pissing about and undermining of my authority. He initially thought I was joking but when he realised that I was being serious he began begging and pleading for one last chance to prove himself. I sent him packing and he had to suffer the indignity of walking out of the auditorium while the rest of the cast watched him in silence. It was a very powerful moment.

I have replaced Spike with Barryl in the role of Mark Antony. Barryl was over the moon with the promotion and promised to learn his lines by tomorrow morning. It's a marginal call. What you lose on Barryl's articulation you gain on the high comedy value for the way he walks with his chest puffed out and his unnaturally deep voice.

Wednesday 16th June

Mrs Bishop handed back our maths 'redemption' test papers and I was shattered to see that I had mustered only 41% after expecting at least 65%. Convinced that there was a logical explanation for my low marks, I approached the chaplain's wife and told her that I thought there had been some sort of mistake with the marking of the paper. Mrs Bishop grew snotty about things and quipped, 'The only mistakes on this paper, Mr Milton, are yours, and they are plentiful.' I would be lying if my deterioration in maths wasn't a concern, but right now *Toga* worries me more than passing matric.

Boggo was hauled into Viking's office after lunch to explain the ridiculous number of punishments that he has dished out since being made a prefect on Monday night. I'm not sure what transpired in Viking's office but the meeting seemed to make no difference as Boggo walked straight out and punished both Runt and Barryl with hard labour for lurking. Plump Sidney reckons Boggo being made a prefect and losing his virginity in the same weekend may have short-wired his brain and made him a megalomaniac.

A further complication for the new prefect is that Vern is refusing to give up slaving for Boggo despite the matric dance being over with. Rain Man attacked Near Death when he tried to take Boggo's laundry this afternoon, and later gave the poor slave a wedgy when he caught him shining Boggo's brown Grasshoppers. Plump Sidney reckons Vern's side guy from the prostitute may have flipped him out too.

19:00 Final Dress Rehearsal. Rambo still doesn't know his words. More worryingly, for the first time he didn't promise to have learned them by tomorrow night. Instead he now reckons that he has a foolproof plan for delivering his lines without learning them. The sight of my lead character still reading from his script on the eve of the performance was the most disappointing since Mermaid passed out on Saturday night after promising me a romp.

Strolling back to the house after the rehearsal, the night was clear and chill. I glanced up at the Milky Way and silently prayed that Rambo wouldn't let us down.

Thursday 17th June

HOUSE PLAYS

19:30 Everything was helter skelter. Barnes started late and overran their time limit with a dreary play that nobody understood. This meant that our set-up was cut from ten minutes to zero minutes. I tore about the stage hissing directions and orders, while the actors fussed about where to stash their props.

Eve slipped through the curtain and tapped her watch. 'John, we quite simply have to go up right now.' I told everyone to break a leg and bolted for the lighting box to assist Rowdy who has a bad habit of losing focus and missing crucial lighting and sound cues. Most of all, I felt sick with worry about Rambo not knowing his words. I could only pray that he really did have a plan and that it would work.

I bashed myself quite badly on the door of the lighting box, ripping off the scab on my left knee. Blood seeped through my school pants but I ignored it and cued Rowdy.

'Music fade, house lights down, cue curtain up, and go with the sound, and ... lights up!'

Rinse the Blood off My Toga was a hit from beginning to end. Rambo was faultless and didn't fluff a single line. Boggo had everyone roaring with his witty asides and the applause from the school was the loudest by far for any of the plays. Afterwards I sprinted down the ladder and congratulated the cast backstage after the curtain came down.

'Rambo!' I hollered. 'How did you manage to pull that off?' He grinned but didn't reply. Albert Schweitzer pointed up towards the theatre roof. High above me, suspended by ropes from the fly bar, was Plaque, dangling down and dressed in his school uniform. In his trembling hands was Rambo's script.

'Um, guys,' he called in a high and desperate voice, 'please could I come down now?'

Whispered lines from above – so that's how he did it.

To complete a night of miracles, *Rinse the Blood off My Toga* won the inter-house play competition and Boggo was awarded the trophy for best actor. Viking was beside himself with joy and gave me a hug of congratulation. The adjudicator said she was highly amused by our play and that it stood head and shoulders above the others for its slickness, excellent performances and clever direction.

Tonight I finally drowned the memory of *Noah's Ark*.

Rambo carried the trophy back to the cop shop and stood it on the shelf above the fireplace. We ordered tea and toast and the Crazy Eight gathered in chairs around the fire. Since we had won a famous victory for the house and tomorrow is the end of term, we agreed to share out a tot or two of Rambo's leftover

vodka. He may have charged me an acting fee, spiked my girlfriend's drinks at the matric dance, and put me through hell as a director, but it was impossible to stay angry. He just has that way about him.

22:45 I dawdled back to my room soaking in the night air. Yes, it may only have been a house play and, yes, the competition in general was pretty poor, but once again it made me feel like the theatre is calling me to follow its path, and that is exactly what I am determined to do.

Tomorrow Mermaid and freedom await.

Friday 18th June

06:30 It's a measure of Viking's pride and excitement at winning the house play competition that our victory has already been recorded and engraved on the house honours board.

At breakfast Boggo noted that he had received three massive strikes of good fortune, what with losing his virginity, becoming a prefect, and now achieving best actor in the house plays.
    'It always goes in threes,' he observed in a smug tone, flicking a stray piece of scrambled egg from his jersey onto the floor.

But Boggo was dead wrong because this week his luck was going in fours. Unbelievably, he was also awarded his rugby colours at the final assembly without so much as having played a single game of rugby for the school. Since when does a linesman receive rugby colours? Rambo thought it hilarious, but then he would do because he received his rugby honours.

I bumped into The Guv after assembly and asked him

what he was doing for his holidays. 'Sampling fermented grapes,' he intoned. When I told him that I was certain to go fishing he gripped my arm and asked, 'You've read the Hemingway, Milton?'

I nodded.

'This requires ponderage,' he said and off he went without saying goodbye.

After a final prefects' meeting with Viking, I strolled across the main quad, through the great archway, and followed Pilgrims' Walk to where Albert Schweitzer was waiting with my bags. He shook my hand and wished me a good holiday.

'The Guv asked me to give you this,' he said, handing me a slim book with a green cover.

Three Men in a Boat by Jerome K Jerome.

I bade him farewell and boarded the bus that would take me home.

SPUD MILTON'S TEN AIMS FOR THE HOLIDAYS:

1. Seduce the Mermaid in her white underwear
2. Pass my learner's test
3. Begin revision in earnest for trials exams
4. Decide on my future
5. Read *Three Men in a Boat*
6. Develop huge muscles thanks to regular workouts
7. Strive to be less cretinous at maths
8. Get a suntan
9. Stay sober
10. Avoid embarrassing situations

Saturday 19th June

Mermaid invited me to the movies at the La Lucia Mall. Her best friends Tarryn, Melly and Michaela were there too. I felt quite impressive striding into the cinema with two blondes and a brunette in tow, but my posse soon became a liability when I spent precious little of the evening alone with my girlfriend. On the one occasion that I had her to myself and was moving in for a passionate kiss and possible grope, Melly interrupted us citing desperately important news that had to be told.

'What happened, Mel?' urged the Mermaid, looking incredibly concerned.

Melly took a deep breath before steadying herself to break the big news.

'Emma and Greg have just broken up.'

'Oh Melly,' gasped Mermaid, 'that's so shocking.' Tarryn and Michaela appeared from nowhere and joined in the heated discussion about the sudden demise of Emma and Greg's relationship. We never left the parking lot.

Later, when Marge dropped me off, I didn't feel that I could snog or feel up the Mermaid with her mother watching and the car running so all I got out of an excruciating night was a peck on the lips.

Sunday 20th June

12:00 Wombat was in a foul mood at the Milton Sunday braai. Not even three double gin and tonics could cheer her up. Despite it being on the verge of the winter solstice, she said it was too hot to sit outside and decamped to a rocking chair in the lounge. Poor Mom had to join her mother inside, while Dad told me fishing stories around the braai and we imagined what we might catch on our upcoming trip to Zombelo's Neck in Zululand. After lunch Wombat accused Mom of stealing her foreign currency, and when it was time for her to go she refused to kiss either Dad or me goodbye and for no reason whatsoever accused us both of being boorish.

After my grandmother left I cycled to Mermaid's house. We hung out in her room for a while and listened to music. Then the phone rang and it was Melly to say that Emma and Greg were now officially back together. I sat in Mermaid's room for what seemed like ages while she responded to all the calls about Emma and Greg's reunification. Eventually I lost patience and made up an excuse of being needed at home. Cycling around Durban North I thought three rather troubling thoughts about the Mermaid:

1. Our phone conversations are better than our real conversations
2. She finds Emma and Greg's relationship more interesting than she does me
3. She hasn't uttered a word about the matric dance nor our 'seconds away from having sex' moment

To make matters worse, Mermaid is leaving on a school hockey tour to Bloemfontein tomorrow. The Miltons are heading off on holiday the day after she gets back and that leaves only five days at the end of the holiday for us to reignite our stalling relationship.

Monday 21st June

Mermaid left for her hockey tour this morning without calling to say goodbye. This smells very much like the beginnings of chronic Mermaid bat. It always begins with a subtle but distinctly noticeable cooling off period and then the guillotine hurtles down and unexpectedly chops off my head. I know I ordered myself last night not to obsess about her, but maths revision is exceedingly difficult when your first serious relationship lies in tatters just weeks after it has begun.

Friday 25th June

My army call-up papers arrived in the post. Mom was rather alarmed at the thought of me setting off for war and threatened to tear them up until Dad stopped her by snatching away the envelope and saying that her actions could amount to treason and get us all hanged. My father didn't seem at all concerned about his only son (and child) being conscripted into the army and fighting guerrillas on the border. He crashed around in his garage for some time before staggering out with his old army trunk which contained his uniforms and various artefacts from his own two years in the army. My father even pulled out his gun which no longer works because he lost a few crucial pieces while cleaning it a few years back. He still keeps it under the bed so that he can scare off would-be intruders, despite the fact that it's harmless and doesn't fire. Nevertheless Dad took me out into the garden and we pretended to shoot a beer can which he placed on the gatepost. While pretending to shoot another round, Dad told me a series of stories about his army days in Oudtshoorn. Nearly all of them involved stealing cigarettes from the captain and chatting up Afrikaans girls from the typing school down the road.

Sunday 27th June

Sunday Times headline:

'Wife cuts off sleeping husband's penis!'

Dad was so agitated that he made me read the story to him while he paced around the room holding his nuts in sympathy. An American woman called Lorena Bobbit apparently slashed off her husband's penis on Thursday after busting him cheating on her.

'This feminism business is getting out of hand,' grumbled Dad and shook his head dolefully. 'I see the same signs in your mother.'

I pointed out that, although a grim story, at least the doctors were hopeful of sewing the man's dongle back on. Dad grimaced, snatched up the paper and stalked out. I glanced at the time on my alarm clock: 6:30.

Today Mermaid returns from Bloemfontein. I would think that if I don't hear from her tonight before going away fishing tomorrow I can consider our relationship dead in the water. I have sworn to myself that I will not cave in and call her first.

12:30 Dad says it takes eight hours by bus from Bloemfontein to Durban. If they left by 6am she could be home by 2pm. If she truly loves and missed me she should call by 3pm.

15:15 Thinking of it now, it's highly unlikely that the hockey team would have left Bloemfontein before breakfast. 9am would be a far more realistic time to depart a hockey festival. That would mean she'd be home by 5pm with the call coming in around 6pm.

17:30 There was no sign of life at Mermaid's house. I didn't linger in case that was the very moment that she returned and caught her boyfriend skulking around the garden.

18:25 I am beginning to grow a little concerned that Mermaid won't call at all and I'll be facing a brief and gutting end to my first proper relationship.

19:15 Dad said the trip might take even longer than eight hours depending on what type of bus was used. He could obviously see that I was waiting for the Mermaid to call because he very kindly made up a number of reasons why she had most probably been delayed on her travels home. These ranged from possible (a puncture) to the impossible (bus driver becoming disorientated after inhaling methane gas from a truck in front and taking the slip road to Welkom by mistake). Nevertheless I appreciated my father's absolute conviction that the Mermaid would call and that it was only trifling details that delayed her.

20:10 I'm losing hope that she'll phone and I'm losing hope that she still loves me.

21:05 Lay on my bed and depressed myself further by listening to REM's Everybody Hurts on my Walkman at full volume. It was comforting to hear the sound of somebody else in pain. I was returned to the present by a violent shaking of my shoulders. My father was grinning.

'I told you,' he said triumphantly. I tore off my headphones, leapt from my bed and scampered down the passage.

'Hello, Johnny,' she said and I could tell immediately from the tone of her voice that it wasn't over. I wished like hell that the Miltons weren't going away tomorrow because right now kissing my girlfriend is all that really matters in life.

Marge kicked Mermaid off the phone after half an hour. It felt just like old times.

Monday 28th June

ZULULAND FISHING ADVENTURE

06:10 Despite towing his new Venter trailer, my father seemed determined to reach Zombelo's Neck at lightning speed. (He later conceded that he and his brother had a one hundred rand bet riding on who would arrive first.)

06:25 I had to step in to avoid a major row blowing up just minutes after leaving home. Mom harangued Dad for being irresponsible and declared that his ridiculously fast driving was bound to wipe the family out. The old man didn't take kindly to having his driving skills or the Mercedes questioned and began demonstrating a number of dangerous swerves that only aggravated the situation. Eventually, I made Mom switch on the news which thankfully quietened them both down.

06:50 Dad has just been pulled over for speeding and fined 500 bucks! The cop maintained my father was driving at 151kph. Dad was appalled at this and accused the policeman of corruption and malpractice as he reckoned he was doing at least 175kph, if not more. The policeman denied his equipment was faulty but my father said the German Mercedes speedometer would be far more reliable than the policeman's speed camera which he said was probably made by Yugoslavs. When Dad's questioning of the speed camera didn't work, he changed tack completely and offered the policeman a bribe. The cop threatened to arrest Dad for corrupting a police officer but my father wisely backtracked by playing dumb and confused and managed to get off with just his original speeding fine and a stern warning. Back in the car Dad shook his head in dismay and cried out, 'Now you can't even bribe the cops!' He stared at Mom with a look of astonishment and asked, 'What's this country coming to?'

Zombelo's Neck

Zombelo's Neck lies on the northern Zululand coast a mere fifty kilometres as the crow flies from the border with Mozambique. The final stretch of driving took an age as Dad had to negotiate numerous sand drifts and potholes that lay in wait to ambush the Mercedes and trailer. The dust road ahead revealed fresh tyre prints which my father grumpily reckoned was Uncle Aubrey's Land Rover and boat trailer.

'Bloody swine,' muttered my father. 'He always gets in first.'

11:30 Uncle Aubrey was waiting for us when we arrived, hooting madly and flashing the lights.

'Ja, you bastard amasende bokwe!' shouted my father out of the window to his brother.

'What does that mean?' asked Mom suspiciously.

'It means he has the balls of a goat,' replied my father triumphantly and hurled further Zulu insults out of the window.

Dad nailed Uncle Aubrey a good shot when he slammed open the car door and caught his older brother on the kneecaps. Uncle Aubrey sank to the gravel with a groan and looked to be down for the count. Dad realised that he may have taken things a little far and leapt out of the car to check if his brother was all right. But Uncle Aubrey was only feigning serious injury and landed a telling blow when he unexpectedly head butted Dad in the nuts. This time it was Dad who collapsed groaning in agony. With the pleasantries out of the way, Aunt Peggy introduced Mom and me to a large beaming man with rosy chubby cheeks named Cousin Rattie who farms next door to them in Namibia.

Soon we were all unpacked and gathered in the boma. Uncle Aubrey had a potjiekos bubbling in his cast-iron pot and despite it being 11:30am, drinks were flowing and colourful stories were already being told. It feels sensational to be out of the suburbs and back in wildest Africa once more.

16:25   I was sent off to find more cold beers and further hilarity followed as Uncle Aubrey told an extremely long but funny story about a man in the Northern Cape named Gert 'Skaapsteker' Groenewald who had an eland crash through his back windscreen while he was driving through the bush. The dead animal was too large to remove so Gert drove it all the way to Kimberley to find assistance. Unfortunately, he was stopped by the cops in the main street of the diamond mining town and arrested for poaching.

Before it grew dark the men took a stroll along a path through the bush that led to the beach. The place was wild and deserted. In fact it appeared like we were the only people in the area. Standing on a dune overlooking the ocean, Uncle Aubrey pointed out where he would launch his boat and the wide channel that would take us out to sea tomorrow morning. I gazed out at the blue expanse of the Indian Ocean and contemplated a duel with an enormous swordfish of Hemingwayesque proportions.

Uncle Aubrey and Cousin Rattie didn't stop drinking or telling stories until after 10pm when everyone abruptly stood up and went to bed. Despite being exhausted, my senses were alive and I could hear wild creatures outside my hut scavenging around among the dry leaves. I needed the toilet during the night, but thanks to my fear of things that lurk in the dark and the ominous signs around the camp warning us about hippos at night, I slashed out of the window with great velocity instead.

Wednesday 30th June

'Sea's on its head,' observed my father and pointed towards the horizon which admittedly was bumpy.

Uncle Aubrey and Cousin Rattie joined us at the tidal line and there followed a long period of staring at the sea, with the odd soft whistle thrown in when a particularly huge wave reared up before crashing back down in an explosion of foam.

It was generally agreed that there must have been a storm out to sea overnight and that conditions were bordering on dangerous and unfishable. I'm not sure if it was because I am only seventeen or if the boat could really only take three people in stormy seas, but it was decided that the men were going out and I was being left behind. Although I was rather bleak about being forced to walk the plank before even stepping on board, the choppy waves weren't exactly inviting and the winter land breeze was bitingly cold.

The sun rose and my uncle's boat *Skipjack* was pushed off the trailer and into the water. Dad had a hard time holding the vessel steady in the shore break as the waves crashed and boiled about him. He was soon drenched from standing waist deep in the choppy water and must have been freezing in the chilly morning air. Uncle Aubrey lowered the two 75 horsepower Yamaha motors into the water and started them up with a rev and a plume of blue smoke. After loud shouting and waving of arms from Uncle Aubrey and Cousin Rattie up front, my father leapt on board – or at least partially. His waist and legs remained dangling wildly but Uncle Aubrey made no allowance for this and with a grating roar the ski boat charged forward, hurling my father into the air with a screech and dumping him back in the ocean. There was jolly cheering and laughter from the two men at the front of the boat while they looped around to pick up my father who was thrashing about desperately in the water and gasping for air. Cousin Rattie, despite holding a beer can in one hand, pulled

Dad out of the water with the other, and onto the deck. More cheering and shouting ensued. Rattie passed my father his beer and almost magically another one appeared in his other hand.

'Hey, Johnno!' shouted Uncle Aubrey. 'Where on earth did you find this maniac father of yours, because he sure isn't related to me!'

The engines roared again and *Skipjack* thundered into the oncoming waves and flew high into the air with three lunatics clutching on for dear life.

I heard the sickening roar before I noticed the boat marooned on the rocky outcrop where the breakers were crashing down with great force. I didn't know what to do besides running up and down the beach shouting and waving my arms. I could see the terrible newspaper headlines rearing up in front of me:

'Boy Watches as Father, Uncle, Cousin Drown!'

A second before the wave smashed down on the boat an ear-splitting explosion filled the air, followed by a flash of light as *Skipjack* disappeared into a cascade of white. The giant wave dislodged the boat from the rocky outcrop but miraculously it didn't topple over. I could hear the desperate metallic whine of the sickly engines as the boat limped ashore with three ashen faced fishermen aboard. Cousin Rattie made it to dry land still clutching his beer and it appeared that the only injury, a bleeding elbow, was Dad's. *Skipjack* was winched onto the trailer and we inspected her bent and distorted propellers. There was also a long and nasty scratch under the boat but Uncle Aubrey said that was from a previous incident when he had mistakenly ridden over a whale shark near Coffee Bay back in '87.

Dad drained his beer and burped loudly and, perhaps noticing the concerned look on my face, patted me on

the shoulder and said, 'Don't worry, my boy, the fishing will definitely improve.'

Thursday 1st July

Uncle Aubrey and Cousin Rattie were up early with their beers and spanners and spent the morning tinkering with the damaged outboard motors on *Skipjack*. Dad woke up in a foul mood and accused the cleaning maids of stealing his Disprins moments before Mom found them under a facecloth in the bathroom. There were big plans to fish from the beach in the afternoon but a howling wind struck up around lunchtime and fishing was cancelled.

I returned to my little hut surrounded by dense coastal thicket and spent the afternoon reading *Three Men in a Boat*. The Guv is a genius. He always knows exactly the right book to give me.

Saturday 3rd July

Interesting facts learned from discussions with Uncle Aubrey:

- My father sounds like he was a complete loon as a child
- Dad once allowed Uncle Aubrey to shoot him out of a cannon to impress some girls
- Dad's nickname at his Afrikaans primary school was 'Hang Bal'. (Having a nickname pertaining to one's nuts obviously runs in the family.)
- Uncle Aubrey reckons he has a leopard living on his farm
- He also suspects that Aunty Peggy may be having an affair with the dominee

- It hasn't rained on the farm in 9 months
- Cousin Rattie despite the name isn't related to us
- Cousin Rattie's real name is Albert
- Cousin Rattie has divorced three times (twice from the same woman)

Sunday 4th July

In the night I dreamed that I was riding a gondola in Venice. I had travelled back in time to the Renaissance where I cut the figure of a strapping young artist clad in a billowing white shirt and dark beret. For a young man who hasn't started shaving that regularly yet, I was particularly impressed with my bushy moustache and hairy armpits as I paddled down the moonlit waterways between dimly lit inns and buildings with shuttered windows. After hearing a mysterious plop, I gazed into the silvery water and noticed a black marlin riding the wake of my gondola. Luckily I had a fishing rod on board but to my rising horror I realised that it was only a trout rod with a mere four pound breaking strain line. It was sheer lunacy, the equivalent of fighting Jaws on a reel of cotton. Despite the insurmountable odds, I flicked in the orange fly and the marlin immediately snapped it up and disappeared into the depths of the shimmering water. The reel screamed in my hands as the line peeled out. I hollered for people to help me but there was nobody around. By the time the line reached its end the fish was running so hard that my reel exploded in my hands and the gondola caught fire. I woke up screaming and thrashing about in the sheets at 4:30am. I didn't fall asleep again and waited in the darkness for the footsteps that would be Dad bringing in coffee and telling me to rise and shine.

05:30 After some last minute tinkering, *Skipjack* launched and made it out to sea, this time avoiding the outcrop of rocks that had caught her out before. It felt slightly unsettling to be out on the ocean beyond the breakers gazing back at the beach in the distance. Our first task was to catch live bait which proved moderately successful as we captured a few small mackerel but nothing nearly big enough to entice Hemingway's black marlin.

We trolled with the mackerel for two hours and caught nothing. Unfortunately, Cousin Rattie became seasick and had to lie down. He didn't stop drinking his beer, though, maintaining it was the only thing keeping him alive under the circumstances.

The morning wore on and the fishing remained in the doldrums. Dad blamed the Japanese for raping our coastline for its riches and turning our seafood into chop suey. Uncle Aubrey reckoned the water temperature was too cold for game fish while Cousin Rattie maintained that the air pressure had dropped after blocking both his ears with his fingers and gulping in air like a fish.

Just when it seemed that all was lost, one of the reels screamed off in an electrifying manner. It was an immensely exciting but brief moment as a black fin shark threw itself out of the water and crashed back into the sea. By the time Uncle Aubrey had the rod in his hands, the line had been snapped and we all agreed that it was a bad omen and headed back to dry land where breakfast awaited.

Tuesday 6th July

I was sorry to leave camp for the final time after waving goodbye to uncle, aunt and cousin. Zombelo's Neck has been just the ticket (as Wombat would say) and despite the poor fishing, I feel nothing but positivity for the world around me. We're heading home and the thought that the Mermaid awaits sends my inner and outer organs into convulsions. I can safely say, without a shadow of a doubt, that a week away in the bush has cleared my mind, provided much needed perspective, and made me extremely horny. I hope Mermaid doesn't react badly if I feel her up during our first kissing session.

Home, Jerome (K Jerome)

18:00   Just had an intense hour of chatting, feeling up and kissing with the Mermaid although her 'no sex before marriage' motto is proving a tough nut to crack. I fear that I am becoming obsessed and desperate with the physical side of our relationship and she may begin to think I'm a pervert.

Wednesday 7th July

In the post:

- More army call up papers
- A housemaster's report from Viking
- A subject report from each of my teachers
- Application forms to various universities for enrolment next year

Maths (Mrs Bishop)

It confounds me that a school scholarship winner and such a seemingly reasoned and intelligent individual should fail to grasp even the simplest tenets of basic mathematics. I have found John's continued struggle to be one of the most frustrating individual cases that I have encountered in all my years as a maths teacher. Indeed his poor performance this term has given rise to concern that his results in mathematics may compromise his entire matric year and quite possibly his academic future. I have as such suggested the following two possible courses of action to his housemaster.

1. John should undertake an extensive course of

extra maths lessons to remedy his failures in all the various basic disciplines of mathematics.

2. John should consider dropping to standard grade which would unfortunately compromise his future in the fields of science, engineering and commerce, but would guarantee at least his matric exemption and a pathway forward into a lesser field possibly in the arts.

GA Bishop

SPUD MILTON STATES HIS CASE:

I Spud Milton do solemnly declare that I am not a maths cretin as suggested/implied by Mrs GA Bishop above. It is deeply telling that the third possible course of action, which Mrs B has glaringly neglected to mention, rears up like the trunk of the proverbial elephant in the room. Considering her abject failure in teaching a 'seemingly reasoned and intelligent individual' such 'basic mathematics' surely the woman should fall on her sword at the nearest possible moment and resign as a maths teacher.

I would also like to state that mathematics is a very poor subject indeed that scores lowly on the excitement stakes. I suggest it should be removed altogether from the syllabus and left to bearded bean counters and people with bad breath and lab coats.

Furthermore, there are reports from a recently elected house prefect that Mrs B bullies her chaplain husband Reverend Bishop and forces him to dress up in her underwear at full moon.

Spud H Milton

Housemaster's Report (Viking)

It has been a storming term (mathematics notwithstanding) for John Milton. His masterful direction of the house play, where he served the house with great distinction (under my close personal guidance)

241

by bringing home the much coveted inter-house play trophy, was a triumph. Congratulations, Milton.

Unfortunately, the boy's desperately poor mathematics marks are a terrible stain on what is a fine academic record, and it is deeply disappointing to see a marked deterioration in this field. I ask you his parents and John himself to ponder deeply on the situation and contemplate what I and his teacher Mrs Bishop have stated on the matter. I would like it to be known that the school is not in favour of John as a scholarship winner considering a drop down to standard grade. (My personal thoughts on the matter may or may not reflect the above assertion.)

Otherwise, John continues to perform his prefecting duties with aplomb. He is popular around the house, particularly with the juniors, and sets a fine example to all.

If he could just sort out this blasted mathematics one would find only positives to describe this lad. Well done and continue to strive for the greater good of house and school.

V A Richardson BA (Hons) UED etc

My housemaster's report was as close to a rave review as one could ever hope for, and if it weren't for the lingering stench of my maths failure it surely would have been cause for celebration in the Milton household. Instead, I was interrogated by my parents for over an hour in the dining room. They seemed astonished that my maths was so poor despite the fact that it has been dodgy for years. Mom shook her head and clicked her tongue like we were in the middle of a family crisis, while Dad looked suspiciously into my eyes and asked me if I was getting into drugs. I attempted to reason with them. I would probably not even use maths again after leaving school, I said, because I was embarking on a career in the theatre in any case. This didn't aid matters. My parents looked like I had wounded them terribly and went on at length about all the sacrifices that they have made for me over the years. Dad reckoned for me to spend my life 'poncing' about in the theatre would be a terrible waste of a good education and that I should consider going into business instead. I pointed out that my course forward had already been charted in second year when I chose drama and history over science and biology for my matric subjects. My parents didn't seem to know this either. I eventually agreed to attend extra lessons and improve my dismal maths marks at the matric trials. Privately, the thought of spending the coming term slogging over maths books made my brain instantly fantasise about eloping with Mermaid, buying a combi with yellow flowers on it, and turning into a hippy. If she agreed, I would leave tomorrow and never look back.

Exhausted from the interrogation, I retired to my room for an afternoon nap. Attempting to figure out one's own future is a dreadful business.

16:30 I cycled across to Mermaid's and we spent the evening lying on her bed, talking, laughing and studying for our learner's licence test tomorrow. Cramming road signs is a damn sight easier than cramming calculus. Lying with her on her bed in such a relaxed manner made me feel that somehow our relationship has grown more serious and intense. In fact I don't think we've ever been closer.

Thursday 8th July

Marge drove us off to Verulam to sit our learner's test. We were given an hour and a half but it was seriously easy and I finished in forty minutes. A traffic officer swiftly went through my answers and stamped my paper with a large PASS. I was sent to another room for paperwork and less than ten minutes after I left the office, a grinning Mermaid burst out into the sunlight waving her PASS. We are officially learner drivers.

Marge made Mermaid drive us home after taping a white L on her back windscreen. Mermaid isn't a very good driver and stalled the car frequently when under pressure. After a kilometre of people hooting and swearing at us, she burst into tears and Marge had to take over for the rest of the way home. Unfortunately, this took some of the gloss off the morning.

15:00   Mom is in a state because Guinea's Rest has had a board meeting and they have unanimously decided to kick Wombat out of the old age home. The official excuse is that Guinea's Rest has no facility to deal with dementia and that Wombat would be better taken care of elsewhere. Mom did her best to persuade the manager otherwise but he said the decision was final and Wombat has to vacate her unit by the end of the month.

'She's not bloody coming here!' announced Dad less than a second after Mom had hung up the phone. 'And that's bloody final!'

Friday 9th July

First driving lesson with Dad

09:45   'Remember, it's only a pile of metal and rubber,' advised my father as he held the driver's door of the Mercedes open for me. I slid in behind the wheel and felt like a fighter pilot with numerous knobs and switches on display before me.

'The key is to be calm and relaxed at all times,' said Dad as he closed my door and darted around to the passenger side. I wasn't so sure that learning to drive in my father's beloved Mercedes was a good idea, but Dad seemed unnaturally calm and encouraging and it was his car and his decision to teach me to drive so I went along with it.

'You're going to be great, Johnny,' he said, patting my leg encouragingly.

There was a great atmosphere in the vehicle. I had managed to set my seat at the perfect level to account for my slightly short body and slightly long legs. Not only that, I became convinced that undertaking one's first drive in a Mercedes Benz was surely a good omen for one's driving future.

Unfortunately, everything went pear shaped after I started the engine. My struggles to get the car into reverse gear instantly riled my father and he began screaming orders at me and accusing me of being an idiot. His sudden mood swing forced me onto the back foot and I stalled when attempting to reverse down the driveway.

'Arse!' he barked.

I apologised and started the car again before stalling immediately once more.

'Oh for shit sakes!' swore my father and threw his hands in the air like I was well beyond stupid. I informed Dad that his sudden rage wasn't making things any easier for me, but he said that he wasn't angry, only excited. I gave it another go, stalling for a third agonising time. Dad grew instantly livid but managed to bite his tongue and look out of the window with his eyes tightly shut. Eventually I succeeded in reversing us down the driveway and began edging the Mercedes out onto the lawn with Dad shouting, 'Easy! Easy! Easy!' In a bid to change from reverse to first gear I must have slipped into third by mistake because there was another terrible jolt and the car stalled. This was one blunder too many.

'You're in third gear, you prick!' he boomed while thrashing the gear lever around to demonstrate the different gears. Things grew even worse after I finally managed to edge the car between the gates and out into the road.

'Clutch petrol clutch petrol clutch petrol!' chanted my father as if it might help me get my timing right. Out in the street there was so much to think about that my driving went to pieces. How is it possible to see what gear you're changing into when you have to keep your eyes peeled on a lady walking her dog and trying to judge whether the miserable little mutt may suddenly jump into the road in front of your tyres?

'Watch where you're going, you silly ass!' screeched my father.

'I'm trying!' I replied in a desperate voice.

Some brainless old man with no hair parked his car in the middle of the road for no apparent reason. This meant that I had to stop the Merc and then try and get it moving again. I stalled it once more and somebody started hooting from behind. Dad was furious and wound down his window to scream out some nasty abuse. The man behind us hooted again and flashed us the finger before screeching past and tearing off down the road.

'Chase him!' ordered my father while retrieving a hammer from under the passenger seat. 'Let's teach that lefty-pinko a lesson.' Despite the lefty-pinko having turned the corner into Broadway, Dad lunged out of the window once more and screamed, 'I'm going to hammer your bloody face in!' He pulled his head back into the car and hissed, 'Come on, boy, let's pick up the pace.' The car stuttered forward and stalled. My father screamed in agony and looked murderous. I couldn't take it any more. I leapt out of the car without saying a word and ran home. Dad drove alongside me, all the while trying to coax me back in to continue our driving lessons. I took a short cut through a park which threw the maniac off my tail.

If that's a taste of driving, then I'm not surprised there

are incidents of malicious road rage all over the place. Quite frankly, I'd rather swallow my pride and take the bus instead.

Sunday 11th July

I should have used my final day of holidays constructively by working on my maths. Instead, I spent the day madly in love with the Mermaid. When the time came for me to say goodbye and cycle home with Blacky she started crying. We kissed and I promised her that the time until the long weekend would fly by.

'It's a whole month,' she sniffed.

'In four months we'll be free,' I reminded her. She smiled and kissed me again. This time I couldn't resist squeezing her bum through her jeans. She giggled and blushed and said I was naughty. I kissed her again and left quickly because Blacky was doing his infamous worm dance on Mermaid's grass verge.

Monday 12th July

Shopping list

1 jar Bovril
1 block Gouda cheese
1 tin Horlicks
1 tin Milo
1 Nescafé
1 bag Five Roses
3 bottles Bioplus
1 bag Cremora
3 packets pasta and sauce
1 condensed milk
1 Complan
10 Build-Up Energy sachets
2 dumbbells (5kg)

I am officially broke.

HOLIDAY SCORECARD

BOGGO	Read numerous books on leadership which he says are all rubbish. He reckons his own 'punish first, avoid questions later' method is still the best way forward to ensure respect.
GARLIC	Lake Malawi/wind surfing/girl with enormous boobs sun tanning topless on the shores of Lake Malawi/clearer water than Mauritius/best holiday ever/best place on earth/etc etc
RAMBO	Rambo reckoned he only 'chilled and mooched', but the manner in which he said it made one believe that he may well have done the opposite.
SPUD	Passed his learner's licence, hung out with his extremely hot girlfriend, and had a surprisingly excellent foray into the bush of northern Zululand.
SIMON	Went to Paris, Lisbon and Geneva with his family. Reckons Portuguese girls are surprisingly hot despite not shaving.
VERN	Is no saner than before. (Unless of course your definition of sanity is someone who wears his underpants on his sleeve.)
PLUMP SIDNEY	Has returned to school a new man after being dumped once again by Penny, packing considerable weight, and rediscovering his personality. Even Boggo conceded that Plump

Sidney may have shaken off the anorexia-paedophilia for good.

Plump Sidney wasted no time in calling in slaves and instructing Shambles to cook him up pasta and eggs. Small & Freckly was dispatched to find Fat Graham and issue notice of an impending weigh-in, while Rambo ferreted out the Scales of Injustice from the stuffing of the old sofa.

Fat Graham as the reigning champion was weighed first and despite appearances had in fact added over three kilograms to his girth during the holidays. Fat Graham seemed mightily pleased with his tally of 106,8kg and smiled across to Plump Sidney as if daring him to eclipse it. But Plump Sidney wasn't going to take any nonsense from a second year and with a look of extreme defiance he strode forward and stepped onto the Scales of Injustice. The dial shot this way and that before settling on the princely weight of 110,0kg. Amidst wild whooping and slapping on the back Fat Graham was demoted back to Plump Graham and Plump Sidney returned to his rightful Fatty.

Plump Graham wasn't at all thrilled about his sudden demotion and declared it rigged. Rambo added to his woes by issuing Plump Graham fingertongs for questioning the integrity of the Scales of Injustice.

In more ways than one, Fatty is back.

Tuesday 13th July

One by one the teachers have taken their turn to warn us severely about the importance of our trial exams next month. Not only that, they threatened us with a diabolical future should we not immediately commence swotting. Mrs Bishop gave a particularly sour speech and declared our maths class to be sloppy, lazy and dim, all the while staring directly at me. Only The Guv didn't appear to give a fig about our looming examinations because he is so excited about tomorrow's debates. He reckons it's his one chance in the year when he gets to sit back and be entertained by a bunch of cretins. I passed Simon on the way to the bogs and asked him how he was feeling about our debate. He stared at me coldly and said, 'I'm gonna wipe the floor with your face tomorrow, Milton.' I hadn't realised my opposition would be taking things so seriously so I fled back to my room to rehearse.

I slipped in to dinner late and only Fatty was left at our table devouring his third helping of chicken curry. I asked him if he was still going to Malawi with Garlic in the holidays.

'No way,' he garbled with his mouth full. 'Nobody is.'

'Nobody?' I questioned.

'Only Vern,' he replied.

The thought of spending two weeks of my holiday with Vern and Garlic wasn't at all tempting. Fatty advised me to break my promise to Garlic immediately.

'How?'

'Tell him your old man refused.'

I listlessly chewed away at the curry on my plate and considered breaking my word to the Malawian.

'You could even blame your terrible maths marks,' added Fatty thundering more salt down onto his plate.

'How do you know about my maths marks?' I asked in a voice that rebounded off the walls of the great hall and made a harsh echo.

'Everyone knows about your maths marks,' shrugged Fatty. 'It's like the school joke.'

'It is?' I replied with rising indignation.

Fatty must have noticed that I didn't look too happy

about his delighted sniggering and said, 'Come on, Spud, surely even you can see the funny side of a scholarship winner failing matric?'

I did concede that there was a certain irony in my situation, but still, being the school joke for my academic performance in an institution of lunatics and cretins was a tough one to swallow. I gave up on the curry and elected to have tea and toast in my room instead. I worked all evening on geometry and when I was done I had almost lost the will to live.

Thursday 15th July

THE GREAT DEBATE

Thankfully, Simon and I weren't picked to kick off the debates. That honour was awarded to the Fatty/Geoff Lawson match-up in their debate about legalising euthanasia. The Guv wore his tweed suit especially and finished his outfit off with a loud red and yellow tie, and dark emerald green shoes with pointy tips. As was expected, he was in a delightfully jolly mood and declaimed, 'Speak the speech, I pray you, as I pronounced it to you, trippingly on the tongue,' before motioning Geoff Lawson up to the front of the classroom with a dramatic wave and immediately collapsing back into his chair like he had rigor mortis.

Lawson was nervous and perhaps startled by The Guv's sudden rigor mortis as his notepad noticeably trembled in his tightly clutched hands. Arguing against euthanasia, Lawson made a few pertinent points about God and the afterlife, but was too easily rattled when The Guv loudly rang the three minute warning bell and continued chiming it with greater velocity every few seconds thereafter until Lawson's statement ended in a garbled heap of nonsensical words. Fatty reared up to support the motion for euthanasia and in my opinion did a far better job of arguing his case. Using quite a few of his deceased grandfathers as case studies, Fatty came to the conclusion that sending a sick or old person to sleep was far more humane than allowing them to suffer and die in a nappy. The Guv made no comment after the debate was over, but scribbled various notes on his clipboard before calling up Spearmint and Martin Leslie for their ding-dong battle on the morality of zoos.

Simon was called out first to defend the motion of school traditions and initiations. He made a compelling statement, but in my opinion became a little over emotional when talking about school spirit built on his so-called 'pyramid of respect'. I fired back with my three minutes of scathing criticism of some of the school's finest traditions. With only a few sentences left to complete before my planned climactic finish, a furious looking Glock stormed into the classroom and angrily forced me up against the blackboard.

'How dare you bad mouth this school in such a loud voice and in front of all these other boys?' he cried, glaring at me in a murderous fashion. I tried to reply to the headmaster but I was rather shocked at being ambushed during my opening statement by the head of school and very few words came out of my mouth.

'You're a prefect, Milton. How dare you set such a bolshie example,' he hissed, growing red in the face.

'Steady on, Headmaster,' droned The Guv from the back of the classroom.

The Glock swung around in surprise and his mouth fell open when he spotted The Guv seated at the back of the room with his feet up on a footstool.

'Edly?' he shouted. 'What is the meaning of allowing Milton this unholy revolt against the institution?'

The Guv drew on his pipe and examined the riled-up

headmaster like he was a basket case.

'It's a debate, Headmaster,' he replied in his droning voice, 'on school traditions. Milton is arguing against the motion and Brown, whom you missed but will be pleased to know, was very much for them.'

The Glock paled as he realised his embarrassing blunder.

'I didn't mean to intrude,' he said, inching towards the door. 'It's just that I might have had prospective parents with me and that wouldn't have been the sort of loose talk that I would have liked overheard. Particularly from a house prefect.'

The Glock glared at me once more, making me think that he didn't have the slightest notion of what a debate was. Despite having just been told that Simon was opposing me in the debate, the headmaster still demanded to know who was defending the school against my heinous attack. Simon solemnly raised his hand.

'Good man, Brown,' responded The Glock. 'Knock him dead.' The headmaster stalked out smiling grimly, but our debate was ruined and I no longer felt comfortable lambasting the school's traditions with the door open.

The Guv called a five minute break while he went off to the staffroom and the rest of us mingled in the quad and openly questioned the sanity of the headmaster. Fatty's right – The Glock should have been a National Party politician with his anti-democratic scare tactics. Boggo reckons the headmaster had most probably been sniffing glue in his office after breakfast this morning.

After the break The Guv returned from the staffroom with crumbs on his jacket. He brushed them off and maintained that he had been seduced by a delectable female biscuit over tea. The arguments raged on, but it was the debate on limiting couples to one child that brought violence to the classroom. The temperamental Pig spoke vehemently against the motion and reckoned that it was morally wrong and criminal minded to stop people having children. Boggo stood up to support the motion and retorted with a rather clever argument of his own, which leant heavily on statistics he said were from the World Health Organisation but later admitted to have made up. Boggo's fictitious WHO statistics proved conclusively that if humanity continues breeding at its current rate, the entire world will starve to death by 2011.

When it came to the general argument section Boggo became even more controversial when he argued that couples morally had an obligation to keep one child and drown the rest in a bucket. Pig retorted by citing his own family of five children. 'Does this mean my four sisters should have been drowned in a bucket?'

Boggo sniffed rather haughtily. 'It would have to be a big bucket, Pig,' he said. 'I've seen the size of your sisters.'

Pig flew at Boggo who screamed in fear and tried to make a break for the door. Pig grabbed the scrabbling Greenstein by the collars of his tracksuit top and hauled him to ground where he commenced strangling Boggo in a bid to get the population down by one. Before Boggo's windpipe was closed he threatened to tamper with Pig's mom in front of his dad. Thankfully, The Guv stopped the murder in its tracks when he cracked Pig sharply on the head with his walking stick and called for another five minute break.

The final session of debates went largely without incident, although there was raucous laughter during the Rambo vs Garlic debate on capital punishment, with Garlic arguing for and Rambo against the death penalty. The Malawian was called up first and with a bright pink face and gleaming eyes set off with his three minute statement.

'Let's face it, guys, we all need a jolly good thrashing from time to time.' The Guv applauded heartily. Garlic beamed proudly at our English teacher, shuffled through his notes for a few seconds and shouted, 'Oh yes!' following that up with, 'Where would school discipline be without the power of the cane?' He nervously looked towards the door as if fearing that his loud comment might see The Glock steaming in again but there was only silence from the empty quad. 'Ban capital punishment,' he stated, 'and you can kiss school discipline goodbye!' Garlic's three minute statement was met with cackling laughter and insulting chirps from Boggo at the front. Clearly the idiot had confused capital punishment with corporal punishment and was heading for dismal failure. When Garlic finally realised his blunder he thumped his palm into his forehead and loudly berated himself for his stupidity.

In the end, Rambo didn't have to do much to win his debate against the Malawian. Garlic tried to bounce back in the general argument section but loud shouting on about unfair hangings didn't hold water because everybody knew that up until five minutes previously Garlic had believed caning and execution were one and the same.

Friday 16th July

During assembly The Glock raged against silly season for over twenty minutes and threatened that anyone trying any 'funny business' would be dealt with to the full extent of the law. The manner in which he spoke made one feel that he was more than willing to break the law if push came to shove.

Over lunch Boggo called the rest of the house prefects a bunch of pacifists and castigated us for not punishing anybody yet this term when he was already well into double figures. 'Come on,' he implored, jamming the back of his fork into a hole in the table cloth, it's silly season. Let's catch somebody doing something hectic and ruin their life and career.'

'I wouldn't mind taking down Plump Graham,' said Fatty rather bitterly. 'He's got a serious attitude problem.'

Boggo proudly stated that he had just punished Plump Graham this morning.

'Good,' grinned Fatty. 'What did you ping him for?'

Boggo looked immensely chuffed with himself and said that he had given Plump Graham a 5 000 word essay on hygiene for standing too far from the urinal and sliming out the step.

17:00 Vern attacked Near Death again after he caught the youngster sweeping Boggo's room. Rain Man punched poor Near Death in the chest and followed that up by biting his arm so hard that Near Death was sent off to Howick for a tetanus injection. After the commotion Vern continued sweeping Boggo's room like nothing had happened. As I was the prefect on duty I ordered Boggo immediately to resolve his slave problems. Either he had to fire Vern once and for all or, if Vern insisted on slaving for Boggo for his entire matric year, then he and Near Death should be assigned separate duties and work together in harmony. Boggo reckoned that he had already fired Vern three times but the cretin refused to listen, and that it didn't matter which roles were assigned to either of them because Vern became angry and violent no matter what Near Death did for Boggo.

I knocked on Vern's wall. 'Spud,' said the maniac when he saw me. He removed his hand from the front of his pants and held it out for me to shake. I ignored the outstretched hand and warned him about hurting Near Death but Vern played dumb and ended my lecture by announcing 'Side guy!' and pretending to fall asleep standing up.

Saturday 17th July

Revised drama and geography.

Sunday 18th July

Maths, maths and more maths! Quadratic equations may have taken years off my life. Called Mermaid and felt a little better – I sense her voice may have healing qualities.

Monday 19th July

Viking called a house meeting in the common room after prep and a rumour immediately spread about that Garlic was to be made a prefect. The Malawian became swept up by the grapevine and spent the evening preparing his acceptance speech. Thankfully the rumours were unfounded as our rabid housemaster was merely engaging us with his version of the annual shout about silly season.

Viking seems to have become unhealthily obsessed with winning house trophies. With Rambo claiming the senior weightlifting competition and Meg Ryan's Son inspiring the house juniors to a narrow victory over Barnes in the badminton finals, we have thus far collected ten trophies, which equals the house record of 1979. Nobody apart from Viking and Simon seemed particularly interested in this news and yet our housemaster led ten lacklustre applauses for each house trophy won so far this year. I kept my head bowed when he mentioned me and *Toga* yet again. Viking rattled off five more approaching house competitions, announced the captains and ordered them to win at all costs. The maniac pointed at the house honours board with its newly inscribed victories and began chanting, 'More! More! More!'

Tuesday 20th July

15:20   I asked Simon what the sudden obsession with winning house competitions was all about. 'Viking is completely crackers, Spud,' he declared like I might not already be aware of this. He reckoned that at least our housemaster was no longer obsessed with naked boys committing suicide. 'Oh, by the way,' he added rather nonchalantly, 'I kicked your arse at the debate.'

Simon maintains that Rambo saw the scores over The Guv's shoulder. I decided not to rise to the bait and quipped, 'I thought you and The Glock put up a convincing argument.' He tried to kick me in the knees but I avoided his swipe and high-tailed it downstairs.

'Stop running!' barked a voice. 'Come here immediately.' For an instant I felt like I was in first year again and something dreadful was about to happen. But it was only Boggo encamped on a chair at the foot of the stairs with an exam pad, his linesman's flag, and a hockey stick.

'What are you doing, Boggo?' I demanded.

He motioned like the answer was obvious.

'I've set up a speed trap,' he replied.

When I asked him why, he looked at me like I was a moron and said, 'It's the best spot for it, that's why. You can catch okes out 360 degrees, twenty-four seven.' He motioned wildly with his arms as he outlined the different routes that intersect at the foot of the stairs. 'I've already nailed like six okes in less than thirty minutes and it's not even rush hour yet.' Boggo showed me his exam pad on which numerous boys' names had been written along with their crimes, punishments and time of capture.

Boggo's Speed Trap Victims

Name – Plump Graham
Crime – Running down the stairs on the way to the tuck shop
Time of capture – 14:29
Punishment – 4 strokes H stick and fined two Tempos (fine doubled at Fatty's request)

Name – Small & Freckly
Crime – Running down the stairs after being urgently summoned by Boggo
Time of capture – 14:57
Punishment – 1 stroke H stick and cop shop hard labour

Name – Stutterheim
Crime – Running to the bogs because of runny guts
Time of Capture – 15:04
Punishment – cop shop hard labour

Name – Thinny
Crime – Tipping off people about Boggo's speed trap
Time of capture – 15:09
Punishment – severe rebuke, double fingertongs and 3 strokes H stick

Name – Albert Schweitzer
Crime – Running around desperately looking for Spud
Time of capture – 15:13
Punishment – 1 stroke H stick and cop shop hard labour

Name – Spike
Crime – Running on the spot in the cloisters prior to jog
Time of capture – 15:17
Punishment – Severe rebuke, 4 strokes H stick (2
suspended), double fingertongs, 3 000 word essay
on respect and R20 fine (fine doubled for possibly
molesting Fatty's under-age ex)

Vern was keeping watch over the three boys in the cop
shop performing hard labour. I poked my head around
the door to find Stutterheim and Small & Freckly hard
at work scrubbing the floor with Albert Schweitzer
instructing the others and having a marvellous time
rearranging the furniture. Vern stood over them dressed
only in his underpants and brandishing his own hockey
stick.

　'Hi, Vern,' I said.

　'Cop shop,' he replied and turned away to watch
the hard labourers. I closed the door only to discover
a small but riveted crowd watching Boggo preparing
to beat Enzo Ferrari one stroke with his hockey stick
after the first year had stumbled through the house
door after being deliberately tripped outside. While he
was booking the pleading first year, Boggo glanced up
at me with a cheeky expression and said, 'Hey, Spud,
check it out. I just pulled over Ferrari for speeding.' He
sniggered away at his own joke and signed off on Enzo's
punishment. After the beating he ushered the crestfallen
boy into the cop shop and ordered him to join in with
the hard labour. Before the door swung shut I could
clearly hear Vern's delighted announcement of 'Enzo!'

Wednesday 21st July

15:15　I am mildly dreading my future career meeting
with Eve for a number of reasons. Firstly, she is bound
to act all pouty and play terrible games with my raging

libido. This means the entire night is a write-off because I'll end up thinking about bonknometry instead of trigonometry. Secondly, I'm growing tired of having to justify myself as a future theatrical to all and sundry. Why does everybody in this world need to be a scientist or a businessman? If so, who would ever entertain them? Surely my father is living proof that you don't need to have a proper job or any qualifications to drive a Merc. It's like your whole life hangs on this one decision which is ridiculous seeing as though I'm only seventeen and three months old and haven't seen much of the world at all.

17:00   The meeting itself was far better than expected and thankfully I didn't have to justify my career in the arts again. Eve has set me up with an end of term two-day work experience with NAPAC at The Playhouse in Durban where I will closely follow a group of actors in rehearsal for a professional play. I thanked her profusely for finding me such an excellent work experience and she smiled at me in a manner which made me unsteady and slightly feverish. She finished me off when she leaned suggestively over her desk to water her pot plant with a small ethnic teapot.

Before leaving her office she reminded me that in just four months' time my school career would be over.

'I know,' I replied, unsure of how I really felt about my life changing once again. Eve may have sensed my hesitation because she smiled at me and said, 'John, have you considered the option of coming back to school and doing a post matric?'

I shook my head. 'I want my freedom,' I replied and boldly stood to leave her office.

'You still have time to reconsider,' she purred with a devious smile on her face. No wonder they call her Eve.

As predicted, I was too distracted to do any work after that.

Friday 23rd July

It's silly season but silliness is nowhere to be seen. Rugby season is a thing of the past and with trial exams looming and new work piling up along with two years worth of revision, I felt badly in need of an idiotic conversation with somebody. I headed for the cop shop.

I poked my head around the door fearful that I might be interrupting Vern attempting to give himself a side guy. I was surprised and rather deflated to find the place deserted. All the slaves were in prep so I switched the kettle on in the annexe and returned to the cop shop where I set about building a fire. I found matches (along with Rambo's cigarettes) on the edge of the shelf obscured by the curtain. After lighting the fire I returned to the annexe and made tea. The milk was definitely on the iffy side of passable but I braved it all the same. Back in the cop shop I settled myself in my favourite faded blue armchair and examined the fire. Minutes ticked by and nobody came in. (When you want to read in peace the place is a mad house, but when you arrive in the cop shop looking to talk a load of nonsense, the lunatics are all working.)

'Spud!' Vern was at the door wearing a grey polo neck jersey and white underpants.

'Spud!' I shouted back. My imitation of Vern set the cretin back. It was quite clearly not the response Rain Man was expecting. His hand moved to his head and began twirling up a lock of hair. Concerned that I may lose my only companion, I quickly pointed out the roaring fire and that thankfully distracted him. 'Where's everyone?' I asked.

'Cop shop,' replied Vern.

'Do you want some tea or something, Vern?'

'Hot water,' he replied.

The siren wailed for the end of prep and within a few seconds the door flew open. It was Boggo, brandishing his hockey stick. 'My oath to God the Normal Seven will never walk again.' He noticed Vern and me sitting beside each other at the fire and jibed, 'What's this, the annual general meeting of the gibbering idiot foundation?'

He threw open the door once more and hollered, 'Slave! Tea and toast immediately!'

Boggo leant his hockey stick against the wall and collapsed onto the couch. 'Had phone sex with Christine today,' he sighed. 'Gave her three orgasms in eight minutes my oath to God.'

'Side guy,' ventured Vern.

Simon kicked the door open and guffawed at the three of us. 'Ah, the desperadoes,' he chortled and shouted for a slave. Albert Schweitzer appeared. 'Tea and toast,' ordered Simon.

Boggo forced Schweitzer to call in all the other slaves because he said he wanted a conveyer belt of food and tea running for the entire evening.

Rambo came in next, wearing a tie-dyed T-shirt and white long-johns. He appeared to have just woken up and was as grumpy as all hell. He ignored all our greetings and headed straight across to the window sill.

'Who stole my matches?' he demanded in a croaky and unpleasant voice.

I fished them out of my pocket and threw them across to him. Rambo glared at me for an unnecessarily long time before lighting up a Peter Stuyvesant and crouching before the fire.

'Hey!' boomed a terrific shout from the doorway. 'Everyone's in here!'

'Oh God,' grumbled Boggo. 'It's the central African.'

Plaque entered soon after Garlic carrying a tray of tea mugs. Either he didn't notice Rambo's smoking or perhaps he's used to it being his slave. We pounced on the tea and Garlic leapt in to claim the extra cup.

'What a complete ball breaker!' barked Fatty as he pushed through the cop shop door in a bustling bad temper.

'Who?' demanded Garlic, his top lip hanging over the edge of his tea mug.

'Penny,' Fatty cried, lurching into the far end of the sofa. 'I guess she didn't think I'd notice if she invited Spike to her junior social.' Fatty continued bemoaning Penny's two faced behaviour but visibly cheered up when Albert Schweitzer entered with a plate of toast with peanut butter and honey.

'Hey,' roared Garlic, 'how about getting some juke in here?'

'It's jute, you retard,' snapped Rambo.

'I could bring in my ghetto blaster,' ventured Garlic.

'It's like a 1978 tape deck, dude,' said Simon rather dismissively.

Plaque was called in again and ordered to bring down Rambo's Sony mini music system which his dad had imported for him from Hong Kong. Once the system was plugged in a loud and abusive argument followed over what music to choose:

Crazy Eight Music Demands:

RAMBO:	Prince
BOGGO:	Duran Duran
SIMON:	Crowded House
SPUD:	REM
FATTY:	Take That
VERN:	Johnny Clegg
GARLIC:	Dr Alban

Prince's Purple Rain soon filled the cop shop and despite some arousing flashbacks about my Sarah Silver snogage (SSS) I joined the others as we kicked back with our tea nodding our heads at the fire in time to the music.

'Amazing song,' said Simon as the music faded after the final chorus which a few of us had sung raucously along to.

'And she's flippin' hot, too,' added Garlic, looking seriously impressed.

'Who's hot?' asked Simon.

'Prince,' replied the Malawian.

Rambo paused the song. 'Er ... Prince is a man, Garlic.'

Garlic obviously thought Rambo was joking because he howled with laughter and waved his hand like he wasn't about to fall for any of his practical jokes, not today.

'Okay, Garlic,' said Rambo, 'if Prince is a woman then how does she sing this?' He aimed his remote control at his fancy music centre and flicked ahead to another track. I wasn't familiar with the song but it certainly started in a deep and manly fashion. Garlic's moronic grin began to fade and his eyes grew a little concerned and bulgy. Rambo threw Garlic the CD case and instructed him to closely examine the picture of Prince on the back cover.

'How many chicks do you know who have goatees, Garlic?'

The Malawian examined the picture and his half-smile disappeared altogether. His face grew dark pink and his expression contorted into one of terrible agony. In a voice of anguish and disgust, he cried, 'But I once pulled my wire to Prince!'

Mayhem broke out in the cop shop. In fact it was the most that I have laughed in weeks, if not months. I doubt in fact that I have ever laughed harder. Eventually I was laughing at the sheer fact that I was laughing so hard. Even Rambo was laid out on the couch clasping his stomach with Boggo, as always, like a machine gun piercing the laughter of the rest of us.

After the mass hilarity at Garlic's expense, the cop shop fell into a lull as more food and drinks were consumed and I added more coal to the fire. Rambo played REM's Automatic for the People which soon had us reminiscing about some of our more insane moments over the years. We agreed that the spirit of adventure was slowly dying out in the school. Rambo lit a cigarette and said he was deeply concerned by the distinct lack of rebellion about the place in general.

Later, when Crowded House's Woodface was playing, Plump Graham knocked and entered. He had a rather cocky expression on his face. Astounding us all with his sheer insolence, he threw down the gauntlet to Fatty and demanded another weigh-in. Rambo was all set to pull out the Scales of Injustice but Fatty refused the challenge citing general suspicion about Plump Graham's bona fides. 'He could have spent the afternoon swallowing lead sinkers for all I know,' he said, before sending Plump Graham off to the dormitory and threatening him with fingertongs for his impudence.

Fatty has taken a dim view of Plump Graham's recent behaviour and admitted to having had him followed. 'Sidewinder's been doing some surveillance work for me,' he confirmed. Rambo suggested that Fatty may be running scared of losing.

'You figure it out,' protested Fatty, while making his way through yet another slice of toast. 'Plump Graham has only spastic colon foods for tuck, seldom has seconds, and spends no more than R20 a week in the tuck shop.' He chewed meaningfully and added, 'And, he doesn't do gym or weights or anything and yet he has put on like twenty-five kilos this year alone.'

He concluded that only two logical answers presented themselves. Plump Graham possessed granite bones or he was an alien.

An extended discussion about alien sex ensued. This was followed by lively debates on cross breeding animals, unusually tall women, and who possessed the longest penis in the house.

It felt like a night that would never end.

Sunday 25th July

Reverend Bishop had a pathetic breakdown during his sermon at morning Eucharist. While waffling on about his favourite topic of lost sheep, he entered the darker territory of his own personal sins. He then seemed to backtrack somewhat and pretend that he hadn't said anything about his sins in the first place, before asking us to bow our heads in prayer. During the prayer he began weeping, and in a fit of desperation cried out, 'Forgive us, Lord.' The Glock, dressed in his lay minister's robes, quickly jumped in and loudly began reciting the Lord's Prayer while the chaplain gathered himself and readied the communion wine.

After the service Boggo suggested that it was more than possible that Mrs Bishop had forced the chaplain into some warped sex game last night. This he was certain had blown the chaplain's mind and made him thoroughly ashamed. When Garlic begged to know what the sex game was, Boggo, who had by now convinced everyone that his hypothesis was true, refused to give any graphic details. All he was willing to say was, 'She's a maths teacher, she would have gone about abusing the chaplain in a logical manner.'

16:00 Had an extremely long conversation on the phone with Mermaid that's bound to get us both grounded.

Dreading a three hour extra maths lesson with Mrs Bishop tomorrow afternoon. After what Boggo said she did to the poor chaplain, I'm even more terrified of her than the maths. Fatty advised me to pack my compasses. Not only is it a genuine mathematical instrument, he said, but it makes for an excellent weapon of self defence should things turn nasty and Mrs Bishop pull out her straps and leathers.

Monday 26th July

During assembly The Glock announced that the school would be undertaking renovations and upgrades to all the houses and school buildings. He said it was thanks to the generous donation of an anonymous old boy that the school was considering building a new house in the good man's honour. He concluded by stating that his own office would be the first building to be renovated because it was 'the nerve centre of the school'.

Outside on the bench in the sun we wondered whether the new house would now be called Anonymous House. Boggo said he had reason to believe that a Malawian may be the anonymous sponsor, stating that it was more likely that it would unfortunately be called Garlic House.

By lunchtime Boggo's rumour had spread. Garlic's father is definitely the sponsor and Garlic himself is certain to be made a prefect within the week. The

Malawian said he knew nothing about his dad making a multi million rand donation to the school but, after being swept up by the rumours, later declared that he wasn't going to be caught with his pants down, and began preparing his prefect's acceptance speech.

14:30   Three hours of extra lessons with Mrs Bishop were every bit as excruciating as feared, although she didn't pull any of her kinky stuff on me. She went on for ages about what a sacrifice she was making of her time for me and how I was a great disappointment to the school. I had to bite my lip to avoid snapping back with something sarcastic because it's common knowledge that she charges a fee for her extra lessons and it's her dodgy teaching that landed me in this mess to begin with.

If I'm honest, despite all the extra maths work, I don't seem to be getting any better at it. Perhaps all my drinking over the last few years has retarded my brain in that dark corner where logical thought is created.

Tuesday 27th July

Why the school wants us to undertake yet another round of athletics trials is beyond comprehension. Perhaps they are hoping that I'll miraculously begin sprinting like Carl Lewis, or that Vern will astonishingly cease throwing the javelin sideways and nearly killing people. With all the pressure of looming exams and decisions to be made about my future, I fail to understand what good can be gained from making me do the 400m hurdles other than to see whether I fall over on my face or not. I carried out my trials with minimal enthusiasm and a sullen attitude, and my protest seemed to rile-up the powers that be because Mongrel called me a monkey naaier and Viking blamed the Crazy Eight for ruining any chances of him winning the house athletics trophy.

Wednesday 28th July

Renovations on the headmaster's office have already begun. According to a rather rattled Rowdy and Stutterheim, The Glock is now conducting his office work from the main desk in the library. The poor second years were only returning history books to the librarian but The Glock called them over and fired up the Spanish Inquisition. After much stammering and gesticulating, Stutterheim was finally able to convey to me that the headmaster had even asked him if he had had sex.

'What did you say?' I demanded.

'It ... told him the t ... truth, John,' stammered Stutterheim. 'O ... o ... obviously I've had sex.'

I didn't mean to shout out 'What!' quite so loudly but I was amazed by what I had just heard. Thinny, despite his gaunt appearance and acne I can just about accept, but Stutterheim losing his virginity before me is completely unacceptable.

'When?' I demanded, fixing the second year with an accusing glare.

'W ... with my girlfriend C ... C ... C ...Cindy. W ... we've been boning since Christmas last year.'

I realised that he was telling the truth. I'm a disgrace to mankind. I can't even brag about a side guy.

Thursday 29th July

Mom called this afternoon and was overly friendly and interested in my affairs. Doubts were raised when she went on about how much she and Dad have been missing me lately, and I became mightily suspicious when she finally revealed that they were coming up to school on Saturday for a 'nice family picnic and chat'. Something is definitely up with the Miltons and I can bet on it being unpleasant news.

Friday 30th July

In between bouts of laborious revision I've come to the inescapable conclusion that Wombat may have died. Tomorrow's lunch is merely to break the news to me face to face so as not to unsettle me so close to my exams. Wombat wasn't looking at all well the last time I saw her so I won't be surprised to hear that she's on her death bed or recently kaput. Either that, or Mom is attempting to stir up more talk of emigration now that I am just a matter of weeks (17) away from finishing school. While debating what nasty surprise tomorrow's Milton picnic might throw up, my attention switched to the window sill where a grinning pink face was observing me.

'Who were you talking to, Spud?' Garlic asked at a good volume.

'Myself,' I replied.

This amused him because he slapped the window pane with his hand and guffawed so loudly it echoed. 'It's a sign of madness, you know, mind if I come in?'

My heart sank as I realised that the time had finally come for me to break my promise to Garlic about coming to Malawi. He took my resigned silence as an invitation and shimmied up the wall and dived through the window, landing awkwardly on the floor.

'The door is unlocked,' I pointed out but he was too busy rubbing his knee to notice. He recovered himself slightly and collapsed into my chair beside the desk where he examined his injury at close quarters.

'There's ice in the cop shop annexe,' I suggested rather helpfully, hoping that he might shuffle off to find some.

'I once bashed my other knee just the same on my windsurfer,' he said. 'I was just checking that you'd remembered to ask your folks for permission to come to Malawi?'

In an extremely serious tone I explained that my parents were extremely unsupportive about the idea because it was too expensive and too close to my final exams. Garlic looked crestfallen so I focused myself on his forehead instead of his sad eyes and attempted to appear heartbroken myself.

'But September is still ages away from finals, Spud, and my dad said he's willing to pay for everything.'

I assured Garlic that I had argued the case for Malawi with all my cunning and might, but my parents had still given me the thumbs down. Just to add substance to my lie, I cited my terrible maths marks as the straw that had broken the camel's back. He nodded sadly and said that he had heard about them.

'So that means only Vern is coming,' he lamented almost to himself. The reality of the situation seemed to dawn on him for the first time, and to my horror he burst into tears.

At that moment there was an urgent rap on the door and an angel appeared in the shape of Albert Schweitzer.

'Um, sorry to interrupt, John, but Viking wants you in his office right now for an emergency prefects' meeting.'

'Why, what's going on?' asked Garlic, wiping the tears from his eyes with the back of his right hand and fingers.

'He didn't say,' replied Schweitzer, opening my cupboard and disappearing from view.

I was almost unable to believe my good fortune and after another heartfelt apology to Garlic for letting him down, and further abuse for my unreasonable parents, I ran off to Viking's office.

I knocked and entered on Viking's angry shout of

'What?'

'Sir,' I said and waited for Viking to say something.

'Yes, what is it, Milton?' he asked in a rather irritated tone.

'I'm here for the prefects' meeting, sir.'

'What prefects' meeting?' he said crossly, paging through his diary. 'I didn't call a prefects' meeting.'

The penny dropped and I realised that my slave was, as always, one step ahead of me. Schweitzer had lied about the Viking meeting to save me from Garlic pleading and crying. What a genius!

'While I have you in the office, Milton, the headmaster has asked me to sound you out about your possible interest in returning for post matric next year.'

I informed my housemaster that I had no interest in returning for another year of school. Viking said the post matric programme could be very beneficial for people such as me. He motioned up and down my body with his pen and said, 'You know, for late developers.'

When I returned to my room, Garlic was gone and Albert Schweitzer had just finished his late afternoon clean-up. I thanked him for using his initiative and offered him tea and toast as a reward for his quick thinking. He grinned with pride, and sped off to cash in on his prize like I might be on the brink of changing my mind.

Saturday 31st July

After a vivid dream involving Wombat on her death bed and a disturbing yet unrelated dream about failing matric and having to join a freak circus, I found myself dreading the arrival of the Miltons.

12:15 I spotted the white Mercedes approaching at exceptional speed and screech to a halt rather reluctantly as the white gates swung slowly open. I waved and the car flashed its lights in return. Mom was out of the passenger's door before the engine was off and gave me a huge greeting and complimented me on how much I had grown and how handsome I had become in the last few weeks. Dad looked less cheery. In fact he looked downright miserable as he began setting up the picnic table and sullenly uncorking the wine and smashing the packet of ice on the tar road.

Mom kept up her ultra happy demeanour but I wasn't about to fall for this sudden exuberance and river of charm. Something was up. My mother made a big thing about her snoek pâté which she said was the snack of choice for the crème de la crème of society. When I refused a second biscuit Mom accused me of being 'otherwise' and 'morose'. I couldn't take the senseless conversation about pâté any longer so I laid it on the line and told my parents that I suspected that they had something to tell me. Mom immediately denied this and ordered Dad to top up her wine. She seemed wounded that I could be suspicious about their motives and said in normal families friendly picnics happen all the time. I began to wonder whether I hadn't in fact overreacted and that my parents were indeed only here because they missed their son and wanted to share some time with him. I caught Dad trying to whisper something to Mom, but when I asked him what he was saying he denied saying anything and hid his face behind the open boot.

After a silence Dad returned to his deckchair where he busied himself with opening another bottle of wine. After numerous eye signals to Mom he finally admitted that they did have some news. Terrible news. Mom dropped her 'thrilled to see me act' and explained that they had wanted to break the news to me face to face so that I wouldn't freak out so close to my exams. I had of course worked this all out days ago but now that the moment was finally upon me I found myself stricken with fear to the point where I doubted if I even had the strength to stand up.

'Did Gran die?' I blurted, unable to contain myself any longer.

Dad's eyes locked onto mine and he shook his head slowly. 'I'm afraid it's much worse than that, my boy.'

Mom reached out her hand and placed it sympathetically on my shoulder. 'Johnny,' she said, 'your grandmother is coming to live with us.'

Even worse, Wombat was moving into my bedroom and I was being shunted into the lounge.

'The sleeper couch is surprisingly comfy,' Mom added. 'And the hi-fi is there so you can listen to your music whenever you want to.'

'The lounge doesn't have a door,' I said grimly.

'It has the front door,' replied Mom rather optimistically.

I could see that Dad was an emotional mess about this. Wombat moving in has clearly hit him hard.

'She's my mother and has nowhere to go,' sniffed Mom. 'I have no choice.'

I knew that arguing would be fruitless because the decision had been made, but I still pointed out that my exams were approaching and working in the lounge wouldn't exactly be ideal.

Mom promised that Dad would hang a curtain up or make a plan so that I had some privacy. She also assured me that this was only a temporary measure until she had found somewhere suitable for Wombat to live and that it would probably only affect the long weekend next week.

'Maybe I can stay at Mermaid's?' I suggested, but Mom shook her head and said that Marge wasn't very happy about me staying over.

'She's quite old fashioned about that sort of thing,' Mom added.

'So she doesn't trust me?' I asked, placing my mother on the spot once more.

'No, no, she trusts you ...' replied Mom quickly. 'Marge loves you to bits. It's just she's a little worried about ... you know.'

'What?' I demanded.

'She's worried about, you know ... you and Debbie ...'

'Me and Debbie what?' I persisted.

'You know ...' she stammered. 'You and Debbie ...'

'Playing hide the sausage,' interrupted Dad rather loudly to put Mom out of her misery.

'Exactly,' said my mother. 'I think you'll be very happy in the lounge, Johnny. It's one of the nicest rooms in the house.'

'East facing,' added Dad, without much vigour.

After the second bottle of wine was finished, my father loaded up the deckchairs and Mom began packing away the picnic. The snoek pâté had barely been touched.

Walking back to the house after saying goodbye, I found I didn't feel angry. In fact it was generous of my parents to drive all the way up here to tell me the news about Wombat moving in. I could see my mother was greatly relieved that I hadn't freaked out but had taken the setback of losing my room to Wombat with relatively good grace. I thought about staying at school for the long weekend but missing out on seeing the Mermaid would be too harsh to bear. I'll just have to grin and bear it.

Sunday 1st August

As always with Rambo's birthday, great plans and bold statements about a hectic birthday present were everywhere. I found Fatty in Boggo's room after breakfast and they were both in agreement that attempting to coerce Rambo into anything, especially a dunking in the school fish pond, was a bad idea. With the Crazy Eight showing little interest in inflicting some sort of humiliation on the now 18-year-old Rambo, it was left to the Normal Seven to take up the baton. Spike and JR Ewing nominated themselves the leaders of the lynch mob and vowed to pounce on Rambo after dinner and dunk him.

The birthday boy as per usual slept until lunchtime on Sunday and thereafter ordered Plaque to make him a late brunch of tea and an egg snackwich. He only emerged from his room in the afternoon, whereupon he sat suntanning for hours minus a shirt on the house bench and always seemed to have company.

18:20 The Normal Seven made a terrible cock-up of dunking Rambo in the fountain after dinner. Their initial mistake was having too few people (Spike, JR, Thinny, Barryl and Runt) and their second was the obvious way they loitered outside the dining hall while Rambo was eating. Although he didn't let on that he was expecting trouble, he must have been aware that most of the Normal Seven were lying in wait to ambush him. Instead of exiting through the main doors, he sauntered through the kitchens to the junior dining hall and made his exit from there. He dawdled across the quad and was well past them before the useless lynch mob took notice. Barryl spotted him first and, rolling his r's in a deep voice, cried, 'Rambo!' The Normal Seven sprinted towards Rambo who turned to face them down instead of running away. 'Get him!' ordered JR Ewing and led the charge, but Rambo simply seized Spike around the neck and Runt by the arm and began dragging them towards the pond at the centre of the quad.

After hurling JR Ewing, Spike *and* Runt into the pond, Rambo made a bid to catch Barryl and Thinny, who abandoned the cause and high-tailed it through the giant archway and out into the night. Rambo swaggered around the house bench inviting people to take him on. With no takers he strolled back into the house and took up residence in front of the fire in the cop shop.

Later, Boggo goaded Rambo into accepting a birthday challenge. To celebrate his 18th birthday and passage into adulthood, Rambo has to do something radical by the long weekend on Friday. After exhaling a cloud of cigarette smoke, Rambo leant back in his chair with a devious smile and reckoned that bringing the school to a standstill shouldn't be much of a problem.

Monday 2nd August

Endured another painful and laborious three hour extra maths session with Mrs Bishop. I also had a sampling of her dark and sadistic mind games that cracked the poor chaplain last Sunday. Luckily, I was wise to her psychological warfare and didn't allow myself to become rattled by her blatant schizophrenia. Boggo was dead right about her cold, logical ball-crushing tactics. Today she revealed three distinctly different mood states, exactly sixty minutes for each one. The first hour was a rough ride with Mrs Bishop rattling my confidence and goading me for my poor maths skills in general. After softening me up with Mrs Hostile, she proceeded to bring out Mrs Sullen for the second hour, and barely uttered a word to me, even when I asked questions. At the end of the silent hour I excused myself and staggered off to the loo to splash my face, take a leak and psyche myself up in the mirror. I returned to the classroom only to discover that Mrs Bishop had now morphed into the most disturbing character of all – Mrs

Ultra Supportive. Maths is a shattering business.

17:30 I hurtled back to my room bedevilled by the fact that I'm still just as crap at maths as I was before, perhaps even crappier. On the credit side, though, that was my last extra maths lesson for a while as next Monday falls on the long weekend and trials begin the Monday after that. I have fourteen days left to revise and master everything that I have learned since the beginning of last year. Overcome with the monumental task that now faces me I grew instantly depressed and lacklustre and lay on my bed for hours staring at the ceiling with unblinking eyes.

Albert Schweitzer seemed to be rather affronted by my slide into melancholy and forced me off the bed and into the showers. My mood wasn't aided by the lack of hot water, nor Vern trying to hand me a blue chit for bad form in the bogs and surrounds. I returned to my room with heavy footsteps knowing that I had to study tonight but feeling like I was physically and mentally incapable of doing so.

'It's pickled fish and boiled potatoes,' announced Schweitzer returning from dinner and mildly liverish. 'I'll knock up some pasta and sauce,' he added, and left my room before I even had time to reply. Settling in at my desk I was determined to crack on with an astonishing amount of revision. I lunged for my geography file, read a few lines on maize farming in the Orange Free State and snapped it shut. I closed my eyes and tried to meditate but all I saw was a vivid image of Mermaid in white underwear. I realised that I had lost complete control when I caught myself two pages into a passionate love letter that I was writing to my girlfriend. Cursing my own stupidity and probable slide into madness, I tore the letter up and sprinkled the pieces in the bin. My head became heavy and I rested it on the desk. Albert Schweitzer returned some time later with a large bowl of pasta and sauce and must have been quite disturbed by what he saw because he asked if I needed help with eating.

I alerted my slave to the fact that I had lost the will to live, thanks to a deadly cocktail of too much revision and an over-exposure to Mrs Bishop. He said he immediately knew how to cure the problem and commenced rifling through my drawers. While I worked my way through the pasta, he managed to pull out an impressive array of paper and stationery and announced that we were working out a revision schedule. The boy is a great believer in making lists and, weirdly, seems to take immense pleasure in crossing items off with a ruler. My slave divided up the next fortnight into blocks of time. I assisted by shouting out all the sections that I still need to revise for history and was rather surprised when Albert Schweitzer reckoned that he had it all done and dusted.

'It fits perfectly into the time remaining,' he stated rather proudly, slapping the evidence down in front of me.

I pointed out the rather obvious fact that he had filled my entire schedule with only history and I still had another five subjects to study for. This was a severe setback for Schweitzer who suddenly realised the seriousness of the situation. He stared vacantly at the page for a few seconds and softly said, 'Shit.' He wasn't deterred for long. He set to work creating a new schedule that would encompass my full workload and, unbelievably, pulled it off. Unfortunately, the new schedule required me to put in twenty-one and a half hours of work a day which meant ruling out sleep, meals and attending classes for the next fortnight. With the holes in his new schedule horribly exposed, Albert Schweitzer fell into a great depression too. The pair of us sat there in my room staring out at the wall.

'It's not right for there to be so much work,' Schweitzer lamented after a while.

'It's a catch-22,' I said.

'How's that?' he asked.

I explained the bitter irony of spending all one's time in matric working on grasping the present, but it's the past that ends up biting your balls.

Schweitzer nodded solemnly like he understood my line of thinking. 'It's just not right at all,' he agreed. My slave realised that he was on the verge of being late for prep and that Boggo was on duty, so he bade me farewell and sadly but hurriedly left the room.

After realising the hopelessness of my academic situation, I raised the white flag and spent the evening thinking of Mermaid and reading Asterix.

HMS Spud is sinking.

Tuesday 3rd August

13:40 I asked Darryl (the last remaining) why there was an unusually large crowd standing about in the cloisters outside the house after lunch. 'Rambo's doing something radical,' he replied. We were soon joined by Runt, Barryl and other onlookers. The crowd swelled and we waited for something dramatic to happen. Minutes ticked by and just as it seemed that all talk of radicalism was severely misplaced, the Harmless Half-Dozen (HHD) shot out of the house door, noted the large crowd gathered in the quad and hastily disappeared back into the house.

'They're getting cold feet, those first years,' observed

Vern.

Vern's moment of normality diverted the crowd's attention and we didn't initially notice the HHD re-emerging through the house door and making their way nervously along the cloister.

'There they go,' barked Runt and we watched them disappear through the archway. Convinced that something radical was certain to take place, the crowd followed along behind the new boys at a safe distance.

The first years scuttled into the headmaster's vacant office and, after a lengthy delay, reappeared, staggering under the weight of the mounted wildebeest head the headmaster had infamously stolen from Mad Dog before expelling him in second year. The sight of the HHD carrying the animal's head out of The Glock's office in broad daylight elicited general sniggers and sporadic applause from the onlookers.

Norm (I don't believe in spinners) Wade called out angrily from across the driveway and strode towards the Harmless Half-Dozen with serious intent. There was a moment's hesitation where it appeared that the wildebeest head would topple and fall to the ground. But Enzo Ferrari's hoarse shout of 'Run!' galvanised the first years into action and they set off across the driveway and down the grass bank at a surprisingly nimble speed considering the size of the trophy they were carrying.

Initially, Norm (I don't believe in spinners) Wade pursued the HHD across the driveway but soon realised that his gammy knee wasn't going to withstand the chase and hobbled into the administration building instead where he set off the fire alarm. While the Harmless Half-Dozen lurched across the lawns towards the squash courts, pandemonium broke out in the main quad where people became convinced that a blazing inferno had erupted and was sweeping through the school. The wailing alarm and smell of fire, which was later attributed to the ground staff burning dry leaves on the far side of Trafalgar, sent Viking on a panic-stricken yet fruitless search for the house fire extinguisher. (It's common knowledge that Boggo sold the fire extinguisher last term to Rhino McDouglas in return for a Jaffle maker and some vintage pornography.)

Meanwhile, according to eyewitness sources (Runt and Garlic), the Harmless Half-Dozen, realising that their plot to steal The Glock's wildebeest head was doomed, dumped the stolen booty in a hedge behind the squash courts, fled across the railway line and didn't return until nightfall.

But the farce didn't end there because Reverend Bishop, while taking a breather after a vigorous game of squash against himself, spotted the wildebeest head looming out of the foliage and immediately phoned the school switchboard to report a wild animal trapped in the hedge behind the squash courts. This only added to the mayhem in the house and around the main quad where Viking was busy ordering people to gather up their possessions and run for the hills to avoid the fire. Meanwhile, Norm (I don't believe in spinners) Wade was hurtling around trying to convince people that the fire was fake and that a major crime was under way. Further trouble was that Rogers Halibut, in his haste to reach the school and save it from the blaze that wasn't, skidded his car off the road and collided with a tree. He wasn't seriously injured but his accident only heightened the confusion now raging about the school.

Meanwhile, the man who had started it all was peacefully drinking jasmine tea from Kuala Lumpur and smoking cigarettes in the cop shop, greatly enjoying the sounds of distress and carnage about him.

To complete the idiocy, upon hearing rumours of an escaped wild animal, Mongrel loaded his double barrelled shotgun and charged to the squash courts wearing his army fatigues. Believing the wildebeest head was a wild animal caught in the hedge, he ordered terrified onlookers to stand back while he leopard crawled forward to gain a vantage point before unleashing two loud gunshots that echoed around the valley. Mongrel blew the entire face off the wildebeest head and leapt up proudly to inspect his kill once he was assured that the animal was a goner. Discovering that he had in fact shot the stuffed and mounted head of an animal that had been shot and killed three years previously, he flew into a terrible rage and threatened to shoot anyone he caught sniggering about the incident. Mongrel later crossed the railway line to hunt for the Harmless Half-Dozen instead. A further few gunshots were heard from the forest over the course of the afternoon but the first years all reported back to the house unwounded before dinner so it's safe to say that Mongrel's poor hunting form continues.

For thirty minutes Rambo's plan visited sheer Armageddon on the school. Later, when we joined him in the cop shop he naturally took full credit for engineering the entire fiasco. He even managed to convince Garlic that abandoning the wildebeest in the hedge had been his idea from the start. While Rambo smoked and boasted, we listened to a new band called Counting Crows sing a brilliant song about a guy called Mr Jones.

Wednesday 4th August

08:30   Norm (I don't believe in spinners) Wade has been unable to identify any of the culprits from yesterday's wildebeest theft. Wisely, the first years have obeyed Rambo's instructions and maintained their silence.

Thursday 5th August

20:30   Over thirty boys turned out for Boggo's erotic auction in the cop shop so it had to be moved to the common room instead. Up for grabs was Madonna's *Sex* book which Boggo claimed to be finished with. He reckoned the book would fetch a high price at the auction as it was bloody sexy, a collector's item, and not only unavailable in South Africa, but illegal here too. The cunning Greenstein whipped up quite a fervour when he said the book, which nobody other than himself has read, contained graphic pictures of Madonna. Garlic started up rumours that there might also be wild animals involved. The cunning Greenstein hiked up the already boisterous energy in the common room when he threatened to bounce the Harmless Half-Dozen minutes before proceedings got under way. He reckoned the HHD were not only too young to bid at an erotic auction, but not mature enough to handle the 'disturbing' pictures in the book. In the end he pocketed an entrance fee of R5 each and allowed them to stay.

Boggo opened up the bidding at a rather ridiculous R1 000 and there were absolutely no takers. He slashed the price to R100 and a number of hands immediately shot into the air. Boggo's somewhat erratic auctioneering approach saw the asking price vault up to R300 which left only five of the wealthiest contenders still in the race. Garlic, Meg Ryan's Son, Spike, Runt and Near Death stoically raised their hands to indicate that they were still interested. The bidding climbed to R400 where Spike and Runt gave up the chase. The auctioneer, using his linesman flag to gesticulate wildly, raised the bid to R500 and Meg Ryan's Son reluctantly threw in the towel, leaving Garlic and Near Death to slug it out for the grand prize. Boggo raised the bidding to R650 and it seemed that it was only Garlic willing to pay over ten times the book's probable value. There followed some confusion when Vern seemed to enter the race by raising his hand and shouting 'Sex!' As it turned out he was only imitating Garlic but Boggo nevertheless took Vern's interruption to signify interest and raised the bidding to R750. The grinning Garlic shouted 'Yes, please!' once again and raised his hand extremely high as if Boggo might miss it if he didn't. Just when it seemed that *Sex* was Garlic's, Near Death tentatively raised his hand.

'Near Death!' screamed Garlic in frustration. 'Come off it!'

The bidding went on higher and higher with the same pattern repeating itself until Near Death could take it no longer and pulled out, leaving Garlic the sole owner of Madonna's most depraved fantasies for the princely sum of R950. This is more money than I have to my name after ten years of saving.

Garlic was hugely thrilled with his 'score' and after handing over a down payment of R300 to a feverish Boggo, he disappeared to his room and wasn't seen again for the rest of the night. After Garlic had sprinted off to his room with Madonna, Boggo was seen handing over R20 to Near Death and later admitted under constant questioning that he had hired his slave to be a stooge at the auction. Boggo also handed over R180 to Rambo because the *Sex* auction/stooge plan was apparently his.

This place is worse than the Mafia.

Friday 6th August

It wasn't the usual start to a long weekend. This time, there was no feeling of relief to be going home and a large part of me wanted to remain behind at school even if it meant extreme loneliness and going mad like Jack

Nicholson in *The Shining*. To while away the time and hopefully inspire me for the weekend ahead, I came up with a good old pros and cons list.

Weekend Cons

- Wombat has occupied my room with a forced removal
- Sharing a bathroom with my grandmother
- Sleeping (and working) in the lounge
- Dad acting strangely because of Wombat's presence
- Mom being on edge because of Dad acting strangely
- Wombat's unruly behaviour
- More 'debates' on my future career
- Another driving lesson with my father

Weekend Pros

- I get to see Mermaid

15:20 Dad was obviously winding down the clock when he picked me up from the bus terminal in Westville. He demonstrated absolutely no desire to head for home and we only made it back to Milton HQ after dark, having taken a suspiciously circuitous route home via Stanger.

17:35 Wombat was waiting for me in the passage, leaning heavily on a stick. She seemed thrilled to see me in my school uniform.

'Such a handsome boy,' she sighed to my mother. I didn't feel very handsome standing around awkwardly while my grandmother looked me up and down.

'He must be driving the girls berserk,' she observed.

'Oh yes,' replied Mom joyfully. 'You've met his girlfriend Debbie, Mum.'

Wombat nodded like she knew the Mermaid well and

said, 'Lovely girl, that Wendy.'

After being examined and talked about in the passage I dragged my bags into the lounge where my makeshift couch/bed had been pushed up against the wall in the far corner. Unfortunately, the others followed me in. Dad opened the liquor cabinet and commenced pouring drinks while Wombat and Mom settled into chairs and went on and on about how good looking John Major was. Dad slipped in a CD and soon the sound of Roger Whittaker's trumpets filled the room.

'Not too loud, love!' barked my mother while attempting to remain sweet. Dad lowered the volume and handed out the drinks. I made a quick escape to the passage and called Mermaid. There was no answer at her house. Instead of returning to the lounge, I opted for a lengthy bath that saw my fingers and toes crinkle up and only pulled the plug after Dad banged on the door and called me for dinner.

After a meal of Mom's infamous and largely inedible onion tart, I made a great scene out of demonstrating how exhausted I was just in case some bright spark suggested the party move back to the lounge. Dad demonstrated the privacy curtain that he had erected to cover the passage. Unfortunately, the contraption collapsed as soon as he touched it which sent Dad into a furious rage. He ripped the entire rail off the wall and savagely gathered up the curtain before storming off to the garage where I could hear banging and drilling late into the night.

At some stage in the early hours I was shaken awake by my grandmother. 'David,' she whispered hoarsely, 'David! There's a fire in the bathroom.' Wombat had caught me in a deep sleep and I was utterly disorientated and momentarily confused as to why she was standing over me and why I was sleeping in the lounge in the first place. After gaining control, I led Wombat, who was dressed in a brilliant green night robe, to the bathroom to show her that there was no fire. I even opened the bathroom cabinet to demonstrate lack of fire and helped her back to my room and into bed. 'David,' she whispered, 'I think there's somebody else moving about the premises.' I assured her that it was only Dad. 'What's your father doing in my house?' she asked in alarm. I told her that Dad was on a security patrol and hoped to leave it at that. 'Who's after us?' she asked, squinting at me in the darkness.

I wasn't quite sure what to say so I took a leaf out of Viking's book and said, 'Bad elements.' This seemed to strike a chord with my grandmother for she nodded and allowed her head to fall back on the pillow. I thought she may have dozed off so I quietly stood up and began slinking towards the door.

'You're not going off to fight, are you, David?' she asked.

I opted for the truth. 'I've already had my call-up papers, Gran.'

'Don't go, David, don't go,' she wailed, sounding a bit like Garlic's Calpurnia in *Toga*. Thereafter there was a brief period of silence before my grandmother commenced snoring in a loud and wretched fashion.

Back in the lounge I couldn't sleep because the streetlight snuck through the crack in the curtains and lit up my bed. No matter how I pulled and teased them I couldn't shut out the light. I lay awake for what seemed like hours and at last dropped off but dreamed that I went off to the army and had my legs shot off in World War Three.

Saturday 7th August

House Party with Mermaid

19:00 Arrived at Melly's house in Glenashley to discover about eleven girls, four boys and no parental supervision.

19:03 Mermaid introduced me to the legendary Emma and Greg who famously split up but are now back together again.

19:05 Melly handed Mermaid and me drinks and told us that we were far behind everybody else. Mine tasted like vodka and lemonade.

21:30 I found myself entertaining the crowd with a succession of stories about the Crazy Eight. Nobody thought I was being serious about Vern's cretinism, even when Mermaid declared Rain Man to be even more insane than the portrait I was painting. This was the first time that I noticed Mermaid was slurring.

22:15 Mermaid and I shared a riotous snog in the garden beside the pool. When I slid my hand hesitantly over her left boob, she responded by sliding her hand over my crotch and I momentarily stopped breathing, thinking Armageddon was under way.

22:16 A tipsy Michaela and Emma burst into the garden and dragged Mermaid away, citing vitally important news that had to be discussed. I prayed Greg and Emma hadn't broken up again.

22:23 Returned inside to find Mermaid and hopefully drag her back to the garden where she would be more than welcome to grope me further with that same naughty look in her eye.

22:28 Discovered Mermaid and her friends were locked in the bathroom together.

22:35 Found Greg and Kelvin (Melly's boyfriend) playing pool in the games room. I entered boldly and made friendly conversation while they played. The friendly conversation soon ran dry and I watched them play numerous games in silence. They never asked me if I wanted to join in and largely pretended that I wasn't there.

23:05 Knocked on the bathroom door once more and called for Mermaid. There was shrill giggling from inside. Finally Michaela emerged red faced and bedraggled.

'Um, hi,' she giggled, 'I think you'd better call your dad to fetch you and Debs.'

When I asked why, she giggled again and replied, 'Um ... Deb's kind of ... passed out.'

23:10 Dad answered the phone like he'd been startled from a deep sleep. When I asked him to pick us up a bit earlier than midnight he asked me who I was.

23:30 My father arrived and I helped the staggering Mermaid to the car. She seemed hugely excited to see my dad and gave him a generous hug and kiss on the cheek. I guided her into the back seat and she giggled loudly before emitting a loud snort which cracked her up.

23:45 Thankfully, Marge was sleeping because my girl-friend was in terrible shape by the time I guided her into bed.

23:48   Returned to the car where Dad whistled to himself and noted, 'You have a helluva girl there, my boy.'

Three things I now know about the Mermaid:

1. She doesn't handle booze very well
2. She becomes a borderline sexual predator when drunk
3. She passes out minutes after becoming a sexual predator

Boggo would call this a small window of opportunity.

Sunday 8th August

17:00   The sadness of seeing Mermaid off for the last time this weekend was soured by the fact that I had to dedicate my evening to the most extreme case in the history of senility. Wombat has an interview with a fancy old age home called The Caister tomorrow afternoon. Unfortunately, the place doesn't accept demented people so my grandmother has to attempt to appear sane and impress the interviewer. I have been bribed by my mother to conduct a mock interview with my grandmother as a trial run for tomorrow.

19:15   Wombat insisted on dressing to the nines for the rehearsal which was utterly ridiculous considering Mom was dressed in her nightie, I was barefoot, and Dad had his shirt open to the stomach. Wombat berated us for our dress and reckoned we looked like a family of poor whites.

'We are a family of poor whites,' Dad replied.

I put on my school blazer to add some respectability to proceedings and set off with the questions Mom had written out for me. My grandmother answered them all brilliantly and sounded completely sane. Even Dad was impressed with Wombat's cleverness and poured another round of drinks at the liquor cabinet in the lounge/my room while whistling Roger Whittaker's *Durham Town*. The final line of the chorus turned from a whistle to loud singing.

'She'll be leaving, leaving, leaving, leaving!'

Monday 9th August

16:00 Last night's rehearsal was in vain. Wombat completely botched the interview with The Caister. Not only did she call the man David instead of Brian, she admitted to having an affair with Winston Churchill who, she said, was currently double parked on a yellow line on Essenwood Road. Suffice to say Wombat was sent packing. Dad was devastated by the news and although he intended to drop me off at the bus stop in Westville, he forgot and drove me all the way back to school instead. My father seemed very down in the dumps and didn't even take a shot at his up-run record. On the contrary, it was almost as if he was dragging out our journey for as long as possible. He mentioned to me that things between Frank and him weren't going so well and that he was thinking of selling his share in the pub.

'Never get into business with friends, Johnny,' he said solemnly. 'And never live with family.'

I watched the white Mercedes gliding down Pilgrims' Walk in the fading light. I felt for him. The poor man has to return home to Wombat and all her madness. I turned to face the school buildings and I swear I almost heard them hissing me a warning: 'Watch out, Milton, for terrible trials lie ahead.'

Tuesday 10th August

The Crazy Eight have been scarce since returning to school. Rambo and Garlic haven't made an appearance from their long weekend yet, Fatty is hard at work, and Boggo isn't taking any visitors. Simon wasn't exactly friendly when I knocked on his door and asked how his weekend went, and Vern is in trouble with Viking after thumping Near Death on the head with a piece of drain pipe while the poor boy was watching the news in the common room last night.

Wednesday 11th August

I am at peace with the fact that trial exams are a mere six days away and there is no way that I will have the time to revise everything. After hearing how little work I achieved over the weekend, Albert Schweitzer flew into a panic and I was forced to eject him from my room because his desperation was rattling my new chilled out mojo.

Rambo has returned but didn't let on why he was two days late. Garlic is due back tomorrow. Rumour has it that there is a hole in the runway at Blantyre airport which has taken the entire week to fix. The house is strangely peaceful without the Malawian's constant shouting and pleading.

My new chilled out mojo is no more. As if trials being five days away isn't bad enough, I am being tortured by another type of trial altogether. Moggy Mongrel has scheduled compulsory cross country trials for Saturday morning. That's exactly what we all need a mere 48 hours before kicking off with the second most important exams of our lives. To make matters worse, Fatty has been crowing on about Friday being the 13th and how it's the last chance saloon for the Crazy Eight to embrace our spiritualism and access voodoo vibes. For some reason, Rambo is agreeing with him and now a Friday 13th Crazy Eight mission has been scheduled. Surely we're getting too old for these sorts of things?

Thursday 12th August

Garlic has returned and rumours of the hole in the Blantyre runway have been confirmed true. Thankfully, he didn't mention me going to Malawi in the holidays so perhaps he has taken the hint and given up on the idea altogether. Mind you, if Wombat keeps failing her interviews with old age homes, a few weeks away in darkest Africa may be preferable to sleeping in the lounge and putting up with her demented behaviour.

Enjoyed the first hearty laugh of the week when it was revealed that Garlic thought trials were starting the week after next and flew into a terrible panic. After galloping around in shock he locked himself in his room for three hours of hard graft, but when he emerged he was even more distraught than when he'd entered. He reckons Madonna's *Sex* book has been distracting him so badly that he's losing his mind. Boggo offered to help out by purchasing the book back at half price but Garlic refused to give it up, admitting to having fallen madly in love with the material girl.

Friday 13th August

The potent combination of Friday the 13th, silly season, and a Crazy Eight mission had everybody on edge at breakfast. Rambo refused to explain what his ingenious plan was but ordered us to report to the cop shop at 8pm dressed in presentable civvies. Boggo warned of dire repercussions if we were bust but Rambo threw half a slice of toast at him and said, 'Dude, we are the prefects, who exactly is going to bust us?'

THE CRAZY EIGHT FRIDAY 13TH MISSION

20:00   When the moment came, I didn't feel like going. Mist was swirling in the quad and the thought of tearing about the area hunting for ghosts on a chilly evening wasn't at all thrilling. I slipped on jeans and my navy polo neck jersey and reluctantly made my way to the cop shop. The fire was blazing away as usual and I would have dearly loved to have encamped with a cup of tea and listen to ghost stories, but Rambo seemed so inspired one could almost describe him as excited.

'Where are we going, Rambo?' asked Garlic.

Rambo didn't reply and kept up his steady march through the main archway and down the grass banks.

'Will it be spooky?' tried Garlic once more.

'Probably,' came the cold reply.

'Why are we heading towards the railway line?'

Rambo grabbed him roughly by the collar of his jacket. 'Another question, Garlic, and I'll eat your face off.'

The Malawian fell into a troubled silence.

We crossed the railway line under the dim light of the stars. There was no moon and yet there was nothing particularly ominous or supernatural in the air. We waited in the bushes for a car to pass and crossed the main road into farmland on the other side. Fatty hissed us to silence and pointed out into the night, saying that he had noticed a large figure moving away to our left. Rambo trained his torchlight through the long grass, revealing nothing. I could hear from Fatty's voice that he was uncertain, if not making it up entirely in a lame attempt to hike up the general spookiness. A few years ago this might have been highly exciting but without the threat of being caught it all seemed a little pointless.

The path met a dust road and we followed it for a few hundred metres. It was leading us to a clump of trees where we could see lights glimmering. I couldn't be sure, but it appeared that Rambo was guiding us towards a farmstead. A dog barked as we drew closer to the trees and buildings. Boggo picked up a stick to protect himself and we attempted to do likewise.

'The dog doesn't bite, you wankers,' hissed Rambo in a dismissive voice.

A security guard in a trench coat met Rambo at the gate. They shook hands and Rambo handed the man some money.

'Hawu, ngiyabonga, Nkosane,' hollered the guard and opened the creaky old gate.

'I bet you the farmhouse is haunted,' whispered Garlic. Fatty agreed and admitted that he was picking up some seriously intense supernatural vibrations from the place. Rambo continued up the driveway in which large tufts of grass stood up in a middle mannetjie.

'Stop!' hissed Simon. 'There's something on that pole.'

Rambo shone his torch and illuminated a beautiful owl with a white heart-shaped face glaring at us.

'It's an owl!' shouted Garlic, sending the bird flying off over our heads in fright and releasing a piercing screech.

'How spooky was that?' whispered Simon.

'This place is definitely haunted,' agreed Fatty.

'Spook!' shouted Vern while staring up at the sky and holding his groin.

Once again Rambo ignored all talk of the supernatural

and led us further up the overgrown driveway which abruptly came to an end at what looked like an abandoned barn. Rambo popped open the lock and the door wheeled open with some plaintive squeaking.

'Now this will blow your mind,' he promised and we cautiously followed him into the darkness of the barn.

It was beautiful. In that moment I felt so envious that I might have given up my right leg just to be Rambo for a single day. Standing proudly in the centre of the barn, illuminated by torchlight, was a brand new jet black Golf GTI with cream leather seats.

'Anybody up for a spin?' asked Rambo with a smug grin.

'Shotgun!' hollered Fatty, Simon and Boggo simultaneously and a bitter argument erupted over who would ride up front. Rambo bleeped the alarm and slid into the driver's seat. With a healthy roar the engine fired to life and the barn was awash in harsh yellow light. The arguments over seating were eventually resolved by order of seniority. Simon up front with Rambo, the prefects in the back, and the two non prefects in the hatchback boot.

Pulsating excitement was everywhere. Our night had rapidly progressed from lame to insane. Our mission seemed epic, even life changing. Rambo drove slowly back down the driveway and through the open gates. Once we reached the main road he hurtled off and cranked up the music on his front loader Panasonic CD player. An ominous guitar riff thundered about my ears and Kurt Cobain's haggard voice shot us through the Midlands, the cold night wind in our faces.

'Oh no, not me, I never lost control

298

You're face to face
With the man who sold the world ...'

Initially, I thought he was just driving us around to show off his car but once we hit the freeway, Rambo confirmed that we actually had a destination – The Stables nightclub in Pietermaritzburg. Friday the 13th and the Crazy Eight were bunking out for a night on the town. I felt fear, thrill and freedom. In that moment I felt dangerous, like I might do anything and not give a damn about the consequences.

The only thing that I was dreading was getting bounced at the nightclub and letting the team down, but the tactic of walking directly behind Fatty and Rambo with my head bowed worked like a charm and I drifted into the throbbing club without detection. A large sign at the door read:

Friday 13th Pig's Night Spooky Special!! Beers R2 Shooters R1!

I didn't have any money so Garlic fronted my cover charge and I promised to pay him back. The place was full of people dressed up as goths and vampires and with the ridiculously cheap prices for booze I wasn't surprised that everyone seemed to be screaming and going wild. Boggo reckoned the only way we would get into the swing of things would be to engage in some panic drinking and he set off to the bar with Fatty and Garlic. Rambo and Simon were already mingling with a group of vampires near the dance floor and I stayed with Vern where the others had left us. Vern seemed a little mesmerised by the chaos going on about him and tapped his foot in time to the music while working away at a clump of hair.

'Cool place, hey?' I shouted to Rain Man over the din.

'Pig's night,' he replied and pointed at the whirring mirror ball above our heads.

Fatty and Boggo each returned with a tray laden with dark brown shooters.

'Jack Daniels!' hollered Fatty handing out the shot glasses.

We drank so many so quickly that it didn't take long for the world to begin spinning in step with the mirror ball. Dr Alban's It's my Life kicked in and there was a roar of approval from Garlic.

'Dance floor!' screamed Boggo and with his right hand held triumphantly aloft he led us into the mad throng of gyrating bodies.

It was a night of insanity.

Saturday 14th August

07:45   Albert Schweitzer shook me awake with a cup of tea. I felt revolting. He reminded me that it was the cross country trials today and with that news I truly felt like dying. My head swirled with hazy memories of last night. I don't remember the drive back from Pietermaritzburg at all but I do remember Fatty forcing us to investigate the abandoned farm house for ghosts. I have a sketchy memory of horsing about on the railway line in the insane hope that a train would come but I have absolutely no recollection of returning to my room, getting undressed and into bed.

09:00   Viking called the entire house to an emergency meeting in the common room and for a sickly few minutes I thought he had somehow found out about the Crazy Eight bunk-out mission. Thankfully, it was a psyching-up session before the cross country trials which doubles as the inter-house cross country competition. Viking went on at laborious length, explaining that every single boy's effort was vitally important and that it was a test of the entire house and not just a few good runners. He pointed at the honours board and reminded us that with one more success we would break the all time record.

'Remember, gentlemen,' he declared, 'there is no short cut to greatness.'

'Oh yes, there is,' retorted Rambo seconds later in the cop shop where he invited anybody who was feeling hungover to join him in cheating.

Fatty (peptic heart murmur) and Boggo (forgery) were both incredibly smug about having a doctor's certificate. In my opinion, they rubbed the matter in excessively by ordering coffee and toast and lighting a fire in the cop shop despite it being a balmy morning. Their smugness, however, was their downfall. Viking marched into the cop shop and was appalled to see the pair settling in for a leisurely breakfast in their pyjamas when the rest of the house was demonstrating their commitment to the cause. They quickly stood to attention and each produced his doctor's certificate. Viking took one look at Boggo's forgery and screamed, 'What the hell is testecloritis?'

'Swelling of the balls, sir,' replied Boggo immediately. 'It's chronic.'

Viking demanded to know how Boggo could charge up and down the rugby field as a touch judge if suffering from swollen nuts.

'I can get away with it in short bursts,' explained Boggo, 'but anything over a kilometre and they swell to the size of Jaffa oranges, sir.'

Viking eventually gave up on making them run but ordered the pair down to offer support for the house and set an example to the juniors.

The walk to the athletics field nearly killed me and I made up my mind to cheat long before Mongrel fired his starter's pistol and screamed, 'Run, you pinky bastards!'

We hid in the same bush that Mad Dog had utilised so successfully in first year when he hadn't waited nearly long enough and broke the junior cross country record by well over ten minutes. This time Rambo was careful with the timing and we succeeded in jogging across the finish line towards the back of the field. When the results were tallied we came in second last in the house competition and an irate Viking was seen furiously and repeatedly kicking the dust under a tree and then stalking off home in a huff.

I promised to allow myself a two hour nap to right the ship, but ended up snoozing all day. After a scorching hot shower and dinner I felt utterly refreshed and ready to hit the books. Unfortunately, *Arthur* starring Dudley Moore, John Gielgud and Liza Minnelli was the Saturday night movie so I allowed myself to watch the first half an hour, intending to crack on with the revision thereafter. I ended up watching the entire film because Dudley Moore was hilarious. I still planned to work late into the night revising English lit and possibly a smattering of the Russian revolution of 1917. But then Rambo brought out the Scales of Injustice and Fatty and Plump Graham had another weigh-in which Fatty narrowly won by 700 grams. The cop shop was buzzing with laughter and stories and I just couldn't drag myself away.

I'm in trouble.

Sunday 15th August

Exams begin tomorrow. If my spotting isn't correct I fear a massacre approaching.

16:00 Mermaid called to wish me luck. It was the only bright spot in a very dark day. Her trials begin on Friday and she sounded rather down about her chances.

During Evensong I prayed for clarity of mind and the energy to get me through. I didn't ask for my spotting gambles to come up because I thought that might be tempting fate.

Friday 27th August

Spud Milton narrowly survives trials!

EXAM RECAP

My hand is arthritic from over writing so Albert Schweitzer kindly supplied the following:

Subject	Difficulty Rating/10	Comments
History	4/10	Straightforward
Geography	6/10	A couple of unexpected questions
Maths / Algebra	9/10	Torrid
Maths / Geometry	10/10	Far worse than torrid!
English / Literature	2/10	A breeze
English / Language	3/10	Cool
Drama	4/10	Simple but long
Afrikaans	7/10	Taxing

Boggo riled the rest of the prefects by accusing us of dropping the ball during exams. 'We haven't had anyone beaten in weeks,' he said. He reckons that the house is running amok before our very eyes and that certain individuals are laughing in our faces with their blatant criminality. He claims to have secured Viking's permission to conduct an intensive house search during prep tonight to weed out the rotten apples, punish them harshly, and save this silly season from being the lamest in living memory.

'My oath to God tonight is going to be bigger than Nuremburg,' declared Boggo with some finality, before flooring his Oros and striding from the dining hall with a look of deadly intent.

19:30   The prefects' search party was joined by Vern and Garlic who thought the entire event to be the equivalent of a murder investigation. The Malawian kept shouting 'Busted!' the moment he found anything that could be construed as even remotely dodgy. Vern spent most of the hour-long search desecrating Near Death's bed and possessions. Among other acts, the cretin ground salt into the poor boy's sheets, licked his tuck, and ate most of his toothpaste. Boggo was ecstatic with the results of the search, reckoning that we had gone a long way to redeeming our respect. The inspired Greenstein led us back to the cop shop where he wrote out his lengthy charge sheet listing the irregular items found in each boy's cubicle, and triumphantly stuck it to the wall.

Busted
Spike – a clear bottle of alcohol (gin?) inside his rugby boot
Enzo Ferrari – three fake IDs
Rowdy – a silver suitcase of theatre sound equipment

To be interrogated
Plaque – one of Rambo's first team rugby socks
Darryl (the last remaining) – porn mag of women with

freak boobs
Albert Schweitzer – framed picture of young boy
Shambles – Playboy magazine
Plump Graham – lack of tuck
Meg Ryan's Son – bottle of hydrogen peroxide
Thinny – 108 condoms
JR Ewing – Small & Freckly, discovered under his bed

Shady but legal
Small & Freckly – unnecessarily large jar of Vaseline
Near Death – a pair of stone washed jeans
Stutterheim – suspicious looking cream called Funganex
Runt – numerous body building magazines
Barryl – a plastic bag containing his own hair

Boggo's interrogation of Plaque went on for half an hour despite the boy pleading that Rambo's rugby sock had merely become entangled in his own laundry. Eventually Rambo grew tired of the constant questioning and told his slave that he was free to go. Boggo was incensed with the let-off and accused Rambo of being a soft touch and showing bias.

'Call in the last remaining Darryl,' ordered Boggo and the door flew open.

Simon thrashed Darryl (the last remaining) two strokes with a cricket bat for being in the possession of pornography. The sentence was initially four strokes but Boggo demonstrated rare leniency after reluctantly admitting that he had sold the pornography to Darryl (the last remaining) in the first place.

Albert Schweitzer became quite rattled when Boggo accused him of keeping his boyfriend's picture in his locker. When the blushing Schweitzer declared the boy in the picture to be his brother Anthony, Boggo promptly accused him of incest. In the end he wasn't beaten but Boggo instructed him to write a five page essay on why girls are hotter than boys. My slave left feeling ashamed and I told Boggo to take it easy on the first years. He snorted like a machine gun and reckoned Schweitzer and I were probably bum chums. I didn't bother to reply.

Shambles was beaten two by Simon after he pleaded guilty to owning the porn mag under his mattress. Once again, it had been purchased from Boggo.

Fatty took over the interrogation of Plump Graham while Boggo had a break from his high intensity cross examinations to drink tea and eat toast. Plump Graham was put on the spot immediately when Fatty demanded to know how he was able to weigh 113kg when he had not a stitch of tuck in his locker. Plump Graham didn't appear very concerned by Fatty's questioning and used his usual excuse of having heavy bones.

'How can your bones have put on 4 kilograms in a fortnight?' demanded Fatty, pointing at Plump Graham with Simon's cricket bat and beginning to lose his cool. Plump Graham shrugged, seemingly enjoying Fatty's growing irritation. He even laughed when Fatty accused him of having a freak spleen that could cover the surface area of Belgium. The ultimate indignity was when Fatty ordered Plump Graham to be beaten but was overruled by the rest of us. Even Boggo agreed that you can't thrash someone for having no tuck in their locker. Plump Graham was released without punishment but before he left the cop shop Fatty grabbed him roughly by the shirt and hissed, 'I'm gonna get you, Plump Graham, my oath to God I'm going to bust your scam if it's the last thing I do!'

Meg Ryan's Son admitted to owning the hydrogen

peroxide which he said he had bought at a pharmacy in Randburg over the long weekend.

'Which pharmacy?' demanded Boggo, now well rested and back to his aggressive prosecuting.

'The pharmacy near my house,' was the reply.

'Give me a name, Meg Ryan's Son, I want a name!'

'Link Pharmacy,' replied Meg Ryan's Son hesitantly.

Boggo bored into the second year's eyes like he was searching for the merest glimmer of untruth in his soul. Abruptly he said, 'I believe you,' and paused for a sip of tea. Meg Ryan's Son said he used the peroxide on his hair to make it blonder and score more chicks.

'So you're not a real blond then?' blurted Garlic.

'Just like his mom,' added Fatty through a mouthful of toast.

Simon thrashed Meg Ryan's Son one stroke with his cricket bat for vanity and harbouring potentially dangerous fluids.

Thinny's explanation for needing 108 condoms because he enjoyed boning didn't stand up to scrutiny. In fact it aroused raucous laughter at the acne ridden bean pole with an inflated ego. While Boggo applauded Thinny for his commitment to safe sex, he nevertheless found him guilty of gross arrogance, having a condom fetish, and wiping out the sanatorium's supplies which could be better used by people who really do have tons of sex – such as himself.

JR Ewing didn't seem very surprised that we'd discovered Small & Freckly hiding under his bed. He was rather nonchalant about the matter and reckoned Small & Freckly has been doing it all year.

'What!' exclaimed Fatty in utter confusion.

'He mostly just sleeps there when he's feeling nervous,' added JR, like it made little difference to him either way.

'So you like sleeping on a slave then?' goaded Boggo to no effect whatsoever.

'As long as he doesn't snore or wake me up, it doesn't bother me.'

Nobody knew quite what to make of all this so Small & Freckly was summoned to state his case before the prefects. The boy was nowhere to be found.

'He's probably under my bed again,' said JR Ewing helpfully. Sure as eggs, the boy was found sleeping under JR Ewing's bed and was hauled straight to the cop shop.

Small & Freckly was extremely nervous and under a barrage of questions from Boggo soon appeared to be hyperventilating. All we could glean from the boy is that he sleeps under JR Ewing's bed for safety because JR plays for the first team and nobody will mess with him. Boggo asked him why he didn't sleep under Rambo's bed if he wanted security.

'Because Mr Rambo might eat me,' replied the boy with great earnestness. All eyes turned to Rambo reclining in his armchair beside the fire. Rambo shook his head and said, 'I'll eat Garlic, but I'm not mad about ginger.' It was agreed that the case was too bizarre to hand out punishments so the boys were sent packing and we were left scratching our heads.

'I guess it's official,' sighed Simon once the boys were gone. 'Small & Freckly is the new Vern.'

Enzo Ferrari was thrashed by Simon for his fake IDs and the final two offenders, Spike and Rowdy, will be reported to Viking tomorrow morning for their sins of theft and alcohol possession.

It was close to 11pm and for a brief moment it seemed that Boggo's reign of terror was over until he announced that it was only right that Vern and Garlic's rooms be searched too, as they were non-prefects and as such couldn't be trusted. Vern looked terribly guilty when Boggo and Fatty rifled through his cupboard but aside from a suspicious stain on the ceiling he was given the all clear.

In Garlic's room Boggo immediately spotted Madonna's book lying open on the desk. 'Ah ha!' said Boggo pointing his bony finger at a picture of Madonna tied up in chains and wearing only black suspenders. 'And what might this be?'

Garlic chuckled because he thought Boggo was joking, but his good humour faded quickly when Boggo found Garlic guilty of harbouring illegal pornography and confiscated the book.

'But I paid you a thousand bucks for it!' shouted Garlic growing decidedly pink. Boggo denied all knowledge of book or auction, and threatened Garlic with a savage beating and a lawsuit should he attempt to take it back. The Malawian was distraught and commenced with some desperate pleading. 'I love her!' he shouted down the stairs, causing further hilarity. Back in the cop shop Boggo discovered an un-posted letter written by Garlic hidden in the back sleeve of *Sex*.

Dear Mrs Madonna
    It's Garth again, I was just writing this to check that you got my previous letters which I sent to the fan address at the back of your book SEX – which is truly excellent by the way. It's easily the best book I've ever read despite it having not that many words in it. Still the pictures are awesome and (I hope you don't mind me saying so but ...) they frequently give me a boner when I should be studying for biology or geography or English or something else. And you sing as well! Your song Like a Virgin sounds incredibly naughty. By the way I am a virgin too, how's that for a coincidence!!!
    As I said in previous letters, I come from Malawi. You ever

been to Malawi? The Lake is massive and you would love it. People can never believe how clear the water is. It's the best country in the world – by far – although they tell me America where you come from is very good as well.

Please write back soon and I'm serious, you should be asking yourself, why not come to Malawi? I double dare you!

Lots of Love

Garth Garlic (Matric)

PS: I see by a few of your pictures in the book that you like kissing hot girls. I just want you to know that although I am a confirmed Christian, I have nothing against girls kissing other girls because I understand it's totally natural.

Sunday 29th August

11:00 Viking was thrilled that Boggo had ferreted out two errant boys during the silly season. It was almost as if he was itching to punish somebody and now with two serious crimes landing on his doorstep he flew into a rage so powerful that even three closed doors and a pillow over my head couldn't keep out the rampage. Fatty was ecstatic that Spike was on the verge of following in the footsteps of his vile older brother and being expelled. It seems Viking was unsure what type of alcohol had been discovered in Spike's rugby boot so he took numerous sips of the liquid until there was barely anything left in the bottle. He eventually declared it to be gin which Rambo could have told him just by sniffing it. Spike is already sitting on a final warning and it seems a foregone conclusion that he will be forced to pack his bags and hit the road.

Investigating Rowdy's offence of stealing an entire suitcase of expensive sound equipment from the theatre proved a tougher nut for the housemaster to crack. Despite Viking's hideous verbal abuse Rowdy, true to form, said absolutely nothing.

'Answer me, boy!' mimicked Vern outside the common room where an intrigued crowd had gathered to follow Viking's ranting and Rowdy's silent retaliation. Our housemaster's controversial tactic of beating Rowdy six strokes to make him sing didn't work. Rowdy remained stubbornly silent. Further silence forced our housemaster into attempting an unusual method of attack. As Simon sagely noted, if Viking had attempted this new gentle tack initially, it may well have yielded results. Even Vern could see the folly in thrashing Rowdy first and asking soothing questions later, because he circled his finger around his head like he thought Viking was nuts.

14:30   Rambo was away with his car this afternoon so Garlic was roped in to make up a fourth at the tennis courts. After a typically complex process of drawing lots from under the grip of Boggo's tennis racket it was decreed that Fatty and Boggo would team up against me and the Malawian. Despite the events of Friday night, Garlic was in an excellent mood and his tennis game was surprisingly good too. He admitted to being over the sudden loss of Madonna and no longer in love with her.

'Look, she still turns me on like a light switch,' he admitted, but shrugged as if it was just one of those things.

We thrashed Boggo and Fatty 6-3, 6-1 and after the game Garlic gave me a meaty high five and shouted, 'We did it, partner!' The opposition squabbled all the way back to the house over who was to blame for the defeat. When they couldn't agree, they accused us of cheating.

Monday 30th August

Rowdy has been let off for his sound equipment thievery by The Glock after Eve came through and saved the day. She admitted to the headmaster that after the house plays at the end of last term she had instructed Rowdy to pack up and take care of the sound equipment. She had assumed Rowdy would pack it away in the AV room but he had misinterpreted her instructions and hidden the equipment under his bed (?)

Boggo claimed Eve's intervention was a stitch up to save Rowdy's bacon and was gutted that he hadn't scored the first expulsion of his prefectship. He was somewhat comforted, however, by the fact that Rowdy had been the first boy in living memory to be caned six for keeping silent.

The bottom line – Rowdy got lucky. And if Runt is to be believed, Spike also got lucky and has merely been placed on Absolute Final Warning. How do these Pikes get away with it?

I'm off to the NAPAC Playhouse next Monday for a two day taste of what life in professional theatre is all about. Perhaps I can impress people when I'm there and will be offered a contract to join the theatre company. This could be the biggest break of my career yet. I became so excited about the thought of spending two days inside the greatest theatre complex in the province that I was only semi aroused when I left Eve's office.

Wednesday 1st September

Grim, cloudy weather welcomed in the first day of spring. School is a waiting game:

9 days until the holidays

Thursday 2nd September

Viking summoned the Crazy Eight to an urgent meeting in the common room after dinner.

'Gentlemen,' he began, 'let me start by saying that this is the most interesting senior year that I have ever had the pleasure to housemaster.' He conceded that most of us were as mad as snakes but maintained that we had thus far worked as a team and led the house with distinction. He reckoned the record equalling heroics in house competitions this year was a testament to the way in which he (and us) had led the house without fear or favour. We were all a little nonplussed by our housemaster's compliments which made for a change from his usual violent insults and frothing at the mouth.

'We heartily deserve this marvellous reward for all our endeavours,' he continued, rocking backwards and forwards on the balls of his feet, 'and by God what a great reward we shall soon be enjoying.' I glanced at the others. Talk of great rewards illuminated Boggo's face and even Rambo leaned forward slightly in anticipation of what great stroke of fortune awaited us.

'Your parents have been notified and have granted their permission ...' I imagined a conversation between Viking and my mother over the telephone with her nodding, grinning and repeating, 'Not a problem.' Go, Mom.

'... I myself and Mr Edly will be overseeing this tour of a lifetime and making sure that you keep up the highest standards.'

I felt shivery with excitement at the thought of travel to an unknown destination. For some reason Borneo came to mind.

313

'All expenses paid, and I have been assured that our every whim will be catered for. However, although a scintillating holiday, this will also be a trip of charity and goodwill.'

It just seemed to get better and better. It felt like God was bestowing on me a great gift for passing all the trials that I have encountered in this place.

'The value of every single cent spent on the trip shall be donated to a local school charity. And as such it shall be compulsory for all of you.'

On a compulsory tour with the Crazy Eight, The Guv and Viking – that can't be all that bad.

'For which we are eternally thankful to one boy and his parents who have come up with this brilliant and generous idea.'

I was so swept up in the moment that I wondered which boy's parents were insane or rich enough to pay for us all to go on a magical holiday together. The answer wasn't long in coming.

'Pack your bags, gentlemen,' Viking roared, a great beaming grin spreading across his bearded face, 'for in a mere eight days we depart for Malawi!'

'Oh fuck,' gasped Rambo and covered his face with his hands.

'What's that, Black?' Viking snapped.

'Nothing, sir,' groaned the shattered Rambo. 'I just said what a slice of luck.'

'Indeed it is,' replied Viking. 'Indeed it is.' Then he handed out our flight tickets and itinerary while we all sat dumbfounded in our chairs wondering how this had ever been allowed to happen.

'Garlic,' said Viking in the most gentle of his voices, 'may I once again take this opportunity to thank you and your parents on behalf of all of us for the hard work and unrelenting single-mindedness you have displayed in putting together such a sensational tour.'

With another elated grin, Viking turned on his heel and strode out of the common room.

'You guys are going to love Lake Malawi!' shouted Garlic, leaping out of his chair with unrestrained delight. As one, we pounced on him, but he was too quick and squirmy for us. He bolted out the door, galloped across the quad whooping like a madman and disappeared through the great archway before anyone had a chance to catch him. The rest of the Crazy Eight filed into the cop shop in stunned silence, still wondering how Garth Garlic had managed so cunningly to outwit us all.

19:00 Simon instructed everyone to call home and double-check that Viking and Garlic weren't bluffing. Mom confirmed that she had spoken to both Viking and Garlic's dad, whom she called a wonderful and generous man.

'It's probably just as well, Johnny,' she added, 'because Gran is still in your room.'

I asked my mother if this was permanent, but she said a suitable place for Wombat was bound to turn up soon. It was hardly convincing.

After the call I didn't feel so bad about being hoodwinked into a free holiday in Malawi. I suppose there could be worse things to have happen to a person.

21:15 Boggo made a desperate effort to excuse himself from the Malawi trip, informing our housemaster that his swollen ball syndrome could erupt mid flight and that he sadly had to cancel. This backfired spectacularly when Viking said he would book Boggo a seat on a bus to Blantyre, a ride of some 42 hours. Boggo wisely opted to double his medication and risk the flight instead.

Friday 3rd September

I didn't sleep very well, what with the trials marks coming out this morning and the dark shadow of maths circling my mind like a hungry vulture. While sauntering across the quad on the way to breakfast with Fatty, Boggo charged past us looking flushed. 'History marks have just been posted and I got an A!' he announced and raced off towards the house. In an instant breakfast was forgotten and Fatty and I set off to the history department where an urgent crowd had gathered to survey the list.

History – A!

Fatty was chuffed with his B and we shook hands, happy with an excellent start. We were about to make tracks for the dining hall when Gomez Simpson hollered down news from the bell tower where he was raising the Barnes House flag that the Afrikaans marks had been posted last night and they were shocking. With rising dread we were off again. Fatty kept up a surprisingly rapid pace despite the terrible gasping sound that he was making in his throat. We eventually made it to the Afrikaans department where a far smaller crowd was gathered.

Afrikaans – C

Fatty also scored a C which he was more thrilled about than I was. Still, it could have been worse and, besides, Afrikaans is practically a semi-foreign language for Durbanites. Then Scum Rogers swore on his life that the maths marks had been posted, too, so we hared off once more with Fatty falling well behind, such was my terrible desperation to get it over with. Unfortunately, Scum was taking the piss and maths hadn't been posted yet. Fatty and I arrived late for breakfast and with all the sprinting around all I could manage was orange juice and a spoon of granadilla yoghurt.

Drama – A
English – A
Geography – B

One by one the results trickled in until maths was the only subject outstanding. Typically, Mrs Bishop was holding back the marks until last, no doubt to wear us down mentally. She eventually posted the results just as it was getting dark and I was bummed to see that I only scored an E. Not quite a fail, but pretty close to it. This means all the hard work and extra lessons have been a complete and utter waste of time and I'm just as vermin at maths as I was last term. It was a real let-down to otherwise solid marks and I would be lying if I said that I wasn't disappointed.

At least if I had done no work then I could shrug and put my E for maths down to neglect, but after grafting so hard I can only come to the conclusion that there is something wrong with my brain. I feel stupid.

Sunday 5th September

13:30   Instead of playing tennis with Boggo, Fatty and gloating Garlic, I strolled down Pilgrims' Walk and crossed the bog stream. The Guv had just finished lunch and his kitchen looked like a bomb had gone off. I asked him what he had knocked up. 'Tuna sandwich,' was the reply. He noticed me surveying the catastrophe of his kitchen and added, 'I scored a narrow victory after a lengthy tussle with the tin opener.'

I nodded in sympathy.

'So it's off to Nyasaland for us, Milton!' The Guv declared, pouring me a cup of tea. I explained how Garlic had hoodwinked us all into the holiday and he chuckled heartily. 'He'll do well, that Garlic, for it is the destiny of this world to underestimate him.' He drew himself up to his full height and with an astonished expression, said, 'Are you aware that he scored a very polished B for English?' We shook our heads in disbelief. 'He's a bit of a pink Houdini if you ask me,' added The Guv which made me laugh like a maniac.

Spread out on the dining room table were a number of open books on Malawi. One was called *Lake of Stars*, another simply entitled *Livingstone*, and yet another called *Livingstone's Lake*.

'Very intriguing man, this Livingstone,' The Guv remarked. He asked me if I was aware that the city of Blantyre was named after Livingstone's birthplace in Scotland. I nodded and said that Garlic had already told us that. 'Of course he has,' he replied.

He congratulated me on my fine results in the English trials. I thanked him but said that they had been overshadowed by bagging an E for maths after working at it like a slave for the past six weeks.

'We all need an Achilles heel, old boy, it's what keeps us interesting.'

I asked The Guv what his Achilles heel was. 'I have several,' he told me, 'three of which are ex wives.'

When I informed him that I was off to Durban tomorrow for work experience at NAPAC he cried, 'Break a leg, Milton, and don't let anybody roger you in the toilets.'

Monday 6th September

WORK EXPERIENCE DAY 1

Highlights

- The Playhouse in Durban is a beautiful complex
- I enjoyed a personalised tour around the entire building
- Was blown away by the epic nature of the opera theatre
- Free coffee and lunch in the coffee shop
- I met a troop of extremely pretty ballet dancers in the foyer
- Being introduced to the head of NAPAC
- Was allowed free run of the place after 3pm
- Nobody tried to roger me in the toilets

Lowlights

- Monday is a day off for actors and artists so nobody creative other than the dancers were around
- The head of NAPAC advised me to avoid becoming an actor unless I dreamed of being poor and destitute (hardly the kind of attitude that I was expecting from the boss of a performing arts council)
- Having an embarrassing knack jump when greeting the troop of pretty ballet dancers in the foyer
- Becoming lost and panicked after enjoying the free run of the place after 3pm
- The abusive drunk man in Smith Street who screamed blue murder at me for no apparent reason as I was getting into Dad's car

- Dad trying to swat the madman with the Merc's logbook just as the ballet dancers exited down the stairs of the Playhouse

Tuesday 7th September

WORK EXPERIENCE DAY 2

Observations of a read-through rehearsal of a professional play *The Coal Miner's Daughter* by Gregory Maynard:

Observation 1:	So as to avoid sniggering and mockery from intellectual types, it may be necessary to change my name.
Observation 2:	Theatricals have numerous coffee breaks.
Observation 3:	There will be no easy rides when it comes to earning a living in the theatre. By the sound of things the entire world is out to schnaai you.
Observation 4:	If you walk out of a rehearsal room and you're the director, chances are you're being slagged off.
Observation 5:	Playwrights get all the glory and all of the chicks, even if they have greasy hair and a hooked nose.

Wednesday 8th September

WORK EXPERIENCE SCORECARD

SPUD	A revealing two days on the state of theatre in South Africa. Despite a life of certain poverty, I have decided to become a playwright/actor and use this cachet to seduce

numerous actresses and become locally famous.

RAMBO

Was flown to Cape Town to experience two days in parliament after conning Eve into believing that he wanted to become president. Typically, he didn't even show his face in Parliament and spent two days on a bender in the mother city with two friends he called Johnny the Jackal and Steve the Sleeve.

FATTY

Had a relatively tedious time working at the Natal Museum in Pietermaritzburg. He said the man in charge was an old timer called Humphrey who was continually harsh about Fatty's weight. He reckons old man Humphrey wouldn't let him anywhere near any of the rare exhibits because he was worried that Fatty might crush or eat them.

GARLIC

Worked at the sailing club at Midmar dam. Apparently there wasn't a single sailor around on the first day so he and the manager sat around telling stories. On the second day the manager called in sick and Garlic had to return to school early.

BOGGO

Informed Eve that he intended to be a doctor in the hope that it would see him stationed at a hospital and having lots of sex with hot nurses wearing suspenders. His plan backfired badly when he volunteered to assist in a Caesarean section and he reckons he's now

	thinking of giving up cunnilingus altogether.
SIMON	Had a brilliant two days training with the Natal cricket team. Even luckier for him was that he got to hang out with Jonty Rhodes and Malcolm Marshall. Marshall famously hit England's Mike Gatting in the face with a bouncer and found a piece of Gatting's nose embedded in the ball.
VERN	Must have told Eve that he wanted to be a farmer because he was packed off to a Jersey cow stud farm near Nottingham Road. Unfortunately, the cretin was sent home early due to bad behaviour. Boggo reckons it was because Vern attempted to insert his head up a cow's backside, but I doubt that's either likely or possible.

Thursday 9th September

Attitudes have begun to change towards the Malawi trip. Anger at Garlic's trickery has subsided and the thrill of travelling to another country with the Crazy Eight, The Guv and, to a lesser extent, Viking has kicked in. There has also been general mirth about Garlic's new Guv inspired nickname which I casually threw out in the cop shop last night causing an ecstatic uproar. The Malawian himself was less than impressed at being branded The Pink Houdini, but was so deliriously excited about us seeing his beloved lake that he couldn't stop jumping up and down and striking up with inane stories and demonstrations of what awaits us.

Rambo eventually grew so riled with Garlic's constant assertions of 'You guys are going to love it!' that he pounced on him and tried to bite his face off. The Pink Houdini squirmed out of Rambo's grasp before bolting from the cop shop in terror but within seconds the door flew open again and Garlic was back with more advice on essentials to pack for the trip. Rambo screamed in frustration and hurled an empty coffee cup at him and Garlic fled once and for all. Plaque was called in to clean up the shattered pieces of crockery.

19:00 I called home to double-check that my parents hadn't forgotten to meet me at the airport tomorrow to collect my files and hand over some extra clothes, money and my passport. Just as well I did because Dad sounded like he was in a dwaal and didn't know what was cracking. Mom seized the phone from my father and promised that she hadn't forgotten anything and that my stuff was packed and ready at the front door. When I asked her about my passport there was a long pause followed by an uncertain, 'I'll have to double-check.'

19:15 Fatty was waiting for me to finish my call so that he could phone home too. He appeared rather concerned about life and said that he had fallen asleep this afternoon and dreamed that there was a bomb on our plane. It exploded as we were coming in to land in Blantyre, killing everyone except for Garlic who escaped without a scratch.

Albert Schweitzer was genuinely concerned when I said my goodbyes and wished him an excellent holiday. It looks like he doesn't think I'll make it back from Malawi either.

I have decided to lock my diary in my cricket bag which

will be handed over to Dad at the airport. Fatty and Schweitzer are right. This is a foray into darkest Africa and there's every chance something could go wrong and if the plane does explode all evidence of my matric year would be burned beyond recognition. As a replacement tour diary, I have a notepad that looks rather promising and jolly, on which I have written:

THE MALAWI DIARIES

Friday 10th September

I thanked my father for bringing my necessaries to the airport and handed over my cricket bag. Dad reached into his pocket and began counting out bank notes. He was more generous than I could have hoped and I felt a bit bad about taking it all. He said I was heading into darkest Africa so he was adding a little extra in case I needed to bribe the police or hire a mercenary. 'Give Mugabe hell!' he hollered jovially and ran off like he was desperately late for something.

There was a scene at the security check-in because the alarm sounded as Vern's sports bag went through the X-ray machine.

Items found in Vern's hand luggage:

- A Swiss army knife
- 4 pairs of Near Death's underpants
- A jar of water with ten dead flies floating in it
- Half a dozen books on ants stolen from the school library
- 7 tubes of Aquafresh toothpaste
- His door handle

Security confiscated Vern's Swiss army knife and asked Rain Man some probing questions about the jar of floating flies and seven tubes of toothpaste. Vern answered all the questions with a stentorian 'Malawi', but as the security man grew more irritated and confused, he changed all his answers to 'Garlic', apart from when security asked Vern for his place of birth to which he replied, 'Cop shop'.

Despite it being well before noon, The Guv and Viking left our group on the chairs and said they were going to the toilet. They strode off in the opposite direction towards the airport bar. I sat next to The Guv on the flight up to Johannesburg, and he declared himself to be madly in love with the air hostess. After slotting back two dinky bottles of white wine, he plucked up the courage to ask for her hand in marriage when she came to clear his empties. She blushed and giggled and The Guv ordered another bottle of wine. The hostess said it was too close to landing but my English teacher cajoled her into bringing one more.

'Don't drink it now,' she ordered, fighting a smile. 'We've already begun our descent.'

The Guv promised he wouldn't dare, but took a large gulp from the bottle the moment her head was turned.

'By God, what a woman,' he cried knocking back the rest of the wine. 'She would be welcome in my cockpit any time.'

After landing at Jan Smuts in Johannesburg we had a long walk with our bags to the international terminal. The Guv and Viking were given a lift on a golf cart after The Guv informed airport personnel that Viking was blind and needed help. Viking could certainly have passed himself off as blind with his wild beard and dark glasses, although the manner in which he leapt onto the golf cart unaided and waved at somebody he recognised in a car driving past rather let him down. Without any teachers present Rambo and Boggo initiated a 200 metre trolley dash along the pavement. After waiting for a gap in pedestrians, Boggo yelled, 'Catch me if you can, dwarf lickers!' and set off with a healthy lead. Fatty unluckily selected what he called a 'sidewinder trolley'. It veered off the pavement and across the road despite Fatty heaving away at it with all his might. Rambo won the event after maliciously forcing Simon off the pavement metres away from international arrivals.

The Guv and Viking's blind act didn't manage to get them into first class, although they were given the first row so that blind Viking had extra leg room. Once again our housemaster dropped his act rather badly when he filled out his departure form without any assistance. While the masters drank in the bar, the Crazy Eight darted from shop to shop buying goods because they were duty free. Simon, who has the use of his father's credit card for the trip, bought himself a new Walkman and a bunch of CDs. Fatty purchased so many sweets and chocolates that it took him four attempts to fit everything into his rucksack and even then a giant Toblerone stuck out the top like a ship's mast. I didn't buy anything. Even though Dad has given me extra money I have no idea how much I might need for the trip or for any possible briberies that lie in wait. Rambo bought himself a bottle of J&B whisky and nobody batted an eyelid.

18:06 The sun had just set and outside Blantyre airport I soaked in the sounds and atmosphere of dusk on foreign ground. Blantyre's airport was minuscule compared to Jan Smuts and all the trees and wild bush around the airfield immediately made me feel like I was in Africa proper. Under the fading orange sky I finally felt like I had taken a manly step on Jack Kerouac's road to nowhere.

Two Mitsubishi Pajeros pulled up and we were introduced to a pair of smiling Malawian men called Dickson and Transport. I double checked with Garlic that the man's name really was Transport. Garlic grinned and explained that Transport had been with the Garlic family longer than he had. Dickson was immensely friendly and has one of the largest grins I've ever seen on a person. He kept smacking his hands together and shouting 'Lubbly jubbly!' before erupting into merriment.

In the fading light I gazed out at the passing landscape with great interest. There were no streetlights and the roads were narrow and potholed. It was wild and rugged and felt how Africa should.

The Garlics' home would be better described as a compound as it covers an enormous area and seems to house vast numbers of people. Garlic claimed that there were eleven servants living on the compound with their families, and he didn't appear to be lying as a swarm of people dressed in white surrounded the car to welcome us and help us with our luggage. We followed the deliriously excited Malawian through two huge wooden doors into an entrance hall where his parents were waiting to welcome us. Mr Garlic (Stewart) was extremely friendly and relaxed and with grey hair and dark eyes looks nothing like his son. Mrs Garlic (Alison) has wild and woolly blonde hair and huge blue eyes and she shouted 'Wow!' when we entered the house. (No guessing where Garlic got the genes from ...) The Pink Houdini took great pride in introducing us individually to his parents. After the introductions, The Guv, who was well pickled after his day of drinking at altitude, started up a raucous chorus of 'For they are jolly good fellows'. Thereafter Viking made a slurred but heartfelt speech, thanking the Garlics for their generous hospitality in sponsoring our cultural tour and the generous charity donation. Garlic's mom had that look on her face like she thought we were all incredibly delightful people. Little did she know. There was some sniggering when she hollered, 'Hands up who's ever been to Malawi before?' Only her son raised his hand. Alison Garlic's face grew slightly pink and she shouted 'Wow!' once more. 'You guys are going to love it!' she boomed, wrapping her arm around her son's shoulder.

'I see the apple doesn't fall very far from the tree,' noted

The Guv over the top of his specs. Alison and Garth roared with laughter while Stewart smiled warmly. Dickson entered the room carrying drinks and a bucket of ice.

'Hey, don't forget to move your watches two hours back,' Garlic reminded us with an earnest expression.

'Good Lord – we're not on Greenwich, are we?' retorted The Guv, squinting at his watch like he was reading hieroglyphics.

'Gotcha, sir!' shouted Garlic triumphantly and both he and his mother laughed like drains. In fact they thought it was so funny that they missed when they attempted a high five, causing further hysterics. While seizing a glass of champagne for himself and Viking off Dickson's tray, The Guv said that he was now considering changing Garlic's B for English into a D.

'You got a B for English?' roared Alison Garlic. The Pink Houdini punched the air with his fist and his mom yelled, 'Wow, Garth, wow!'

'Oh God, now there are two of them,' grumbled Rambo with a sickly smile.

'This is going to be so bad,' added Simon as the Garlics celebrated with more high fives.

The Garlic house is never ending and there were plenty rooms spare although only three had been made up for the Crazy Eight. Rambo and Simon claimed the largest. Fatty and Boggo paired off after Fatty had assured me back at the airport that we would be sharing. With Garlic sleeping in his own room that left Vern and me in the smallest room at the very end.

'Spud,' said the cretin happily after entering the room to find me already there. I asked Vern which of the beds he wanted. He lay down on one and pointed at the other.

Saturday 11th September

A morning tour of Blantyre and surrounds in the two Pajeros. Garlic and Alison were our self-assigned tour guides. Blantyre has very few landmarks, although The Guv spent considerable time analysing the Livingstone Monument.

The visit to Nestlé Malawi was rather underwhelming and wasn't at all like my lifelong imagining of what a Roald Dahl chocolate factory should look like. The tasting room was the highlight, though, and Fatty ate so many chocolates in our twenty minute tasting session that he later complained of blurred vision, numb tongue and, more alarmingly, shrill Christmas beetle-like ringing in his left ear.

The tobacco auction on the other hand was excellent fun. Boggo became heavily involved and made it his mission to find and purchase a sample of the best tobacco in Malawi. He even became embroiled in some pushing and pulling after accusing one of the farmers of setting up with sub-standard goods. Vern loved the auction, too, and shadowed the auctioneer as he made his way up and down the rows of tables laid out with bunches of tobacco. It was impossible to hear what the auctioneer was shouting although everybody else seemed to understand him perfectly. Vern's sporadic shouts of 'Sex' and 'Side guy' attracted a few confused glances from the farmers, but nobody fell for his fake auctioneering which, in truth, sounded more like a horse race because he had blocked his nose with his two middle fingers.

After hours of haggling, Boggo returned with a clump of tobacco which he declared to be the finest in Africa if not the world. It smelled much like any other tobacco but he held it up to the light and demonstrated its bluish tinge which meant that it had psychedelic properties. He ended up selling the tobacco to Rambo for a greatly inflated price. Rambo broke off a piece for himself and sold the rest to The Guv for double the price Boggo had charged him.

When it grew dark Rambo forced us to accompany him to the far reaches of the garden where we all had to smoke his psychedelic tobacco. Apart from burning my throat and making me slightly nauseous, the tobacco had no impact, although Fatty later claimed to have seen the face of God in the sky.

Sunday 12th September

MALAWI!

Nkhata Bay

LAKE MALAWI

Lilongwe

THE SHACK!
Cape Maclear

Zomba

Blantyre   Mount Mulanje

According to Garlic's hand drawn map we headed in an easterly direction from Blantyre to Mount Mulanje which has the highest peak in South Central Africa. The area around Mulanje was green and mountainous with many tea plantations and we spent the afternoon having a braai and sampling various types of tea at a large rambling farmhouse. After lunch an excellent game of baseball broke out on the sprawling lawn. Even Viking and The Guv got involved, although Viking took the whole thing far too seriously and The Guv never once hit the ball despite repeatedly swinging in a violent fashion and being allowed twelve strikes before being given out. He retired grumbling to his deckchair and declared, 'It's just not cricket!'

While Transport drove us back to Blantyre, I remarked to Garlic that I was very impressed with the beauty of Mount Mulanje. 'Mulanje is nothing,' he replied. 'The lake completely kicks Mulanje's butt.' I nodded but Garlic perhaps thought that I didn't believe him because he added, 'You can even ask my mom.'

In the evening I pined for Mermaid for the first time since being in Malawi. I wonder how things will be between us when I return home.

Monday 13th September

06:00   Departure for Lake Malawi

Judging by all the provisions being loaded into the trailers attached to the Pajeros, we won't be starving. 'Lubbly jubbly!' shouted Dickson as he started our car and we all shouted it back. The doors closed and we were waved off by Alison Garlic and a large crowd of grinning servants. Vern, seated close beside me, waved vigorously like he might never see Garlic's mom again. Fatty took the other window seat at the back while Boggo was up front having set his alarm for 5:15 to make sure that he was the first to shout 'Shotgun' and secure the passenger seat in writing.

It's been bugging me since arriving on Friday and I've finally put my finger on it. The cars are different here. More to the point, there are hardly any German cars at all, whereas at home every second vehicle is a Golf or BMW. Before leaving Blantyre I counted eleven Nissan Sunnys, all of which were cream or yellow in colour.

06:45   Vern kept winding down the window and sticking his face out like a dog. It wouldn't have been so bad if he hadn't had to clamber all over me in the process. Aside from surprising people on the road, his antics seemed to concern Dickson greatly as he repeatedly swivelled around to check that Vern hadn't jumped out.

07:15   'There's the lake!' declared Boggo in a triumphant voice. Dickson hooted with laughter and said that Boggo had just spotted the edge of Lake Chilwa which was very small in comparison to Lake Malawi. 'What a wally,' chortled Fatty. Vern sniggered too and repeated, 'Wally'.

07:30   The area around the town of Zomba is stunningly beautiful. The plateau to the west is spectacular and, as Boggo accurately observed, it possesses a very similar shape to Eve's buttocks when viewed sideways.

07:45   The Pajero in front pulled over rather suddenly and we followed suit. Judging by the agitation of Viking and The Guv, who were both walking around the car gesticulating wildly, there must have been some sort of problem. Garlic was taking a pee in the bush at the roadside and waving at us with his other hand while shouting something about the Zomba plateau. Abruptly the two masters leapt back into their Pajero and it sped off with a screech of tyres. Simon stuck his head out of the back window and shouted, 'Enjoy, suckers!'

'Hey! Hey! Hey!' shouted Garlic, running down the road

after them while attempting to zip himself up. 'You left me behind!' he screamed. After staring at the road for a while, The Pink Houdini darted up to our car and hollered, 'Anybody need a tour guide?' Despite the groans, Garlic squeezed in between me and Vern and called out, 'Full steam ahead.'

08:25 I found myself irritated with Garlic's incessant prattling and utterly revolted by Vern picking his nose and having gross nasal problems.

08:35 We stopped once more and shifted Vern to the boot with the supplies. He seemed happy enough. To drown out Garlic, I slipped Automatic for the People into my Walkman and eliminated the excited voice of our pink faced tour guide.

REM did the trick and when I reached the end of the CD I didn't want it to end so I played the final track Find the River over and over again because it felt like it somehow explained everything about my life that I couldn't.

The further we travelled the flatter the terrain became. Mile upon mile of mango and litchi trees sprouting up around small round huts and makeshift homes. I think Mr Bosch would say this is a good example of subsistence agriculture. People lived and hung out near the roadsides, while away from the main road the vegetation became wild African bush as it must have been when Livingstone was here.

10:35 Dickson halted to show us a massive baobab tree growing beside the road. While Garlic had another slash, Fatty measured the circumference of the trunk which came to 22 paces which, by unrelated coincidence, is also the length of a cricket pitch. It somehow defied anyone even to think about trying to chop it down. And on we went.

11:30 Boggo attempted to stop the car because he swore on his life that he'd spotted a sign warning people to beware of crocodiles. Garlic and Dickson did their best to calm Boggo down and assured him that there were no crocodiles in Lake Malawi and that swimming is over 100 per cent safe.

11:40 While relieving himself in long grass, Boggo said that there was no way that he was setting foot in the lake. He proceeded to tell me various grisly things that a crocodile will do to your body when both dead and alive.

'I dunno about you, Spud, I don't want to be boned by a crocodile before he eats my liver.'

He seemed astonished that I was still willing to swim and advised me never to go further out than Fatty who would most certainly be taken first. I reminded Boggo that crocodiles hunt from the bank so he advised me to make sure that Garlic was in shallower water since he was bound to attract the reptile. 'A croc can smell pork from a mile off,' he concluded, shaking his pecker and taking in his surroundings.

12:45 'There's the lake!' trumpeted Boggo pointing to a broad expanse of water to the right of the road. 'I saw it first, you gonads,' he bragged, all the while sniggering like a machine gun. Garlic and Dickson erupted into a cacophony of laughter because once again Boggo had been stitched up by a fake lake.

'That's Lake Malombe,' cried Dickson, shaking his head like Boggo was a fool.

'You wait, Boggo,' promised Garlic. 'My oath the real lake will blow your balls off.'

The journey never seemed to end. Dickson drove sedately except for when there were children, animals and people in the road, when he would speed up and hoot urgently. In fact it's a miracle that we didn't run over a dog or a goat, because in Malawi they're kamikaze.

13:10 'There's the lake!' blurted Garlic with unrestrained delight. 'Isn't she beautiful?'

Stretching out to the horizon was Lake Malawi. I stared at its sheer size – in fact if you had told me it was the ocean, I would have believed you. It was immense.

14:00 Dickson and Transport wouldn't so much as let us carry our own bags into the Garlics' lake house, which they call 'the shack'. The place was a large and rambling beach house, not at all fancy but very comfortable, with beds, couches and old magazines piling up in the corners. Garlic led us out onto the wide veranda. The lawn became white sand dissolving into crystal clear blue water.

'Not too bad, Garlic,' remarked Rambo grudgingly. 'Not too bad at all.' There was a mad rush for baggies and we followed Garlic into the warm water where we thrashed about and took turns in dunking the Malawian. Islands almost seemed to erupt out of the lake before our eyes and a small dugout canoe carrying a wad of thatch slipped by. Boggo sat in a deckchair with The Guv and Viking on the veranda watching us swim and keeping a sharp eye out for crocodiles.

Rambo caught sight of a fancy ski boat moored a bit further down the beach. 'Should we steal it?' he asked Simon.
     'You don't have to steal it,' cried Garlic. 'It's ours.'

The Malawian showed off a large shed crammed with water sports equipment, and personally introduced us to his yellow and blue windsurfer. He also showed off the chest fridges in the dining room. The one on the left contained cold drinks and the one on the right Carlsberg green. He told us to help ourselves whenever we were thirsty. There was some debate about whether or not we were allowed to drink beer in front of Viking. Rambo made a scene of cruising out to the veranda, cracking open a beer and swigging it lustily. Viking glanced up but returned to his magazine without making any comment. The rest of us weren't as brave and instead we hid our beers under our shirts and drank them further down the beach.

We played touch rugby on the white sand when the sun was setting. Jazz played from the music system in the shack and a few locals gathered around to watch us and to laugh at Vern's antics. When it grew dark Dickson switched on the floodlights and we played on into the evening with only the gentle lapping waves and a swarm of flying ants for company.

I slept out on one of the camp beds on the veranda with a mosquito net tucked in around me. Before falling asleep I soaked in the incredible stars and imagined the dark islands rearing out of the centre of the lake.

Tuesday 14th September

After a breakfast so large that it had the Crazy Eight laid out on the grass begging for mercy, we began a gentle amble up the beach towards the infamous Monkey House. If Garlic had told us that it was four kilometres away, we never would have gone, but his assurances that it was the Mecca of cool on Cape Maclear and the place where hot chicks tan naked drove us on. When we eventually reached 'the Mecca' it was fairly deserted apart from a man with long grey hair who looked like Gandalf smoking on the deck and staring thoughtfully out at the water. There were no naked ladies. In fact, there were no ladies at all. Boggo was about to unleash a torrent of abuse all over Garlic when Simon spotted something promising written on a chalk board positioned on the beach:

Monkey House Full Moon Party
Friday 19h00 till Late
Happy Hour 21h00 – 23h00
Live Music/DJ/ Beach Log Fire/Pool Competition
Happy times! All welcome.

14:30 Even The Guv and Viking left their chairs on the veranda to witness this one. We had taken turns attempting to water ski – which looks rather easy on TV but is actually not. I took three attempts to stand up and even then it felt like every tendon in my arms was on the verge of explosion. I enjoyed about fifteen seconds of skating across the surface of Lake Malawi before losing my balance and crashing into the water.

The time, however, had finally arrived for Vern's maiden attempt. The cretin was clearly nervous before setting out as he devoured nearly half a tube of Aquafresh and had some stern words with himself in the shallows. Dickson swam him out into deeper water and helped him attach the skis to his feet while Transport, piloting the boat, slowly took up the strain. When Vern signalled that he was ready by shouting 'Garlic' the boat roared off. Vern was taken aback by the sudden force visited on his arms and screamed like he had been stabbed. His head jerked back and the front of his skis pitched forward into the water. Against all odds Vern kept hold of the rope and much to the delight of the expectant crowd, he proceeded to ski a considerable distance across Lake Malawi on his face.

Garlic is surprisingly nimble with his windsurfer. The

rest of us (bar Boggo) took turns skiing behind the boat on a tractor tyre. It was the most radical fun I can ever remember having.

The Guv told some ripping stories over dinner, after which we were all so exhausted from the feast and the day's activities that we went off to bed. Only Rambo sat out on the beach until late smoking his tobacco and occasionally throwing things into the water.

Wednesday 15th September

The boat scythed across the endless waterscape. The wind wasn't up yet so only a thin ripple disturbed the surface of the lake. The Guv, dressed in what he called 'Livingstone khaki' and his hat from the Boer War, sat up front with Transport who handled the controls. The boat soon slowed and we beached on a rocky island that urgently needed exploring.

Garlic led us up to a rock face high above the water and said it was called Daredevil Ledge. It used to be a popular spot to jump off until a local boy died in 1988 and since then only the suicidal and the insane have taken the leap. Naturally Rambo immediately insisted that we all jump and that anybody who didn't wasn't worthy of being in the Crazy Eight. This kind of peer pressure may have worked in second year but not now. Boggo was the first to refuse, but claimed not to be frightened of the ten metre plunge nor the large boulders lurking at the bottom, but the submerged crocodile that would seize him into a death roll the moment he hit the water. Fatty was the next to bail, citing his well-known fear of heights. Garlic also shook his head, saying that he'd seen pictures of the dead boy's body in the newspaper and his whole head had caved in after he'd slipped and smashed into the boulders below.

'I wonder which rock he hit,' pondered Rambo without demonstrating too much sympathy for the poor lad. Vern didn't exactly say that he was backing out but revealed his state of mind by grasping his crotch and hiding behind a shrub. Rambo tried to guide him out onto the ledge but the cretin shook his head vehemently and scuttled off on all fours to catch up with Fatty and Boggo who had already started back down. Simon pretended to be keen for the leap but his lame excuse of having a sudden ear infection after too much swimming saw him backing down and joining the rest.

'Spuddy?' asked Rambo, grinning mischievously.

'I'll do it,' I said boldly.

I could tell from his expression that he didn't believe me. He stepped aside and motioned to the rock as if it was all mine. 'Don't worry,' he said comfortingly, 'it's still a good six weeks until the dying season.' If I had thought it through I would have backed out like the others but some inner desire to test the world was driving me on. I vaulted off and flew like Icarus through the air with the turquoise water calling me in. I didn't make a sound as I plunged into the lake. When I finally surfaced there were wild whoops from the others standing at the water's edge. I gazed up at the ledge that I had leapt off and it didn't look nearly as intimidating from below. 'Come on, Rambo!' I hollered. But Rambo was already down at the beach and maintained that he had only been joking about jumping. I couldn't help asking him if he was scared. He didn't reply so I made a chicken noise and he threw a rock at me. It's the first time in living memory that I have ever out Ramboed Rambo.

My heroic moment was cut short by Vern's wild screaming. The cretin had begun fishing on the point and hooked something of note. His mad reeling and shouting eventually produced a fair sized butter fish which Garlic said was excellent eating. Transport made a fire on the beach and we settled in for a delicious picnic of roasted butter fish, chilli beans and fresh bread rolls.

Viking is the most chilled that anyone can ever remember him. Today he was even spotted suntanning and whistling. The Guv meanwhile, on a camp chair in the shade, continued with his reading of David Livingstone's expeditions up the Zambezi.

After lunch we snorkelled in the cove. Garlic wasn't kidding about all the multicoloured species of fish and we even discovered the one with the upside down evolutionary face that Garlic is always on about. No wonder the fish is so rare, it must be nigh impossible to score chicks with a face like that. Simon and Rambo eventually talked Boggo into getting wet and there was high comedy when he tiptoed into the water in his underpants wearing a pair of goggles. His long furry white legs made him appear like a hesitant salamander on the verge of a long migration. At one stage he even lowered his face into the water so that he could conduct an underwater search for crocodiles. His short-lived and rather painful swim ended abruptly when Simon charged across the beach waving his arms and shrieking, 'A croc! A croc! Boggo, a croc!' Boggo scorched up the beach and took refuge behind Fatty who was seated under the shade of a mango tree licking fish skin off the braai grid.

Thursday 16th September

CULTURAL DAY

Nobody was very keen to leave the lake and embark on a day of cultural interaction, charity and learning.

Boggo tried his best to persuade/bribe Viking into cancelling, but our housemaster turned down his offer of two thousand kwacha and a back massage from Vern, declaring our cultural day to be a matter of conscience. Typically, it was a beautiful day on the lake with not a breath of wind. I was forced to wear shoes for the first time this week and pulling on jeans and a smart shirt felt rather against the spirit of things.

Cultural Highlights

- Playing soccer with the kids from a local primary school.
- The Guv's brilliant and witty speech to the teachers.
- Making a grand donation (R15 000) to the local orphanage on behalf of our school and Nestlé Malawi – the headmistress cried with gratitude.
- Visiting a traditional craft market.
- Buying some excellent bracelets and a beaded necklace for Mermaid.
- Enjoying a tasty traditional meal at a local village.
- The extreme friendliness of every single Malawian we met along the way.

Cultural Lowlights

- Viking taking the match against the primary school way too seriously. His aggressive tactics were unnecessary and we took little joy out of beating the kids 2-1.
- Viking's booming and unnecessarily intimidating speech to the staff of the primary school.
- Vern crying because the headmistress of the orphanage was moved.
- Boggo's unpleasant haggling with the poor old man selling wooden tables at the craft market.

- Only discovering after we had eaten that the traditional meal was made out of goat.
- Realising how many poor people there are in this country.
- Vern being reprimanded by a policeman because of his ridiculous and lengthy saluting at a poster of the Malawian president Hastings Kamuzu Banda.

Sunset touch rugby, nightswimming, drinks on the beach around a campfire, a huge feast of a dinner, crazy talk, staring at the stars, and restful sleep. Another tough day in Africa.

Friday 17th September

Monkey House Full Moon Party

The Monkey House was unrecognisable from the place we visited a few days ago. It was lit up with fairy lights and crammed with people laughing, drinking and having a wild time. I couldn't help but notice how locals and tourists blended together like race doesn't matter here. It immediately made me feel in a harmonious mood with my surroundings and relaxed about whatever direction the night may choose to take. We bought drinks and gathered around the fire on the beach while eyeing out the other revellers and scanning the party for beautiful girls. 'Ten o'clock, the brunette standing by the bar,' alerted Garlic. 'Even better,' chimed Boggo, 'two-thirty, slutty looking blonde playing darts.' The Guv and Viking were already well ensconced playing pool against Gandalf and a heavily built lady wearing a Monkey House T-shirt.

The full moon broke free of the clouds and lit up the shimmering lake in shafts of silver and white. I had a terrible wrenching pang for the Mermaid.

Later, some girls arrived and joined us on the beach around the fire. They were Canadians conducting aid work in Malawi and having what they called a 'gap year'. Two of them were pretty but they were all 21 and 22 and too old for us. That didn't stop Boggo, Rambo and Simon from pulling out the spade and digging up a few suspect pick-up lines.

Fatty and I broke away from the fire and ambled down the beach to check out what was happening at another bar further along the bay which turned out to be a guest house with an old guy singing loudly into a microphone.

'Penny would love this place,' said Fatty rather mournfully once we had begun our retreat to the Monkey House.

'Anybody would love this place,' I agreed, thinking of Mermaid once more.

'Whatever you do, don't tell Garlic,' he said earnestly, 'or we'll never hear the end of it.'

Fatty mentioned that Rambo has threatened to stab anyone overheard telling Garlic that they are impressed in any way with Lake Malawi. 'Simon reckons it's better than anywhere in Europe and Simon's travelled lank,' he added, beginning to puff from the exertion of our slow amble. Fireworks began exploding at the Monkey House so we paused our musing on the merits of Lake Malawi and hurriedly returned to the party.

When Dickson arrived to pick us up at midnight only Viking and a reluctant Guv went back in the car. The Guv reckons he was making bangworthy inroads with the blonde at the dartboard. 'One more drink and I was bound to hit the bull's eye,' he declared, hoisting himself into the Pajero with a grunt. He reckoned his dodgy knee wouldn't withstand a night of lovemaking and a 4km walk home, so he said that he was retiring to bed where Livingstone impatiently awaited.

I bought the Crazy Eight a round of shooters and added a further six for the Canadian aid workers encamped with us at the fire on the beach. One of them was playing intense Tori Amos songs on a guitar and was being totally ignored even by her friends. There was a great roar when I arrived with the shooters and I soon found myself embroiled in a discussion on apartheid with one of the Canadian girls whose name was Skye. She seemed rather astonished that I was so liberal in my general outlook. It probably helped that she had just been chatting to Boggo who isn't liberal at all. At one stage she drew a map of Canada on my leg with her finger to show me where her home town was. I kept reminding myself that she was nearly 22 and that I am only seventeen and a half and that I was under no circumstances allowed to even think about kissing her. Besides, minutes before I was having love pangs for Mermaid.

Later, after more drinks and discussions about poverty in Africa, I told Skye that I respected her for giving up a life of luxury to help poor people. This made her misty eyed and she leant in to kiss me. Luckily, I had my wits about me and within seconds of our lips meeting I pulled away and explained that I had a girlfriend back home whom I loved and couldn't cheat on. She said she understood and respected me even more for my resolve. I returned to the bar to buy us more drinks and, while waiting to be served, I considered how splendid it is to find somebody unexpectedly on your wavelength. Not only that, I had demonstrated strength and dedication to my relationship with Mermaid and overcome Toronto temptation of the highest order. I returned to the fire with an extra spring in my step only to find Skye sitting between Simon and Boggo, laughing her head off. She was already holding hands with Simon.

Long after last rounds had been called and the Monkey House had extinguished its fairy lights, our group on the beach decided that it was finally time for home. Simon and Rambo left with Skye and her friend in a car while Fatty, Boggo, Vern, Garlic and I began the long walk home along the sand. The moon was riding high and Garlic never ceased telling us stories about the lake. Perhaps we had drunk too much, or it was merely the power of the full moon, but for the first time we really listened to his stories. Tonight was the first time that I have ever gone out without my watch.

Saturday 18th September

I was awoken by loud shouting and the sound of a stick being bashed into the floor. I heard The Guv hollering, 'I'll have you, serpent!' There was a snake in the house which The Guv was trying to kill with his walking stick. Unfortunately, he seemed to be bashing just about everything else in the lounge aside from the snake. Eventually Dickson brushed the reptile out of the kitchen door and it slithered into a nearby flower bed. It was already 11am. Feeling exhausted from last night's revelry, I ate breakfast and zacked out on a sun lounger beneath the mango tree. Simon and Rambo arrived at lunchtime looking smug. Apparently Simon had rampant sex with Skye who he said was an animal in the sack. Just my luck!

Garlic spent the entire afternoon teaching me how to windsurf. We both met with limited success.

Sunday 19th September

It's all ending too quickly. It doesn't feel right or real that we should be leaving this place tomorrow. Poor Garlic was so overcome by all the things that we still had to do or see that he became overwrought and we were forced to dig a vast hole and bury him in the sand to calm him down. It was quite a sight to see a bright pink shouting face sticking out of the beach and passers-by took a noticeably wide berth around him. We pretended not to hear his screaming and pleading that we were running out of time and hadn't even been to see Dog-leg Gorge. Rambo was hoping that Garlic would remain buried until it was time to leave tomorrow, but The Pink Houdini somehow escaped his sandy captivity and joined us for lunch on the veranda in a far more settled mood.

It was a beautiful evening so Dickson lit a fire on the beach. He and Garlic had earlier erected a volleyball net so we played into the night. Simon instituted a rule that any cretin attacks would be met with an instant fine of a lake plunge. Vern was the first to break the rule when he got his head stuck in the net, freaked out and pulled everything down. He didn't seem too unhappy about being hurled into the water. Fatty was next in after sinking too deeply into the sand and having to be pulled out. He willingly leapt into the water with an almighty crash. Boggo's was the third and final cretin attack when he punched his service far too long, sending the ball careening into the fire which doused a furious Viking in fiery sparks. Boggo refused to pay his fine of leaping into the water. Instead, he took flight down the beach, threatening to scratch out people's eyes if they pursued him. Rambo took off after Boggo like a bullet, and the rest of us charged after Rambo anxious to see what would eventuate.

Boggo was horrified when he realised Rambo and the rest of us were in hot pursuit and began screaming obscenities about our mothers. As Rambo closed in, the obscenities became a long and terrible scream of panic. There was an audible smack as Rambo launched himself at Boggo with a flying rugby tackle. Greenstein went down in a heap and came up wailing in pain and reckoning that his spine was broken. But Rambo wasn't finished because he picked up the whining Boggo and slung him over his shoulders like a large sack of pale potatoes. Boggo didn't fight back but did note that he may also have internal bleeding. It was only when Rambo carried Boggo down to the water's edge and began whistling and calling for the crocodiles that Boggo commenced screaming and kicking once more. We all gathered around to offer assistance but Rambo seemed to have things covered and hurled Boggo some distance into the water, shouting, 'Fresh meat, boys!' Boggo did an excellent hovercraft impersonation and didn't stop moving until he was safely in the house where he locked himself in the bathroom for 40 minutes.

After dinner we swallowed our malaria pills and Fatty raised his glass of water and declared, 'To Gecko.' I'm not sure if it was the mention of our late comrade or just our last night on the lake but things were more serious around the fire tonight. We began to chat about the future and what we might do with our lives. Rambo dragged things down even further by saying that statistically one of us would die before we were twenty-five and another would live to ninety. We decided that Fatty would be the first to kick the bucket due to his excessive girth, and the only one of us cunning enough to cheat death for so long would be Boggo. The man himself wasn't much buoyed by the promise of a long life and reckoned he probably wouldn't last the night, what with his broken spine and internal bleeding.

Monday 20th September

I was awake before the sun climbed up over the lake. I lay propped up in my bed watching the orange ball rise over the mountains of Mozambique and change the colour of the water from grey to silver then shimmering blue. I reminded myself to soak in my last few hours in the Great Rift Valley which has made me feel like no other place ever has.

'A final stroll with a tick infested old dog, Milton?'

I turned to see The Guv dressed in a grey tracksuit and wearing what appeared to be a jockey's cap. I scampered out of bed and threw on my baggies and didn't bother with a shirt. We walked north along the shoreline with the sun in our faces.

'Glorious, Milton. Bloody glorious,' exclaimed The Guv, gesturing out over the lake with a broad sweep of his arm.

'Better than a bed full of blondes, hey, sir?' I retorted, throwing one of his own lines back at him.

The Guv roared at that and wrote in the sand with his walking stick:

Here paused the village idiots.

We sauntered on. I told The Guv that I felt like this holiday had recharged my batteries which had become badly run down with all the demands of school and home life. The Guv agreed and said that he, too, had a new lease on life and despite battling his dark demons this year, he had resolved to live so long that he would eventually have to be murdered.

I almost stopped walking because in that moment he had revealed something to me. I waited for him to continue but he didn't and I was too polite to ask him any further questions so we walked some distance without speaking.

A small bird with metallic blue wings and a bright pink beak shot past us.

'Great Scott, Milton,' he cried, 'I do believe that was the malachite kingfisher.' My English teacher declared this an excellent sighting and told me to remember the name.

We walked on but I didn't realise how far we had gone until we turned for home.

'So, come year's end, it's the old exit pursued by a bear for you, Milton?'

'Yes, sir,' I said.

'No post matric then?'

'No, sir.'

There was a pause. It was as if The Guv either didn't know what to say or was afraid to say it.

'I fear your leaving, boy,' he said, looking out at the lake so that I couldn't see his eyes.

When I replied, my voice was gruff and choked up.

'Sorry, sir.'

'I lie, Milton,' he said. 'I fear the moment of your leaving even more.'

'Me too, sir.'

We walked the rest of the way in silence. It wasn't awkward or odd and it felt that no more needed to be said. With the sun at our backs, we gazed ahead and our eyes drank in the splendour around us.

Tuesday 21st September

Dad was waiting when I exited the airport terminal with my trolley. He made quite a scene of waving me down and pretending to be having an almighty tussle with a large fish over the railings in front of everyone at arrivals. I felt embarrassed as I had just noticed a beautiful blonde woman in a business suit standing right there watching us like we were freaks. I responded with a dignified wave and kept my cool traveller's composure.

'How was Kariba?' asked Dad, seizing control of my trolley. I hardly ceased with my Malawi stories all the way home and Dad reckoned it sounded just like his youth in South West. My father was in all round excellent form and far calmer about life. The answer to his significant and sudden improvement in mood came when I arrived home to find Wombat's packed suitcases and large boxes of trinkets piled up and waiting at the back door.

Dad was so filled with joy and rapture that he began toyi-toying in the driveway. Blacky became hugely excited by Dad's vigorous movements and barked madly before losing control and urinating all over himself. Swept up in the moment, I toyi-toyed along too.

'David!' screeched my grandmother. 'How was Kenya?' When I corrected her she didn't appear to register and asked, 'Did you see the running of the wildebeest?' It soon became apparent that nobody in my family has the first clue about Malawi. No wonder Garlic is always so exasperated.

I assumed Wombat's packed suitcases to mean that she has finally hoodwinked an old age home into thinking that she isn't crackers. As it turned out Mom, under duress from Dad, decided to check Wombat into the Royal Hotel so that I could have my room back for the last week of holidays. Mom encouraged me to tell further stories about Malawi on the drive into town and these were frequently interrupted by Wombat asking ridiculous questions such as, 'Did you see the Sphinx, David?' and, 'How old is Kenneth Kaunda nowadays?'

Tell-tale Wombat evidence in my room:

- The book on Winston Churchill's private life discovered on the bedside table
- Three empty plates stashed under the bed, all of which smelled suspiciously of fried fish
- My clock radio tuned into the 'A' programme instead of Radio 5
- My semi-naked Heather Locklear poster being turned back to front
- My completely naked Sharon Stone poster being removed entirely

19:00 In a state of great nerves and apprehension I made the long awaited call to my girlfriend. When Mermaid came on the line she sounded so soft and distant that I immediately thought she was drugged out on antidepressants. She said she had a migraine and wasn't feeling well so I promised to try her again tomorrow. It was a case of worst fears confirmed and I immediately began dreading tomorrow's phone call.

Wednesday 22nd September

PM Had a meeting with my parents around the dining room table to discuss my immediate future (ie what I am going to do with my life). My initial statement that I intended to travel the world with a backpack went down like a lead balloon. Dad said it was a terrible idea because I would run out of money and end up becoming a boemelaar on the street ransacking people's garbage bins and smoking 'cracked cocaine'. When I suggested that I would find work along the way to fund my travels, Mom said I was bound to be interfered with by 'funny men in train stations'.

Bizarrely, when I informed my parents that I wanted to study drama they seemed greatly displeased, and yet when I mentioned the possibility of a BA degree at university (which is where one studies drama) they were mightily supportive. I realised that I wasn't going to be able to decide my future then and there around the dining room table so I agreed to send in applications for the Universities of Natal and Cape Town. Both Mom and Dad made it quite clear that I would have to win a scholarship for UCT because, although they were willing to pay my tuition with Wombat's money, they couldn't afford boarding and living expenses. Before the meeting was adjourned my parents brought up the option of post matric which I think they both secretly thought was my best path forward. I shook my head vehemently and replied, 'I want my freedom.'

Dad made a last desperate bid to pretend that the big wide world was far less free than school is because of all the obligations that mount up on your shoulders as you get older. I pretended to be taking note of what he was saying but there was no way in hell that I was falling for that one.

Thursday 23rd September

19:35 Just had a long and extremely heavy chat with Mermaid on the phone. She said that she couldn't see me before I go back to school because it will take too much out of her emotionally. She blamed my constant coming and going in her life for her emotional state. With finals looming, she reckoned seeing me for a few days and then not seeing me for six weeks could send her over the edge. So we are sort of together but not really together.

Girls (?)

Saturday 25th September

17:00   I debated the matter for some time and eventually decided to be impulsive and call the Mermaid. Not only that, I planned to sweep her off her feet and take her out on a romantic date tonight. This is always the kind of stuff that guys do towards the end of movies and it nearly always turns out well (except in films with serial killers where the young couple are always brutally murdered after kissing in the woods).

I didn't count on Marge bailing me up and talking about my relationship with Mermaid like she was involved. She advised me to give her daughter some space until exams were over. 'She's very sensitive at the moment,' she said, and wouldn't even let me speak to her.

Since he was the only possible option left, I asked Dad for some advice on the matter which he kindly said he would pass on if I fetched a six pack from the fridge in the garage. After listening to my entire story about the Mermaid's most recent descent into fragility, he clicked his tongue like the matter was beyond any of us. 'Women are no different to mosquitoes and golf balls,' said my father, staring sagely up at the ceiling. 'They all need a bloody good thrashing.' I nodded as if this helped, although I could hardly see how giving Mermaid a thrashing would help her to become less emotionally sensitive.

'It's that bloody mother of hers,' blurted my father suddenly. 'She's mollycoddled that child into thinking it's a depressive.' He drained his beer and cracked open the next. 'If I were you,' he said, 'I'd be bloody shot of her.'

Mom, who had obviously been eavesdropping at the lounge door, could take it no longer and burst in. 'Do not listen to your father!' she warned, waving a threatening finger at me. She declared I should cease hounding the poor girl with phone calls and visits. (I would hardly call two telephone calls and zero visits to my girlfriend in five days 'hounding'.) Later, when my mother set off to fetch her nail kit, Dad looped his finger around his head and slapped his hands together to indicate that he still thought the Mermaid was a nutter and most probably needed a thrashing to see her right.

Sunday 26th September

Revised algebra, made study lists, exam timetables and wrote a long letter to the Mermaid offering love and support which I dropped in her letter box with her necklace from Lake Malawi. Finally I prepared myself for my ultimate term as a schoolboy.

Hard to believe that a mere six days ago The Guv and I were walking along the shores of Lake Malawi without a care in the world. Too much life happens too fast.

Monday 27th September

18:30 I stepped off the bus onto the cobblestones of Pilgrims' Walk and took a brief moment to soak it all in. I may just have experienced my final bus journey back to school. It was an odd thought. Everything inside me has been so geared to leaving this place and yet being back felt strangely comforting. I wondered in that moment if I shouldn't delay the end by one more year. I gazed up at the red brick walls once more and, after a few deep breaths, walked on.

Tuesday 28th September

At the prefects' meeting Viking ordered us to begin compiling our own prefects' lists for 1994. 'And please note, gentlemen, that the 31st of October is the deadline to apply for post matric.' His gaze lingered on me for a second, but I boldly stared back so that he could see that I wasn't to be tempted.

11:00 The 1st cricket team has been called to a meeting tomorrow evening at the pavilion. Word is circulating that The Guv is resigning as our coach. When I questioned him about the rumours after English class he called me 'An ironing maid and a poo sniffer'. Garlic interrupted his insults, demanding to know what The Guv thought about Lake Malawi now that he has experienced it with his very own eyes. He glared at the grinning Garlic over his spectacles and declared that his un-flushed toilet bowl at home held more interest for him than Lake Malawi. Garlic was badly wounded by The Guv insulting his beloved lake and chased our English teacher across the quad arguing his case all the while. The Guv finally silenced the Malawian by striding into the staffroom after furiously kicking the door open and hollering, 'Who will rid me of this pestilential menace?'

Wednesday 29th September

Albert Schweitzer seems thrilled to have me back at school and even thumped the dust out of my fake Persian carpet with the rim of his tennis racquet. While

I did a series of strengthening exercises on a towel near the door, he prattled on about his holiday in the Kruger National Park where he said he had met the girl of his dreams. I asked him if he had fallen in love with a warthog but he didn't get the joke and showed me an out of focus photo of her which he kept in his back pocket. 'Very nice, Schweitzer,' I said. He blushed and took one last look at the photograph before stashing it away.

'Bianca,' he said with reverence in his voice. After the chat about his new girlfriend, Albert Schweitzer's work rate dropped off rather alarmingly. He would frequently stop whatever he was doing and lapse into a bout of unblinking staring at the wall or cupboard. His pathetic expression of love led to thinking of Mermaid which made me unhappy so I sent him on an unnecessary mission to buy me a fizzer from the tuck shop.

18:45   We arrived at the cricket pavilion to discover it locked up and deserted. We sat on the benches outside the change room awaiting The Guv.

'What the hell is he playing at this time?' asked an irate Stinky, peering uncertainly into the gloom of the empty cricket field. Martin Leslie, after sitting in silence for an extended period, suddenly remembered that his key ring had a pen light attached. We craned our necks to peer through a curtain-less crack of window in case our coach had fallen asleep inside the pavilion. There was no sign of him. Rambo was about to call it off when Dog Johnson let out a yelp and swore that there was somebody standing on the cricket field. We galloped out there to find The Guv perched on his shooting stick in the centre of the pitch. His neck and most of his face were hidden by an enormous scarf and in his hands he cradled his hip flask.

'Ill met by moonlight, proud cricket team.' I was the only one to laugh at his *Dream* reference. We gathered tightly around The Guv because he said he had an important and possibly life changing announcement to make and that he wasn't much in the mood for shouting.

'Gentlemen, this will be a cricket season like no other,' he said without sounding too thrilled about matters. 'Gone are gentle Saturdays of young men dressed in whites battling willow and leather through the infernal drizzle.' After further complaints about modern cricket, The Guv announced that we had been entered into the first ever inter-school limited overs night series to be played every Wednesday at the Jan Smuts stadium in Pietermaritzburg. He went on to say that should we make the finals we shall be playing at Kingsmead. There was an audible gasp from the team at the thought of playing on one of the world's great Test grounds. Simon asked The Guv why he had entered us into the competition if he was so much against night cricket.

'Because the winning school, and for that, Brown, you can read coach, receives two thousand rands worth of home equipment.' We laughed but The Guv silenced us once more. 'Most importantly, gentlemen, I entered us into this hideous competition because I believe we can win it.' He paused for a moment and I could feel him regarding his team in the darkness. 'The question is,' he whispered, 'do you believe we can win it?' We assured our master that we could and a wave of excitement washed over our excited huddle, especially when he said our first game was against St Giles next Wednesday and that earnest practice would begin forthwith.

'There is a catch, however,' added The Guv before sending us on our way. 'Lose a single match and the game is up.'

More exciting still – it's a knockout.

The team ran along the edge of the field towards the school buildings pumped with excitement. Night cricket – it sounded more exciting than life itself!

Thursday 30th September

Fatty tore after me to catch up and have a word after breakfast. 'Wait up!' he gasped as he staggered closer looking somewhat alarmed. 'Have you heard the big news?' I was still trying to swallow a large piece of apple that had frustratingly lost its juice and become floury, so I just shook my head and grunted.

'Rambo's coming back for post matric!'

'What?' I blurted, sending a volley of Golden Delicious onto the paving stones of the main quad.

'It's official. He's going to be head boy.'

I thought Fatty was done with his astonishing news but unfortunately he wasn't. 'Hey, I saw your Mermaid on Saturday night.'

'What?' I repeated in much the same tone as before.

'At the ice rink with her friends.'

'Oh really?' I nodded, wondering what exactly I should be thinking about this.

'She's a bloody good ice skater, hey.'

I nodded like I knew all about this and in case Fatty brought out any further astonishing news I glanced at my watch and made a break for the safety of my room.

Friday 1st October

11:30   Garlic has announced that he, too, is staying for post matric. He has implored the entire Crazy Eight to join him in another year of school.

11:33   Rambo has declared that he is no longer returning for post matric. He said that while the lure of being head boy was great, the thought of another year with Garlic made him want to vomit up his own insides.

11:35 Now Vern has announced that he is doing post matric. Although funny, this is impossible because Vern is on functional grade and barely literate.

By lunch Boggo had concluded that Rambo's story about being offered head boy was a myth and that he was only winding people up and being his usual otherwise self.

'How do you know he won't be head boy?' questioned Garlic.

Boggo smiled knowingly and replied, 'Because I know for a fact Simon was offered head boy on Monday.'

All this maniacal talk about head boy and post matric was frying my mind so I ducked out and sauntered across the quad and back to my room where I planned to do some mental preparation before cricket practice.

'Milton,' called Viking and beckoned me over to where he was standing with his legs astride in the cloister. 'Inside.' He motioned with his left arm and closed the door of his office behind us.

He said he wasn't going to beat around the bush and he didn't.

'If you stay for post matric, Milton, I'll offer you the position of head of house. What do you say?' I couldn't believe it and had no words for the housemaster. Eventually he said, 'Think it over and get back to me by the end of the weekend.'

Today is Friday which means I don't have much time. I exited Viking's office and was met with some curious glances from JR Ewing and Thinny who were making their way back to the house after lunch. I lay down on my bed and took some deep breaths to clear my mind but almost immediately there was a loud knock. 'Come in,' I groaned. The door flew open and it was an intense looking Boggo and Garlic.

'I heard Viking just offered you head of house?' accused Boggo with a hugely raised eyebrow. It was then that the thought first occurred to me that Boggo might have bugged Viking's office.

'What's it to you anyway?' I countered.

'I want to be head of house,' he replied.

'But I thought you weren't coming back for post matric?'

'I'm not,' he said, 'but if they beg I will.'

'And I'm going to be a house prefect even if Dad has to pay for it,' added Garlic with a determined expression.

I couldn't shake Boggo off until he had his answer. Eventually I lost patience and admitted the truth. Boggo seemed to be chewing his gums as he processed my revelation. He eventually stopped chewing and said, 'I'll give you five hundred rand if you don't take it.'

'Five hundred bucks!' roared Garlic so loudly that Boggo was forced to silence him with a cheap shot to the ribs. Boggo held out his hand but I didn't shake it. I needed time to think this all through before making commitments to people.

Saturday 2nd October

It felt odd practising rather than playing cricket on a Saturday afternoon but our first night match is looming. The Guv, who is notoriously lax when it comes to extra practices, has spent every afternoon perched on his shooting stick in the nets. He even has us practising with white balls which he had a friend pilfer from the Natal Cricket Union stock room. I think it must be the mouth watering grand prize that has him so inspired because at one stage when I was walking back to my bowling mark he whispered, 'Milton, do you think I would derive more rapture from a talking fridge or a vibrating waterbed?'

My bowling is still erratic. Usually it comes back to me quite quickly after the winter lay-off but this time it feels like my arms and body are refusing to cooperate with each other. At least the batting is improving. I seem to have more strength than before and greatly enjoyed smashing Simon's trundling medium pacer onto the pavilion roof. After years of being plundered by him in the nets I took immense pleasure in advising Simon where he could find a ladder so that he could climb up to recover his cricket ball.

Sunday 3rd October

Mom phoned to say that Wombat was back at home after being kicked out of the Royal Hotel. She didn't say why my grandmother was given the boot but I could hear in her voice that it must have been a shocker. I nobly suggested that I wouldn't come home for the long weekend and Mom sighed with tremendous relief and thanked me profusely. 'She'll be gone by the end of the year,' she said but I could hear in her voice that she didn't quite believe what she was saying. 'Of course your father has driven off in a terrible state.' Mom said Dad was coming up to watch the night cricket but had to end the call abruptly because she could smell Wombat frying fish and was worried about her starting a fire.

18:15 I could see Viking working in his office with the lamp on and made my way down the cloister to his door. Boggo obviously didn't think that I would spot him hidden behind the *Sunday Times* on the house bench, nor Garlic who was pretending to be riveted by a two month old notice outside the vestry. How Vern thought that he was in any way disguised by the small flower pot right outside Viking's office only the cretin will know.

'Sir, I've thought it over and I'm not staying for post

matric.' Thankfully, Viking didn't argue and nor did he seem too upset by my decision. He asked me to keep an open mind and let him know if I had a change of heart.

'Sometimes the end plays tricks with the mind,' he added knowingly.

Boggo manhandled me into the cop shop where he threatened to impale me with a burning stick if I didn't tell him the news immediately. When I broke it to him that I wasn't taking the position he hurled down the smoking stick and hugged me with delight. Garlic was so overcome for no apparent reason that he attempted to join the hug. I broke free and crashed into Vern who had been hiding behind the curtain. Boggo studied me with uncomprehending eyes and asked why I wouldn't take the money. I told him it was a matter of integrity, leaving him in a state of utter confusion. Suddenly his expression changed as a realisation came to him and he gripped Garlic's shoulder like he was on the verge of a vital announcement. Even Vern stepped out from behind the curtain with his left thumb forcing his nose upwards into a disturbing pig's snout. Boggo waited until the laughter had died down and uttered, 'He'll be asking Fatty next.' With that, the three of them scampered out of the cop shop leaving me happily alone with the fire. No regrets. The end is the end, and the end is nigh.

Monday 4th October

08:35 The Glock made a big scene about the night cricket during assembly and announced that a transport list would be going up for anybody wanting to head down to PMB on Wednesday to support the cricket team.

15:30 Mrs Bishop became nasty and unnecessarily sarcastic when I had to leave her extra maths revision early for cricket practice. She demanded to know how my trials marks justified me leaving. There was no answer to that question so I blamed it on The Guv and said that it was a direct order. In an icy voice she said she would be having a word in the ear of my English teacher. The manner in which she said this was highly disturbing and, despite the risk of incurring a Shakespearean tongue lashing, I decided to alert The Guv to the threat before practice started.

Tuesday 5th October

It has been nine days since I left a letter of support and love in Mermaid's post box. Not so much as a word of thanks for the Malawian necklace. Perhaps she's too busy ice skating with her friends to care.

Despite Fatty's assurances that he had no plans whatsoever to stay on for post matric, Boggo nevertheless offered him seven hundred rand to turn down head of house next year. Fatty grew exasperated and cried, 'But he hasn't even asked me yet!' Boggo reckoned that Fatty's use of the word 'yet' was telling and hiked up his bribe by a further hundred.

14:30 A scuffle broke out at the laundry after Vern caught Near Death checking in Boggo's dirty clothes. According to Albert Schweitzer, who was a witness, Near Death threw down the laundry bag and took flight towards the science block with Vern in hot pursuit, his Swiss army knife poised for a stabbing. Rogers Halibut eventually broke up the fight but not before Vern had smashed a beaker of potassium nitrate in the chemistry lab and Near Death had wet his pants.

On the way back from practice I checked the notice board to see how large our support would be tomorrow. Only about 40 names. If it were rugby it would 400.

Wednesday 6th October

We boarded the 1st team minibus just minutes before the rest of my class shuffled into double maths. For that moment alone, eleven years of cricket have been worth it. The Guv was less thrilled about my bunking maths as Mrs Bishop had shared some menacing words with him in the staffroom and he had sworn on his mother's grave that I would miss no more classes. 'I fear the dreaded calculus dragon will have my testicles for this, Milton.'

We utterly devastated St Giles under the lights of the Jan Smuts stadium. It was a brilliant performance by our team with Simon scoring 88 runs off just 91 balls and sending the small but lively crowd in the stadium delirious with all the sixes and fours he was smashing. Although there were only 50-odd boys from our school present, they were treated to some excellent cricket and a surprising number of schoolgirls from the PMB area who turned up to watch. Thinny reckoned the evening was better than a social and when we bowled St Giles out for less than a hundred runs there was a great roar of appreciation around the ground. I didn't take a wicket, nor did I even get a chance to bat, but being a part of that team under the floodlights of a proper cricket stadium with hundreds of spectators looking on was thrilling enough. Afterwards, The Guv treated the team to a celebratory slap-up dinner at the Golden Egg Grill in Scottsville.

Friday 8th October

During my afternoon duty check Garlic halted me at the top of the stairs and urgently beckoned me over to where he was eavesdropping at the door of Fatty's room. 'Listen,' he whispered in a state of great delight.

I leant in a little closer and could hear Fatty speaking to somebody in his room, 'My oath to God,' he said, 'you've got to see Lake Malawi, it's like the best place in the world ...'

'What's going on?' came Boggo's strident whisper and he too leant in to eavesdrop. 'Has Viking finally popped the question?' Fatty was talking again. 'Check this pic out, Sidewinder, how clear is that water?'

'Bloody clear,' added Garlic outside, nodding vociferously. 'Hey, Spud?'

'Very clear,' I agreed.

The unsettling face of Vern loomed in and I was becoming a little claustrophobic anyway so I left the others to their eavesdropping and continued with my house inspection.

21:00 Rambo walked out into the night with his hair slicked back and dressed for a party. He said he was only taking a stroll but it was obvious that he was going out again. Talk about living the life of Riley.

Sunday 10th October

I gave Albert Schweitzer a stern dressing-down for his shabby service of late. After listing the litany of tasks which he hasn't even attempted this week I threatened to swap him with Near Death and make him slave for Boggo for the rest of the year. This immediately struck fear into the youngster and he swore on his life that he would regain his former efficiency immediately. He went on to concede that his new girlfriend Bianca was to blame. 'I think I'm in love,' he declared, looking despairingly at the mountain of mess piled up on the desk. 'I've written her sixteen letters in the last week alone.'

I thought I would save Albert Schweitzer an era of

pain and turmoil and warn him off about girls before he lost his mind completely. I graphically laid out the full history of my dealings with the Mermaid and, if I'm honest, I may have lingered on her madness and depression a little longer than her good points because when I'd finished Schweitzer said, 'I suppose it's the price you have to pay for dating a Hustler girl.' When I asked him to clarify what he meant, he backtracked slightly and said Mermaid was very beautiful, with excellent boobs, and any guy would be delighted to have her. 'As a girlfriend, I mean,' he added quickly.

I had my first experience from the other side of the fence today of third years pushing for prefect. I returned from lunch to find Thinny and JR Ewing standing on the backs of Shambles and Plaque soaping down my bedroom window with facecloths. When I asked them why they were doing this they replied that I was by far their favourite prefect and the pleasure was all theirs.

Over a tennis rematch with Garlic against Fatty and Boggo, various other incidents of pushing for prefect (PFP) were discussed and noted:

Blatant acts of PFP

- The entire Normal Seven attending confirmation classes
- Runt walking a round trip of four kilometres with a sponge and a bucket of soapy water in order to wash Rambo's car
- Darryl (the last remaining) sliding an admiration letter under Simon's door declaring the head of house to be the greatest human being that he has ever encountered
- Barryl walking around proclaiming Lake Malawi to be the best place on earth having never been

there (quite why he has chosen to brownnose a non prefect is a mystery)
- Thinny and JR Ewing cleaning Spud Milton's windows
- Thinny buying Fatty a box of Belgian chocolates
- Thinny offering Boggo full use of his bike
- Thinny offering Boggo full use of his sister

Boggo spent the evening in his room with Garlic, Fatty and Vern working out how much Rambo owed him on a two and a half year bet. With a complicated formula involving astonishing compound interest being multiplied by inflation times eleven, Boggo finally settled on the figure of R2.3 million.

'But why did Rambo take such a stupid bet about the last remaining Darryl?' asked Garlic who was consistently amazed with each unfolding development in the saga.

'It was 1991, Garlic,' replied Fatty in an ominous voice. 'They were dark times.' He went on to explain how the first two Darryls had dropped like flies due to the menace of Pike, their fear of Rambo, and being hung out of the window frequently by Mad Dog.

'Rambo thought it was only a matter of time until the final Darryl cracked and he took the bet expecting to make a healthy profit,' added Boggo, showing off Rambo's signature on a page stamped by a commissioner of oaths, three lawyers, a priest and Viking.

Garlic was amazed by this and blurted, 'Wow! Three brothers all called Darryl in the same house in the same year, now that's what I call a coincidence.'

'They weren't brothers, you retard,' spat Boggo.

'And they weren't called Darryl either,' added Fatty.

Garlic was aghast that the real name of Darryl (the last remaining) isn't Darryl. When he asked what the boy's real name was, Fatty replied, 'Nobody knows.' He paused and added, 'Not even Darryl.'

'All I know,' interrupted Boggo, 'is that the last remaining Darryl may look like a wet blanket but inside he's as hard as nails.' He sniffed and looked superior. 'I've always been an excellent judge of character.'

The bottom line is that Rambo owes Boggo R2.3 million payable by the end of term.

Monday 11th October

I received a letter from Mermaid which has somewhat righted the ship as far as my view of 'us' is concerned. We are still in a relationship although she said that between now and the end of exams it's in hibernation – like a bear. She mentioned that the Malawian necklace was beautiful and promised to wear it for me as soon as we were reunited.

On the positive side, Mermaid's promise of a reunification suggested that we have a future. Unfortunately the realisation has just hit me that barring Eve jumping me in her office, I will be leaving school a virgin.

21:00 Viking's obsession with breaking the house trophy record knows no bounds. After a screaming start to the year, victories in all disciplines have dried up, leaving our house marooned on ten trophies for months. I thought it unnecessary for Viking to explain to the house the entire children's story of *The Tortoise and the Hare* as an analogy, although Garlic, Boggo and the Normal Seven were nodding along like they were hearing it for the first time. With only five competitions left in the year, Viking declared it imperative that we get the monkey off our back as soon as possible. He wished the house chess team under Runt's captaincy well for their clash tomorrow and loudly barked out the house's Latin motto which nobody had ever heard of.

Tuesday 12th October

Boggo has taken his punishments to a new level. He issued Meg Ryan's Son and Enzo Ferrari three hundred lines each for not showing enough excitement when he announced his B for a science project in the showers. Thanks to Boggo's constant flow of petty punishments, use of the urinal has dried up completely, while the constant queue at the house phone has been greatly reduced since the rumour spread that Boggo split the wires and is listening in on everyone's calls.

Runt's chess team came third in the house competition. He reckoned they may have done better but having to witness their own housemaster being ejected from the chess room for repeatedly shouting advice rattled the team's concentration. Now there are only four competitions left and Viking is becoming desperate.

Thursday 14th October

The Guv called an urgent cricket meeting around the fountain at tea break and delivered the news that Westwood College would be our night cricket opponents next Wednesday. To keep us sharp and in form he has also organised a forty over game against Lincoln on Saturday. Apparently Lincoln lost quite badly in the first round of the night series to King's College. The Guv said that by his reckoning a win next Wednesday evening against Westwood should see us into the semi-finals of the competition. He sent us on our way by declaring, 'A waterbed, a waterbed, my kingdom for a waterbed!'

It's less than three weeks until our final exams start. That doesn't quite seem real to me even as I write it.

Friday 15th October

13:50   Rumours have spread that JR Ewing has been offered the position of head of house for next year. After an hour long meeting with Viking he left the office sporting a smug grin and refused to comment on the matter.

14:10   Upon hearing the rumours about JR Ewing, Boggo complained of a blinding headache and took numerous pills and teaspoons of medicine which he said was certain to right the ship.

15:30   Boggo has been rushed to the san complaining of acute chest pains, breathing problems and double vision. He's convinced that he's either been poisoned by Rambo or has contracted cerebral malaria.

15:35   Sister Collins decided to take no chances and called for the school ambulance. Rambo continued with his good humour and said it would be best if the doctors checked Boggo out for syphilis while they were about it.

15:42   Boggo's last word while being carried out on a stretcher was to accuse Rambo of murdering him to avoid his R2.3 million debt. Rambo pretended not to know what Boggo was talking about and Sister Collins agreed that Greenstein was hallucinating and ordered the driver to set off at once and show scant regard for the speed limit.

'Gee, I hope it isn't cerebral malaria,' chirped Rambo breezily as we watched the ambulance making its way down Pilgrims' Walk. 'That would be a real bugger.'

19:30   Boggo has returned from hospital and is back in the san. He hasn't been poisoned nor does he have malaria or syphilis. After numerous tests at the hospital the doctors have come to the conclusion that he suffered an acute panic attack brought on by sudden stress. How we laughed in the cop shop when Fatty told us the news.

Saturday 16th October

08:15 A rejuvenated Boggo returned from the san in complete denial about his embarrassing panic attack yesterday. He assured us that he really did have cerebral malaria, but instead of succumbing like Gecko had, his superior immune system had knocked it off before dinner time. Rambo showed no mercy for the recently hospitalised and enacted a great scene of mockery around the house bench pretending in a high-pitched girl's voice to be Boggo having an emotional meltdown. Boggo attempted to silence the mockery and laughter by taunting Rambo about the R2.3 million bet. Rambo reminded Boggo that the dying season was only two weeks away and either he or Darryl (the last remaining) was bound to kick the bucket in suspicious circumstances. Boggo's snigger was clearly fake and he strode unsteadily into the house clutching his chest.

The mighty juggernaut smashed Lincoln in our practice match today. I scored thirty-two runs but bowled poorly and didn't take a wicket. When I asked The Guv for some recommendations to improve my bowling he advised me to stay positive and double up on my intake of eggs. He reckoned that trying to tamper with the complicated mechanics of leg spin bowling was as futile as reading Chaucer to an Italian.

Sunday 17th October

Just completed eleven hours of gruelling maths revision. I have barred myself from thinking I'm improving because thus far I have only been fooling myself. Nevertheless, I think I'm improving.

Tuesday 19th October

21:00 We spent a good deal of the cricket team talk in the cop shop sharing stories about Mad Dog and the old days. Just when it seemed that it was merely a tea drinking exercise, Simon let loose a passionate speech about how this could be our last meaningful match for the school. 'Do yourself a favour,' he said lowering his voice. 'On the way back to your rooms tonight take a look at the cricket notice board and see how many boys are coming to watch tomorrow.'

It wasn't really on the way to my room but I went to check the cricket lists anyway. I lost count of all the names, but the number must be close to 200. I returned to my room where I struck a quick-fire imaginary century with my bat in front of the mirror.

Wednesday 20th October

We are in the semi-finals! What a night it was at the Jan Smuts stadium with a crowd of at least a thousand packed in to watch us.

Highlights

- The roar as Simon hit the winning runs with five balls to spare.
- My brief but fluent innings of 26 runs.
- Being asked for my autograph by a small and possibly deranged young boy.
- The Guv umpiring the whole match in sunglasses.
- The thrill of playing cricket at night in front of over one thousand screaming fans.
- The look I received from a beautiful girl with long brown hair as I was walking to the bus with my cricket kit after the game.

- A cross-bred Dalmatian charging onto the field of play during the game. Much to the crowd's amusement the spotted animal avoided a vast army of ground staff and security guards for at least five minutes before leaping over the boundary fence and scampering under a wall and into the bowels of the stadium.

Lowlights

- Dad's weird belly dancing on the grass bank every time I struck a boundary.
- The bald Westwood opening bowler who now must be well into his late twenties.
- The bald Westwood opening bowler being called Dad by the rest of the team.
- Vern's attempt at streaking with his underpants pulled up his bum crack.
- The loud and endless droning on by the stadium announcer over the PA. It sounded like the man was drinking heavily on the job because during the drinks break he played Forever Young, dedicated it to his ex-fiancée, and started blubbing on about how he missed her.
- Having to head back to school in the team minibus directly after the match when the throbbing music from Take 5 could be heard in the distance. It sounded hedonistic and wild.

Thursday 21st October

I was rudely awoken by Albert Schweitzer and his friend Wingnut Wilkens when they snuck into my room at 6.15 to examine my cricket bat and watch me sleeping. After driving the vermin out, I sipped on the mug of tea that Schweitzer had left on my bedside table and replayed last night's match over in my mind. It was without doubt one of the most epic nights of my life.

After breakfast Viking had some stern words with Vern in his room. Since the cretin has no door a large crowd gathered around the foot of the stairs to eavesdrop.

'It's just not on, Blackadder!' roared Viking, his voice echoing off the walls of the bogs.

'Lubbly jubbly,' replied the cretin in an extremely nasal voice that also rebounded off the walls and set off stifled sniggers on the stairs and surrounds.

'You can't just run around in public with your underpants wrenched up your crotch.'

'Pig's night,' replied Vern and pulled down his shorts revealing no underpants in his crotch whatsoever.

'Good God, boy!' barked Viking in alarm.

'Answer me, boy!' shouted Vern in reply and slammed his missing door in the housemaster's face.

Viking threw his hands in the air like he was giving up on life entirely and roared, 'One more bloody month!' He pushed past the crowd of boys all pretending to be standing around at the foot of the stairs studying old house photographs on the wall.

'I want all the prefects in my office immediately!' he snapped at nobody in particular.

Once the prefects were seated in his office Viking began rolling up his sleeves. 'What will become of that simpleton I have no idea,' he muttered leafing through his diary. Quite why he started in January and paged forward when he could have started in December and worked one month backwards is anyone's guess. After some feverish paging and licking at his fingers he arrived at the highlighted date.

'Sunday the 14th of November. Mark it down in your diaries, gentlemen, for that is the day that you shall be leading the rest of the house up Inhlazane.'

'Oh my crap,' mumbled Fatty like he had just been alerted to the date of his own demise and it was far earlier than expected.

'Barring being on the verge of death, I shall accept no excuses.' Viking halted Boggo's raised hand by declaring outright that swollen testicles would not be accepted as a legitimate excuse.

'Unless I can see your scrotum hanging out the bottom of your shorts, Greenstein, you'll be marching with the rest of them.'

He droned on about it being a house and school tradition and as the last year group from our house to complete the mission, it was beholden on us to lead from the front and guide the others.

Depending on whom you speak to, the round trip up Inhlazane is anything from 46–101 kilometres. I remember it being the most gruelling day of my school career and like everyone else I'm determined to avoid it at all costs. My plan is to keep close to Rambo and pray for bad weather.

Saturday 23rd October

Further complaints about the third years pushing for prefect have surfaced.

Pushing for prefect (PFP) Part 2

- Runt sweeping the cloisters outside Viking's office on a daily basis.
- Barryl painting Viking's gate without even being asked. The idiot ended up with hard labour and a tongue lashing when Viking ruined his favourite jersey after leaning on the gate not realising it was covered in Barryl's paint.
- Spike giving Shambles a long lecture on school

spirit at the house bench while Simon was attempting to read the *Weekly Mail*.
- Thinny promising to bring a coffee machine back for the cop shop annexe after the long weekend.
- Thinny offering to make Fatty a bronze plaque to commemorate his house farting record in first year.

Other more sinister reports include Thinny offering Albert Schweitzer a large sum to hang himself from the rafters in the dormitory while stark naked in a bid to stoke up Viking's old naked boy committing suicide phobia. Despite Thinny promising to heroically save Schweitzer from suicide at the last minute, my slave wisely refused the offer. JR Ewing was also overheard bragging about the changes he would make about the house once he was officially announced as head of house. He's obviously banking on his status as a first team rugby player swinging the vote in his favour. He may not be wrong.

I'm not exactly sure what led to the deal being struck because I found myself drifting deep into my own thoughts. Suddenly everyone was jumping up and down in astonishment and Boggo and a grinning Rambo were shaking hands.

'You'd better mark this down in your diary, Spud,' advised Fatty, 'because I don't quite believe it myself.'

Unbelievably, Boggo had shaken on it and written off the entire R2.3 million Darryl debt. In return, Rambo has promised the following:

1. Rambo won't murder Boggo as he earlier swore on his life to do
2. Rambo will drive Boggo to Inhlazane and back on

November 14 in his car
3. Boggo will be elected head of house

I cleared my throat and Boggo's head jerked around suspiciously.

'Sorry, guys,' I said, 'but Viking offered me head of house yesterday and I've decided to accept his offer and return for post matric.' It wasn't just Boggo glaring at me in horror, Rambo looked murderous too. I allowed the seconds to tick by, greatly enjoying their discomfort, and then with a cheeky grin, I said, 'Gotcha.' For once the joke was on them. Just in case, a mightily relieved Boggo offered me a side guy from Vern's hot granny if I didn't come back, and Rambo threatened to slit my throat if I did. Boggo seems convinced that with Rambo's blessing he has head of house all sewn up because he immediately enquired about the exact date Simon would be vacating his room.

Monday 25th October

Final exams begin in just eight days. During assembly The Glock laid down the law to the school about respecting absolute silence around the theatre while matrics were writing their finals. He rambled on at length about the school's phenomenal academic record and produced an enormous trophy which he said would now be awarded to the house that had distinguished itself in the field of academics. Viking had his eyes fixed on the headmaster and he sat forward awkwardly in his chair on the stage awaiting the result.

'Congratulations to Barnes House for pulling off one of the narrowest margins of victory possible.'

Viking jerked back violently in his seat and pretended to clap but didn't. After assembly our housemaster disappeared into his office where, by the sound of things, he attacked his filing cabinet. To make matters worse, our house had come second, losing by the tiniest of margins.

13:25 'Poor guy,' sighed Fatty, glancing up to the staff table where Viking sat dejectedly not eating his lunch. 'If Vern had only been on standard grade instead of functional grade, we would have won and broken the house record.' The cretin himself didn't appear too concerned about his stupidity changing the course of house history as he was more focused on lapping up a saucer of gravy like a cat.

Wednesday 27th October

The entire house turned out for the inter-house tennis championships. For the Harmless Half-Dozen it was compulsory. The Normal Seven arrived because they are all in PFP mode and want to show off their sudden house spirit to Viking. The Fragile Five turned up because they realised that it would look like desertion if they were the only ones who skipped proceedings. Garlic, who was being followed by Vern, turned up to support because he was pursuing Boggo who in turn was following Rambo who was following nobody and merely felt like watching an afternoon of tennis.

Despite numerous renditions of the house song and Simon's unbeaten afternoon, we didn't win the inter-house tennis competition either. Viking marched off after the cup had been handed over to East and was seen kicking a small plant to death near the top end of Pilgrims' Walk.

Thursday 28th October

SPEECH DAY

The folks were in high spirits upon arrival at speech day. Aside from Dad parking the Merc in the chairman of the board's parking spot and having to be called out to move it shortly before the ceremony began, there were no major embarrassments. Wombat looked resplendent in one of her blue ball gowns, black hat, red sash and white gloves, although she thought we were in England meeting the high commissioner at a garden party. After shaking hands with The Glock, she asked me if he was the man himself. To avoid having a lengthy conversation, I mentioned that he was Austrian.

'Bloody kangaroo shaggers the whole lot of them,' added Dad, picking up stompies.

I received the English and drama prizes, but lost out to Squirter Kennedy in history which was mildly galling since he only arrived at school this year and won most of the prizes, including dux and merit achiever of the year.

After the prizes and speeches The Glock stood up to announce the head boy and vice head boy for next year. Dog Johnson seemed mightily shocked when he was called up as vice head boy and was embarrassingly chipped out by the chairman of the board for having the back of his shirt untucked.

'And the head boy for 1994 is ... Simon Brown.'

Simon, on the other hand, appeared as cool as a cucumber as he strode down the steps of the amphitheatre to shake the hands of the dignitaries. Dad whispered loudly in my ear, 'He's a bloody good cricketer, he deserves it.'

Wombat had a few too many at the buffet lunch and became weepy when it came time to say goodbye. My grandmother took one last look at the school and said it was probably the last time that she would ever lay eyes on old England.

'Goodbye, Winston,' she wailed and waved a gloved hand at the chapel. Distraught, she sank into the car dabbing at her eyes with a handkerchief. Dad tooted the horn and my parents wished me luck for the exams. I watched the Merc until I could no longer see it and returned to the house where Rambo was pumping heavy weights in his jocks and blaring out ACDC on his imported hi-fi in the cop shop.

Saturday 30th October

18:00 I knocked on the door and heard a loud bang followed by squeaky footsteps on a linoleum floor. The Guv was wearing an old green tracksuit and cream sheepskin slippers. His hair was curiously standing up on end and his eyes were wide and alert. 'Ah, Milton,' he said ushering me in. 'Just been rewiring the plug on my egg poacher. The dining room table was littered with tools and odd pieces of rusted metal.

'Working weekend, I see, Milton,' he said, violently heaving the cork out of a bottle of red wine and filling two glasses. 'All set for English language on Tuesday?'

I told The Guv that I was feeling more confident about finals than I had about trials. He appraised me over his glasses. 'That's what I've always enjoyed about you, Milton, you're a thoroughly otherwise little sod.'

My English teacher let out a long sigh and showed off a pile of pages. 'You're not the only one who has been scribbling, you know.' He confided that he has at last begun writing his memoirs which he reckons would be billed as a comical tragedy in many acts, most of them obscene. The first bottle of wine was finished before I was halfway through my glass and he led me to the kitchen to find another and show off the splendid lamb shanks which we were eating for dinner. 'That fellow Thinny had his mother ship in a freezer load of fine dining for me. Either the boy is pushing for prefect or the mother is pushing for a rogering,' he declared, heaving away at the cork of a second bottle. I alerted him to the fact that Thinny has taken pushing for prefect to a new level, but The Guv cut me short and proceeded to lambaste me for ruining his fantasy about Thinny's mom leaning over his stove wearing nothing but red high heels.

We returned to our chairs in the lounge where The Guv asked me if I had any regrets looking back at my four years at school. I listed a few things but it was my mentioning not losing my virginity when considering that stuttering second years are shagging loose women with gay abandon that caught his attention. The Guv seemed amazed that Mermaid and I hadn't done it yet and when I said that she was saving herself for marriage he lurched forward and cried, 'She's not a crackpot, is she?' I admitted that she might be and The Guv pondered the situation deeply before saying, 'Milton, there are two golden rules to sex. One, be spirited at all times even in a losing cause, and two, never allow anybody to dress you up in a leather pig costume.'

Thinny's mom's lamb shanks were so delicious that I've decided to vote for her son as a prefect.

Sunday 31st October

Hammered history and geography today. It feels like I have been over the notes so often that I may be developing a photographic memory. Unfortunately the same theory doesn't appear to work for maths.

15:30 Just about every matric at school for the weekend joined the sprawling game of touch rugby on Trafalgar. I even managed to intercept a weak pass from Chris Plant and score a try. After the game Rambo took us through our moves for the farewell haka/war dance. Mostly people messed about and pulled funny faces at each other but the rehearsal was enough to bring Garlic to the verge of tears. 'It's all ending too fast,' he wailed and shook his head like life may never be better than this.

19:15 The first years were at a life skills lecture in the theatre so Vern, as Boggo's surrogate slave, was placed on tea making duty. After the cretin was seen eating three Rooibos teabags and destroyed the kettle by continually boiling it with no water inside, he was replaced by Garlic who made a vast amount of sweet milky tea after boiling over ten litres of water on the stove.

'Well, gents, tomorrow the dying season begins,' stated Rambo in a rather jovial fashion. Fatty peered into the fire and admitted that he had a feeling that something shocking and terrible was going to happen.

'What? You going to take off your shirt?' quipped Boggo.

'My oath to God,' said Fatty, 'I've got this sinking feeling.'

'You mean one of us might die?' asked Garlic earnestly, carrying in numerous mugs of tea on a tray.

'Could be,' Fatty replied and threw another log on the fire, causing numerous sparks to fly out onto the carpet. 'It's not like it hasn't happened before.'

'Maybe we will all die together,' ventured Rambo, 'in my car in a blazing wreck on the side of the road?' He glanced at the uncertain faces around him and added, 'You have to admit it would be a classic way for the

Crazy Eight to go out.' He nodded at us like the idea appealed to him. 'A bang, not a whimper.'

I made a mental note not to ride in Rambo's car during November.

As the gathering broke up, Fatty wished us luck and safety for the first day of the dying season. I'm not sure why, but I felt nervous heading back to my room and sprinted off like I was being chased. Once safely inside, I said a silent prayer for everybody I knew and battled to sleep with all the thoughts and luminous shapes flipping around my subconscious when I closed my eyes.

Monday 1st November

The Dying Season

After a morning of maths, a lunch of lasagne and an afternoon of cricket practice, I languidly made my way across the quad soaking in the clear evening and the swallows diving above the fountain catching their invisible insects. Boggo exited the house door carrying an extremely full cup of tea which occupied his entire focus. Under his arm was the evening paper and his destination was the house bench. I watched him balance his tea on a small concrete ledge and stretch his legs out while unfurling his paper.

'Fatty!' hollered Boggo, sounding distressed. 'Fatty, get out here!' There was a note of desperation in his voice. Fatty came bursting out of the house doors and rumbled across to Boggo, closely followed by Garlic and Vern.

'What is it?' cried Garlic charging along in confusion.

Obviously there was something astounding in the paper and I quickly made my way over to the bench to find out what was so captivating. The headline read:

River Phoenix dies!

Underneath it said:

Young Hollywood star collapses outside nightclub.

We all sat there in silence staring out at the quad to the sound of Pissing Pete's trickle.
'It's already got one,' gasped Fatty.

The dying season has struck.

Tuesday 2nd November

Final exams begin

This is the beginning of the end. Twelve years of relentless toil and at last I arrive at the final exams I shall ever write as a schoolboy. English language was a gentle start and I was kept amused throughout the three hour paper by The Guv who, as one of the invigilators, paced around the theatre auditorium in a variety of different characters. First he limped past my desk like Richard III, later as the cruel undertaker in *Oliver!* and finally he dragged his toe behind him like some satanic beast of the underworld. Mr Ashleigh-Meyer didn't approve of my sniggering and asked me if I had a problem with the paper. I shook my head and tried my best to block out The Guv who by now was swinging his right leg around like he was in the ministry of funny walks.

Thursday 4th November

Wrote history today. Lennox was invigilating and after the exam he asked me how it went. 'No surprises,' I replied. He said that it was fortuitous that the Hani trial got under way this morning. 'I hope they string them up,' he muttered, despite not believing in the death penalty.

'These days, days they run away
Like horses over the hill.' U2

Friday 5th November

King's College has been announced as our semi-final opponents next Wednesday. What a night awaits!

Monday 8th November

Since Boggo has convinced himself that he is destined to be head of house, he has grown even more totalitarian. Yesterday he thrashed Shambles with a belt for drinking straight from the tap without using his hand. This morning he beat Rowdy for making a noise outside his room (the chances of which are extremely unlikely). He also made Plaque cry before lunch after threatening to have the poor lad expelled for using the urinal during office hours. Simon says he isn't surprised that even Vern received more votes for head of house than Boggo. In fact the only people who voted for Boggo were Vern, Rambo and himself. Enough said.

Tuesday 9th November

Our cricket team has attained legendary status. Such is the demand for spectator transport that The Glock decided to make tomorrow a half day and hired buses for the whole school. This kind of announcement is usually reserved for Rhodes Scholars (occasional) or a blanket of snow in the quad (never). I did my best to focus on the glory and glamour of tomorrow and not think about the mutant maths monster lying in wait on Friday.

Wednesday 10th November

Semi Final of Night Series against King's College

14:45   We made our way from the bus, down a corridor and into the change rooms where we migrated to the same areas that we had occupied before. After lacing up my spikes and conducting a few stretches, we followed Simon down the tunnel and out onto the field to check the pitch and warm up with some fielding practice. We were met with an almighty roar from the grandstands where the entire school stood to salute us.

'Crikey!' shouted The Guv above the din. 'This is worse than Eden Gardens.'

15:00   Another almighty roar went up when King's College marched out in their blazers. 'What a bunch of vaginas!' chirped Rambo rather loudly. With King's running out onto the field Simon decided to call us in to the change rooms so as to keep up our mystique. The entire school rose to applaud us as we made our way back down the tunnel and the pale hairs on my arms stood to attention.

'Remember we beat them in the first term. They are more scared of us than we of them,' our captain repeated once we were back in the bowels of the stadium.

Simon lost the toss and King's decided to bat first. This was a big advantage because batting in the bright light of the afternoon is far easier than under floodlights at night.

15:30   We started flat and King's College piled on the runs. My single over of bowling was clouted for 14 and the other bowlers were just as bad. Even the repeated and increasingly desperate war cries from the school weren't enough. The King's batsmen had an answer for everything we bowled at them.

18:00 King's rattled up 217-4 in their forty overs which suddenly seemed like a vast amount of runs. The situation was so desperate that The Guv even dusted off Henry IV's Agincourt speech during the dinner break. The wind had been taken out of the sails of our supporters. King's College spent the break shouting and chanting while our school hung around behind the stadium eating pies and spading girls. Sitting there in the change room 218 runs for victory felt like an improbability unless Simon could pull off yet another innings of a lifetime.

18:45 The school sang Happy Birthday to Martin Leslie as he made his way out under the floodlights to face the first ball. He raised his bat to the crowd and there was loud chanting of 'Eat! Eat Eat!' The positivity ended right there because Leslie was clean bowled first ball. It was a terrible way to start and King's unloaded another echoing war cry. Simon strode to the wicket and our supporters began a slow chant of 'Si-mon Si-mon Si-mon!' Wickets began to tumble although Simon held firm at the other end. It all seemed so dismal as I walked to the crease with our score on 69-6 after 18 overs. I could hear the disappointment around me and knew in my heart that our unbeaten record would be lost tonight in front of all these people. The realisation that we were doomed removed the terrible pressure of expectation and I stroked two fours off my legs which pleased the crowd and led the belly dancing madman on the grass banks to flash the lights of his car distractedly in my eyes.

The sight of me scoring runs and playing with confidence had an excellent effect on Simon who began smashing the ball around the ground like he was playing park cricket with a tennis ball. When I first came to the wicket he said that we could not disgrace the school and needed to salvage some pride. Half an hour later, he met me in the middle of the wicket and reckoned that it still wasn't impossible to win this. After another belligerent flurry of strokes by Simon the stadium announcer blurted out that we had reached our 50 partnership. Despite only scoring 11 of the runs myself, Simon seemed hugely impressed with my contribution and warned me against trying be a glory boy. I made a great show of blocking my next ball. Unfortunately, I couldn't resist having a swat at the short ball that followed and top-edged it to fine leg towards the fielder waiting on the boundary with his hands cupped. I could hear the groan from some of the crowd and the mutter from myself at my own rashness and stupidity which, I decided in that moment, was born as a result of gross insecurity thanks to a string of failed relationships with the same woman and lingering virginity issues.

The ball sailed clean over the fielder's head for a six and another chorus of 'Eat! Eat! Eat!' echoed around the ground. The rest was a blur of excitement and danger. I can remember Simon's century and also nearly running out my captain with a suicidal single. But there was no stopping us as we coasted to victory with an entire over to spare. Out of a 131 run partnership I had scored only 38 runs but from the manner in which the stampeding crowd hoisted me aloft one would have thought I'd made a double century.

Back in the change room we danced and sang and drowned out The Glock who was trying to make a speech from the door. I couldn't do much but sit there exhausted and astonished by what had just happened. Everywhere I could hear voices chanting, 'We're going to Kingsmead.'

I felt Rambo's strong hand on my shoulder. 'Spuddy, you wanna come to Take 5?' I grinned and nodded. The Guv was too excited and overwrought to deny me heading off with Rambo and Simon. He knew that we must have been going out because we were dressed in civvies and he said, 'Have one for me, Milton, and remember the luck of the Irish.'

21:30 Take 5 was throbbing by the time we made it to the doors. My fantastic run of luck continued when I evaded the bouncer's attention and followed Simon and Rambo up into the club. We hung around drinking beer and talking about the cricket but then Rambo and Simon started chatting to some girls they knew, leaving me feeling a little spare. I decided the only place I wouldn't look like a loser was among the crowds on the dance floor so I headed over and attached myself to a large circle grooving to Funky Town. After a few songs I began to regret coming out at all. It had felt like such an exciting thing to do but now I was stuck with Rambo and Simon and hardly knew another soul. The adrenalin from the cricket was also beginning to wear off and my legs felt like heavy tools unfit for dancing. I didn't last long on the dance floor and made my way back out to find the others. I skirted the crowded bar area and almost crashed into a tall brunette.

'John Milton!' she cried, her eyes wide with amazement. I recognised her immediately.

'It's you!' she hissed, pointing at me like I was the criminal in a witness parade. All at once I felt incredibly anxious. I was caught in the harsh headlights of Sarah Stalker Silver.

'Why didn't you write back?' Sarah demanded, advancing on me in a threatening fashion. The night was deteriorating rapidly. I had run into the worst possible person imaginable and I now fervently wished that I hadn't let my ego get the better me when Rambo invited me out.

'Why didn't you write back?' she hollered louder this time. I was left with no other choice but to play dumb and deny everything.

'What do you mean?' I bleated in a shrill voice.

'You didn't get my letters?'

'What letters?' I replied this time sounding a little more convincing.

A vast smile broke out of her unsettling expression. She reached out and took my hand, leading me forcefully outside onto the open deck.

'You promise you didn't get my letters?' she asked, staring meaningfully into my eyes.

'I do.'

Unfortunately my response sounded eerily like I was accepting a marriage proposal. Without further ado she pulled me towards her and kissed me passionately. I tried my best not to respond. Thereafter she gazed into my eyes and creepily whispered, 'I'm so into you.'

'Me too.'

I don't know why I said that because it sounded ridiculous and it set Sarah Silver off with more psychotic happiness. After further vigorous kissing she declared that she wanted to have children with me. She obviously noticed my horrified expression and shouted, 'Kidding!' before punching me really hard on the shoulder. She hooted like a maniac.

Thankfully, Simon and Rambo approached just then and announced that we were leaving.

'This place is so dead,' reckoned Simon despite the club being packed to the rafters behind him.

'You're Rambo,' blurted Sarah Silver. He grinned casually and flicked his car keys in the air, catching them nonchalantly in the back of his hand.

'Come on, Spuddy, let's hit the road,' he said.

Sarah Silver whispered 'Call me' in my ear.

'Definitely,' I lied again, and followed the others out of the club.

Sarah Silver may be a total psychopath, but she remains a bloody good kisser and possible nymphomaniac.

Thursday 11th November

After sleeping until lunchtime, enjoying a thirty minute shower, writing up yesterday's events in my diary and receiving lengthy compliments from the Normal Seven, I retired to my room and realised that I had a mere three hours left to prepare for my algebra exam tomorrow. I became rather panicked at the lack of time I had left myself but Albert Schweitzer made me see reason with his strong tea and sage advice. 'John, if you don't know your algebra by now,' he ventured, 'you'll never know it.'

Friday 12th November

A Milton mathematical hypothesis:

Everybody agreed that the maths algebra paper was a stinker.

Mrs Bishop said she thought it was fair and reasonable.

Therefore Mrs Bishop is a stinker.

17:00 Albert Schweitzer hurtled up to me on the lawn outside Barnes House where I was in an involved discussion with Flip-Flop Scott and Moose Mabbett about the maths paper.

'There you are,' he gasped. 'I've been looking for you

all over the place.'

My slave explained that a girl called Sarah had called seven times this afternoon and had threatened numerous boys including Small & Freckly with serious repercussions if he couldn't locate me immediately.

'Small & Freckly is now hiding under JR Ewing's bed,' he panted, 'and everybody's too scared to answer the house phone and it keeps ringing and ringing.'

I advised Schweitzer to refer all calls from Sarah Silver to Vern. I reasoned that the only way to fight insanity is with even greater insanity. My slave nodded uncertainly and sprinted off along the cloister like he had been tasked with carrying the Olympic torch across Europe.

Saturday 13th November

Tomorrow the torture of Inhlazane awaits. Most of the house are running scared after Boggo spread the rumour that the hike was 130km each way and that the mountain itself was so high that you needed oxygen to survive it.

After two conversations with Vern on the telephone, the incessant calls from Sarah Silver have dried up completely.

Sunday 14th November

INHLAZANE SCORECARD

The Good

- Fatty's idea to force our slaves to carry a back pack. This enabled us to have extra water and Fatty to bring along an entire three course meal.

- The view from the top was magnificent and it made me strangely euphoric about life and leaving school.
- The Crazy Eight having a compulsory slash on the trig beacon at the top of the mountain. An important Crazy Eight tradition instituted by Mad Dog.

The Bad

- Waking up at 2:30 in the morning.
- Boggo and Rambo pretending to have walked to the foot of Inhlazane when they spent the day driving around the Midlands having picnics.
- Fatty forking out large amounts of money to hitch a ride back from Inhlazane in Rambo's car. He called it a matter of life and death.
- I forewent the offer of a free drive back to school. After my heroics on Wednesday night I didn't want Schweitzer and the others to think I was merely a lucky big hitter who went AWOL in tough situations.
- Viking's smug welcome back to school after limping in at 20:15.

The Ugly

- Plump Graham throwing up before reaching the Three Sisters.
- Fatty's constant complaining.
- Being the only prefect on the return leg meant I was inundated with complaints of people collapsing and dying of thirst.
- My blistered feet soaking in a bucket of water.

- Vern insisting on hiking in his full school uniform.
- Vern drinking his own urine out of his black school shoe.
- The school's belief that any good could come from forcing boys to traverse half the continent in a day on account of house spirit.

Monday 15th November

Woke up in agony. I'll never hike again. I swear.

15:30 Up to my ears in geography swotting, I took a break and visited Fatty in the archives. Despite the fact that Sidewinder has single-handedly kept the place running for the last year while Fatty has been besotted with Penny, he predicted a dim future for the archives after he left. 'Sidewinder works hard,' he conceded, 'but he's not right in the cranium.' He tapped his forehead and shook his head dismally.

'Knock knock who's there?' It was Garlic grinning and pink after a hot shower. 'What's happening?' He seemed rather confounded by our lack of response. 'Just chilling,' said Fatty drily.

'What do you mean just chilling?' he questioned. 'We have geography tomorrow!' As the conversation inevitably does with Garlic nowadays, matters turned to post matric.

'Think about it, Spud. You could play cricket for the firsts, come back to Malawi in the Easter holidays, park off in the cop shop talking shit and go on Crazy Eight missions.'

'But we've done all that, Garlic,' I said.

'But you can do it again!' he cried throwing his hands up like I just didn't get it.

'But I want to go out and do something for the first time.'

'Boggo's right, Spud, you're not right in the head.' He turned on his heel and stormed off down the stairs.

'What a muppet,' muttered Fatty glancing at his watch. 'Come on, Spuddy, the tuck shop opens in five.'

20:00 We are taking on St James in the finals of the night series. The Guv says there is a good chance the match will be postponed until Friday night because of all the rain around in Durban.

I immediately called home to check on the weather. Dad said it was peeing down and that our garage roof is leaking. Mom reckons the weather is set in all week and that I shouldn't get my hopes up. I heard Dad in the background blaming El Niño which in turn he blames on the Russians for nuking Chernobyl.

Tuesday 16th November

I heard on the radio news that Chris Hani's killers have been sentenced to death. Luckily for the murderers, there is a moratorium on the death penalty so they will get life imprisonment instead. Lennox reckons one should write down a list of countries that carry out executions and that same list will double for the world's worst warmongers.

Geography was far easier than our trial exam. Another one bites the dust.

17:00 Mom says it's still raining but the weather forecast says it will start clearing on Friday.

Thursday 18th November

What a damp squib! The night series final has been called off because the field is waterlogged and the Natal Cricket Union doesn't want it damaged because there's a big provincial match being played on Sunday. The team was mightily disappointed, especially when we heard that the game had been cancelled rather than postponed. We tried to brainstorm ideas about relocating the match but The Guv said it was over with and best accepted, although he did concede that we had finished the competition with a whimper rather than a bang.

'What about the prizes, sir?' asked the Stinkmeister.

'Never fear, Stinky, my vibrating waterbed is on its way,' he replied. 'And I intend to christen it with Thinny's mother.'

We were rewarded for our unbeaten heroics on the cricket field with a sumptuous tea in the staff room. If lurkers such as Mongrel and Sparerib hadn't been hanging around stealing our chocolate éclairs, it might have been an enjoyable occasion. Once we had finished our sumptuous tea The Guv asked how many of us would be staying after the exams to take part in the Natal trials week down in Durban. Despite stroking a few memorable shots through the covers last Wednesday evening, if I'm honest with myself I don't have a prayer of making the side. My leg spinning has deteriorated with my advancing years, and besides who in their right mind would want to hang around school for a further two weeks doing nothing? As it turned out seven of the team did, but neither Rambo nor I signed up. The Guv called me traitorous and tried to cajole me into coming back by declaring me to be in the form of my life at the moment.

To complete a disappointing day we had to write Afrikaans all afternoon. It was a terrible grovel as per usual, but I know I pulled through – *sonder twyfel*.

Friday 19th November

Poor Viking is in a terrible state. Sunday sees the inter-house tug-of-war which is the last chance to break the infernal house trophy record. To make matters worse for our housemaster, Fatty has refused to take part because he says that he is solely focused on completing his finals and doesn't want any distractions. Rambo has unsurprisingly refused to take part unless Fatty takes part. The entire house overheard Viking's shouts, taunts and pleas but Fatty was having none of it.

'What a sheep shagger,' grumbled Fatty later in the cop shop where we had gathered to stare at the fire and NOT work.

'Poor Shouty is getting desperate,' grinned Rambo, sipping at hot Milo.

Minutes later Viking burst into the cop shop and made another bid for Fatty and Rambo to sign up for the team. Our housemaster let rip with an emotional speech about history and the importance of this moment for our house, making himself rather tearful in the process.

'Sorry, sir,' replied Fatty sadly, 'but I really don't want to do it.'

Viking nodded like he understood that it was Fatty's right to refuse. 'Black?' he asked hopefully, looking across to where Rambo was reclining in his armchair with his feet up on the table.

'Sorry, sir,' Rambo said. 'I'm only in if Fatty's in.'

'But why, Black? Why?' boomed Viking, desperately clutching at his umbrella.

'Because Fatty is setting the example and I would like to respect that position, sir.'

Viking nodded and said he understood when he patently didn't.

'Sir,' called Garlic, 'if you're really desperate I'll be happy to help you out with a tug.'

'Side guy!' trumpeted Vern from behind the curtain.

Viking left amidst hooting laughter and slammed the door behind him.

I lay awake listening for the night train which passed at 23:06.

Saturday 20th November

08:15 Viking flagged Fatty down after breakfast and hauled him into his office. Our housemaster mentioned he had by stroke of luck found a surplus in the house funds account and since he was asking Fatty for such a huge favour he would like to hand over some money to help change his mind about the tug-of-war. After counting out R250 (which is two and a half times my house play budget) Fatty agreed to sign up and thereby guaranteed Rambo's involvement too. Fatty immediately ran up to Rambo's room where he found him lying naked on his bed shaving his belly button. He handed over R200 because the whole thing had obviously been Rambo's idea in the first place. Fatty was thrilled with his R50 profit and wrote up a long list of things that he was going to purchase in the tuck shop. Viking was delighted about the unfolding developments and marched up and down the cloisters barking on about us all making house history tomorrow. He had every right to be excited because Rambo pulled out the Scales of Injustice and weighed the house tug-of-war team:

Tug of War Team (in kgs)

Fatty	118
Plump Graham	117
Rambo	97
Barryl	91
JR Ewing	83
Total	506kgs

That's over half a ton.

The final weekend at school threw up numerous conundrums. I didn't know if I felt like watching the house movie, talking rubbish in the cop shop or relaxing in my room listening to music. I think the word for this is surreal.

Sunday 21st November

A day of incessant geometry was broken up by the inter-house tug-of-war competition on Trafalgar. Our juggernaut half-ton team barely raised a sweat in smashing all comers and claiming the trophy. Viking demonstrated some unnecessary screaming and pumping of his fists, especially considering how casually most of the other teams took the event. Larson House even sent out a joke team by choosing the smallest collection of first years possible. The joke team were so overwhelmed by our heavyweights that most of them were airborne when being hauled across the line.

19:30   This evening in chapel I soaked in every stained glass window and sang the hymns with everything I had, knowing it was the last time. There was no rush by the matrics to leave the chapel after the service. Perhaps they, like me, could feel the sudden and terrible finality of it all.

Monday 22nd November

08:00   'And now it gives me great pleasure to announce
the heads of houses for next year,' intoned The Glock
as he stood regally at the lectern in his academic gown.
I wondered what it would have been like to be called
up as head of house. What would I have felt? Would it
have been worth another year at school? Names poured
out of the headmaster's mouth. Our house's name
was read out. 'Please put your hands together for Alan
Greenspan.' There were some sniggers as Boggo strode
towards the stage like a man of power and wisdom.
Once again the headmaster had bollocksed his name
up (last time it was Alan Einstein) but Boggo didn't care
because he had what he wanted and Rambo's bet had
been repaid. It would be fair to say that Boggo's election
to head of house wasn't at all popular as a number of
boys groaned and covered their faces with their hands.
I pity them all.

Viking was hauled up to receive a commemorative
plaque for the house wall to reward our achievement for
winning a record eleven competitions this year. The idiot
was meant to have shaken hands with the headmaster
and return to his seat but instead he took over the spot
at the lectern and embarked on a long-winded and toe-
curling speech about how great our house was. There
was some feeble applause after he had at last finished
and loud whooping from Garlic and the Normal Seven.

Later, when Rambo questioned Boggo about the headmaster calling him Alan Greenspan he reckoned it
was another private joke between him and The Glock.
He said that the headmaster was alluding to Boggo's
economic savvy while simultaneously welcoming him to
the cabinet. It was difficult to watch Boggo's extensive
gloating spree around the house door so I retired to

my room to hit the maths books. I look forward to the exam tomorrow afternoon because then the world's most torturous subject will be finally done with. Dead and buried.

Tuesday 23rd November

I thought I had done quite well in the geometry exam until I realised that most of my conclusions were different to Simon's who scored a B during trials. I am now convinced that I have failed and only hope that my algebra paper will be good enough to scrape me through with an E. Nevertheless I feel elated that the dragon has been slain and that I'll never have to see Mrs Bishop again. I predict the chaplain will commit suicide before the decade is out.

As I started off for the touch rugby match on Trafalgar I could hear music blasting out of numerous windows about the quad. Down on the field the entire matric year had turned out for the game. With only English literature standing between us and our freedom, there was a joy in the way we played and mocked. Afterwards we practised our leavers' haka for Friday which everybody took incredibly seriously.

18:30 While in discussion with Boggo about the leavers' party at Joe Kools on Friday night I noticed that he was walking further away from me. While I crossed the paving at the centre of the quad he strode across the grass as is now his privilege as head of house elect. 'You're going to have to speak up, Spud, I can't hear you,' he said, making a great show of his grass walking.

Wednesday 24th November

Awoke from a magnificent dream about making love to Amanda beside the fire in the cop shop. I do hope our futures collide at some stage. Even for just one night. Spent the morning going over my English lit notes and cleaned out the drawers of my desk.

I took a long walk around the grounds, soaking them in for the final time. I lingered on the theatre and my old cricket fields the longest. I suppose they carry the happiest memories.

Thursday 25th November

16:00 Albert Schweitzer was thrilled with all the books, clothes and money I presented him. He was a tad emotional about my approaching departure and did his best to talk me into returning for post matric. I thanked him for his fine service over the year and said I would miss his efficiency and attention to detail. This set him off with some embarrassing sobbing, so I gave him all of my excess stationery, which cheered him up considerably. He asked me if I minded if he kept in touch once I had left school and we shook on it. It seemed that he was becoming emotional again so I sent him off to make me tea which I didn't really feel like drinking. My bags are packed and my army trunk lies locked and waiting behind the door along with my box of books and cricket bag.

When Schweitzer returned he asked me what he should do with all the files containing my many notes.

'Take them to the cop shop,' I ordered. When he questioned why I replied, 'Rambo's orders.' He nodded uncertainly and went about his business.

20:00   Our final night as schoolboys began with a bang because of Rambo's insistence that we incinerate all our notes. A bottle of vodka was being passed around but I only mimed drinking because I really didn't feel like it. Vern became carried away with burning stuff and ended up throwing his pencil case, wallet and blue jeans into the fire too.

When I thought the night was over Rambo insisted we carry out one final mission and he led us to the front of the school where his black bullet was brazenly parked outside the chapel. We were all dressed in our khakis so we surely weren't heading to a nightclub but Rambo refused to let on where he was taking us a matter of hours before our final exam. We sped along and I grew uncomfortable as I recalled Rambo prophesying us all dying together in his car. Here we all were, racing along a narrow road in the dying season. Boggo complained the entire way about Rambo risking Boggo's future as head of house with his mad rebellions. He did, however, perk up considerably when Rambo parked his car under a tree opposite St Catherine's, the very Mecca of hot girl schooling.

'Last chance to lose your virginity, Spud,' quipped Simon as Rambo switched off the lights and engine. Rambo twisted his body in the driver's seat to address us at the back. 'Ever heard of the VC?'

'Victoria Cross!' bellowed Garlic from the boot.

'The ultimate challenge. Razor wire, electric fences, security guards, dogs, police patrols – you name it.'

'No frikking way!' hollered Boggo. 'I'm head of house.'

'Not yet, you aren't,' Simon replied with a devious grin.

'Chips! Chips! It's the cops!' hissed Fatty and we all sank low as headlights washed over the car.

'It's a tow truck, you wop,' scolded Rambo, checking up and down the street for any other cars.

'Okay,' he whispered. 'Kit off, and I mean everything.'

I took a sip from the nearly finished vodka bottle for Dutch courage and began stripping off.

'Let's go,' hissed Rambo and set off across the road butt naked and leading the way. The line of boys approached the gate and I noticed that the guard hut was dark and deserted. Just as I was considering how we might break into the school, the main gates slid open. Rambo showed off his green clicker. 'It's come in handy over the years, trust me.' We laughed and trotted through the main gates of St Catherine's School for Girls. Rambo picked up the pace and made a beeline for a large building to our right. Around the back we climbed over a wall and found ourselves in a corridor with locked classrooms to the right. We descended a flight of stairs and paused as Rambo searched for a rock to break the fire alarm glass.

A long and foreboding air raid siren started up and we galloped after Rambo who led us along another dark corridor and up a flight of narrow stairs.

'Let's do it!' he shouted and sprinted out across the lawn of the quadrangle towards the boarding houses. It must have been quite a sight for the crowds of girls gathering on the balcony above because the floodlights were switched on and the Crazy Eight streaked by, butt naked and whooping with joy. The girls went bananas.

We ran on, following Rambo as he looped around the back of the school. Then we found ourselves at the open main gate with four security guards standing between us and freedom.

'Charge!' screamed Rambo, and we ran straight at them. Rambo bounced one of them out of the way and another leapt out of the path of a stampeding Fatty. A hand grasped at my shoulder but I shrugged it off and made it through the gates and across the road to the car.

But Garlic wasn't so lucky because he had stopped to ogle the girls and the security guards had regrouped by the time he reached the gate. Two of them rugby tackled the screaming Malawian and the others jumped in to subdue him.

'Shit!' swore Simon as we feverishly pulled on whatever clothes we could find.

'I'm not going down for Garlic,' cried Boggo. Rambo must have been in agreement because he started up the car and began driving down the street.

'Garlic!' shouted Vern with his head out of the window. And there he was, The Pink Houdini, his white hair gleaming like an orb of light madly waving his hands for Rambo to stop with the security guards in pursuit now some distance behind. Garlic dived through the open window and we set off with his legs still outside. The car was complete bedlam and I found myself riding up front with Rambo with the others chanting and screaming at the back. Midnight Oil's Bed Are Burning played us back to school and we never tired of chanting the words.

I stood gazing around the quad for some time. Only Pissing Pete broke the silence and up above was a vast sky of brilliant stars. It was all too much for me.

Friday 26th November

D-DAY

08:00   Viking began his house meeting by congratulating Simon on being elected head of school and Boggo head of house. The difference in the applause for each of them was marked. Rambo, Fatty, Vern and myself were called up to receive our old boys' ties.

'Salvete, John Milton,' said Viking and shook my hand firmly.

I glanced down at striped navy blue tie hidden in plastic. This is what they call 'the old school tie'. Somehow it didn't feel very powerful in my hands.

'... and now the house prefects for 1994 who shall commence their duties as of midday.' A great hush fell across the room as the Normal Seven paled and clutched at their hands.

JR Ewing
Runt
Barryl
Darryl (the last remaining)

For a moment it seemed that there were only four prefects because Viking paused for an exceedingly long time to scratch his beard before continuing, 'And the final prefect for next year is Garth Garlic.'
    'Me?' roared Garlic, scrambling to his feet and whooping with delight. Thinny was shattered about not making it. I put my hand on his shoulder and reminded him that Boggo had been in the same position a year ago and was now head of house. This only made matters worse.

In all the excitement I almost forgot that I had a final exam to write. 'One more dragon boys,' called Rambo hauling up his stationery and notepad. The clock above the giant archway ticked over to 8:55.

'Once more unto the breach dear friends, once more.'

12:00   A great roar exploded around the theatre. It felt like the end of an era. Outside we hugged and chanted and tackled each other. Then we marched into the main quad and took up our positions. The rest of the school had gathered in anticipation in the cloisters and with one final cry from Rambo, the class of 1993 kicked into our haka. Mass cheering and applause dissolved into fighting my way through the throng while shaking hands and saying goodbye. Even Viking was emotional and embraced whoever he could, including those who would be coming back. I said my final goodbyes to Albert Schweitzer who was doing a lousy job of fighting back tears. He promised to send my trunk and bags down with the Durban bus in a fortnight. I thanked him once again for everything and shook his hand.

This is it, I kept reminding myself. This is where it all ends.

I found myself running through the archway, along the passageway and past the crypt. I circled the swimming pool, crossed Trafalgar, vaulted the bog stream and arrived at the gate. I was panting so hard that I couldn't immediately reply when I heard his hoarse voice from the veranda.

'So you've come to put an old syphilitic swine out of his misery.'

'I've come to say goodbye, sir.'

'Indeed, young man,' he replied standing to his full height. There was a pause because neither of us knew what to say. What could we say?

'Sir,' I said eventually, 'thank you for showing me absurdity.'

'The absurdity was all mine, Milton.' The Guv tried to

tempt me into more of Thinny's mom's lamb shanks but I said that I had to go because the others were waiting. I asked if he had any final advice for me as I started my journey into the big wide world. He gave it a moment's thought before declaring, 'Never stop bowling your leg spinners.'

He tapped me on the shoulder with his walking stick and said, 'Right, be off with you then and allow this old man to quench his broken heart.'

I gave him a hug and stepped back to say our old line of farewell.

'Exit ...' I began but he couldn't reply because he was too choked up and I couldn't continue because the words wouldn't come. With one final and triumphant raising of his walking stick The Guv turned and disappeared into the house.

The Crazy Eight were waiting impatiently at the house bench. Snatching up my bag, I joined them as we privately said our final goodbyes to the house and all that is familiar. With long strides we ran across the sacred grass of the main quad and ducked through the great archway. On we went, jostling, mocking and laughing down Pilgrims' Walk where the last of the matrics were loading their bags into their parents' cars. While Fatty rested, I turned back and gazed up at the school's red brick buildings. The very place my parents left me as a small boy four years ago.

On we ran past the tennis courts and Trafalgar. Finally we reached the white gates where the security guard was laughing and shouting joyfully at us. With Vern's piercing and triumphant shout of 'Side guy!' the gates were heaved open and the inmates ran hysterically from the asylum. I didn't dare look back again.

Spuddy, shot for all the memories.
    Keep a straight bat.
        Simon.

Spuddy! What a trip
it has been. So thrilled
    you got it all down in the
diary. One day when we're old
and grey, I'm going to pull
in and read back over the crazy
    days. Good luck with your
future. I hope you finally make
    it to Hollywood! Fatty.
(House Farting Champion 90 –
        93. Ha Ha.)

SPUD!

So sorry (not) you couldn't
come back for post matric cos
Boggo, The Cat Greenstein
would've taken you down.
Regards Head of House 1994.
Boggo The Cat Greenstein.
Professional Shagger.

I can't believe this is it. What
a ripping 2 years! Come visit at
    Lake Malawi anytime.
Love Garth Garlic
(The Pink Houdini.)
PS. Up the Europeans!

YOU'RE NEVER TOO
YOUNG TO DIE
SUDDENLY.
    RAMBO.

Afterword

They say that all good things come to an end. I have no idea who said this or who exactly 'they' are, or even *why* all good things should stop. Who decided this – the Glock? So, yes, *Spud – Exit, Pursued by a Bear* may be the fourth and final book in John van de Ruit's series of Spud titles, but the beauty and the strength of the Crazy Eight and their scribe, whose diary entries have given thousands and thousands of readers a glimpse into a rich, strange, sometimes wildly unbelievable world of boys shakily navigating their way towards manhood, will, I predict, ensure that this good thing will not come to an end, or at least not any time soon.

When the first book in the series – *Spud* – arrived on my desk in manuscript form and I began to read it, I felt a small spark of excitement deep down inside, that spark that reminds a publisher where everything begins. It all begins with the words. Contrary to popular opinion, the sound of till points jingling is not the first music to a publisher's ears – at least not to this one's. It's the music of the words themselves and the harmonies they weave that grips you. If you find yourself immediately caught up in the imagination of the writer and feel a connection with the characters whose lives and struggles resonate on some fundamental level with your own, then that is a feeling like no other. *Spud* did that instantly for me. *Spud – The Madness Continues* ratcheted it up another few notches, and *Spud – Learning to Fly* took wing and soared to new heights. And finally, *Spud – Exit, Pursued by a Bear* brings the series to a poignant yet fitting close.

John van de Ruit and I have been on a long journey together. In publishing terms, the Spud books have been massively successful and deservedly so. They have given pleasure to many readers, across gender and generations, and will continue to do so long after both of us have moved on to other things.

For me personally, however, the collaboration with John has given me so much more than book sales. The friendship we have forged over years of conversations deep and shallow; the many working sessions at unlikely rendezvous spots, where storylines were created, laughed off, embellished and risked; and the celebrations shared when the fans applauded and queued for their books to be signed – these are the things that make it all worth while. These are the good things that will not come to an end.

Alison

Alison Lowry
Chief Executive Officer
Penguin Books South Africa
June 2012

Acknowledgements

As I sit here and write this, I am surrounded by a pervading sense of the surreal. That this should be the end of the road for Spud Milton and my second stab at youth, and the conclusion of the most wondrous and, at times, confounding decade of my life. It began as a scribbled page on a pad of paper in a hotel room in Harare in 2002, and ended up utterly changing my very way of life. One day I was hopefully thumping away at my old PC in Wombat's flat in my underpants, and the next I was being whisked around the country in smart trousers, being gaped at by complete strangers and developing arthritis in my signing hand. The sudden success was intoxicating, as was the tantalising thought of constructing a series that traced the awkward years from boyhood to manhood. The challenges shifted, how do I find the humour without repeating myself? How do I go about subtly ageing Spud's voice, losing neither his character nor the sense that he is growing up? These and other questions occupied my mind, but I relished it all, even the toil and the moments of doubt and insecurity.

Take a bow, Alison Lowry, who wears many hats as Penguin CEO, publisher, my trusty editor and sounding board. Your sharp wit, black humour and sage encouragement kept me searching for the ever elusive garden of comedic perfection. Thanks go out to all the Penguins over the years who have worked so hard to sell Spud and make him look beautiful. To Tracey McDonald, the dark mastermind who wreaks havoc with my anonymity, and Reneé Naudé for her excellent design work and for bending my deadlines. My appreciation to Pam Thornley for straightening the crooked, and Ellen van Schalkwyk and all the present and former publicity penguins for taking care of me when I lose my marbles, and taking care of my marbles when they lose me. A shout out too for the booksellers of this grand nation, you did what nobody thought was possible. Salute!

Many thanks to my literary agent Roy Sargeant who first passed on my manuscript to Penguin and has handled my Spud dealings with aplomb. Your faith in my writing has been unshakeable, good sir. To those that I have mentioned in previous books and to the many who have been a part of the Spud army, I thank you. To Ross Garland, for his amazing movie crusade, along with fellow horsemen Brad Logan and Don Marsh who have offered Spud a life beyond the page and attracted new readers all over the world. A humble bow to HRH John Cleese for saying yes, and turning a wild and ridiculous dream into reality. A special mention, too, for my beautiful alma mater Michaelhouse, and the insane men who have frequented her cloisters. Thank you all for seeing the funny side. To my amazing and inspirational sister Cath, and my strong and characterful mother Ros, thank you for riding this wave with me and handling it and life's sometimes brutal curveballs with such grace and humour. You both keep me humble, grounded and relatively sane. To Jules whom I love, who walks every step of the road with me. Without you this wouldn't mean half as much, and I wouldn't laugh every day.

Finally, I thank you, the reader, for falling for Spud and the mad people that surround him. Although I cannot hear your guffaws and sniggers, I am reliably told that they do happen on occasion and the thought of that derives me much pleasure. Thank you, Spud fans, for forcing your friends and families (on occasion at gunpoint) to read these books. You have allowed me to build a life around my writing, and that, more than anything, is a gift and a unique privilege.

John van de Ruit
June 2012

Join
THE SPUD *Charitable* **TRUST**
and help to promote imagination,
reading and creativity to young
South Africans.

Visit:
www.thespudtrust.com
and make a difference today.